Margarita, How Beautiful The Sea

a novel by
Sergio Ramírez

translated by Michael B. Miller

CURBSTONE PRESS

A Lannan Translation Selection
with Special Thanks to Patrick Lannan and
the Lannan Foundation Board of Directors

Spanish original: *Margarita, está linda la mar*
©1998, Sergio Ramírez
Grupo Santillana de Ediciones,S.A.Torrelaguna 609, 28043 Madrid

Cover design and artwork: Les Kanturek

This book was published with the support of the
Connecticut Commission on Culture and Tourism,
 the Connecticut State Legislature through the
Office of Policy and Management, the Lannan
Connecticut Commission Foundation, and donations from many individuals.
on Culture & Tourism We are very grateful for this support.

Library of Congress Cataloging-in-Publication Data

Ramírez, Sergio, 1942-
 [Margarita, está linda la mar. English]
 Margarita, how beautiful the sea / by Sergio Ramírez ; translated
by Michael B. Miller.
    p. cm.
 ISBN-13: 978-1-931896-41-2
 ISBN-10: 1-880684-84-5 (pbk. : alk. paper)
 I. Miller, Michael B., 1941- II. Title.

PQ7519.2.R25M3713 2007
863'.64—dc21   2001004097

CURBSTONE PRESS   321 Jackson Street   Willimantic, CT 06226
phone: 860-423-5110   e-mail: info@curbstone.org
www.curbstone.org

Translator's Notes and Acknowledgments

The translation of Sergio Ramírez's award-winning novel *Margarita, está linda la mar* (*Margarita, How Beautiful the Sea*) (co-winner of Spain's prestigious Alfaguara Prize) is a project that I began in December 2000, finishing the first draft in September of the following year. From October 2001 to December 2006, the initial version, with several time-outs in between, saw numerous corrections and a fair amount of editing and rewriting before reaching the definitive version. The experience was both exhilarating and painstaking. But no work reaches its final draft without a great deal of help from those who can take the time to do a careful reading of the text and offer suggestions and changes.

I owe a special thanks to my editor, Sandy Taylor, for his painstaking work in coordinating all the diverse and difficult elements of the text editing. Also, a special thank you is owed to Nicholas Caistor, who has translated other works by Sergio Ramírez and who added his valuable support to a most challenging project, in reviewing the translation and making important contributions to it; to the author, Sergio Ramírez, for his many clarifications and explanations along the way; to Professor Emeritus Nick Hill of Fairfield University for his careful reading of the translation and many valuable suggestions and corrections; to Professor Matias Minambres of North Georgia College for his spirited help in clarifying many other points that required his expert help, and to my former colleague at Gallaudet University, the late Dr. Silverio Muñoz of Chile, and to Gastón Hernández. All the individuals named provided invaluable help in offering critical suggestions, corroborations, and clarifications of the more esoteric points in the Spanish original.

Bending the complex and often subtle text to extract from it the exact meanings and making it conform to the English while preserving the flow of language in the original was often a demanding but equally rewarding experience. The novel makes frequent references to Greek mythology and biblical characters and quotations, material that often sent me scurrying back to search out the exact meanings in English.

The title of the work is taken from an event in 1907: Rubén Darío's triumphal return to his native land. At a celebration in his honor, at the Hotel Lupone at the Port of Corinto, he wrote verses on the fans of seven-year old sisters Margarita and Salvadorita, daughters of Doctor Debayle, the physician who attended the poet in his last hours of life. Eleven years later Margarita's sister, Salvadorita, at the age of eighteen, marries the future dictator of Nicaragua, Anastasio Somoza, at the time a meter reader for the Power & Light Company of Nicaragua.

The title, which comes from the verses written on Margarita's fan, serves as a leitmotif for the work, in that the verse embodies the glory and culture of an age past, juxtaposed against the agony and misery of a later era, embodied in the years of the first period of the Somoza dictatorship (1937-1956) and the conspiracy that is mounted to bring it to an inglorious end. Ironically, the plot, rather than ending the dictatorship with the assassination of Somoza merely perpetuates it as Salvadorita and her children gather their forces, allowing the sons––Luis, the Good and Anastasio, Jr., the Bad—to maintain the family's tight grip on Nicaragua for another twenty-three years.

M.B.M
Burke, Virginia

To Mercedes Estrada

The Chorus

This, then, is the proclamation that is heard everywhere: "A talent for him who shall kill the tyrant Diagoras of Melos, and a talent for him who destroys one of the dead tyrants." We likewise wish to make this proclamation: "A talent to him among you who shall kill Philocrates, the bird-seller; four, if he brings him to us alive. For this Philocrates skewers the finches together and sells them at a rate of an obolus for seven. He tortures the thrushes by inflating them, so that they may look bigger, exposes them, sticks their own feathers into the nostrils of blackbirds, and collects pigeons which he shuts up and then forces them, fastened in a net, to decoy others."

Aristophanes, The Birds

Preface

1907. León, Nicaragua. During a tribute which he delivers to his native city, Rubén Darío writes on the fan of a little girl one of his most famous poems: Margarita, how beautiful the sea

1956. In a café in León, a group of literati gather around a little table in a corner of a restaurant-bar named Casa Prío, a hotel in the time of Rubén Darío, run by Captain Prío's father. Captain Prío stands on his balcony at Casa Prío overlooking Plaza Jerez as an observer of events as they unfold on the critical day in question: the rally in the plaza for Somoza who has come to León to declare his candidacy for president one more time.

This group of literati has been meeting at Casa Prío for several years, dedicated, among other things, to the rigorous reconstruction of the legend surrounding Rubén Darío and his life. Erwin, the owner of the Cara Lutecia print shop; Norberto, a failed businessman, in debt and owing money to the bank from his ill-fated cotton growing venture; Rigoberto, a journalist, and a dead ringer for a famous Cuban singer of the time; Bienvenido Granda, the singing moustache—all in their early twenties—and the goldsmith Segismundo, owner of the Pearls of Basra jewelry shop, comprise the group. Along with a Cordelio Selva, a Nicaraguan exile in El Salvador, for whom Somoza's security people are on the lookout should he return, all are involved in the plot to kill Somoza, a plan mapped out by Erwin at his home, which also houses the Cara Lutecia print shop.

Through their comments and discussions on the journal entries Rigoberto has collected about the life of the great poet and the dictator Somoza, the reader gradually forms a picture of the two men, a mixture of fact and fiction: Darío, the national glory of Nicaragua in his day, and Somoza, the national shame of Nicaragua.

Anastasio Somoza, president since 1937, is visiting the city of León, accompanied by his wife, doña Salvadorita, to declare himself a candidate for president for yet another term at the Great Convention that is being held in Rubén Darío's native city and where a statue of the great poet has recently been erected after having been lost for several years in San Salvador where it had been unloaded by accident by the stevedores at that port and left on the docks of the Customs House, until it was purchased by a don Manlio Argueta, the owner of an ice cream parlor in San Salvador. While in El Salvador, Rigoberto discovers the long-lost statue and informs Dr. Balthazar Cisne, President of the Rubén Darío Honor Society, whom he met at his rooming house and who happens to be in El Salvador, searching for the statue, of its whereabouts. It is then brought back to Nicaragua, its rightful home, aboard the Salvadorita, a ship owned by Somoza and named after the First Lady. Cordelio Selva is aboard the ship, posing as a Protestant evangelist. Also aboard the ship, packed away in Rigoberto's little cardboard valise, is the "little black beast," the gun purchased by Cordelio Selva in a San Salvador gun shop, the gun that will be used by the assassin.

In the meantime, a banquet of pomp and splendor is being planned to celebrate Somoza's announcement earlier that day, at which the little group from Casa Prío will carry out its attempt against the dictator's life, and that little girl with the fan, from a half century before, Salvadorita, the wife of Anastasio Somoza, will not be a disinterested party to the events that occur on the night of September 21.

In Margarita, How Beautiful The Sea, *Sergio Ramírez manages to bring together, in a complete metaphor of reality and legend, the entire history of his country. In a language whose brilliance captivates the reader, with flashes of humor and irony at once astonishing given their poetic meticulousness, the action and plot move along roads a half century and apart between two levels of narrative, creating a temporal continuum between past and present which seems to belong to the best realms of the myth of Rubén Darío. And within this literary landscape, with much greater reality than the facts themselves, the author has us come to know characters of unmistakable identity, at once original, tender, indispensable, and inscribed upon the mind of the reader in the best tradition of the great personalities of Latin American literature.*

A perfect novel, abounding with nobility. An exceptional work, written with overtones of a Greek tragedy.

Nick Caistor

Margarita, How Beautiful The Sea

PART ONE

Return to the Native Land

Captain Agustín Prío had just finished adjusting his best bow tie, the one that made him look like a boxing referee, when the sound of wailing sirens filled the room, and his mirror flooded with red reflections. When he went out on the balcony, the sudden gust of hot air threatened to push him back inside. On the far side of the square crowds of alarmed campesinos were scattering from the bestial roar of Harley-Davidsons as they thundered forward under the fiery sun, clearing a path for the caravan as it came to a halt in front of the cathedral. Climbing down from the cotton trucks and orange-colored Department of Public Works dump trucks, the demonstrators took the placards, still dripping with wet paint, being handed out by the men in charge, and hoisted them aloft or used them to shield themselves from the heat. Behind them came the women, clasping infants to their gaunt breasts and holding older children by the hand as they disappeared into the throng of other equally disoriented campesinos who had been ferried in from the surrounding rural areas, as well as those who had walked there from the outlying districts of the city wearing their red caps, broad-bottomed stall-holders, women street-vendors in palm hats, municipal street-cleaners in big heavy boots, school teachers under their parasols, shaven-headed military recruits, and civil servants in drab ties.

Then there was a slamming of doors, bodyguards baking in black cashmere under the hot glare of the sun rushing forward, a ring of Thompson submachine-guns circling the armored limousine, as funereal and black as they. Somoza stepped out—white Palm Beach suit, a silver cigarette holder between his teeth—and raised his Panama hat to greet his supporters, who from a distance unleashed their applause. There was a cry of: *Long Live The Man, the best goddamn*

3

man there is. You're The Man, you're The Man, goddamn right! then the echo swelled in a cavernous wave that engulfed Captain Prío out on his balcony. Behind Somoza came the First Lady, standing there in a bottle-green silk dress trimmed in a deeper green, a soft green toque over her coif of curls, its veil covering her heavily made-up face. The couple quickly ascended the cathedral steps between the barricades of soldiers and bodyguards, up to the main entrance where the Bishop of León awaited them. The last thing Captain Prío saw from his vantage point was an explosion of flashbulbs as the entourage entered and made its way along the central aisle of the deserted nave, with soldiers guarding every inch of it.

The wreath of papier-mâché lilies and felt roses, arranged on a tripod, was waiting at the foot of the statue of Saint Paul opposite the tomb guarded by a weeping cement lion, its mane draped over a coat of arms, also made from cement. Tortured by the corset that dug into her flesh, the First Lady leaned close to gain the ear of her husband who, out of respect for the surroundings, had handed his silver cigarette-holder with its half-consumed *Lucky Strike* to his aide-de-camp, National Guard (NG) Colonel Abelardo Lira. Somoza—thinning hair, double chin, liver spots dotting his nose and cheeks—was also tortured by a tight-fitting corset, but his was a lightweight vest of woven steel that J. Edgar Hoover had sent him, with his personal card attached, by way of Sartorius Van Wynckle.

Nobody heard what she said. But I presume, Captain, that she wasn't reminding her husband that the brain of the person laid to rest under the weight of the weeping lion had been stolen on the very night of his death: a troublesome piece of family history. It is far more likely her thoughts had drifted off to the verses our beloved poet had written on her fan one far-off day in her childhood:

The written phrase, the new pearl,
Thanks to infinite celestial light,
Will one day show their splendor;
Oh, Salvadora, Salvadorita,
Don't ever kill your nightingale!

The well-fed nightingale assented and smiled. If he had been allowed, the goldsmith Segismundo—one of the guests at the cursed table who still carries on the tradition of meeting in the Casa Prío, the very same place where Captain Prío was standing on the balcony gazing out across the square— would have been bold enough to ask her, even though he already knew the answer: *When did that happen, Salvadorita?*

But such familiarity is not permitted. Therefore I'll let the First Lady's face—mercilessly powdered and aging with even less mercy—peer into the fleeting mirror of the waters of time; let an invisible stone create ripples on its transparent surface so that in its depths she can glimpse the quivering image of a girl aged ten, dressed in organdy just like her sister Margarita, both in Italian straw hats with two ribbons falling over their shoulders; where some of you will also have to hurry to find a place.

It is the morning of October 27, 1907. In the distance can be seen the *Pacific Mail*, and as many of you as possible should gather on its deck, because it is carrying the man who now lies in eternal rest beneath the statue of the cement lion, on his return to his native land.

As the dawning sky puts on its display of flaming foliage for the passenger, the steamer heads into the Bay of Corinto. He stands gripping the starboard rail, where he had stationed himself before sunrise, eager to discern the details of the coastline as it emerged in shades of gray. As the stars dimmed, he could see far off all the volcanoes of the Maribios Cordillera, which he had seen from the sea for the first time when he had sailed for Chile on an earlier distant dawn.

He had gotten dressed, with uncertain fastidiousness, by the weak light from the bulb in his cabin. He chose the white silk suit that had cost him thirty louis d'or, hand-tailored by Maurice Vanccopenolle from the Faubourg Saint-Honoré; a pale blue tie held in place by a gray pearl pin, and a striped sportsman's cap. The moustache and goatee, neatly trimmed by the barber scissors he keeps in his *nécessaire*, frame a bloated, discolored face.

The hangover from the two-star Martell cognac bought from the Dutch sailors—which he drank alone straight from the bottle long after midnight in his cabin, hot as an oven—is still drilling his skull. His giddiness is made even worse by the odor of tar and the stirred-up vapor of kitchen waste which the salt breeze drags along the ship's bridge all the way from the hatches at the stern.

When the bathymeter indicates a depth of 30 fathoms, the stokers hear an order through the intercom from the first officer on the bridge and, standing on their shovels, stop feeding the boilers. The incessant pumping of the pistons slows, and a thick stream of black smoke issues from the funnel as the engines slacken before being shut down. Then the whistle howls three times, like a beast being led to the slaughter. The heavy links of the chain speed out through the prow, dragging anchor, and when the hooks reach the sandy bed of the estuary, the *Pacific Mail* jerks to a halt. Its rough pitching quickly turns to a soft rocking motion.

On one of the promontories of Cardón Island there's a brief flash of light, followed by a puff of smoke. The sound of the howitzer, manned by two barefoot artillerymen in blue uniforms, echoes along the hot, bushy coastline and, as it scatters in the hazy air, startled seagulls fly off toward the mangrove swamps.

The first boats draw close, keels dipping into the violet-and crimson-tinged foam—their canvas sails stowed, powered by rowers and steered from the rudder by bare-chested sailors. Drawn by the enthusiastic shouts from down below, the passenger leans over the rail. At his back, the copper-colored funnel for the boilers looking like a brass tuba sways languidly in the breeze as he waves his cap to return the greetings of the gentlemen who raise walking sticks, stringed instruments, and hats in his honor, and of the ladies who, under their French lace parasols, are shrieking in feigned alarm at the bobbing waves.

In the lead vessel, the learned Doctor Louis Henri Debayle is trying to keep his balance as he energetically waves his Panama hat like a semaphore flag, all the while encouraging the bishop, Monsignor Simeón Pereira y Castellón, crouched fearfully beside him, to get to his feet as well. Bishop Simeón, his soutane and cloak soaked by the churning waves, barely dares let go of the gunwale to raise his skull cap, but at last he lifts his buttocks just enough from the crosspiece to shout at the top of his voice: "Long live the Prince of Swans, gentlemen!"

The battery continues its salute, and the boats maneuver to come alongside the barnacled hull of the steamer. Indifferent to the cannon fire and the shouts, the deckhands open the metal cage, and once their passenger is safely inside, they start to lower it, using all their strength to operate the cable pulley. Dangling from the ship's crane, the cage spins round and round while its passenger closes his eyes and feebly grabs hold of the bars, like an ailing wild animal. He has counted fifteen cannon salvos to this point. The women toss him fistfuls of flowers that glance off the bars and fall into the water. Doctor Debayle manages to grab hold of the spinning cage and, unfastening the lock, helps the returning hero into the boat. The flowers now find their mark, and strike him gently and delicately on chest and chin.

He tries to make room for himself on the transom next to Debayle's wife Casimira, who kisses him on both cheeks and has her daughters, Salvadorita and Margarita, do likewise, and then receives a hasty embrace from Bishop Simeón. Long, tremulous arpeggios on mandolins greet him, while on the boat next to his a tall, dark woman, with thick, knitted eyebrows and a diadem on her forehead, clasps her hands together and starts to recite some of his verses, which the breezes of the Pacific immediately snatch away:

> *As I steered my boat for Cythera*
> *I greeted the waves, and the waves replied*
> *with the happy sound of female voices ...*

He turns his head towards the woman, and moves his lips along with her recitation of the verses.

"She's like a Beardsley painting," he says softly. "Snow, charcoal, and ash."

"She's my niece, Eulalia," Casimira whispers to him.

"Married?" he asks, also in a whisper, and the impact of his cognac-laden breath makes her wrinkle her nose.

"Rubén Darío, the incorrigible!" she laughs obligingly. "Married, very much married..."

The battery stops firing. The boats sail over the bar into the estuary, leaving behind a trail of flowers scattered on the foam. Blinded by the fiery morning sky, the returning hero narrows his puffy eyes.

The crossing from Panama aboard the *Pacific Mail*, a cargo ship with just a few passenger cabins, has been an infernal torment for him. It was full of sordid bandits, rogues more than sailors, and he found himself obliged to share a table with the captain, a bad-tempered Lutheran from Leiden, a Bible preacher with poor Spanish, who to top it all was a teetotaler, and the only other passengers, a Salvadoran landowner don Leandro de Sola and his daughter Clelia, a scrawny girl, perfumed at all hours with heady essences, who kept insisting he write verses for her in her album, or even on the napkins from the miserable dinners they were served, always a cabbage stew like in an orphanage.

How different had been the trip between Cherbourg and New York aboard the Compagnie Générale Transatlantique's imposing *La Provence*! There, the Neapolitan valet was attentive to his every need, and he had enjoyed the place of honor every night at the table of the genteel captain, Monsieur Daumier, with 1903 Rhône and Chinon wines, a superb vintage, a chamber orchestra playing from afternoon onwards on the stage of the dining room, stuccoed with garlands of fruit, imposing Flemish still-lifes on rich Florentine silk panels, and Bohemian crystal chandeliers whose glass teardrops multiplied their burnished splendor, and the discreet bustle of the female passengers, strings of Basra pearls dangling amidst curls on foreheads cool as marble, a magical and absentminded touch of fans to their lips, an invitation to *flirt*...

And before that, the express Pullman coach that carried him from Paris to Cherbourg, the copious, cheerful celebration on the night of his departure with his intimate circle in the restaurant at the Gare Saint-Lazare, all of them there to protect him from her, *La Maligna*, fearful lest she suddenly appear and carry out her threat to splash his face with the dark little phial of vitriol always squeezed tightly in her gloved hand. She had appeared at the last minute when he was already safely tucked away in his compartment, and from behind the lace curtains he saw her on the station platform, arguing with Julio Sedano, his private secretary, who was blocking her path. A real *copain*, Sedano. And he saw her turn for a moment towards his compartment window, beheld the Lucifer-like glow of her green eyes...

"*La Maligna*, what a nickname!" Casimira laughs. "Did you know? She returned to Nicaragua ahead of you, and she's waiting for you at Corinto, *mon pauvre ami*; they say she's a changed woman."

"What?" he asks, his face growing pale. "But I left her in Paris...she had a job at Madame Garnier's millinery shop."

"I don't know...I only know what I've heard she's been saying...that you were having fun in New York, and she was a step ahead of you all the way..." Casimira laughs again.

And the stream of his singsong laughter says a lot. What does someone like that have to do with me? A vulgar and quarrelsome woman, quite fitting that she works in a milliner's shop, a woman who wears an ermine stole in the tropical sun. What have I to do with riffraff like that?

So *La Maligna* is back. Why go on trying to explain? Fun in New York, yes...in a club called *The One, Two, Three*, where he paid for love with a Dominican woman of pleasure with a sonnet...then the Port of Colón in Panama, the cranes at work building the canal against the backdrop of a slate-colored sky, the workcamps thronged with a mixture of races: Chinese and Blacks tossed together, mosquitoes incubating in the swamps, the heat from the tar and the odor of creosote, toilets marked For Coloreds Only; Yankee progress, aseptic wisdom. Then finally, the nightmare of the *Pacific Mail*.

The boats cut swiftly through the surf, ride the crest of the waves, and reach the shore where the tide dies away on the sand. The sailors leap into the water to pull the boats onto the heavy logs that serve as a slipway, and once aground, they carry the passengers and deposit them onto the coast's soft mirror at the foot of the shimmering dunes.

And when he sets foot on the sand under the panoply of coconut palms, he sees before him a garish crowd, struggling to contain its adulation and finally breaking into wild, happy cheering just as the National Military Band begins to play the "Welcome" march composed especially for the occasion by its director, maestro Saturnino Ramos. While the musicians, of all ages and heights, dressed in blue uniforms, work their fingers on the keys of their instruments and blow into the mouthpieces, they cannot take their eyes from the recently arrived guest. A barefoot boy comes out of the crowd and staggers towards him, his thick mop of bushy hair blown by the sea breeze, struggling with all his might to carry the flag of Nicaragua waving defiantly on the flagstaff that is topped with a tin spear on a crescent moon.

Dazed, the newcomer manages to shake the wet sand from his trousers while he fearfully searches for the face of *La Maligna*, but she is not there, and now he has to banish all unpleasant thoughts from his mind because the crowd is drawing nearer, engulfing him, a noisy mob, and the shouting, the ecstatic hurrahs and the swell of cheers drown out the music so that all he can hear are the harsh snorts of the burnished copper tuba that flashes as the rays of sunlight reflect off it, and suddenly he feels his arms filled with bouquets that dampen his silk suit, handfuls of them, baskets of flowers and fruit which he accepts one after another with a courteous nod of the head before leaving them in the hands of his entourage as he tries to climb the dune, using the cambric handkerchief to wipe the sweat dripping from his face and neck as he opens a path for himself among all these devotees pressing around him, wanting to touch him, to feel his clothes, to kiss his hands, while the little boy with the thatch of curly hair leads the way, still clutching the flag of Nicaragua, and the musicians of the National Military Band bring up the rear of the parade, struggling to stay in step as their feet sink into the soft sand.

Bishop Simeón, who is shouting *Long Live the Prince of Swans!* over and over, and the learned Debayle, haughty and circumspect, are walking alongside him, trying to shield him from the enthusiastic mob. Annoyed but pleased, he turns to ask Debayle the meaning of all this madness. And with a restrained smile, the man of science smooths his moustache and says that this is nothing, that León will be the real madhouse.

"My Palm Sunday, monsignor!" he says, turning towards Bishop Simeón.

"Your Rome and your Jerusalem!" Bishop Simeón says, gathering up his soutane and hastening to catch up, because he is falling behind amidst the jostling throng.

At last they reach the wooden fence surrounding the luxuriant garden of the Hotel Lupone, filled with palm, mango, and coconut trees. The balconies of the whitewashed wooden mansion peer out from amidst the vegetation, and above the latticework of the top floor stands a turret, crowned with a wrought-iron weather vane. The street beyond is full of puddles where pigs are scavenging for food, while on the far side of the road an express train is waiting inside the station, its locomotive garlanded with flowers, with the presidential coach placed at his disposal by General José Santos Zelaya already hooked up. The soldiers from the port garrison hold back the crowd with fixed bayonets to allow the entourage to enter the hotel where the breakfast to welcome the guest of honor is to be held.

In the dining room, tables have been placed together to form squares and are covered with starched tablecloths that Casimira has brought with her from León. On the tablecloths are porcelain flower vases, painted with hunting scenes, a naked Diana and her hunting dogs emerging from a dark grove. Palm fronds decorate the walls, with roses woven among them.

There are far too many people to find a seat at the table, and several of the gentlemen, among them the harbormaster, erect in boots that smell of shoe polish, have to remain standing behind their companions who occupy cane chairs, stools, benches, and rocking chairs, all taken from the rooms and other areas of the apparently deserted hotel. The guest of honor is seated on a wicker sofa in between Debayle and Bishop Simeón. Casimira, her two daughters, and her niece Eulalia, sit close by.

A toast. Debayle stands up in order to propose a toast, improvising a brief speech. There was no way to chill the champagne, and so, served lukewarm in the stemware, its bubbles quickly go flat. Thirsty as always, Rubén downs his glass and fills it a second time. Debayle finishes his speech and looks at him with gentle reproach.

"*Merde*! You're already fussing about drink! Such a bad habit!" says the poet, raising the glass to his dark lips.

"León awaits you, your León," Casimira tactfully intervenes as she gathers her two daughters on her lap, so bored they wanted to get down from the table. "They're clamoring for you in Managua, and everywhere else, but we won't let you out of León so easily."

Abruptly, he pulls his cambric handkerchief from his coat pocket, badly wrinkled now from so much handling, and wipes his lips. His thick nostrils flare: broad cartilage at the base, powerful nostrils; and his eyes, glinting darkly each time he draws a breath, fasten upon Eulalia. He passes his glass to her with an imperious gesture, and she graciously consents to fill it. But the bottle is empty.

At that moment the barefoot boy, the one with the bristly thatch of hair, comes to the table struggling to carry a fresh bottle as if it were as heavy as the flag. With a resigned gesture, Debayle removes the metal seal from the neck of the bottle to uncork it, then turns away so as not to spray anyone when the stream of foam shoots out. Applause follows the popping of the new cork. Condescendingly, he stands up to serve the traveler himself.

"No, not you," says the poet, and fastens his eyes upon Eulalia once more.

Debayle leaves the bottle on the table and sits down, embarrassed. Eulalia comes over to the sofa, picks up the bottle, and pours the champagne into the poet's glass with impeccable deportment.

"And your husband?" he asks, seizing her by the arm.

"Her husband is an invalid," the learned Debayle interjects. "An irreparable fracture of the sacrum."

"If he was left an invalid, it must have been because you were the one who treated him. Another of your victims," Rubén laughs, without letting go of Eulalia's arm.

Taken aback, Debayle proposes another toast. The bottle circulates around the table and it too is soon emptied.

"I like the way you recite. 'Cythera'! The island of Aphrodite, painted by Watteau! But I like your silence even more," he says, finally releasing her. "More champagne!"

Eulalia returns to her seat. And when the boy appears with another bottle, Rubén reaches across the table and seizes him by the sleeve of his poplin shirt.

"And you, what's your name?" he asks him.

The boy merely looks down at his bare feet. An impatient Debayle informs him that his name is Chiron.

"Chiron?" Rubén's astonished query resonates in the warm air.

"Do you remember the edition of *Profane Prose* you sent me from Paris?" Bishop Simeón asks him.

"I remember it very well," he answers. "The Argentine edition of 1896. It was my own copy. The last one I had."

"So you told me in the letter that accompanied the book. That was when for the first time I could marvel at your 'Colloquium of the Centaurs.' And thus Chiron was born, with your poem, and with the century," a smiling Bishop Simeón says, extending the hand on which he wears the Episcopal ring to signal Chiron to approach. The boy obeys.

"In that case, who is his father?" Rubén asks Bishop Simeón.

There is a strange silence. But after a moment, Bishop Simeón smiles again.

"One day I will tell you, and you alone, the story of Chiron the Centaur," he says.

"Chiron the Centaur," Rubén says. "*The great imperishable figure of the beautiful Muses...*"

He drinks again from his glass, then wipes his mouth on the sleeve of his jacket, his cambric handkerchief forgotten.

"*...and the triumph of the terrible mystery of things...*" Eulalia replies from where she is seated.

He raises his glass to her. Then, in a grave voice, he summons Chiron. Bishop Simeón speaks into the boy's ear

14

and gently pushes him towards Rubén. He sets his glass aside, stands up, and takes the boy's head between his hands.

The boy wants to pull away, but Rubén's implacable hands hold him still, squeezing him harder each time. A distant rumor, like that of seashells, slowly fills the boy's head, and the noise rattles him so much that he staggers and faints.

Casimira barely manages to stifle a scream behind her hands, and Margarita turns to hide in her mother's lap. Salvadorita bursts into tears out of fright. Rubén sits back down. Eulalia, frowning, is the only one who meets his gaze. Bishop Simeón comes to the boy's aid, kneels down next to him and fans him with his skull cap; Debayle also gets up, disgusted, and sends to the train for his little black bag.

When the boy, revived by the smelling salts, sits up on the floor, there are no tears nor is there any look of fear in his eyes.

"Now, suffer the burning, Chiron. The *numen* is in your head, the inspiration of the muses is yours," Rubén says, slurring his words.

Almost no one hears what he says; no one pays any attention to his words because everyone's eyes have turned toward the door. *La Maligna.* Eulalia is the first to spot her. And now he sees her: her thin dark silhouette standing out against the reddish morning light filling the doorway. It is the same pearl-gray suit she was wearing when they said goodbye, following a bitter quarrel, under the vine trellis of La Pagode in Camaret-sur-Mer in Brest, last summer. The same parasol, the same hat with its crest of heron feathers. Her green eyes have been staring at him defiantly for a few moments. She has not uttered a single word, but when she does, he knows that flecks of saliva will form at the corners of her lips. Her brother Andrés Murillo, dressed in black like an undertaker, stands a few steps behind her. The metal tip of her folded parasol is pointed like a deadly weapon straight between Eulalia's eyes, there where her thick eyebrows form a dark knot. And the guests remain frozen in mid-gesture as if under the glare of a flash of magnesium powder.

"Who is that whore?" she finally asks, seething.

"And what did Rubén do then?" asks Norberto, who always appears to have just stepped out of a bath. Under his double chin dangles a small medallion amidst the tufts of hair on his chest. He wears a bracelet bearing his initials on one wrist, and is dressed in white linen trousers and white shirt. His hair gleams with Yardley hair cream.

"He struggled up from the sofa and went over to her, ever so solicitous, with open arms, walking docilely towards her in little steps," the goldsmith Segismundo says from beneath a Tyrolean hat decorated with a sprightly feather. He has gotten to his feet to imitate Rubén's mincing gait towards *La Maligna*, and the patrons still left this late at night at the other tables watch him, amused, out of the corners of their eyes.

"That's how it was," Captain Prío confirms. And being short of stature, he rises in his chair to waft the smoke from his cigarette up into the air, where it hangs like lace. "He wanted to kiss her, but only succeeded in brushing her cheek because she turned her face aside with a look of disgust, reproaching him: 'Scarcely daybreak and you reek of liquor already. Aren't you ashamed?'"

"Don't believe a word of it, maestro," Erwin tells Segismundo. "Rosario Murillo hadn't even returned to Nicaragua. She arrived on another ship, a week later, also from Panama. It was the *Bernardo O'Higgins*, bearing a Chilean flag."

Erwin is sporting a Basque beret. He stutters and trips over his words. Smooth-faced and rosy-cheeked, like the cheerful Mennen Powder poster baby, he seems too big for the table. His fingernails show traces of ink from his print shop.

"I don't have to believe it, my friend; it's all written down right here," says Segismundo, checking the entry in

Rigoberto's journal. "He went up to her, ever so meekly. He had no will of his own. It was as if he had a horse's bit and bridle, like Lohengrin's swan."

"The divine absinth had destroyed his spirit," Captain Prío says, disconsolately, watching the rings of cigarette smoke dissolve at the ceiling.

"I stand by my facts," Rigoberto replies, checking a page in his journal. "The *Bernardo O'Higgins* reached the port of Corinto the 25th of October to load timber, ipecacuanha, and coffee. She was received by her brother Andrés Murillo. They took lodging at the Hotel Lupone in rooms 5 and 7, having decided to wait for Rubén's arrival. The harbormaster's office paid the bill, on orders from the government."

Rigoberto is tall, a dark-complexioned young man, quite slim, with curly hair and a thick moustache above fleshy lips. He's been eating tutti-frutti sherbet and has already had two servings.

"It was completely natural, in any case, for her to remain in the port to wait for him, since they were husband and wife," Erwin says.

"Was it also completely natural for her to want to throw acid in his face?" asks Norberto.

"That's why he called her *La Maligna*," Rigoberto says. "In Paris, she confiscated his salary as a consul, 240 francs. She tried to seize the furniture, his Louis Quatorze pieces, which consisted of a desk and *secrétaire*, 90 francs; and his Pleyel upright piano, 500 francs, his greatest treasure."

"And she burdened him with bills from dressmakers, and even sent him the bill for a medicinal spray—a mouthwash for halitosis—2 francs," says Captain Prío, who has come around to the other side of the table to read Rigoberto's journal entry, too.

"The idea that he could transfer the *inspiration of the muses* to a child simply by squeezing his head between his hands seems like an exaggeration to me," Erwin objects.

"It's no exaggeration," Captain Prío says. "The boy rolled on the floor, seized by a high fever. Dr. Debayle treated him for months. He was suffering from a kind of cerebral palsy."

"Who could possibly have proof of such nonsense?" Erwin asks.

"Here's the testimony of maestro Saturnino Ramos who, as musical director of the National Military Band, was present at the breakfast," Rigoberto says, handing Erwin a folded sheet of paper from among the pages of his journal.

"Maestro Saturnino is the worst witness you could have," Erwin says, tripping over his words. "The old man is blind and he's taken to whistling funeral marches all day in the street, compositions he makes up in his head as he goes along."

"Quite right. It's as if he's always going around wetting his pants," Norberto says.

"Take into account that Rubén was drunk. A man in an inebriated state is capable of all kinds of nonsense, like that thing of the laying on of hands," says Segismundo.

"Well, then, so you don't do anything stupid, don't have that next drink," Norberto says.

"I drink, but I never get drunk," Segismundo replies, head held high.

"The swan drank out of shyness. An insecure, tormented soul. That woman who persecuted him couldn't be called a wife," says Captain Prío.

"The *Maligna*," Segismundo says. "She even wanted to disfigure his face with acid. And him such an elegant man. A prince."

"A prince who always owed his tailor. Vanccopenolle refused to send him the uniform he was supposed to wear to present his credentials to King Alfonso in Madrid, because he hadn't paid. He had to go in one he borrowed. Or am I lying?" asks Erwin, looking for Rigoberto's corroboration.

"We'd best not talk of people who indulge in expensive pleasures, jewels and all that kind of thing, and end up owing money," says Segismundo, looking at Norberto in joking reproach.

"It wasn't his fault. They didn't pay him his salary. He had to abandon the court at Madrid, just so he didn't seem like some penniless ambassador," says Captain Prío. "Even the coachmen on Calle Serrano wouldn't trust him for his fare."

"And aboard that ship, *La Provence*, was it true he traveled in first class?" Norberto asks Rigoberto.

"Sure," says Rigoberto. "I have a published biography with a photograph of the ticket."

"But he was never once invited to the captain's table," says Erwin. "He spent the trip locked in his cabin, drinking. The passengers in the adjoining cabin, a Mr. & Mrs. Delaney of New Haven, filed a formal complaint to the first officer about the shrieking and howling that kept them awake."

"Delirium tremens," says Captain Prío.

"Where did you get that story from?" Rigoberto asks Erwin.

"Highly reliable sources," Erwin says. "I've also investigated the life of the great poet."

"And that Mexican, Sedano, was a good-for-nothing," adds Captain Prío. "He stole from him, tricked him, sold the rights to his books in his name. A swindler."

"They put him before a firing squad in Paris in 1917," Rigoberto says.

"They shot him for being a swindler?" Norberto asks.

"If they shot people for that, there would be no one left in this country by now, my friend," says Segismundo with a sigh.

"He wasn't shot," Erwin says.

"He was shot for being a German spy," Rigoberto says. "It turned out that he was an agent in Mata Hari's secret network."

"He was the secret son of Maximilian of Austria. He also had a blond beard, parted in the middle, like two wings," says Captain Prío.

"So many lies," Erwin says, shaking his head and laughing, compassionate, as if he were excusing the falsehoods.

"Here it is in my journal, if you want to see it," Rigoberto says, resentful. "Sentenced in a military court and placed before a firing squad at Neuilly, the 17th of November, 1917."

"I believe you; you can show me tomorrow," Erwin says, adjusting his beret. "I have to leave now, to correct some galleys. It's night already."

"Somoza's going to be a neighbor of yours, Captain. He'll be staying at the Municipal Palace," Rigoberto said, stuffing his journal into his portfolio, also getting ready to leave. It was a plastic, imitation lizard-skin briefcase.

"I already saw them taking all the desks and filing cabinets out of the offices and loading them onto trucks," Captain Prío said.

"Orders from Van Wynckle," said Norberto. "They're even going to remove the strongbox from the Bank of Nicaragua downstairs."

"It's a big snub for doña Casimira. She's spent a month having the house painted just for her son-in-law's visit to León," Captain Prío said.

"Who's this Van Wynckle?" asked Segismundo.

"Some expert the gringos sent down to take charge of Somoza's security," Erwin said, standing up.

"They even brought Somoza a bulletproof vest, a gift from Eisenhower," said Norberto.

"No, it was J. Edgar Hoover, the head of the FBI, who sent it," Rigoberto said. "It's made of woven steel, and it's lined with washable nylon. It weighs two pounds, seven ounces, and can withstand a bullet from a .45 magnum."

"Don't go putting that in your little journal," Captain Prío said, lowering his voice.

"It's nothing more than you can read in any magazine," said Rigoberto, shrugging his shoulders.

"So now, Somoza will be wearing the latest in fashion, strutting about in his new jacket," said Norberto.

"Those silver-toothed buffaloes up North!" Segismundo exclaimed to the rafters, spreading his arms wide. "Godfathers of the likes of a gangster like him, a man with no asshole who has shat all over Nicaragua!"

"What's this about Somoza not having an asshole?" Norberto remarked, laughing, first checking the street to make sure no one was going by.

"They removed it at the Oschner Clinic in New Orleans, and never put it back," the goldsmith Segismundo said.

"You let your political passions invent such lies," Erwin said.

"Lies?" the goldsmith Segismundo said. "He shits through his stomach, my friend, with a rubber valve. It's a state secret."

"A state secret that's only known at this little table," Norberto said.

"How sad," said Captain Prío, staring at the red tip of his cigarette. "All that money and he can't shit in peace, sitting on his solid gold toilet seat."

"It's called a colostomy," Rigoberto said, pulling out his journal again, although there was nothing written on the page he consulted. "Removal of the rectal tract and the construction of an artificial anus, a method developed by Charles Richet."

With a Trembling of Stars and the Horror of a Cataclysm

Mars was approaching Earth again, wrapped in a glow of blood. On the evening of Thursday, September 6, 1956, when *La Salvadorita* weighed anchor in the Port of La Unión to cross the Gulf of Fonseca en route to Nicaragua, it had already appeared above the truncated promontory of the Cosigüina Volcano, and lightning flashed against the murky sky like the branches of the blasted tree of Good and Evil, unfurling themselves in dazzling silence above the contours of Isla del Tigre.

The Caterpillar engine warmed the oil-spotted planks of the deck where the passengers, unable to find a place for themselves on benches that looked like they were from some abandoned church, maneuvered to spread their sheets and wool blankets among the stacks of crates of Salvadoran products—knitted clothing, plastic plates, and plaster saints. Others slung their rented hammocks from the rungs of the gunwale in preparation for the six-hour crossing to Puerto Morazán. Heavily loaded, *La Salvadorita* pitched and tossed among the churning waves.

"Who's that kid? Anybody famous?" came a woman's voice all of a sudden, as loud as a newsboy's, raising itself above the clatter of the ship's engine.

The beringed finger of the passenger, a merchant woman of ample buttocks and plump arms, pointed to the head of a marble statue, barely visible among the folds of the slicker that covered it. The statue stood on its pedestal in the middle of the deck, directly under the single light bulb burning in its wire cage.

A little man had his arms wrapped around the statue to protect it, not so much from the rough slap of the waves that increased as the lights of the Port of La Unión grew faint in the distance, but more from the vulgarity that was already beginning to threaten it. As childlike in stature as the statue itself, he looked to be about fifty years of age and was dressed in a baggy and wrinkled white linen suit, a black tie hanging down to just above his fly. Drawing closer to the light, the woman recognized him.

"Why, if it isn't Dr. Balthazar Cisne, lawyer and money-lender," she said, at the top of her voice as usual. She tried to give him a big hug, but he rebuffed her, baring his protruding teeth in a disdainful smile.

"A little more respect, please, señora Catalina Baldelomar!" he said, the smile disappearing from his face when he saw she was intent on unveiling the statue. But that did not stop her.

"This kid must have done something important! Just look at that big head of his. Large-headed people are always geniuses," she said, delighted with herself.

In the glow from the light bulb, the uncovered head revealed the sharp features of its face, the intent stare under contracted eyebrows, the mouth puffed with pride and distaste.

"Geniuses! Geniuses, yeah, for setting fires. In León I met a big-headed little sprout who set fire to his house just because they had scolded him for jerking off in the outhouse, and he left his entire family in the street like orphans," came another voice.

It was the melodious screen-idol voice of a cockfighter, who sported a pencil-thin moustache and a curl of hair that peeked out on his forehead from beneath a charro's embroidered sombrero. Squatting, he had just finished securing the rooster cages, aided by an albino boy who seemed to glow like a bright stick of chalk. He strode over, spurs jangling, a cigarette stub in his mouth. He was carrying a bottle of Cuscatleco rum by the neck.

"Who on earth would think of wearing spurs on a boat!" harrumped the merchant Catalina Baldelomar.

"Me," came the artistic voice of the Mexican charro, in a silvery whisper. "Is that a crime?"

Now she could see him more clearly under the light, she wrinkled her brow in an effort to distinguish his features. His left cheek bore the ugly imprint of a stone that had hit him in the fight that put an end to the main event at the cockfights in Sonsonante.

"I'll be damned if it isn't *Jorge Negrete*!" she said admiringly.

"At your service," the cockfighter said, touching the brim of his hat. Then he took a swig of rum, wiped his mouth, and offered her the bottle.

"Thank you, Jorge," she said, and looked around, proud of herself. She drank, wrinkled her face, feigning dislike, and then returned the bottle to its owner.

"Maybe this little fellow, even though he's not of age, would like a drink," *Jorge Negrete* said, and went up to the statue to shove the bottle into its mouth.

"It's hard to believe—a Darío fan like yourself, don Olinto Poveda!" Dr. Balthazar Cisne said, pushing the bottle aside.

Fed up with their mockery, he decided once and for all to remove the slicker, which he folded with great respect, revealing the statue in its entirety. Crowding round, the passengers gazed at the diminutive figure in military dress uniform with a plumed hat tucked under his arm, the front of his frock coat adorned with gold olive branches, and a small dress sword at his belt. The statue was the size of a small child.

"Aha, so the kid's a military officer!" said Catalina Baldelomar. "What battle did he win?"

"He was no military officer, ladies and gentlemen, anymore than he was a kid! Before you stands none other than Rubén Darío!" said a dark-complexioned young man with a bushy moustache and plump lips, who had set down a small cardboard valise with rusted locks at his feet.

"*Bienvenido Granda* in person, the singing moustache!" said Catalina Baldelomar, giving him the once over. "Is the Matanzas Sound orchestra here with you, *Bienvenido?*"

Dr. Balthazar Cisne, who had been about to reveal the identity of the statue himself, looked daggers at *Bienvenido Granda*.

"Rubén Darío! How was I to know it was you when you look so tiny? What a giant he was!" said *Jorge Negrete*.

"You knew perfectly well, don't lie!" said Dr. Balthazar Cisne.

"If I had known, I never would have dared offer him a drink," *Jorge Negrete* said. "So it's none other than Rubén Darío! He tied on many a Paris drunk, one right after another, asleep, at dawn, on the sidewalks of those majestic boulevards!"

"Don't give me away, I'm on the run, in disguise," *Bienvenido Granda* whispered to Catalina Baldelomar.

"What dirty trick did you pull this time?" she asked, already in league with him.

"How can you bear to repeat those rotten lies about Rubén Darío?" Dr. Balthazar Cisne said to *Jorge Negrete*.

"You know very well, doctor, of my devotion to Rubén Darío," *Jorge Negrete* said. "But who's going to deny the fact that Rubén drank to get inspiration?"

"I made off with a student from a convent school of the Aesculapian Nuns; she was from one of the fourteen families of El Salvador, and they set the secret police on me," *Bienvenido Granda* told Catalina Baldelomar.

"And what about your musician buddies, what happened to them?" she asked.

"The police nabbed them all in San Salvador, trying to get their hands on me," he said. "Fortunately, The Gypsy Boys of Spain, who are here on this ship, helped me out," he said. And he pointed to Juan Legido, who was wearing a waist-length jacket, high-heeled boots, and a black Andalusian hat, and who had come closer to get a better look at the statue.

"I haven't noticed any such devotion," Dr. Balthazar Cisne said to *Jorge Negrete.*

"It's going to seem very strange, you singing tropical songs with The Gypsy Boys of Spain. They're the castanet type," Catalina Baldelomar said to *Bienvenido Granda.*

"Of course I'm a devotee!" said *Jorge Negrete.* "He drank, I drink."

"Rubén Darío! Who would have thought it! Didn't he ever get any bigger, then?" asked Catalina Baldelomar, turning to Dr. Balthazar Cisne. "No wonder they call him the boy poet."

Curious, to get a better look, she bent over and gave a maternal pat to the head that Dr. Balthazar Cisne was about to conceal under the slicker again.

Auctions, subscriptions, raffles, festivals, recitals. All fell short of raising the amount of money that the House of Poloni and Sons was charging for a life-size marble statue of Rubén Darío: the sculptors, after studying various photographs sent to Carrara, had recommended sculpting him in his ambassador's regalia before the court of Alfonso XIII.

The exact size was eventually decided upon after a lengthy correspondence between this very same Dr. Balthazar Cisne, president of the Rubén Darío Honor Society, and signor Cesare Poloni of the House of Poloni and Sons, who for reasons of cost was constantly proposing they scale back, until it had seemed as though they might end up reducing the poet to an ignoble miniature, a bibelot more appropriate for a table in the salon of a Madame de

Pompadour than the majesty of a park, as Dr. Balthazar Cisne repeatedly protested in his letters: the statue had always been destined to be erected in the little park with its few benches and trees in front of the Church of San Francisco in León, where Rubén Darío had heard mass as a child.

For several months, the statue had been left out in the open on the Customs House quay at the Port of La Unión, El Salvador, where it had been unloaded due to a crass error by the stevedores, since the markings on the pine box clearly indicated the Port of Corinto, Nicaragua, as its final destination. When nobody claimed it, the bust had been sold off at a public auction and acquired by a don Manlio Argueta, owner of The Thousand Flavors of Chief Atlacatl Ice Cream Parlor, located on Avenida Independencia in San Salvador. It was there that Dr. Balthazar Cisne had finally discovered it by complete chance.

The statue adorned the entrance of the establishment. And it only took one glance for *Bienvenido Granda,* the singing moustache, to realize that it was Rubén Darío; and when Cordelio Selva showed up for their prearranged meeting at the ice-cream parlor, he commented on it, somewhat amused and somewhat sad, with words to this effect: so this is where the great poet came to rest, etc. To which Cordelio responded that if it were true, then the president of the Rubén Darío Honor Society's search had ended.

It so happened that Dr. Balthazar Cisne, president of the Rubén Darío Honor Society, was lodging at the Casa Dinamarca where Cordelio, an itinerant inhabitant of boarding houses for traveling salesmen and students, was also staying. And as he sat down for breakfast one morning, Cordelio had chanced to hear his table companion complaining about the fruitless and weary search he had been engaged in for the past month, spending his money on radio and newspaper ads, paying for false leads, traipsing all around the Colonia Escalón, approaching fenced gardens of mansions with Doric columns, or visiting mausoleums, in the hope that the bust might have ended up adorning some fountain or the grave of a child.

One Saturday, the two men accompanied a happy and grateful Dr. Balthazar Cisne to his meeting with don Manlio, to whom he had to pay a modest ransom, the transaction being facilitated by the happy coincidence that they were dealing with a Darían enthusiast, who knew by heart: *Do you remember that you wanted to be a Marguerite Gautier? Fixed in my mind is your face, when we dined together, on our first meeting, on a joyful evening that shall never return...* but who had never dreamt that the statue of the child he had acquired at a Customs House lost-property auction could possibly be the prince of Castilian letters, as he explained while he treated them to a bowl of mamey sherbet, a specialty of the house, on which *Bienvenido Granda* lavished praise, and won himself a second helping.

"The greatest Andalusian poet of this century and all those to come, a glorious figure of the mother country!" Juan Legido was heard to say as he went in search of his hammock after admiring the statue.

"The Mother Country?" An agitated Dr. Balthazar Cisne flapped his short arms, like the broken blades of a ceiling fan, pleading for the others' support. "The gold of the conquest wasn't enough for you! Now you want to rob us of Rubén, too!"

"Well, of course, Rubén Darío was born in Seville, in the Plaza de la Santa Cruz, by all accounts," Juan Legido insisted, turning away from him in his hammock.

At this, the famous wrestler Manfredo Casaya, better known in the ring as *The Lion of Nemea*, who was trying to get some sleep on the deck, stood up. He strode nonchalantly over to the gunwale to pee, and with the same nonchalance sought out the singer, stooping to make his way through the swarm of hammock ropes, as if he were entering the ring. Naked from the waist up, his bushy mane of hair gave him a terrifying look. Still more frightening was the barber's razor flashing in his hand.

"Repeat after me," *The Lion of Nemea* ordered Juan Legido. "Rubén Darío was born in the humble town of Metapa, later called Chocoyos, and today Ciudad Darío, in the Department of Matagalpa, in the Republic of Nicaragua, on January 18, 1867. His parents were don Domingo García and doña Rosa Sarmiento..."

Unaware of the danger he was in, Juan Legido turned over onto his back in his hammock and covered his face with his tassel-trimmed sombrero.

The Lion of Nemea flipped Legido's hat off with the blade and it rolled quietly on the deck. He grabbed him by the collar of his short jacket and brought the blade up to his neck.

"Repeat what I just told you," he said.

Watching the scene from a distance, *Bienvenido Granda* picked up his little cardboard valise and hurried over. The other members of the Gypsy Boys rushed over too, their shadows flitting through the darkness.

"Hey, Rubén Darío has always been a Nicaraguan, no two ways about it, but put that razor away before you cause needless bloodshed," pleaded Mario Rey, the orchestra's other lead singer.

Ignoring this conciliatory voice, *The Lion of Nemea* stroked the blade across the palm of his hand, as if he were getting ready to shave Juan Legido, who had sat bolt upright in his hammock.

"For the last time. are you going to repeat it or not?" the wrestler demanded.

"Manfredo, you're addressing none other than Juan Legido," *Bienvenido Granda* said, taking him by the arm. "Haven't you ever heard him sing 'El gitano señorón'?"

"Well, OK, I take it all back. Shit, it's no big deal," Juan Legido conceded, in a cowed voice.

29

"Juan Legido?" *The Lion of Nemea* said with surprise, quickly putting away his razor.

"In person, right in front of you." *Bienvenido Granda* smiled. "And here are Mario Rey and Pepe Marcos too. All these you see here are genuine, The Gypsy Boys of Spain."

The Lion of Nemea looked at them in amazement.

"Listening to you sing 'Two Crosses' even brings tears to the eyes of a bumpkin like me," he said. "Why don't you play it for me now?"

"That'll be part of Saturday's show, in León," Juan Legido said, getting up from his hammock and prudently walking over to the gunwale to have a cigarette, which he had trouble lighting.

The Lion of Nemea had presented himself one day at the Casa Dinamarca in San Salvador, offering Cordelio to climb into the ring for a modest sum so that the juicy winnings from the wrestling match might serve the cause of freedom, he had whispered into his ear in a mysterious tone. He was returning from Mexico, where in match after match he had left his adversaries sprawled on the canvas at the Tepito Arena.

Doubtful at first, Cordelio, who was in desperate need of funds for the cause of freedom, ended up being convinced. All he needed was an opponent. And that was *The Red Devil*, who if he won would walk off with half the gate as the purse. But how was *The Lion of Nemea* going to lose? The mere thought of it was laughable.

The Grand Master Mason Segismundo Mestayer, goldsmith by trade and lifelong bachelor, was sharing a room at the Casa Dinamarca with Cordelio because he had been exiled to San Salvador. One afternoon in León he had gone to the door of his jewelry shop, Pearls of Basra, when Somoza's entourage was passing by, and raised his hand to give him the finger. He kept it that way despite the fact that rifle butts were soon raining down on him; and with his finger still sticking up, as if his arm were part of a wooden saint, his bloody body was lifted onto the military jeep. A man of aloof demeanor and gallant manners, always keen on pleasing the ladies, he boasted about the size of his physical endowment and its inexhaustible power as naturally as if one were speaking of swollen tonsils.

It was he to whom Cordelio entrusted the mission of securing 500 colones from *The Beautiful Love Goddess* to set up the match. Widow or spinster, no one knew which, worth millions, — which was common knowledge—and famous for her insatiable carnal appetite, also a fact, *The Beautiful Love Goddess* lived alone in Planes de Renderos, in a mansion built high at the top of a ravine. It was a castle with tall towers and battlements, and protected by a moat she had filled with alligators after winning a suit against the city authorities, who had protested they were a public hazard.

So one night, his old shoes freshly shined, his burlap suit sent to the dry cleaners after everyone chipped in, and having relinquished his little Tyrolean hat so as not to spoil his rakish looks, Segismundo had been dispatched to the castle of the alligators in a taxi. And the following morning, he returned triumphant, although on wobbly legs and somewhat drawn in appearance.

"I got all her kinks out for at least a month," he told them, standing on the sidewalk and holding up the check from the Banco Hipotecario bearing the signature of *The Beautiful Love Goddess.*

The wrestling match took place at the El Salvador del Mundo Gym, filled to the rafters. *The Red Devil*, who smelled like sulfur, came out into the ring with cape and trident; *The Lion of Nemea* climbed in, barely covered with a lion pelt Cordelio had bought from some hunting party in the Guascorán jungle; badly cured, it smelled of carrion.

The Red Devil left his cape and trident in his corner, and then, before the referee had even advised the opponents on the rules of the match, went after *The Lion of Nemea* who, unawares, was roaring mightily and pounding his chest with his fists. *The Red Devil* grabbed him by his long mane of hair and sent him whirling through the air as if he were some pathetic pinwheel; then, after landing him on the canvas, sat astride him, and applied a body lock that made him howl in despair. He started pleading for them to get *The Red Devil* off him, and with each twist of the lock on his arms and legs, as if this were some kind of police interrogation, shouted at the top of his voice that he had never wrestled before in his life, and that if he was passing himself off as a wrestler it was because he had gone hungry for so long. When they heard that, the spectators started to hurl cushions, chairs, and bottles into the ring, while Cordelio, the promoter, and the goldsmith Segismundo, treasurer of the short-lived venture, rescued *The Lion of Nemea* from the gym and carried him to the emergency room of Rosales Hospital where they stitched him up and set splints for him.

In the darkness, *Bienvenido Granda* returned and stood next to Juan Legido who, suddenly aware of his presence, extended him his hand.

"Man, I really owe you. If it hadn't been for you, that animal would have knifed me," he said.

"Nicaraguans are very jealous of their national heroes," he said, with a smile.

"Jealousy over a woman, well, that's worth knifing somebody for. But jealousy over a poet..." Juan Legido tossed his cigarette into the water.

"Listen I have a favor to ask you," said *Bienvenido Granda*, setting his little valise that looked like it belonged to an itinerant barber down on the deck.

"Of course," Juan Legido said.

"I have a friend who would be over the moon if he could have The Gypsy Boys of Spain serenade his sweetheart," *Bienvenido Granda* said.

"That could be dangerous, couldn't it?" Juan Legido asked cautiously. "I mean, suppose the father of the girl is another lunatic who came out with a knife in his hand?"

"The father's a respectable and polite gentleman. There he is over there," he said, pointing to Dr. Balthazar Cisne, who was sitting down clutching the statue. "Her name is Zela, *Zela the Moor.*"

"Then consider it done. Look for me on Saturday at the Hotel América," Juan Legido said. "And your name? What is your name, if you don't mind my asking?"

"Bienvenido," said *Bienvenido Granda*, and he picked up his little valise.

Calm had returned to the deck. *Bienvenido Granda* was already moving on to find a place to lie down when suddenly someone pushed his way through the crush of bodies, got up on a big crate close to the statue, and opened a thick Bible, all the while keeping his balance amidst the rolling movements of *La Salvadorita*.

The light bulb overhead on deck cast a yellow glow on his angular face and prominent cheekbones. His hair was shaved above his ears and there was a bluish shadow where sideburns would have been.

"Mars is again approaching the Earth!" he shouted.

"What's gotten into Cordelio?" Dr. Balthazar Cisne, a bit alarmed, asked *Bienvenido Granda*, who had just sat down next to him.

"Damned if I know," he replied.

"For the love of Christ of the gypsies, how is anyone supposed to sleep?" Mario Rey complained from his hammock.

"Shut up there, you!" the melodious voice of *Jorge Negrete* warned him in mock anger.

The sound of laughter came from the corner of the deck where the cages for the gamecocks were stored, where he was sharing his bottle of Cuscatleco rum with Catalina Baldelomar, seated on her boxes of merchandise. The albino boy was asleep on top of the cages with a towel wrapped around his head so that his white glow wouldn't wake the roosters.

"Mars, herald of woe!" Cordelio was waving his Bible above his head, pointing to the sky. "The ill-fated planet approaches every twenty years for a visit, ever since it was seen for the first time during the reign of King Sharon of Syria!"

"Since when has Cordelio become a preacher?" Dr. Balthazar Cisne asked *Bienvenido Granda*.

"He turned preacher during his exile in El Salvador, to earn a living," he answered.

"And does he think that because he's a preacher they won't throw him in jail as soon as he sets foot in Nicaragua?" asked Dr. Balthazar Cisne. "In *Novedades*, they're accusing him right and left of conspiring to assassinate General Somoza."

"Now he's a man of peace, dedicated to his evangelical preaching," *Bienvenido Granda* said. "Before, when he was a Catholic, he led a corrupt life, all guaro rum and women."

"Let the dictators, the satraps, and the despots remember profane and scornful King Sennacherib, struck down by flames from heaven, as the planet Mars foretold!" Cordelio went on atop his soapbox.

"What's he up to? Listen to him!" Dr. Balthazar Cisne told *Bienvenido Granda*, his voice filled with fear.

"You can see Mars from here, it's that bright red star," said *The Lion of Nemea*, pointing towards the sky. Then he got up, and walked over to the railing where Juan Legido stood smoking, deep in thought.

Juan Legido gave a start. But seeing *The Lion of Nemea* smiling at him in a friendly way, his whole mouth devoid of teeth, on account of the *The Red Devil* having knocked them out in the main event, Juan Legido calmed down and offered the wrestler a cigarette, which he accepted, though he put it in the pocket where he carried his knife.

"I don't smoke, but I never turn anything down," he said.

"I imagine you're a fierce wrestler," Juan Legido said.

"I've only lost one match in my life," *The Lion of Nemea* answered. "And that's because they dressed me in a rotten lionskin that didn't fit right, and its stench made me feel more like puking than fighting."

"Ah, yes, the star they call Nergal!" Cordelio said, consulting his Bible. "'You are the terror, the panic, the one who turns the night sky to fire,' so exclaimed Esarhaddon, the heir of tyranny, before the slain body of his father Sennacherib."

"Give the preacher a drink!" *Jorge Negrete* said, raising his voice again.

The bottle of Cuscatleco rum is passed from hand to hand until it reaches Cordelio and is offered to him amidst much loud whistling.

"And this kid?" asked the merchant woman Catalina Baldelomar. "What happened, how come he's got no color?"

"That's Tirso, my nephew," *Jorge Negrete* said. "He was born that way because Saint Mardoqueo put a curse on him."

"'Thus was fulfilled the sign promised by the prophet Isaiah'," Cordelio said, bending down from his pulpit to take the bottle. "'Yaweh shall bring the shadow of the dial of Ahaz backward ten degrees and the firmament will rise up in a tempest of flames to exterminate the tyrant.'"

"Saint Mardoqueo dealt in curses?" the merchant woman Catalina Baldelomar asked, taken aback.

"It was his only curse, during the time of the Yankees," *Jorge Negrete* said. "That all the women who took up with Marines hoping for fair-skinned children would instead give birth to albinos. Is the preacher going to have a drink or not? If not, please hand me back the bottle!"

Cordelio took a long swallow.

"Mars came again, and the walls of the temple came tumbling down on the head of King Uzziah, the oppressor, as the prophet Amos had prophesied. Because Uzziah had disobeyed Jehovah who had demanded of him bread and freedom for his oppressed people."

He took another swig from the bottle.

"So much for your abstemious pastor," Doctor Balthazar Cisne said, nudging *Bienvenido Granda* with his elbow.

"Let them not forget Mars, those haughty Pharaohs, ravenous crocodiles with prodigious fangs, who, wherever they go, will hear the humble say, "It passed by here!" Cordelio took another, slower drink. "Satraps who, like the Chaldean kings, tread on the vanquished after gouging out their eyes! Who bring the people low, without remembering that one day the fire of heaven will turn them into ashes!"

"So is this Tirso the son of some Yankee from the occupation?" asked Catalina Baldelomar, intrigued.

"My sister Eufrasia Poveda got mixed up with one of those whiteys from the Pendleton detachment; just about the time they were leaving Nicaragua, he got her pregnant, and poor Tirso was born so colorless that he glows," said *Jorge Negrete*. "Holy Smokes, preacher, you're finishing my whole bottle! What kind of religion is that?"

Cordelio measured the contents against the light and saw that the bottle was almost empty. Then he returned it to the chain of hands raised up to reclaim it.

"Poor kid, with no clothes on he must look like a glowworm," the merchant woman Catalina Baldelomar said, watching Tirso the Albino sleep.

"Let the voracious ones take heed, who, already possessing flocks, snatch from the poor his only lamb! Who has told you, wolf, that the republic is yours?" Cordelio raised his voice still higher. "Tremble on your throne, tremble in your lair! Mars is now approaching, with his crown of blood, avenger of heaven! Your days, satrap, are numbered! Amen."

"I don't see him at all repentant," Dr. Balthazar Cisne complained again. "It's a double-edged sermon."

"You're right. I'll have a word with him. Watch my valise for me, I'll be right back," *Bienvenido Granda* said.

Cordelio had already gotten down from the crate, and his laughter echoed in the darkness, mixed with the laughter of *Jorge Negrete* and Catalina Baldelomar.

"What a tiny valise," Dr. Balthazar Cisne said aloud to himself, barely touching it.

"Let's not talk about tiny; you're no giant yourself." It was the voice of *The Lion of Nemea* who had crawled over, and seemed more to observe than talk from his toothless mouth. Dr. Balthazar Cisne didn't deign to answer.

"What in the world could Rigoberto be carrying in that tiny valise?" *The Lion of Nemea* remarked.

The pair of them stared fascinated at the little cardboard valise with its rusted locks. It could barely hold a change of clothes: a shirt, a pair of pants, a pair of rubber sandals, a Gillette razor, a small, half-used bottle of Mennen aftershave, a worn-out toothbrush, a tube of Kolynos toothpaste, crumpled from so much squeezing; and snuggled among the handkerchiefs, socks and underwear that provided a warm nest, lay a snub-nosed *little beast*, all shiny and black, breathing, softly asleep.

Wonders Have Been Seen

From his roost, even without a spyglass, Captain Prío could take in the whole of Plaza Jerez and its surrounding area that tumultuous morning. The plaza itself, veiled in a tenuous vapor as if it were cooking over a slow fire, revealed nothing out of the ordinary: cement benches, laurel trees pruned into globes, and the statue of General Maximiliano Jerez, a distinguished liberal and Rubén Darío's baptismal godfather, who had his back turned to the cathedral for reasons of a long-standing Jacobean enmity; then clockwise from the cathedral, there was the Episcopal Palace, the Academy of the Assumption, the Teatro González, the Provincial Headquarters of the National Guard; and moving beyond the Casa Prío, the Recalde Bookstore, and the Municipal Palace (which housed the Social Club of León), a branch of the Bank of Nicaragua, and the El Sesteo Restaurant; and on the other side of the street, heading back towards the cathedral, the Rambla Hardware Store.

It was now ten o'clock. Somoza, his Panama hat once again on his head, and the silver cigarette holder clamped between his teeth, cut across the plaza diagonally on his way to the Teatro González, surrounded by his bodyguards (their automatic pistols bulging under the coattails of their black jackets), and followed by officers of the Presidential Guard (with their kepis and crisply pressed uniforms, their black ties tucked inside the fronts of their shirts, plus their dark Ray-Ban sunglasses, with the cases tucked neatly in their belts), members of the National and Legal Junta of the Nationalist Liberal Party (the PLN), (some with wide floral ties and striped cashmere suits, others with rumpled linen jackets and a wide variety of hats). To Captain Prío, the entourage looked like a slithering reptile as it moved forward, clearing a path among the red banners, cardboard placards,

38

straw hats, parasols, and red baseball caps. A reptile with its tail held erect: Sartorius Van Wynckle standing out because of his height and his arrow-thin body.

Captain Prío was not able to get a good, up-close look at him, but I'll help him out: dressed in a wrinkled bone-white linen suit, and wearing a bow tie askew in a way that seemed to reflect his way of walking, edging his way forward with the vigilant gaze of his blue eyes hidden under rimless sunglasses always peering ahead in advance of his body; elastic suspenders visible under the suitcoat that flapped open with each hasty and purposeful step, a shirt pocket stuffed with pencils, his big shoes mercilessly crushing the toes of more than one unsuspecting member of the boxed-in entourage, National Guard Lt. Anastasio Morales (Moralitos) being the most likely victim of this bruising because he had to stick close to him to receive his instructions, his starched uniform crackling with his every step.

Moralitos was the second-in-command at the Office of National Security (ONS) being created under the supervision of Van Wynckle, but which, owing to a continued lack of adequate quarters, was still working out of a small sewing room in the rear of the Presidential Palace on Tiscapa Hill, equipped with a desk for Van Wynckle, two telephones, and school desks with hinged tops for each of his three apprentice officers, the same desks General Somoza's children—Luis (the Good), Lilliam (the Queen), and Anastasio (the Bad)—had used for doing homework during their school days.

Moralitos, born in the Calvario barrio of León, was plainly given the name of Anastasio in homage to Somoza, his baptismal godfather, just after he had come to power. A recent graduate of the Military Academy, Moralitos had taken an intelligence course at the School of the Americas at Ft. Gulick in the Panama Canal Zone, where Van Wynckle had been his instructor. He was only twenty-four, though, when he began to show signs of incipient baldness that had already left a tonsure visible on the crown of his head; his taut lips beneath a moustache, a bulldog face, and bloodshot eyes that always seemed in need of sleep, displayed a zeal and a willingness to learn his trade.

Somoza entered the Teatro González with his entourage. On his Grundig radio downstairs in the sitting room Captain Prío could hear the commotion inside the theater rising above the voice of the Gran Cadena Liberal radio announcer, even though he was now shouting, and had abandoned all attempts to imitate the rotund eloquence of Manuel Bernal. Outside in the street, Somoza's supporters disbanded, trampling the placards and banners; and in lines that soon turned into a mob scene, they grabbed for the tamales and rations of aguardiente being distributed from the backs of the trucks. Women breast-feeding their infants sat in solitude on the curbs and watched the tumult from a distance.

And while Somoza ascended the stage, according to the radio announcer's fervent and enthusiastic explanation, the First Lady was leaving her paternal home with her own entourage on the north side of the cathedral to get into her limousine and be driven the short distance to the old Maison de Santé Hospital. Captain Prío, who was watching the discreet stir at the door, consulted his pocketwatch again, verifying that she had spent barely five minutes inside. But she would return later for lunch—an intimate lunch with just a few guests, according to the program that had appeared in the newspapers.

The Maison de Santé, a short distance from the rear of the cathedral, was not within Captain Prío's field of vision. But follow the First Lady with me, if you will; go with her as she walks the dilapidated corridors of the old hospital she so devoutly wanted to convert into a museum, see the damp patch on the wall where once hung in a place of honor the portrait of her ancestor, Stendhal; out in the garden, bushes and prickly-pear shrubs overtaking in a sad exuberance the grass and flowers, while crabgrass grows amidst the shafts of sunlight pouring in through what had once been the roof of the operating theater, where the learned Debayle had carried out his aforementioned operations.

The sole inhabitant of the Maison de Santé was out at the moment of the First Lady's visit. At that hour, he could probably be found wandering aimlessly through the stalls of the Mercado Municipal a block away in search of lunch, a book under his arm as usual, a thick mat of hair, streaked with gray, protruding over his ears like a flowerpot; or perhaps he's gone to the top of the cathedral facade. The massive towers are anchored to the central nave by two supports, each one held up by a pair of columns; from each support hangs a bell, and under one of those bells, where there is no parapet, Chiron enjoys sitting and reading. But he's not there, not yet at least, for if he were, Captain Prío would already have spotted him, unmistakable even from that distance because he always wore white.

Would she remember him if they came across each other in one of those hallways tiled in a black-and-green mosaic pattern like a chess board, tiles which he brought to a brilliant shine with a mop soaked with disinfectant? He had been her father's little servant, the one who served him his champagne, buried the fetuses for him, set the surgical instruments out for him, lined up in perfect order. His name is Chiron, madame, like Chiron the Centaur, Aesculapius's mentor. Rubén transmitted the *numen* to him once by taking the boy's head between his hands and squeezing it. Rubén? Rubén Darío? Rubén Darío transmitted what to him? At the Port of Corinto? What madness is that? He fainted? Smelling salts? When? I don't go around believing in saints who pee.

Now they had reached the farthest courtyard, beyond what used to be a concealed pavilion for the consumptive and the insane. Here, beyond an iron grille, were the stone steps that led down to the morgue. And while Salvadorita complained to the wife of the mayor of León, who was accompanying her on this visit, about the deplorable state of the building: how much was this going to cost, a ton of money, would her husband Tacho, President Somoza, tight-fisted as he was, be willing to provide the budget for it? An engineer there from the Ministry of the Economy and Public Works in a tie and short sleeves, sweating profusely, followed her around notebook in hand, as the echoes of their footsteps gradually merged into voices, voices that seemed to emanate from the crumbling walls. Did Captain Prío hear this conversation from his vantage point? No, he's too far away, and the Grundig radio was still blaring. Does Chiron hear what they're saying? Chiron always hears everything because he's got the starry ear of a centaur. But if that's not sufficient, I also have ears:

Today is November 18, 1907. In the shade of the garden where a pair of peacocks strut about, the cypresses stir in the barely perceptible breeze which portends rain. Chiron is polishing the mosaic tiles of the hallways with a mop.

Rubén and the learned Debayle have just had their photographs taken. You can still see the two lacquered rocking chairs in the garden, their delicate contours and splendid jet-black color outlined against the green foliage. Between the delicate spirals of the rockers, the peacocks peck at the grains of wheat sprinkled over the grass like a trail of foam. Maestro José Cisneros has already passed through the emery-polished glass doors that lead into the waiting room, carrying his tripod and the two large nail-studded boxes where he stores his equipment: the Lumington camera, the plates, the vials of potassium cyanide, and the magnesium powder.

Rubén is seated in the hallway at one end of a cane sofa, next to a little table covered with a crocheted mantle that drapes into points, and on it a bottle of cognac and a glass. He is wearing a beige alpaca suit and a navy-blue tie held in place by the ever-present gray pearl tie pin. On the same sofa, laid out in no particular order, are the photographs of the triumphant reception that Maestro Cisneros handed him on his arrival.

The whole town races toward the small square outside the train station. A swarm of ants dressed in their Sunday best joyfully pours onto the platform and kidnaps him as soon as he appears at the door of the train, raising him on their shoulders to carry him to the open carriage, where they unhitch the horses in a burst of jubilation. A band of artisans immediately grabs the pole and pulls the carriage along the street through a flurry of banners and placards. Palm fronds festooned with Chinese paper-chains on sidewalks crammed with people. Triumphal arches adorned with fruits and sawdust-filled birds silently cawing. The carriage rolls over a soft carpet of cracked wheat, dyed mauve, gold, and hyacinth and fashioned into images of swans, fauns, and Pegasuses. From the triumphal arches, papier-maché pomegranates open to discharge a shower of leaflets with his first childhood verses, and people fight over them tooth and nail as if they were winning lottery tickets.

Now, as he reclines on the sofa with his legs wide apart, his protuberant stomach is as prominent and remarkable as his formidable head. Behind him, the lithograph of Stendhal's portrait in his consul's uniform, painted by Valeri Silvestro, stands out against the gleaming whitewashed wall. Nearby, the learned Debayle, dressed in a black broadcloth suit, paces back and forth, preoccupied, clenching his hands behind his back, muttering in French. He releases his hands and, without interrupting his pacing, waves them round and round in front of him. A shadow darkens his broad forehead.

General Selvano Quirino had insisted on changing the color of his eyes because he wanted blue ones. They called him *The Little President,* as much for the power that the president, General José Santos Zelaya, had given him, charging him with oversight of the country's entire western region, León, and Chinandega, as for his tiny stature; a Subtiava Indian of such proven courage that Garibaldi, under whose command he had fought in the Piedmont campaign, wrote in a military dispatch that *di piccolo non avea altro*

43

che la statura. From Italy he had brought the habit of carrying a vanity-case in his military satchel, and used its little mirror to groom the hairs of his moustache sprouting on either side of his mouth.

The operation had a disastrous result. General Selvano Quirino was left blind and died a short while later, after having made a farewell circuit of his Santos Lugares properties on the back of a mule. Since he had no children, everything went to his sister Galatea Quirino, *Our Lady of the Fields*. And being quite powerful in her own right, *Our Lady of the Fields* initiated a scandalous lawsuit against the learned Debayle.

"But, tell me, why did you insist on performing such a stupid operation?" Rubén maliciously interrogates him, looking up from the photograph album.

"He insisted on it, because even though he was a large landowner, he felt small," replies Debayle without turning around, looking out on the rainy sky. "And it wasn't a stupid operation, Rubén."

"As stupid as the one you performed on your nephew, the inventor Godofredo," Rubén says, leaving his book resting open on his stomach.

"That wasn't my fault, either." the learned Debayle approaches him, quickening his pace. "The manufacturers in Detroit sent me the wrong-size stainless steel sacrum."

"Out of vanity, out of your thirst for fame, you'd be capable of stitching a double penis to the groin of some poor impotent bastard." Rubén laughs, rhythmically nodding his head.

"I followed Van Grafle's method step by step to change the color of his eyes." The learned Doctor Debayle stops very close to Rubén. "I used Kalt's pincer to extract the lens, injected a solution of blue methylene. I washed the lachrymal sac with mercury chloride, at one per three thousand..."

"What colossal nonsense!" Rubén closes the book with a light tap. "Have you caught the tropical plague? Here

44

stupidity becomes a contagious disease. You, a student of Pean, who learned how to operate in tie and tails, wearing white gloves and medals on your chest to be applauded in the operating rooms the same way Gino Tagliaferri is applauded at the Paris Opera!"

"It wasn't nonsense, Rubén." The learned Doctor Debayle waves his hands. "It's a scientific procedure...in Paris, at the Hotel Dieu..."

"In Paris, you'd be in the dungeons of La Défense by now." Rubén makes an effort to appear harsh. "And what do you want from me?"

"A gesture on your part, to President Zelaya, to put an end to this perverse trial." The learned Debayle, looking helpless, sits down next to Rubén on the sofa. "My prestige is being torn to shreds. Zelaya will not deny you anything."

"Me, a negotiator! He's twice denied me the audience I've requested of him! They counsel him against me, they tell him that I'm nothing but an incorrigible drunk." A blue vein bulges on Rubén's right temple, and his nostrils flare.

"You're a national treasure." Debayle pats him affectionately on the knee. "They'll give you your credentials as ambassador to the Court of Madrid. That's a fact."

"A fact just as sure as the one that they'll sentence you to hard labor for leaving a man blind!" Rubén returns to his book, still agitated. "Who will dare to touch someone of your standing? Go on, go on with your butchery. I won't lift a finger to help you."

"I received a telegram from her." The learned Debayle looks at him, measuring the blow he's delivered.

Rubén looks terrified.

"*La Maligna*! What does she want now? I gave her everything I had, in her brother's presence, five thousand francs, in bills, so that she wouldn't get off the train in León, so that she'd continue on to Managua."

"More money. She wants another five thousand francs and she'll finally consent to a divorce." Doctor Debayle crosses his arms.

"Another five thousand francs! She´s crazy! Where will I get another five thousand francs?" The book appears restless in his hands.

"She threatens to return and make a lot of trouble for you." Debayle squeezes Rubén's knee. "I advise you to settle."

"Settle? Will you give me the five thousand francs?" Rubén is seething and the book is about to go flying through the air.

"All you need to do is talk with Zelaya." The learned Debayle presses his hand down harder on Rubén's knee.

"I'm going to ask President Zelaya for money to give to my wife?" Now the book does go flying, and the doctor walks over to pick it up.

"An advance on your salary as ambassador," he says, handing the book back to him.

"My salary? They don't want to name me to the post and you're already talking about an advance!" Rubén laughs contemptuously.

"You have no other recourse than to ask again for a meeting." The learned Debayle shrugs his shoulders and starts pacing back and forth again.

"Yes. And in the process, I'll take up your case with Zelaya." Rubén scrutinizes him when he's turned around again.

"She'll come here and make you suffer." Debayle shrugs again. "You know how jealous she can be. She's capable of throwing her famous little flask of vitriol in Eulalia's face."

"That would be unspeakable!" Rubén is worked up.

"You have to prevent such an infamous act." The learned Debayle extends his hands in a gesture of stopping the perpetrator.

"*La Maligna*. The black torment," Rubén murmurs, his legs wide apart, his head hanging down.

"So?" The learned Debayle smiles, sniffing victory.

"So there'll be two people in jail; you, for blinding an old man, and she, for disfiguring a lady's face." Rubén picks up the glass and downs it in one gulp.

And ignoring Debayle, he lifts his eyes from the book and fixes them on Chiron, who is diligently pushing the mop along the tiled floor.

"Come, come over here," he bids him.

Chiron doesn't move, his hands clinging to the mop.

"Come over here, don't be afraid." Rubén repeats his request with an awkward wave of his hand.

A nurse in a long blue-striped apron and nurse's cap crosses the hallway, carrying a tray of medicines. Debayle comes to a halt to ask her something. From a distance, on the floor's mosaic tiles, the two look like pieces on a chessboard. Then the woman disappears behind a folding screen, draped with a white blanket to obscure any view of the interior of one of the private rooms.

Chiron is standing in front of Rubén now, mop in hand. Debayle consults his watch and again looks out at the cloudy sky. The solemn session of the Athenaeum of León, in homage to Rubén, awaits them.

"Bishop Simeón will be dying to launch into his bit of oratory welcoming you." Debayle pockets his watch.

"Can you read?" Rubén asks Chiron.

Chiron indicates no, shaking his thatch of hair.

"I'll teach you." The odor of old fermented grapes invades the boy's nostrils.

Rubén quickly takes a sip of his cognac, puts his glass down on the little table, and seats the boy on his knees. He turns back to the first page of the book with pink and yellow jaspers on the cover, the same book he has been reading since he left Cherbourg: *The General and Native History of the*

Indies, Islands and Terra Firma of the Ocean-Sea by Captain Gonzalo Fernández de Oviedo y Valdés.

"It's getting late, we must go." Debayle goes to fetch their hats, which are hanging from the deer antlers mounted on the wall.

"You go, and send greetings on my behalf to the august gathering." Rubén, not letting Chiron get down, reaches for the bottle of cognac.

"Stop it! You can play kindergarten teacher some other time." The learned Debayle comes over with Rubén's hat and tries to put it on his head.

"Go to hell!" Rubén slaps his hat away.

"Rubén, I won't let you!" The hat has rolled to Debayle's feet.

"You and your crowd of uncouth know-it-alls, I'm fed up with your recitations and discourses." Rubén throws a scare into the learned Debayle, flailing his arms about, with the book in his hand.

"Bishop Simeón will never forgive you," Debayle wants to continue arguing as he retreats.

"Stop pestering me!" Rubén explodes, and brusquely setting the boy down from his lap, stands as if to throw the book at Debayle's head.

"And what about Eulalia, who's going to recite in your honor? What shall I tell her?" The learned Debayle is trembling with anger. "How noble! Courting the wife of an invalid!"

"Invalid because of you! And don't meddle in my private business. You'd do well to get busy with buying the judges off! Blue eyes! What nonsense!"

The learned Debayle disappears behind the polished glass door, which closes with a thunderous slam. Rubén quickly takes another sip of cognac, lifts Chiron back onto his lap, returns to the book, and with his index finger points to a line, slowly tracing his finger over it.

"Let's read about Pedrarias Dávila, the *furor domini*, who was the one who brought pigs to Nicaragua for the first time," Rubén says, resting his large head against the back of the sofa. "A conquistador who became powerful raising pigs. This is a good country for fattening pigs."

"What does *furor domini* mean? Chiron asks him. Never until now had he heard his voice, like a distant wood flute in the foliage of Pan's forest.

"*The fury of God*. When God blows a gasket, he sends the people a pig farmer. And the pig farmers don't understand anything about poets, just lard and bacon. The muses, Chiron, have nothing to do with chitlins." Rubén has another glass and the cognac tints his lips a dark amber.

The wind kicks up in the garden, now covered in shadows, and tips over the two empty rocking chairs. The peacocks flee. A powerful thunderclap reverberates and silvery streams of rain begin to fall in a noisy torrent from the eaves, to the happy sound of female voices. "Who was there to film those scenes?" asks Erwin, as Rigoberto closes his journal.

"They're historical reconstructions," says Captain Prío. "There's no need to question them."

"Can it be true that Chiron became such an avid reader?" Norberto asks.

"Well, if it means anything, he's always going around with some big heavy book or other under his arm, the kind that puts you to sleep with its small print," says Erwin.

"Let Rigoberto tell us; he was Chiron's distinguished pupil," Captain Prío says.

"Did Chiron take your head between his hands and pass on the sacred *numen* to you as well?" Erwin asks him.

"Not me," Rigoberto says. "I'm just an amateur poet. But he did introduce me to great books."

"A dumb teacher. That's a new one," says Norberto.

"Well, if Chiron sits there in the bell tower of the cathedral, at least he's read that novel about the hunchback of Paris," the goldsmith Segismundo says.

"He has, indeed," Captain Prío says. "He had barely learned to read when he started on Victor Hugo. At Rubén's farewell banquet, at Debayle's house, he stunned the dinner guests when he read aloud from *The Legend of the Centuries,* and in French."

"And what about that pack of lies that Debayle was a descendant of Stendahl?" Erwin says, addressing Rigoberto.

"Henri Beyle was Stendhal's real name," Rigoberto says, turning back to his journal. "De Beyle, Debayle."

"So Somoza is related to the author of *The Red and the Black*! Shit mixed with glory!" the goldsmith Segismundo exclaims.

"And why was it that Stendhal came to Nicaragua?" Erwin asks.

"He was overseer for the cocoa plantations in the Menier Valley in Nandaime," Captain Prío says. "That's where the Menier family made its fortune, the kings of the chocolate industry in France."

"You're mistaken, Captain," Rigoberto says. "It was one of Stendhal's sons, living with a mulatta from Martinique, who came to Nicaragua as overseer. He remained here, and had a family with the mulatta."

"Stendhal's son and the mulatta must have come on the same ship as Giuseppe Garibaldi," says Erwin.

"Garibaldi arrived in 1851, at the port of San Juan del Norte, aboard the *Prometheus*," Rigoberto says. "Stendahl's son and the mulatta, a decade earlier."

"Garibaldi lodged with Dr. Darbishire, on Calle Real," Captain Prío says. "General Selvano Quirino, a boy at the time, went out with him to hunt rabbits."

"Garibaldi came just for that, to hunt rabbits?" Norberto asks.

"He was involved in some commercial dealings, with a friend of his, one Francesco Carpaneto," Rigoberto adds. "They started a candle factory in León."

"And from hunting rabbits with Garibaldi in the mountains of León, Selvano Quirino went on to serve in the Italian campaign in Piedmont," Erwin says.

"He was also a hero at the Battle of Catania," Rigoberto reminds them. "After the campaign in Sicily, he came back a colonel."

"And with a trunk full of gold coins, he made himself into a landowner, that's for sure," the goldsmith Segismundo says.

"The only thing he brought back from Sicily was a clavichord given to him by King Víctor Manuel as a reward for his services," Rigoberto says. "He made his money here, with Zelaya, after the liberal revolution. Zelaya promoted him to general."

"I don't even believe this Selvano Quirino ever existed," Erwin says.

"He existed, of course he did," says Captain Río. And with his hand he traces a huge territory off in the distance. "He owned vast properties, from the Gulf of Fonseca to Lake Managua. The entire plain, from the Cosigüina Volcano to the Momotombo Volcano."

"Let him have his doubts, Captain," Rigoberto says. "Seeing as how he wasn't at my side when I consulted books, underlined, copied until the early morning hours—he's got a right to be skeptical. That's ignorance for you."

"The Santos Lugares properties were fought over in the Holy War," Norberto says. "*Terrestial Light* inherited Cafarnaún when *Our Lady of the Fields* died, run over by an ox-cart."

"That's how you got to be a prosperous businessman, renting those lands from her to grow your cotton," Erwin says. "So prosperous that the bank is still after you."

"When you marry *Zela the Moor*, those lands will pass into your hands," Captain Prío says, slapping him enthusiastically on the shoulder. "*Terrestial Light* will leave it all to your mother-in-law, *The Rose Child*," he added.

"Shed some light on those relationships, Captain," Norberto asks, settling into the chair.

"Goliath, a powerful businessman, had three children," Captain Prío says, in his best professorial mode. "Saint Mardoqueo, Eulalia—*The Rose Child*'s mother—and *Terrestial Light*."

"In that case, the famous Eulalia, she of the joined eyebrows, will become his grandmother through marriage," the goldsmith Segismundo says, pointing to Norberto.

"Exactly. And Norberto will then also become a relative of Saint Mardoqueo, Eulalia's brother," Captain Prío says.

"And probably of Rubén Darío, too, if it's true that the poet got Eulalia pregnant," Norberto says, looking round at everyone with great pride.

"Forget it. *The Rose Child*—*Zela the Moor*'s mother—is the daughter of the paralytic Godofredo," Erwin says.

"Godofredo became impotent after he fell from the horse," Rigoberto says. "In which case, I assure you: *Zela the Moor* is Rubén's granddaughter."

"Their lovemaking took place right up there, in the very same room where I now sleep," Captain Prío said.

"Well, Captain, perhaps you'll find something of Rubén's famous *numen* somewhere in the sheets," said Segismundo.

"Or some bit of pubic hair, which in any case would be my inheritance," stated Norberto.

"The one who was impotent was Rubén. He could never have gotten Eulalia pregnant," Erwin asserted. "By the time of his triumphal return to Nicaragua, liquor had destroyed his virility."

"For me, impotence is an absolutely bizarre experience," Segismundo stated, cocksure.

"If not, then let *The Beautiful Love Goddess* say otherwise," Erwin said.

"How did news of that episode reach here?" the goldsmith Segismundo asked, quite pleased with himself.

"The second half of the story is the best, when they sent you to get the money from her to stage the Judas play, Norberto said. "That's where that viper left you minus your balls."

"You know me well enough to be sure I didn't tell anyone about that unfortunate affair," Rigoberto said, looking imploringly over at Segismundo.

"This young chap," the goldsmith Segismundo said, taking Norberto by the arm, "isn't he the one who entertains himself serenading licentious men?"

"Don't talk to me about serenades or there might be some unpleasant repercussions," Norberto said, glancing at Rigoberto as he bit the little medal hanging from his neck.

"It's a wonder Norberto didn't commission you for an engagement ring for the bridegroom," Erwin said, addressing the goldsmith Segismundo and fanning himself with his Basque beret.

"Quit stirring things up, I've already told him I'm sorry," Rigoberto said, and then made as if he were writing something in his journal while glancing at Norberto out of the corner of his eye.

So Sentimental And So Divine

At midnight, when *La Salvadorita* was approaching Puerto Morazán, navigating one of the narrow inlets of the Estero Real, Mars was already shining brightly above the invisible volcano chain of Los Maribios. The scattered lights of the port could be counted from the deck of *La Salvadorita*, as it came alongside the little wharf perched on top of uneven pilings, while the Caterpillar engine droned on, spewing the odor of burned diesel fuel from the stern.

On a hill, at one end of the horseshoe-shaped estuary, lights were shining from the National Guard barracks, a construction of prefabricated panels donated by Truman's Four Points Program for rural schools. Lower down, set on pilings at the edge of the flotsam left by the incoming tide, stood the Customs Office, and at the other end of the horseshoe, in front of the mangrove swamps, was the Bartola Bar and Restaurant, a kind of embarkation anchored on land. There, as aboard *La Salvadorita*, you could sleep in hammocks hung from the crossbeams, or on deck, or by joining two of the tables together with metal signs advertising Victoria beer. And scattered next to the dunes, the shacks of fishermen and stevedores, the flickering of candles visible between the stalks of wild cane.

Sergeant Domitilo Paniagua, super erect, with bristly, rebellious hair like a porcupine, shone his flashlight on the faces of the passengers as they came down the cedar plank that served as a gangway between the boat and the dock. Behind him, a drowsy private armed with a Garand rifle, a cone-shaped cap on his head, was on watch.

Very attentive to his accounts, the sergeant turned the flashlight away only after they had handed him payment for each bundle of merchandise, and their travel documents—boarding permits which he himself had issued to the merchants—tearing them up once he got them back, for this was the surest way of invalidating them. He also collected all their passports, to take up to the barracks, type out the list on his Remington typewriter, and stamp them.

Later, when the passengers were already asleep in the Bartola, he turned his flashlight back on and stopped again at each face. He was returning the passports. The Gypsy Boys, annoyed, grumbled. Dazzled by the beam, *The Lion of Nemea* rubbed his eyes and shook his long locks. Dr. Balthazar Cisne, on the other hand, at the far end of the room because he didn't want to be anywhere near Cordelio, kept on snoring with his mouth open, a little thread of saliva running down his unshaved chin, and it took some effort to wake him.

The flashlight finally paused on Rigoberto's face, who blinked, dazed. He had remained awake, leaning against the flimsy wall, the little cardboard valise squeezed against his lap. Next to him, Cordelio was also awake.

Sergeant Domitilo Paniagua signaled them to come with him with his flashlight, and they followed him to the edge of the dune, awash in the churning waves on a pitch black night.

"Where have you come from?" he asked in a very harsh tone.

"Me? From San Salvador. As for the preacher, I don't know; I don't know him," Rigoberto said, setting his little valise down on the sand.

"Bullshit. You came together," Sergeant Domitilo Paniagua said, cutting him short. "You were seen drinking beer together in La Unión. If you want more details, in La Cucharita Bar."

"All right, to tell you the truth, sergeant, I know him and I don't know him." Rigoberto looked for corroboration from Cordelio, who nodded.

"What? Do you take me for an idiot?" Sergeant Domitilo Paniagua said.

"We met by accident. We were both looking for Rubén Darío, who was lost," Rigoberto said.

"Rubén Darío got lost?" Sergeant Domitilo Paniagua looked puzzled.

"He'd been stolen. And he was the one who found him," Cordelio said, pointing to Rigoberto.

"Found him where?" Sergeant Domitilo Paniagua, his curiosity aroused.

"In an ice cream parlor, where he was used as a decoration," Cordelio said.

"As a decoration? Do you mean to say they had him there, doing nothing?" said Sergeant Domitilo Paniagua.

"More or less," Rigoberto replied.

"Poets are all a bunch of tramps," declared Sergeant Domitilo Paniagua. "And so that's what you were doing in San Salvador?"

"No, I was really there chasing down the famous wrestler Manfredo Casaya to interview him. I'm a journalist," Rigoberto said.

"A journalist, right. I saw that on your passport," Sergeant Domitilo Paniagua said warily.

"It's true, he was there to interview me." They heard the voice of *The Lion of Nemea*, hoarse with sleep, as he emerged from the darkness, more disheveled than ever.

"You, go back to sleep," Sergeant Domitilo Paniagua ordered, shining his flashlight on him right up close. "This is a private interrogation."

Sergeant Domitilo Paniagua dismissed *The Lion of Nemea*, as if by turning his flashlight away from him he had made the man go away; and then he aimed it at Cordelio's face.

"And you, they say you're a Protestant preacher." The sergeant checked him out from head to toe with his flashlight.

Cordelio's only reply was to press the Bible against his chest and bow his head. Sergeant Domitilo Paniagua pulled out both of their passports from the back pocket of his trousers. Aiming his flashlight, he looked through the pages of Cordelio's passport.

"You're a Honduran citizen?" he asked him.

"Josías Arburola Reina, brought into the world by the grace of Our Lord Jehovah, in Comayagua," Cordelio said, without raising his head. "I preach all over the Chamalecón jungle, from San Juan de Ulúa to Chalatenango. As penance, my only nourishment is wild honey."

"Wild honey? I detect the stink of guaro," Sergeant Domitilo Paniagua said, sniffing him.

"Fermented wild honey," Rigoberto said.

"He became a Protestant after he washed his hands," *The Lion of Nemea* said, butting in again from the darkness.

"What do you mean, he washed his hands?" Sergeant Domitilo Paniagua asked him, and the wrestler came closer, confidently.

"Sure, because he played Pontius Pilate in a Judas play they staged in San Salvador," *The Lion of Nemea* said.

That had been a great event. After the fiasco of the wrestling match, Cordelio got the idea to stage a play for Easter, *The Martyr of Golgotha*, a work by Manuel Pérez Esrich, where the principal actors would be the exiles themselves.

The goldsmith Segismundo was once again given the job of procuring the finance for the undertaking, although it took a lot of work on Cordelio's part to convince him a second time because, despite his manly vigor, he already knew where he stood with that madwoman of pleasure. Nevertheless he went once more to surrender himself to the arms of *The Beautiful Love Goddess*.

They clambered all over one another to see him off at the door of the Casa Dinamarca as he set out again, all powdered and perfumed with Yardley, and his shoes as shiny as cracked mirrors, this time not in a taxi but in a gold Chrysler waiting for him outside. When she learned of his imminent visit, *The Beautiful Love Goddess* had sent the car for him. A chauffeur in jacket and tie and a black chauffeur's cap, as if it were really a hearse, opened the car door for him.

This time *The Beautiful Love Goddess* really did take him apart. He came back a week later, his knees rubbed raw, his sides aching, his shoulders crisscrossed with long scratch marks. He even began suffering from blood in his urine.

"Brothers, I come to you half-dead," he told them as they helped him out of the gold Chrysler and led him up to his bed, undressed him, put on his pajamas, and tucked him in. "I think that other time I must have gotten hold of her when she was ailing, or who knows what, because she let me go after just one slam-bam session, and I managed to get back on my feet, although pretty banged up and feeble. This time, after the first night, when she woke up, I thought I had taken care of her forever because there had been seven onslaughts, one right after the other. Whatever possessed me to boast in front of her! That was only a goddamn dress rehearsal, she said, with an evil cackle. And from then on, she did with me what she wanted: she milked me dry, standing against the walls, squatting in the porcelain bathtub full of hot water, sitting on the toilet, on the stairs, in the Madame Recamier armchairs, on the prie-dieu in her chapel, in the kitchen, down on the floor, on the stones in the garden. The only thing missing was to throw me, already spent, into the alligator pit so they could get their fill of me, too."

But he brought back a check for one thousand colones. The performance was announced all over San Salvador, and on Good Friday the exiles, all cast members, rehearsed and dressed in their Hebrew tunics and Roman soldier gear, waited in vain for the public to show up at the Flor Blanca Stadium, while they sat and sat in the locker rooms, which served as their dressing rooms, turned into ovens by the burning sun. By four o'clock, Cordelio was forced to cancel the performance, leaving the crosses of Mount Calvary planted in the turf of the soccer field; and he took what was left over from *The Beautiful Love Goddess's* check to rent a bus to take the cast to the beach resort at Jiquilillo.

They filled up the Atlacalito bar, sitting under an arbor to the surprise and even indignation of the drunks in bathing suits at the other tables, who coudn't understand this vision of Nazarene tunics and Pharisee turbans surrounding a Jesus who stumbled every time he got up to pee. On Easter Saturday, the still convalescing Segismundo showed up. He told them that for the second performance, which no one had remembered to cancel, the stadium was full to bursting, and there were still lines at the ticket windows that stretched out of sight.

"I played the role of Judas Iscariot because the Italian director they hired needed someone who looked mean," *The Lion of Nemea* said.

"I've got an Italian prisoner right here who's a theater person, too," Sergeant Domitilo Paniagua said.

"And what's the name of this Italian?" a cautious Rigoberto asked him.

Sergeant Domitilo Paniagua beamed his flashlight on a third passport he had pulled out of his pocket.

"His name is Lucio Ranucci," he said, having difficulty deciphering it.

"It's him!" said *The Lion of Nemea,* who had come closer to get a look at the passport picture. "It's great you've got him locked up, sergeant. He almost hanged me for real with the Judas rope during rehearsal."

"Why did you take him prisoner?" Rigoberto asked, still suspicious.

"When I was going to stamp his passport, I heard him mumble under his breath: 'Thank God I'm leaving this shitty country forever,'" Sergeant Domitilo Paniagua said with renewed anger. "I've got him over there in the little cell for his disrespect toward the country, that fairy."

"He's no fairy, sergeant," Cordelio said. "He fucked all the women in Jerusalem between rehearsals."

"And all that money you made from the play, what did you use it for?" Sergeant Domitilo Paniagua asked.

"I never saw any of it," said *The Lion of Nemea*.

"We used it to buy a little black beast," Cordelio said.

"What?" Sergeant Domitilo Paniagua asked, mystified.

"I've got a pedigree baby buzzard; they're expensive," Cordelio said. "Besides wild honey, I like to eat buzzard."

"That's disgusting," Sergeant Domitilo Paniaguas said, with a grimace.

"Only if you let buzzards eat dead animals, sergeant. But if you raise them from chicks and feed them little kernels of corn, it's a very clean meat," Cordelio said.

"And what do you have to do with Passion if you're Protestant?" Sergeant Domitilo Paniagua asked him.

"At the time, I still hadn't converted to the true faith," Cordelio said. "When I saw the wantonness of the Italian with the women of Jerusalem, the eyes of my soul were opened."

"Well, the Italian was hired here to direct the drama segment for Radio Mundial, and I don't know if he would have had time to fool around with the actresses," Sergeant Domitilo Paniagua said. "They got rid of him because he refused to direct *The Right to Be Born*, or so he told me in the interrogation."

"I'll bet you he wanted to put on a play called *Tovarich*," Cordelio said. "It's his obsession."

"*Tovarich*? Yes, he mentioned that," said Sergeant Domitilo Paniagua.

"Do you listen to many soap operas, sergeant?" Cordelio asked him.

"In this part of the world, the only entertainment a person gets is from the soaps," said Sergeant Domitilo Paniagua.

"In San Salvador I gave sermons over the radio, too," Cordelio said. "Do you think that would be possible here in Nicaragua?"

"Who knows?" said Sergeant Domitilo Paniagua. *The Man* doesn't like evangelists. Doña Salvadorita is a devout Catholic."

"By the way, sergeant," Cordelio said, "why's this ship we came on called *Salvadorita*?"

"Are you a little slow? It's named after the First Lady I've been talking about," Sergeant Domitilo Paniagua said.

"And who does the ship belong to, if I may ask?" Cordelio said.

"Well, it's hers," Sergeant Domitilo Paniagua said. "It's part of her own business interests, separate from those of *The Man*."

"Poor woman, she needs security in her old age," remarked Cordelio.

"Look here," Sergeant Domitilo Paniagua said, thinking it over and getting angry. "What am I doing, giving you explanations about anything, anyway? Just be glad I don't report the three of you to Headquarters in León."

"The three of us? Why me?" The *Lion of Nemea* asked from the back.

"For going around in that costume, half-naked like that and with your hair mussed up," Sergeant Domitilo Paniagua said.

"Can I go back to sleep now?" Cordelio asked.

"The interrogation isn't over," Sergeant Domitilo Paniagua said. "What was all that business you were preaching on the ship about some Martians coming down out of the sky to overthrow *The Man*?"

"You were misinformed, Sergeant," Cordelio said. "Each time General Somoza wants to get re-elected, Mars approaches Earth to help him, that's what I said. The magnetic power of Mars is immense! It's the planet of great men!"

"And you, you only write about sports for the newspaper?" Sergeant Domitilo Paniagua asked Rigoberto.

"I also cover crimes, robberies," Rigoberto answered.

"But letters, for example. You know how to write nice letters?" Sergeant Domitilo Paniagua drew closer to him.

"Love letters, especially," Rigoberto said.

Sergeant Domitilo Paniagua fell silent; then he returned their passports to them.

"And what about my passport?" demanded *The Lion of Nemea*. "Me, Manfredo Casaya."

The sergeant looked for the passport, the last one he had left to give back.

"They shouldn't even have issued you a passport, seeing as how scary ugly you are," he said, holding it out to him.

He laughed and flicked off his flashlight. Then he timidly brushed against Rigoberto's elbow, almost guessing it was him in the dark.

"I'll write the love letter for you," Rigoberto told him.

"Are you a seer or something?" Sergeant Domitilo Paniagua smiled to himself.

"Are you asking for her hand?" Rigoberto said.

"I'm already married. My wife is a cook here at the Bartola," Sergeant Domitilo Paniagua said.

"And the other one, then, where does she live? Here, too?" Rigoberto asked.

"No, she works in León, at Baby Dolls," Sergeant Domitilo Paniagua said. "She's an assistant to the owner. She manages the bar and sees to the rooms."

"The owner is *The Alligator Woman*," Rigoberto said.

"Yeah, that butch," said Sergeant Domitilo Paniagua, laughing. "No one's been able to figure out if she's a man or a woman."

"Hasn't anyone ever touched her privates?" they heard *The Lion of Nemea* ask.

"Who? *The Alligator Woman*? How should I know, and I don't care either," Sergeant Domitilo Paniagua said, barely able to locate him in the dark.

"No, not that one, the one you want to screw," *The Lion of Nemea* said.

"No one has ever touched Minerva Sarraceno," Sergeant Domitilo Paniagua said without anger.

"A miracle, a virgin in the midst of so many whores." *The Lion of Nemea* laughed.

"This guy writes the best love letters in the world." Cordelio came over. "When your Minerva Sarraceno gets that letter, she'll come running to you and drop her panties on the way."

"I wish," Sergeant Domitilo Paniagua sighed.

Then he signaled Rigoberto to follow him, and headed straight for the barracks, lighting the way with his flashlight.

"Where have you ever seen an Evangelist preacher who preaches about the planet Mars, goes around with a lousy naked guy, talks about women, and gets involved with putting on a Passion play," the sergeant said as the two of them walked off.

"As far as I'm concerned, all that stuff about the Passion play and costumes is repugnant," Rigoberto said.

"You didn't wear a costume in the pastor's Passion play?" Sergeant Domitilo Paniagua asked, stopping.

"I already told you, I didn't meet the preacher until we went looking for Rubén Darío," Rigoberto said.

"What do you think, do Martians really exist?" Sergeant Domitilo Paniagua asked, directing the beam of his flashlight up into the sky.

"They exist, but they don't have a dick, they don't have anything." Rigoberto, who had stopped to pee, looked up at the sky, too. "They're flat, like wooden saints."

"That's a good one," said Sergeant Domitilo Paniagua. "So, they can't even screw."

"Unlike Italians, who'll fuck men *and* women," Rigoberto said, buttoning his fly.

They were already climbing the dune. A flock of herons flew by in the darkness and they heard the clamor of their wings above their heads.

"So then, this Italian that I've got locked up, you mean he'd screw another man?" Sergeant Domitilo Paniagua asked, anxious.

"Even behind bars, Italians are dangerous. They have a bag of tricks," Rigoberto said. "The best thing you can do is hand him over to me."

Sergeant Domitilo Paniagua turned around, puzzled.

"And what do you want him for?"

"I want him to stage a Judas play in León," Rigoberto said.

"A play? I thought you just said you hated that stuff?" protested Sergeant Domitilo Paniagua.

"But as you just heard, it's a money-maker," Rigoberto said.

"There's still a long time to Easter," Sergeant Domitilo Paniagua said.

"It's important to start rehearsing now. We need a lot of actors," Rigoberto said.

"That's going to be difficult," Sergeant Domitilo Paniagua said. "I was going to contact León tomorrow, for them to come and get him. From there, they'll take him to Managua for Lieutenant Moralitos to interrogate him better."

"Lieutenant Moralitos only interrogates important enemies of the government," Rigoberto said.

"Like a certain Cordelio Selva who wants to sneak into Nicaragua," Sergeant Domitilo Paniagua said. "Tomorrow they're sending me his photo and all the details. If I nab him, I'll earn myself a medal."

They had stopped at the barracks door. The fluorescent tube screwed under the eave bathed them in a pale light. Gnats spun around it in a thick cloud.

"Oh, well. Poor Cordelio Selva if they catch him," Rigoberto said after a moment of silence.

Sergeant Domitilo Paniagua suddenly smiled.

"You look just like *Bienvenido Granda*," he said.

"Many people do mix us up," Rigoberto said. "Well then, is it a deal? The letter for you, the Italian for me."

"You're not one of those perverts are you, and that's why you want the Italian?" Sergeant Domitilo Paniagua asked him.

"Do I look like a pervert?" Rigoberto asked.

Sergeant Domitilo Paniagua remained pensive. He still hadn't remembered to turn off his flashlight.

"It all depends on the letter you write for me," he said. "If I like the letter, then we'll see."

"No, nothing doing with *we'll see*," Rigoberto said, picking up his valise as if he were going somewhere.

"It's just that this is very delicate," Sergeant Domitilo Paniagua said. "Releasing a prisoner, just like that."

"I'll take the letter to the girl myself," Rigoberto said. "What more do you want?"

"You sure are the Devil, *Bienvenido Granda*!" Sergeant Domitilo Paniagua said, and he finally turned off his flashlight.

The Remington typewriter sat on top of the metal desk, which took up almost all the space in the office. The sea air filtering in through the window shutters failed to relieve the stifling heat. Sergeant Domitilo Paniagua opened a desk drawer and handed Rigoberto a stack of letterhead stationery.

"This is National Guard paper," Rigoberto said.

"That way the letter will carry more weight."

Rigoberto sat down on the stool with professional celerity, inserted a sheet of paper in the carriage and was set to begin. The sergeant remained standing next to him, waiting for the first click of the typewriter. But Rigoberto suddenly sat up straight.

"First, I've got to speak to the Italian," he said. "Open the cell door for me."

"Oh no," Sergeant Domitilo Paniagua complained. "Now you're asking for too much."

"It's just that I've got to know if he'd like to direct the Judas play," said Rigoberto.

Very much against his will, Sergeant Domitilo Paniagua went over to the wall and took down a big ring of keys from the nail.

When he heard the screech of the iron door, Lucio Ranucci sat up, his blond locks flopping over his forehead. A confused smile appeared on his frightened face when he saw Rigoberto, who put his finger to his lips to warn him to keep quiet. His red silk shirt revealed a bounteous mat of blond chest hair; his recent growth of beard looked like it had been dusted with gold filings, and even the dirt his clothes had picked up from the cell looked gilt-colored like his wicker valise. Everything he wore was the color of whitewash: his shirt, the jacket folded over his arm, the canvas shoes he wore without socks.

"You're coming with me, but don't say a word," Rigoberto whispered to him, trying to look as though he had never seen him before in his life.

All Mine Were Your Laughter,
Your Fragrance, Your Sorrow

The only time Captain Prío left his observation post the morning of the great commotion was when he had to go downstairs to give orders to the waiters hard at work preparing to receive the conventioneers during the noon recess: hammer and chisel in hand, they were breaking up the blocks of ice to fill the zinc buckets where they piled bottles of Victoria beer, tearing into the boxes of Spur Cola, and breaking the seals on the cartons of Cañita rum to line up the bottles on the bar shelf.

He rushed about his domain, instructing, bellowing, threatening, his hand either adjusting his bow tie or in his shirt pocket, always ready to pull out a cigarette. He moistened his glasses with his breath and cleaned them, holding them up to the light before reading any list or invoice he was handed; when they asked him for something kept locked up, he himself found the key on his key-ring and went to get it.

Satisfied that everything was in order, he returned to his vantage point. He had lost sight of *The Alligator Woman* but she was back again, sashaying energetically along the sun-filled sidewalks, stuffed into a flaming red shirt (the Liberal Party color), hands clasping her belt buckle, the ribbon of her big woven hat tied under her chin, her triangular dark glasses covering most of her face, a sparse, bristly moustache above her fleshy mouth. She (he) was giving orders too, chiding, haranguing, answering queries, handing out vouchers for liquor and food, trying to boost morale among the sleepy-eyed demonstrators, rounding them up to assemble in front of the Teatro González where she needed them again to crowd together with their banners and placards.

But you'd better come with me now to Captain Prío's bedroom. Famous guests lodged on the second floor, a balcony with every room, in the days when the Casa Prío functioned as a hotel under the regency of don José Prío, Captain Prío's father. Among them, Rubén Darío, who had occupied this very room.

The same afternoon of his triumphal entry into León, he returned, with all the pomp of his fame, to his childhood home on Calle Real, nostalgic for memories, only to find after an hour that there were no longer any memories to return to, and that his Aunt Bernarda who had raised him was sinking into a desperate old age. Despite all her devotion to him, hardship had made her mean, and she had lent herself to the ploys of other relatives, working to get money out of him; and to top it all, she had only one good eye now, something that filled him with a mixture of fear, repulsion, and pity.

For the old woman, on the other hand, it was as if a three-ring circus had camped out in her house, a pilgrimage of devotees whose clamor only died down when they saw Rubén leaving the refuge of his bedroom, puffy and bored, to pick up with reluctant nods the reams of paper they handed him, compositions in homage to him or collections of poetry that required his signature. She was annoyed at the streams of people trampling through her rooms, while he was dismayed at the poor comforts of a house too small for his needs, his trunks, lined with cordovan leather, with his initials branded on the lids, sitting out in the hallway: one full-length trunk for his suits, another for his shirts and white clothes, a smaller one for his shoes, ties and hats, and in addition the portable bathtub, a kind of tiled sarcophagus in its sailcloth casing.

And besides that, he needed a valet, a position improvised by a local tailor, Onofre Belloríno, who was as fond of the drink as he was. He moved in with his smoothing irons so he could have the poet's suits perfectly pressed, and after he had picked his way through the jumbles of clothing in the trunks, found he had no option but to iron on a table in the hallway, in full view of everybody.

In the beginning, the old woman used to get up from her seat, quickening her step as best she could, to confiscate the bottles of cognac and Scotch he had purchased from this very same Casa Prío and tip them into the privy. Despite this, the bottles would always reappear, so she had to settle for scolding him, covering her bad eye with her hand so the sight wouldn't upset him. Even so, this terrified him so much that he couldn't stop dreaming about dead eyes falling from the ceiling and plopping onto his pillow with dry thuds.

And so one day he went over to Casa Prío, taking his portable bathtub and his trunks with him in a horse-drawn cart, only to have a worse dream on his first night there. Don José Prío heard him shrieking in terror, and when he went to his aid, followed by his servants, he found him sitting on the floor in a corner, his head covered with a bed sheet. It took a lot of persuasion to calm him down and convince him to remove the sheet.

"What happened?" don José Prío asked, kneeling at his side.

"I dreamed something frightful," he finally answered, the cup of herb tea trembling in his hand. "Two men, cross-eyed with rage, wrestled and punched each other to snatch a head, a red ball, clotted with blood, horrible, a ball with a face. And it was my face, it was my head they were fighting over."

But there's more to tell about that room. So while Captain Prío continues observing *The Alligator Woman*, allow me to send the pages of the calendar flying backwards in a rapid whirlwind. I have an easy way of achieving this (which you'll know soon enough) so that we won't be delayed in coming to the evening of April 7, 1908, just before Rubén's return to Europe.

Now you can see him up close. He's writing something on the mirror behind the candelabra. The bruise from a blow has puffed up his cheek and gives his eye a ruby-like hue that is reflected in the mirror. The guttering candles dispel the shadows in the room, dense with incense and myrrh. A warm gust of air swells the sheer drapes that hang from the window, from which one can see the ashen towers of the cathedral on the other side of the deserted plaza.

With his finger, tinged with blood, he's left the words *Mene*, *Tequel*, *Fares*, written on the mirror. Eulalia, sitting on the bed, is getting dressed, tying up the laces of her corset, and when he, wrapped in the sheet like a Greek tunic, turns to show her his blood-stained finger, she gives him a melancholy smile, her thick eyebrows more closely knit than ever.

Was it true, or was it the dream's undertow? The blood was on his finger, the words were written on the mirror. And yet he was still frightened and amused at the obscenities and blasphemies he had tried to silence in her mouth; and there were her teeth marks on his hand, where she had bitten him in the fury of her final release.

That evening, during the farewell soirée at the Teatro Municipal, Eulalia had recited the poem "The Return," which he had composed the previous afternoon in a nook at the Casa Prío. Barefoot and in pajamas, he had rushed downstairs to ask don José Prío for paper, then he sat to write, his buttocks on the edge of the stool, while the hotel guests went to other more distant tables to watch in reverent silence as he filled the pages. When he had finished, he got up to take a short stroll around the sitting room in an effort to limber up, and on one of his rounds informed them:

"Now I have to write my farewell speech to Nicaragua."

Then the distant reverence became an uproar as he found himself accosted by dozens of poets and orators who began rushing into the cantina, eager to be seen and remembered among those noted in his discourse. They soon got entangled in heated debates about their own merits, and some even threatened fisticuffs.

When the time came, he could barely be heard as he read, his face hidden in the jumble of papers he held between his hands; and upon descending the steps of the proscenium, he tripped and took a spectacular fall, banging his cheek. Terrified by having to give a public recital, he had been drinking since noon in the company of his tailor-valet, and once the evening program had begun, Debayle had to ask for help to get him into the bathtub and then into his tails.

Eulalia, who had done the first reading, arranged for them to put the helpless Rubén into her carriage with the pretext that she was accompanying him to Casa Prío to look after him. It was useless for Debayle to plead that he would take care of him, and her Aunt Casimira's warnings about discretion fell on deaf ears. With the poet safely installed in her carriage, she said goodbye to them with an unflagging smile, and ordered the coachman to give the horses their reins. They took off at a gallop that set her veils fluttering out of the window.

On orders from don José Prío, the waiters carried him upstairs to his room as carefully as if he were the statue of a saint. Eulalia sent for a jug of boiling water, washcloths, and alcohol, and after getting everyone out of the room, she locked the door, lit the candles of the candelabra, put incense and myrrh in the braziers, and began applying hot compresses to his injured face, which was already beginning to swell.

Downstairs in the saloon, the hotel guests, drinking since dawn, directed their curious gazes towards the top of the stairway. And against the wishes of don José Prío, bets were taken and placed in hats: was or wasn't it true that Rubén Darío was a satyr with a goat's hooves, or was that business

71

of being a faun with crude carnal excesses merely innocent adornment in his poetry?

His amorous dalliances with the dramatic recitalist had become famous over the months he spent in Nicaragua. Enveloped in his habitual hangover, he had his valet the tailor, whose hands also displayed a constant tremor, dress him, and then about three o'clock in the afternoon he would exit the Casa Prío, walking stick in hand, to proceed on foot to Eulalia's house, as though it were a proper visit to a fiancée. Everybody peered out their windows to watch him pass by. Women abandoned their embroidery frames, gentlemen laid their unfolded newspapers down on their rocking chairs, billiards players, cuesticks in hand, barbers, and their customers with their faces still lathered and towels wrapped around their necks, pharmacists and their customers, clerks from dry-goods stores with their tape measures, all went outside to watch him walk by.

It troubled Casimira that Rubén made no effort to hide his puerile affection for the recitalist, and it troubled her too that Eulalia should allow herself to be seduced by such a chimera, for despite the eccentricities of her character, she judged her incapable of defiling her marriage vows; her fickle moods, her easy transition from grief to joy, from boredom to enthusiasm, her cataleptic fainting spells, and her sleepwalking through the hallways of her house were manifestations of recurrent hyperesthenic crises, according to her husband, the learned Debayle.

The visits did not unsettle Godofredo, the inventor who had fallen from his horse on Saint John the Baptist day, shattering the base of his spine. That day, he had been trying to win the crown of queen of the races for Eulalia, and only needed to hook one more brass ring hanging from satin ribbons on Calle Real when his horse was spooked by a firecracker at the starting line, reared up on its hind legs and then fell back on its haunches, trapping its rider beneath it. Eulalia had promised to marry him once the crown of queen was on her head, and although she had never intended to carry out her promise, the disaster made her feel obliged to take the crippled man as her husband.

The inventor Godofredo now made his way through the corridors of the house devoid of the noise of children, using his powerful arms to push the high-backed Viennese wicker wheelchair, outfitted with bicycle wheels that squeaked on the floor tiles. The chair, a modern invention, had been imported from Bremen by the commercial establishment of don Desiderio Lacayo, Eulalia's father, known as *Goliath* because of its contrast to his stiff, half-starved figure. His emporium was the first to import wheelchairs, hand chairs, and walkers for cripples and paralytics. Godofredo received the chair as a wedding gift from his father-in-law and went to the altar in it.

In León there wasn't anyone who didn't know that if Eulalia rehearsed dramatic poses in front of mirrors, her eyes riveted on the knot where her eyebrows came together, her hair hanging loose in an abundant cascade like Sarah Bernhardt, it was to cure herself of a surfeit of virtue because the inventor Godofredo had failed as a husband, beginning with their first night together as man and wife. While trying to implant the stainless steel sacrum, the learned Doctor Debayle had punctured his scrotum with the scalpel, tearing it beyond repair.

Beneath an awning in the courtyard behind the house, Godofredo kept himself busy perfecting his inventions, while pigeons cooed all around him. One of these inventions was a talking doll, which, thanks to a Pianola mechanism sewn into its stomach, could sing two verses from a Rigoletto aria:

> *Si, vendetta, tremenda vendetta*
> *di quest'anima é solo desio...*

Dressed as a Neapolitan ruffian, the doll was despatched to the 1900 Paris World's Fair to be put on exhibit in the

Nicaraguan pavilion. It stood next to a fetus of Siamese twins in a bottle of alcohol, provided by Debayle who wrote in French the tract that explained the phenomenon. Also on display were some small handcrafted cups, a dried-up lizard, and a bag of sand from the Momotombo Volcano, praised by Victor Hugo in *The Legend of the Centuries.*

Eulalia finishes dressing, setting the diadem with its plume of feathers on her head, her face covered by veils.

"The finger of an invisible hand traced these words on the wall, behind the candelabra, at the banquet of a thousand guests," Rubén says, pointing to the mirror.

"In blood?" Eulalia asks, barely smiling.

"With a flame that came out of nowhere," Rubén says. "And the concubine of King Belshazzar, son of Nebuchadnezzar, was then filled with fright."

"And what was the name of Belshazzar's concubine?" Eulalia asks.

"I've forgotten," Rubén says. "I have no memory for the names of concubines."

"Alcoholic amnesia," Eulalia then says.

"Or mental ennui," replies Rubén.

Eulalia has returned to bed, without taking her shoes off. She draws her knees up, resting her head on them while her hair falls about her face, once more free of the diadem that lies on top of the sheets.

"They've been placing bets downstairs in the cantina that you weren't capable of taking my virginity," Eulalia says.

"How do you know?" Rubén asks, looking uncomfortable.

"I heard their voices coming up the stairway. You ought to go and show them your blood-stained finger," says Eulalia.

Rubén spreads his arms in a display of annoyance, and as he does so the sheet slips off, revealing his skinny legs and the tense roundness of his stomach. Eulalia laughs out loud at the sight of that vulgar ugliness, accentuated by his tousled hair and beard, his face swollen from the fall, his inflamed eye. The sheet is no longer a tunic, it's just any old sheet. In the air, now devoid of incense, she perceives the odor of exuded alcohol and stale urine. And she finds him shorter in stature, his indigenous features more pronounced, his skin darker.

"Come with me to Paris," says Rubén.

"What would you do with me in Paris? Another concubine? You already have one, that Spanish peasant girl," Eulalia retorts.

Rubén brusquely wraps the sheet around himself once more.

"It's often better to drink from pure fountains than polluted ones," he says.

Eulalia laughs again, lifting her head.

"Polluted! You didn't find your wife from Managua, the one they had you marry at gunpoint, a virgin. But I was," she says.

Rubén wants to take her hand then, very tenderly, but she rejects him.

"What's the name of that harpy, the one who called me a whore at Corinto?"

Rubén's face turns sullen and somber.

"I don't know," he says.

"Wife, concubines, you forget all their names," Eulalia says.

"And you, why did you marry that invalid? You told me you did it out of pity. Pity is a pistol to your head, too," Rubén says.

"I never told you I married him out of pity," Eulalia says, raising her face with a violent grimace.

"Pity, at first. And afterwards, when you found out he was impotent?" Rubén asks.

Eulalia leaps off the bed, tears filling her eyes.

"Look who's talking! Absinthe has sapped your virility; you're useless!" she says.

"Here's the proof," Rubén says, not in the mood for quarrels, showing her the blood on his finger.

"I'm menstruating, that's all," Eulalia says suddenly, and runs out of the bedroom.

Rubén buries himself in the pillows, and with eyes closed hears the dull, hurried thump of her heels descending the stairway. He raises himself up partway. On the rumpled sheets he sees her diadem with its plume of feathers.

"Carnival masks," he thinks, and throws the diadem on the floor.

"You're trying to tell us Rigoberto even knows what Darío was thinking," says Erwin.

"It's all true," Captain Prío says. "There was a black wrought-iron bed in the room with a baldachin above it. And they put incense and myrrh in burners to drive away the mosquitoes."

"The blood-stained finger seems in very bad taste to me," Segismundo says. "Can't you leave that out, my dear poet?"

"What gives you the idea that I can alter the historical facts?" says Rigoberto.

"It's better to leave it out. And all the more so if it's menstrual blood, as Eulalia asserts in the final scene," Norberto says.

"What scene? This isn't a question of scenes," Rigoberto says. "It's not the theater, is it?"

"On stage, with Ranucci as director, this would be better than *Tovarich*," Erwin says. "We take the Captain's wrought-iron bed over to the theater, and that's it."

"Before I forget," Rigoberto says, "we still need one more actor for *Tovarich*. Vasili Ivanovich, captain of the hussars, in love with Princess Natasha Petrovna."

"And who will be the gentle little princess?" asks Segismundo.

"*Zela the Moor*," Rigoberto says."

"Well, then, what could be more natural than for this young man to assume the role, seeing that he's her beau?" Segismundo says, pointing to Norberto. "He also has a soft spot for men, but that's neither here nor there right now."

"He's a little overweight for a leading man," Erwin says.

"We've only got a week until the performance," Rigoberto says. "And the only other person left is Tirso the Albino, *Jorge Negrete's* nephew."

"The one who was born bleach-white because of Saint Mardoqueo's curse?" asks Segismundo.

"It's precisely on account of his lack of color that Ranucci doesn't want to give him the role he's been begging him for every day," Rigoberto says. "Despite the fact that he's got the part down pat."

"We've got a rationalizing theosophist here who believes in the miracles of saints," Erwin says to the goldsmith Segismundo.

"It's just a question of make-up so that he won't glow with his white light," Captain Prío says.

"One minute, my friend," the goldsmith Segismundo tells Erwin. "As a mason, I have to bow before the marvels of the Great Architect when they bring justice to the people. Saint Mardoqueo's curse was directed against the Yankee intervention."

"Saint Mardoqueo isn't an altar saint yet," Captain Prío says. "They haven't even initiated the process of canonization in Rome."

"Precisely because he cursed the Yankees, they'll never grant him sainthood," the goldsmith Segismundo says. "Pius XII is an accomplice of imperialism."

"You politicize everything," Erwin says to the goldsmith Segismundo. "And even if it were true, it would be an unjust miracle. Saint Mardoqueo didn't punish the Yankees with his curse. Not even the women who went to bed with them. The ones who paid the price were the poor innocents. Children who hadn't been born yet."

"Saint Mardoqueo avenged himself on Tirso the Albino, but he couldn't do anything to stop his own sisters," Captain Prío says. "Eulalia, sinning with a faun. And *Terrestial Light*, sinning with a nun."

"Unjust or not, there is nothing to be done. Those children of the intervention, without color, will be an example for generations," the goldsmith Segismundo says.

"And how many more are there in the world who glow like Tirso on account of that curse of my great uncle, Saint Mardoqueo?" Norberto asks.

"Dozens," Captain Prío says. "Every time you see a whitey Tirso's age, it means that he's the child of that curse. If you string them all together, their white glow would reach the heavens."

"Well, Tirso is going to shine by his own light on the stage, thanks to the curse," Erwin says.

"If I were younger, I would be tickled pink to take on the theatrical challenge," says Segismundo.

"There's still one part left where age doesn't matter," Rigoberto replies. "It's the servant Anatole. All you have to do is enter with an oil lamp in your hand, and say: 'Good evening, little father.' Why don't you do it?"

"It doesn't suit me," says Segismundo. "It's too small a role for me."

"I congratulate you on the publicity for *Tovarich*," Captain Prío says to Rigoberto. "That question on the radio and in the papers: 'What will happen on the twenty-first?' has got everybody intrigued."

"Take care, poet," the goldsmith Segismundo said to Rigoberto, "lest the henchmen think that, if something bad happens to Somoza on the 21st, it's because you announced it surreptitiously."

"Perish the thought," Rigoberto said.

"I'm only warning you because I've already heard comments about the publicity," the goldsmith Segismundo says.

"Where did you hear that?" said Erwin.

"A lot of customers come into my jewelry store, and everything gets commented on there," the goldsmith Segismundo said.

"Let's turn the page, to avoid bad luck," Captain Prío said.

"Bad luck? It would be fantastic if someone put an end to that gangster's escapades on the twenty-first," Segismundo said.

"We'd better get back to family matters," Norberto said to Rigoberto. "Who finally won the famous bet?"

"There are two versions, that's why I didn't write either down," Rigoberto said. "One that Eulalia exclaimed, laughing as she crossed the room: 'Pay those who bet on Rubén Darío's virility!'"

"And the other ?" said Segismundo.

"Let Captain Prío tell you the other one," Rigoberto said.

"According to my father, she covered her head and face in her veils and left like a shadow past these very tables without saying a word. It was sad, very sad," Captain Prío said.

"I hope it's true that she left her virginity in the bed where the Captain now sleeps," Norberto said. "I already told you, I want to have a son with the head of Rubén Darío."

"That boy will turn out to be either a saint or a poet," Captain Prío said.

"Or he'll go broke in cotton," Erwin said.

Pegasus Neighs and Is Coming Your Way

The vehicle whose run was between Puerto Morazán and Chinandega, passing through Tonalá and El Viejo, was called The Pegasus Traveler, as indicated by the sign written in Gothic letters above the mud-splattered windshield. It was a Chevrolet pickup truck with a large wooden box built on top of the chassis and attached to the cab, a configuration that looked very much like a Pullman car. The passengers sat on two traverse benches, facing each other. On both sides of the exterior, herds of winged horses, painted by the hand of some anonymous artist, were flying in a pale blue sky dotted with white clouds; coal-black Pegasuses, a blue sky, and white clouds, interrupted by holes for windows.

The truck traveled inland from the Gulf of Fonseca along a winding road flooded by recent rains at the end of the August heat. Puddles as big as lagoons overflowed from the flooded pastures and covered the road in stretches of muddy water, which seemed to leave the barbed-wire fences adrift.

The large puddles of water steamed in the sun, and the sky struggled to be reflected on the chocolate-colored surface which the tires of the truck churned and dug into. A few passengers, including some musicians from The Gypsy Boys from Spain, were standing on the single running board beneath the rear door and hanging onto the iron ladder that gave access to the roof, where the cardboard boxes, stuffed with Salvadoran merchandise and the orchestra's bulkiest musical instruments were bouncing around: the drum set (bass drum, snare drum and cymbals) and the double bass.

The passengers squeezed together on the benches are mostly already known to us: the merchant woman Catalina Baldelomar, suffering from a terrible headache and from regrets known only to her, took up three spaces, thanks to the exuberant bulk of her buttocks; her sidekick, the charro *Jorge Negrete*, now seated at a distance from her, looked downcast, just like his pair of gamecocks, Lucifer and Beelzebub; Tirso the Albino was curled up at his feet, next to the cages, the resplendent glow of his white skin dulled by a veil of dust; Juan Legido, who fanned himself with his Andalusian sombrero, his linen shirt unbuttoned to the waist, the crotch of his skin-tight gypsy pants soaked with sweat; next to the merchant woman, *The Lion of Nemea*, his torso and stomach covered with sticky, repulsive (as one can see by the effort the merchant woman Catalina Baldelomar makes to avoid any contact with his hulk of a body), and indecent sweat; Dr. Balthazar Cisne who, as expected, was busy trying to protect the marble passenger wrapped in its slicker by holding it by the shoulders.

And then there were three who sat together: Cordelio, reading his Bible, holding it very close to his face; Rigoberto, cradling his little cardboard valise on his lap, while he dozed, his head bobbing up and down; and Lucio Ranucci between the two of them, as if they had him in handcuffs, swearing *sotte voce* in a Tuscan dialect—because according to his passport he had first seen the light of day in Arezzo one spring morning in 1924—his blasphemous curses hanging in the air because nothing was stirring in the blistering noonday heat, not even the legendary ferocity of Lucifer and Beelzebub.

"Why do you always go around wearing a black tie?" *The Lion of Nemea* asked Dr. Balthazar Cisne all of a sudden.

"So I won't be caught unprepared if I get news of a wake," he replied, baring his teeth with a look of smug cunning.

Rigoberto smiled, and the others smiled as they dozed.

"I say we make a stop somewhere," *Jorge Negrete* said, without opening his eyes. "I'm dying of thirst."

No one objected, and so before they left behind the four or five roadside bars that clung to the cliff close to the Virgen del Hato waterfall, *The Lion of Nemea* quickly stuck his arm out the window and banged on the red-hot roof of the cab. Then they all carried the statue in a cloud of dust to the first of the thatched lunchstands they could see.

The landscape here was different, with no trace of rain, as though they had entered another country. Scorched scrub-brush, bare hills with no hint of green anywhere. The vehicles coming from El Viejo could be seen by the distant clouds of dust they raised. The few guanacaste and berry trees, the jícaros of the savannah, languished under the dust that also poured from the roof of the cafe and deposited itself on the lid of the cooler, adorned with the Canada Dry logo, where bottles of beer swam among bits of ice. Set down next to the cooler, the cloaked statue was itself soon covered with dust.

All the stools were placed around the three tables so that the whole troupe, including the owner of The Pegasus Traveler, could sit down. Next to Rigoberto's chair rested the little valise; next to *Jorge Negrete*'s, the cages with Lucifer and Beelzebub; very close to Dr. Balthazar Cisne's, the statue. They brought in more beer from the other stands, taken from the other Canada Dry coolers after a friendly agreement among the owners.

After the first round of beers, *Jorge Negrete* began to get festive.

"Tell them, doctor, about that night you showed up at Baby Dolls and asked *The Alligator Woman* to bring you the best of the girls," he said to Dr. Balthazar Cisne. "Tell them why none of them wanted to do it with you, and tell them what that big, chubby, dark-skinned girl—*Day Flower*—finally told you: 'Oh, no, me with you? I couldn't. I wouldn't know if you were screwing me or I was giving birth to you.'"

The guffaws (Rigoberto refused to join in) burst offensively upon Dr. Balthazar Cisne's ears, and he frowned bitterly and shrank back in his chair. The merchant woman Catalina Baldelomar laughed so uncontrollably she announced that she was going to piss her pants, and she actually did. A pool of yellow liquid began taking shape in the dust under her chair.

"And how do you know that?" Juan Legido asked, turning to *Jorge Negrete.*

"Because we ran into each other there several times, right, my dear doctor?" *Jorge Negrete* said.

"I'm not in the habit of frequenting such places," Dr. Balthazar Cisne stated categorically, and he tipped his bottle of beer decorously against his mouth, setting it back down on the table with a dull thud.

"Oh, no. Don't make me out a liar, doctor," *Jorge Negrete* complained. "You remember quite clearly that while you were there that night, you proposed I give you half an hour on Radio Darío for your program *The Muse of the Airwaves*, dedicated to the poetry of Rubén Darío. I did that for you, gratis, and was happy to do it, and out of gratitude you made me a member of the Rubén Darío Honor Society."

Staring straight at his bottle of beer, Dr. Balthazar Cisne remained obstinately quiet.

"Such an odd name. It's strangely beautiful!" Ranucci said. "*The Muse of the Airwaves*! Let me jot that down." And he searched in vain for a place to make note of it. "Does that program still exist?"

"Of course it does, doesn't it, doctor? And I haven't charged him for it," *Jorge Negrete* insisted.

"And the station that bears the name of the great poet, is it really yours?" Ranucci asked.

"And yours, too, my friend," *Jorge Negrete* said with a bow.

"Do you get Radio Darío in Italy?" *The Lion of Nemea* asked Ranucci.

"In Italy, in Spain, in all of Europe. What do you think?" Juan Legido said, mockingly.

"It's true about the program," Dr. Balthazar Cisne said finally, appearing sullen. "But there are times when they don't broadcast it. You go to the studio with your script ready, and Tirso here who's at the controls, growls: 'There's no program today.'"

"Don't shortchange the truth, doctor," *Jorge Negrete* says. "That business of your program being canceled happened only once, last year, when *The Man* wanted to hear the "Beer Barrel Polka" and upset the whole evening schedule for me. Right, Tirso?"

Tirso the Albino assented, belching up his beer. Somoza had arrived in León, and they were honoring him in the home of some supporters by the name of Campuzano from the Guadalupe barrio, and having already had his share of Black and Whites under his belt, he got it into his head to dance the "Beer Barrel Polka," which was a guaracha, a polka, or who knows what the shit it was, with the Campuzano daughter, who was celebrating her fifteenth birthday; and there being no gramophone in that house or anything, except for a radio, Colonel Lira, his aide-de-camp, phoned the station and ordered them to play the "Beer Barrel Polka." The radio host announced: for the pleasure of His Excellency, the President of the Republic, on his visit to our city, with great pleasure, the "Beer Barrel Polka." Colonel Lira called back: the "Beer Barrel Polka" once more; as soon as the record stopped, there was another call: the "Beer Barrel Polka."

"After the tenth call, Tirso sent someone to look for you at the Fuente Castalia," Dr. Balthazar Cisne said, in a conciliatory tone.

"What's the Fuente Castalia?" Ranucci asked.

"A bar I own, a very popular place, run by my wife, María Félix," *Jorge Negrete* said.

"Castalia! What a sublime name! The fountain of inspiration!" Ranucci said, overflowing yet again with admiration.

84

The "Beer Barrel Polka" had been playing over and over for more than half an hour, with the radio announcer repeating: 'And now, for the pleasure of His Excellency, the president, the "Beer Barrel Polka." It wasn't enough with the orders over the phone. When *Jorge Negrete* arrived at the station to try to sort things out, he found a big National Guard Jeep outside, and two armed and mean-looking security agents commanded by Lieutenant Moralitos in the control booth to make sure the announcer didn't stop playing the "Beer Barrel Polka." Moralitos didn't have a very high-level job then. And the "Beer Barrel Polka" was played from 7:00 p.m. until 11:00 that night, four hours of the "Beer Barrel Polka." Finally, *Jorge Negrete* plucked up his courage and approached Moralitos. He asked him, "Do you think *The Man* is still dancing to the 'Beer Barrel Polka' with the young lady at this late hour?" "No," he answered, puckering up his bulldog-like snout. "The cavalcade is already en route to Managua with the young girl riding in the presidential limousine. But we'll keep on playing the 'Beer Barrel Polka' until further orders." And his hand reached for the belt where his automatic pistol hung.

"And you've got the nerve to say I canceled your program for some whim," *Jorge Negrete* said.

"That bar, the Fuente Castalia, was originally the property of the dearly departed *Basilisk*," Dr. Balthazar Cisne said.

"And that's where Rubén Darío drank his rot-gut guaro," added Jorge *Negrete*.

"Again I repeat, Rubén Darío was no drunk," Dr. Balthazar Cisne said with dismay. "Much less would he drink cheap liquor in some cantina."

"Is that so? The glass Rubén drank those burning shots from is in a display case, where my father-in-law, *Basilisk*, stowed it for safe-keeping," Jorge *Negrete* said.

Basilisk succumbed to rage the morning that *Jorge Negrete* eloped with his granddaughter María Félix, his most precious treasure. She happily served the customers easy smiles, with her high cheekbones, her face a perfect oval, her big black eyes, and long braids laced with red and green ribbons, firm little breasts under a blouse embroidered with sequins. *Jorge Negrete* sang for her that Sunday in the bar after the cockfight, and that one song was enough, along with a significant arching of eyebrows and glances, to render her his slave. And the Fuente Castalia came to be an unexpected inheritance. Because of his hernia (he needed a boy to help him up), the *Basilisk* couldn't get out bed when in the darkness of his room he noticed a draft of air from the street coming in through the door that had been left ajar by that devilish girl, nor could he do anything when he heard the hoofbeats of the horse as it galloped off, his granddaughter seated on the rump and *Jorge Negrete* singing "The Festival of Flowers." All he could do was choke on the anger that was dragging him down, each rasping breath a fathom deeper.

His own stool, and the stool on which he rested his hernia in the cantina, have remained ever since in the same corner with the carafes and funnels, where he used to transfer the grain alcohol to the bottles, the same alcohol, flavored with nancite fruit, that Rubén Darío drank on the occasion of his triumphal return to Nicaragua in 1907. *Basilisk* served it to him with his own hand.

"All honor to *Basilisk*, brother, after you killed him with rage," Cordelio said to *Jorge Negrete*.

"Brother, any other kind of anger would have done him in," *Jorge Negrete* said.

"Are you two blood brothers then?" Juan Legido asked.

"We're bosom brothers," Cordelio said. "Because, sometimes, we've sucked on the same tit."

"Better yet, we're sons of a priest," *Jorge Negrete* added.

"What priest is that?" asked Catalina Baldelomar.

"Father Olimpo Lozano," *Jorge Negrete* said. "His best cock is The Archangel Gabriel."

"This brother of mine taught his own father to be a cockfighter," Cordelio said.

"My father has only one other vice that's worse than cockfighting," *Jorge Negrete* said. "Impregnating the Daughters of Mary."

"How can the two of you talk that way about the man who gave you life?" the driver-owner of the truck said.

"He didn't give us life," *Jorge Negrete* said. "He took us in when we were boys wandering the streets. But as for children of his own, he's been more than blessed."

Dr. Balthazar Cisne acted as if he was going to piss, and as he walked past Rigoberto, he whispered in his ear: "Everything they're saying is true. They'll do themselves in, being imprudent like that."

"You, pastor, as a foreigner, be careful with your blasphemies," Rigoberto warned Cordelio.

"I only like women in skirts, 'cause priest's skirts stink," said Juan Legido.

"And as for me, only María Félix's," *Jorge Negrete* said. "She's gotten a bit fat, that's true. But there's no beauty equal to hers."

"One day, dear brother, you must introduce me to my sister-in-law," Cordelio said. "Even if she's a little over-weight, it doesn't matter."

"No, brother, I don't trust you," *Jorge Negrete* said.

"These guys are such skirt-chasers they don't even respect each other anymore," said Catalina Baldelomar.

"Well, with the example of a father like that," Juan Legido said.

"Olimpo Lozano may be weak because he's a womanizer, but he's an artist. He was my violin teacher," Rigoberto said.

"And your literature teacher was Chiron," *Jorge Negrete* said. "A priest, and the son of a priest."

"Stop your profane lies," Dr. Balthazar Cisne said, sitting down again.

"Who doesn't know that Chiron is Saint Mardoqueo's son?" said *Jorge Negrete*.

"Chiron? Like the Centaur?" exclaimed Lucio Ranucci, not expecting any more surprises. "Who's he?"

"A sacristan at the cathedral, who was left mute in a fight perpetrated by the soldiers of the Yankee intervention," Cordelio said.

"You know a lot more about this than you should for a Honduran," said Catalina Baldelomar.

"Fight, hell," Rigoberto said. "It was because of a denunciation he wrote in *The Chronicle*, against the Yankee Marines after they profaned the cemetery of Guadalupe."

"They took a bunch of whores to the cemetery and created a great infantile bacchanal. That was when the only girls in *The Alligator Woman*'s brothel were tender young things," *Jorge Negrete* said.

"*The Alligator Woman* is like a mother to me, so show her some respect," said Catalina Baldelomar.

"I'd take my hat off to her if I hadn't left it in the truck," *Jorge Negrete* said. "But I mean no disrespect at all. It's a fact that came out in the newspaper at that time."

"My father, Escolástico Cisne, was the owner of the newspaper then. *The Chronicle*," Dr. Balthazar Cisne said. "Out of revenge for that article, the American soldiers led a raid on the shop."

"And how could a mute teach you anything?" *The Lion of Nemea* asked Rigoberto.

"By telepathy," Rigoberto said.

"I'm going to see if he'll teach me," said the *Lion of Nemea*.

"The old and wise Chiron, Achilles's teacher!" Lucio Ranucci exclaimed.

"No one's noticed the name of my truck," the owner of The Traveling Pegasus said.

"It's something that astounds me, to see such famous artists traveling in beaten-up trucks like The Traveling Pegasus," Catalina Baldelomar said.

"Those of you who don't like my truck can stay here," the owner of The Traveling Pegasus proclaimed.

"Would you provide the use of the Teatro Darío, without charge, for a benefit performance?" Rigoberto suddenly asked Jorge *Negrete*.

"The Teatro Darío? Hey, everything in this man's life is Rubén Darío," said Juan Legido.

"An outright cult!" Lucio Ranucci said.

"What would this benefit performance be in aid of?" Jorge *Negrete* asked.

"To be able to put up Rubén Darío's statue, which you see here," Rigoberto said.

"Set the date," *Jorge Negrete* said, and his words were awarded with applause.

"Raising that statue should come out of your own pocket, you've got more than enough reales," Catalina Baldelomar said to Dr. Balthazar Cisne. "As for me, you swindled me plenty."

"And what performance are you going to put on?" asked *Jorge Negrete*.

"*Tovarich,* a famous play," Rigoberto announced, standing up. As he got to his feet, he picked up his little valise, as though about to leave.

"What's this about Dr. Balthazar Cisne swindling you?" *The Lion of Nemea* asked the merchant woman Catalina Baldelomar, as if he were going to avenge her.

"*Tovarich* will be staged within two weeks, the 21st of September, directed by maestro Lucio Ranucci," Rigoberto said, still standing.

"Lending me reales at ruthless interest rates, he's left me on the street," said Catalina Baldelomar, staring spitefully at Dr. Balthazar Cisne. "And his brothers Gaspar and

Melchior, another pair of money-lending lawyers, they'll strip you, too."

"Me?" Lucio Ranucci pointed to himself, happy as could be.

"Gaspar, Melchior, and Balthazar? The three kings?" said *The Lion of Nemea.*

"Leave my family out of this," Dr. Balthazar Cisne said, upset by the allusions and the distraction.

"Could you make me a loan?" *The Lion of Nemea* asked him.

"Don't even think of it. He's the worst of the three kings. If you don't have a shirt on your back now, you won't have a pair of pants when he's done," Catalina Baldelomar said.

"I demand more respect from this woman," Dr. Balthazar Cisne pleaded, glancing imploringly at everybody.

"Ranucci doesn't have the balls to stage the work in two weeks," Cordelio said. "A Judas play, all right. That's no big deal. But an artistic work..."

"Don't butt in, preacher," said Rigoberto.

"I've got the balls," Lucio Ranucci said, offended.

"Atta boy!" said Catalina Baldelomar, and thrust her hand under the table, grabbing him by the testicles. Ranucci gave a start and leapt to his feet, bumping against the table, but he couldn't free himself from her grip.

"I've never seen such vulgarity! Let him go!" said an indignant Dr. Balthazar Cisne.

"Oh, go on. It's not your Rubén Darío I've got hold of," Catalina Baldelomar said, releasing Ranucci, and she sat down, quite offended.

"She grabbed Tirso the Albino the same way last night in the dark at the coast," said *The Lion of Nemea.*

"What a big lie!" exclaimed the merchant woman Catalina Baldelomar, burying her face in her hands.

"It's no lie, because when I was returning to the Bartola, I saw the two of them rolling around in the sand," said *The*

Lion of Nemea. "Tirso was hugging you, squirming like some phosphorescent fish gasping out of water."

"So, that's why I heard Lucifer and Beelzebub crowing out there next to the ocean!" *Jorge Negrete* said, casting a stern look at Tirso the Albino. "When you're having yourself a party, don't take the cages with you!"

"I'm so humiliated I could cry!" Catalina Baldelomar said, and she started crying.

But above the merchant woman's sobbing, everything turned into a babble of voices: it was a matter of getting down to work as soon as the train reached León—because there was still the train trip from Chinandega to León—to make typed copies of the libretto that Lucio Ranucci was carrying in his wicker valise, which had to be done no later than Monday, the 10th of September, and today was Friday; they had to persuade Professor Max Somarriba, Director of the Mercantile Student Academy, that his most advanced typing students take it on as a project; and the cast had to be chosen no later than Tuesday, the 11th: he promised that *The Rose Child*, an amateur actress, wife of Dr. Balthazar Cisne, would call a meeting of other amateur artists, men and women, in their home; make sure he doesn't rob the clothes off their backs too, Catalina Baldelomar said bitterly.

"I take it for granted that your wife will play the female lead, doctor. But your daughter can also play a role," Rigoberto said.

"How old is your daughter?" Lucio Ranucci asked him.

"Eighteen," Dr. Balthazar Cisne said.

"Perfect for the young Princess Natasha Petrovna," said Lucio Ranucci.

"Her name is *Zela the Moor*," said the know-it-all Juan Legido.

Surprise and mistrust crossed Dr. Balthazar Cisne's face, as he looked from side to side with a cautious smile.

"The fame of her beauty has even reached Spain?" *The Lion of Nemea* asked, amazed.

"At the Bartola, you were saying your daughter's name in your sleep," Rigoberto was quick to tell Dr. Balthazar Cisne.

"My wife has already warned me that I talk in my sleep," Dr. Balthazar Cisne said, the surprise and distrust vanishing from his face.

"Well...that's how we'll do it then," Juan Legido said, shrugging his shoulders.

"Now that I recall, the twenty-first of September is the day *The Man* declares his candidacy at the Teatro González," said *Jorge Negrete*. "That date won't do for the opening."

"It's an evening performance, the convention is during the day," Rigoberto said, taking a swig of beer.

"We don't want to postpone it," Dr. Balthazar Cisne said to *Jorge Negrete*.

"No one's postponing it," *Jorge Negrete* said.

"Leave the publicity to me. And a small part in the play, too." said Rigoberto.

"I want to act in the play, too," said Tirso the Albino.

"That's all I need," *Jorge Negrete* said.

Despite the fact that he was beginning to look glassy-eyed, the owner of The Traveling Pegasus remembered he had to make the return trip to Puerto Morazán from Chinandega that very afternoon, so he urged everybody to follow him. Some didn't want to move. But the Canada Dry coolers were empty, so the troupe had to return to the pickup, carrying the statue with them.

The Traveling Pegasus had already turned onto the highway when Rigoberto, after looking around and patting himself as if he was missing something, shouted:

"My valise!"

The Lion of Nemea banged on the driver's cab, and even before the pickup slammed on the brakes, Rigoberto was already making his way to the rear door, pushing people aside. Jumping down, he landed in dust up to his ankles and ran along the highway back toward the group of eateries. In the distance, one of the waitresses was waving the little valise in the air.

"Such love for that shitty little valise," *Jorge Negrete* said when Rigoberto had returned to his seat.

"It's because I have a little animal sleeping here," Rigoberto said, hugging the little valise against his chest.

"That's what comes from drinking," said Catalina Baldelomar. "A little animal would have suffocated in there by now."

"It's just a little toy animal," said Rigoberto.

Now I Want To Say to You All,
Until We Meet Again!

From Captain Prío's observatory, one could see the wrought-iron railings of the balconies of Debayle's old mansion, the red roof tiles, and a portion of the interior garden and rear courtyard; the house was located near the noisy municipal market with its smells of rotting onions and sun-cured leather goods.

The movement of soldiers and security agents had increased at the doors to the house. The First Lady was returning with her retinue to have lunch with her mother, and there, according to the radio announcer on the Gran Cadena Liberal, President Somoza would join them afterwards, perhaps for dessert. At that hour he was still reading his electoral manifesto to the Great Convention in the Teatro González, the ceiling fans unable to mitigate either the suffocating heat or his tedium or the flashes of anger that he felt at times, all the while his saliva sprinkling the pages of his text: if he had realized it earlier, he would have ordered those responsible for stitching together such a lengthy declaration to cut it in half at least. And on top of that, the sweat made his tortoise-shell glasses slide down his nose. And the bulletproof vest was producing body sores on his sides. And the heaviness he felt in his bladder.

The limited number of guests invited to the luncheon had already started arriving. Among them one should mention the publisher of *The Chronicle*, Rafael (Rafa) Parrales, his perfectly sculptured chest the result of constant workouts, sporting a tie on which a Hawaiian dancer moved her hips every time he squeezed a little rubber ball hidden at his waist; Father Olimpo Lozano, parish priest of the Church of the Calvary and chaplain for Company 5 of the National Guard, with a military cap, and captain's bars on the shoulders of his white cotton soutane; and doña Leda Sacasa, *The Rose Child*, accompanied by her husband, Dr. Balthazar Cisne, wearing his customary black tie (a habit that was to have tragic consequences later that day, but I'm getting ahead of myself).

The Rose Child couldn't help but be nervous the whole time, given that she had to go on stage that night at the Teatro Darío in her role as Ninoshka Andreyevna, mother of young Princess Natasha Petrovna, a role which her own daughter, *Zela the Moor*, would be playing. To Lucio Ranucci's relief, the cast was finally complete, and because no other options were available, the princess's suitor was to be played by Tirso the Albino in the role of the captain of the hussars, Vasili Ivanovich. *Jorge Negrete* would play the part of Prince Fedor Sergeievich, and he had also agreed to a small role for his wife María Félix as the maid, similar to that of the butler Anatole who merely had to enter and say: "Good evening, sir." The maid would have to clean the chairs with a duster while humming, without ever looking at the audience, and then exit stage left.

Few men were invited because, above all, it was a ladies' luncheon: the wife of Colonel Melisandro Maravilla (NG), Commander of Company 5 (I feel tempted to reveal that on that very night he would be taken prisoner, accused of treason), wives of cabinet ministers who had come from Managua on the presidential train (all of whom would be arrested, along with hundreds of others, and taken to the Plaza Jerez, where they would have to form a circle, taking turns to create some privacy each time one of them had to pee).

If I were to ask Captain Prío, as he returns to his vantage point, he would give me the reasons for certain male guests being invited to the luncheon and not others, or better yet, I ought to hand this topic over to the regulars at the cursed little table at Café Prío. But it's impossible for them to hold court on such a difficult day:

The journalist Rafa Parrales, because he's doña Casimira's godson (my *protégé*, she calls him from her wheelchair, remembering the appropriate words in French, words her husband had accustomed her to using). He, for his part, behaves quite obsequiously, cloyingly so, with the First Lady (*my first lady*, he's constantly calling her), while she delights in his display of familiarity.

Dr. Balthazar Cisne, because he's *The Rose Child*'s husband. He smiles happily at anything and everything as he approaches the circles of conversation. He has spent years with his name listed on the blackboard of León's Social Club, his application turned down year after year under the rigorous scrutiny of the members who never tire of depositing their little black balls in the jar, voting against him despite his marital connection, and without it seeming to matter to them in the least that it was his father, the orator Escolástico Cisne, who had founded *The Chronicle* newspaper.

And Father Olimpo Lozano because he's doña Casimira's confessor. Ever unconcerned about appearances, and seated next to the liquor table in the hallway, his cap askew, he was drinking glass after glass of Black & White mixed with Spur Cola, as if trying to make up for lost time.

Let's go to the table. Rafa Parrales was solicitously manuvering doña Casimira's wheelchair. Next to each plate, the guests found a carbon copy of the menu, typed up in the offices of the municipal government. Served in the garden under the old honeysuckle-covered wire cupola, the luncheon was interspersed with off-color jokes told one after another by the indefatigable Rafa Parrales, in a voice resonating with great authority. The First Lady made him sit next to her so she wouldn't miss a single word, obliging Dr. Balthazar Cisne to give up the seat he had so carefully staked out. She was beside herself with laughter, holding her head between her hands, her chin buried in her chest, and gesturing: no, no more. Her mother, from behind a pair of thick lenses that made her gaze a little misty and her eyes appear excessively large, smiled, resting peacefully in her wheelchair but not seeming to understand and beaming absent-mindedly at everything all the while

On the other hand, Dr. Balthazar Cisne's smile, when he was forced to abandon his place at the table, was truly one of displeasure, and it would remain so until the luncheon was over. While they were passing the plates, he conjured up impossible plots of revenge against the swine who was taking great delight in playing the joker and impeding his chance to convince the First Lady to attend next month's unveiling of Rubén Darío's statue, on whose pedestal would be engraved, in accordance with (guess who?) Rigoberto's suggestion, the verses on her fan:

Oh, Salvadora, Salvadorita,
don't kill your nightingale!

What else could one expect from that degenerate? A bastard son of the Debayle family, a servant brought from a farm on the former dominions of *Our Lady of the Fields*, he now boasted of being a journalist and gave himself illusions of grandeur. He even gave prisoner-release orders, which Colonel Maravilla executed out of fear of the First Lady; he gave recommendations for civil posts and organized a club for shoeshine boys in order to build a reputation for himself as a benefactor, as if he were Saint Mardoqueo.

Dr. Balthazar Cisne was looking at his empty plate because they hadn't remembered to serve him, repressing his darkest thoughts: a First Lady who behaved, in word and deed, like a merchant woman; if Rubén had met her now, he never would have written anything on her fan. And from time to time, he allowed himself a timid glance at his wife, *The*

97

Rose Child, who was smiling out of obligation at the vulgarities, twirling her golden curls with a nervous hand.

But it's time to remember, Captain, that under that same honeysuckle-covered wire cupola, another luncheon had taken place many years earlier. And if the blades of the fans, whirling slowly on the ceiling of the Teatro González across the plaza, can't alleviate the heat that makes the conventioneers despair, as if they had just been bathed in recently boiled bleach, nor alleviate the suffocation of the individual who continues reading his electoral manifesto, stuffed, to top off his ills, inside that bullet-proof vest, which by now must seem to him more like a cloth of thorns, then allow me to use them to make the pages of the calendar fly back before your eyes.

Pay attention. It's April 8, 1908. Under the cupola, supported by Doric columns of cedarwood, its shafts and pilasters adorned with marble-like jaspers, the learned Debayle is offering a farewell banquet to Rubén Darío who is about to leave Nicaragua again for Europe. At the center of the canopy of honeysuckle, above the heads of the luncheon guests, a mass of roses is fashioned into a lyre with seven chords, and from the lyre hangs a haughty *papier mâché* eagle, with outspread wings, in its beak a gold medal that bears the familiar image of a pensive Rubén, one hand resting on his chin.

Between the lace curtains draped over the street doors, curious onlookers are peering in at the celebration. Set up in the sitting room, the string orchestra is playing a waltz, "Loves of Abraham," by the leprous composer José de la Cruz Mena, under the baton of Maestro Saturnino Ramos, and the arpeggios waft fitfully out into the garden. In his place of honor, a sober Rubén appears unusually full of enthusiasm. The mark of his recent injury stains his cheek a cyclamen red, and his eye, now hooded, glows like a bright red ember.

They're already having dessert, and the ladies insist on passing him their fans for him to write a dedicatory verse. Gallant, he sees to all of their petitions while he speaks of the century's new inventions, of the Paris World's Fair, which he covered in 1900 as a correspondent for *La Nación* of Buenos Aires: the imperial German pavilion where they displayed the shoeshine machine, patented in Berlin by the engineer Von Schultze-Kraft; the toilet with mechanical brushes that washes one's posterior when activated by a pedal, a bit of English genius by the learned Victorian, Sir Harold Pinter; the talking doll that sings arias from Rigoletto, the contribution of a home-grown scientist, and he purses his lips in a sarcastic gesture, seeking out Eulalia with a playful look.

Inventions of a fast-paced age, juxtaposed against those more mundane artifacts, fabricated for the purpose of mitigating the desolation of forsaken places...he remembers his first trip to Chile in June, 1886, the port of Chimbote on the arid coast of Peru, where it never rains, and seeing the houses on the coast decorated with painted backdrops and stage curtains that simulated woods and thickets, a bizarre theatrical scene witnessed by him from the deck of the German steamship *Barda*, which had left Nicaragua under the flames of an erupting Momotombo Volcano, the midday sky blackened and the pelicans frightened by the spectacle, seeking refuge in the passenger cabins...yes, he lived in a fast-moving age...the performance of *La Traviata* which he saw at the Metropolitan in New York, with the great tenor Gino Tlagiaperra, and changes of scenery mounted on electric turntables, a festive palace suddenly replaced by a street scene at Carnival time.

"What Yankee invention can do, *messieurs, mesdames!* And what the commercial spirit of these modern behemoths can wrest from invention, which transforms adventure into a *réclame*...you should know that during the crossing aboard *La Provence*, from Cherbourg to New York, my valet came to wake me early one morning in my cabin, to invite me to witness the rescue of a shipwrecked man; I went on deck, where many other passengers had already gathered. But this was no rescue...just a bearded man, tanned by the sun in a flimsy sloop, clinging to the mast, and in a loud voice, letting us know that he was following the route of Columbus sponsored by Sapolio, the bath soap manufacturer...and from his little boat, he even sang us a line from a Sapolio advertisement. Colonel Andrews was his name. He had served in the Yankee Navy during the Cuban war..."

Suddenly, setting aside the fan on which he had begun writing, he again searches for Eulalia and points with his flashing fountain pen toward the petals of a satin rose that covers the top of her *décolletage.*

"*Décolletages, ma chérie,* even for evening wear, have become old-fashioned, so dizzying is the whim of Paris fashion. And I fear that their dictates are final."

As though this verdict had left her naked, Eulalia instinctively brings her hands to her chest. Discreet laughter is heard. Now the poet turns to the topic of corsets:

"Those instruments of torture! Herminia Cadolle, the mother of modern fashion designers, said one day: "So, this is what we've come to!" And, oh, empress of change! She sliced open her corset in a single motion, right down the middle, until she had freed her midriff. The medical reports showed a plethora of cases of women who, after having used whalebone corsets and cords, had broken ribs, or a collapsed thorax. X-rays, that other invention which show in life the naked skeleton of death, do not lie!"

Constrained by their rigid corsets, the ladies suddenly find it even more difficult to breathe. The learned Debayle rewards the substance of Rubén's clinical description with a sober nod of his head.

And in answer to a question, while he resumes writing, Rubén embarks on an extensive discourse on fashion. He ponders the sensuality of soft satin, the voluptuousness of muslin and the dark rose-colored crepe glacé, the charm of gray muslin stoles embroidered with steel-colored pearls, the displays of *passementerie* on the dusters that leave a flowery trail in their wake as they sweep across the floors of the salons, the broad white toques that seem to fly, their great butterfly-loops of velvet moiré; he remembers the delicate waists, cinched tight by golden laces. And for the evening strolls in Luxembourg Park, the *camisas judías*, embroidered on the bottom, on the sleeves, and around the collar, the little jackets *á la* Figaro, and Russian blouses of crude serge...like Garibaldi, he says, who stopped here on his way through León. Did they know that? In his day, he imposed on the fair sex the fashion of his own loose, collarless shirt, the *garibaldi*... Such is the power of masculine charm!

He takes another fan and turns to the topic of hats. Pale gold buttons that flourish amidst white foliage, the Charlotte, crowned with little bells, decorated with blue and silver cherries, like none he had ever seen, and dark yellow *albelíes* mixed with greenish roses. Somewhat foolish, but in the end, *charmant*! Sweet bread, baskets of flowers, sheaves by the handful, the elegance of the *aigrettes,* all straight from a veritable land of Canaan, interspersed with muslin grains of silk and long tufts, the black *aigrettes* of Numidia. The *serre-tête*, though it seems a bit vulgar now, still has its fans. He asks for the little prescription notepad, which the learned doctor keeps in his coat pocket, and draws a cotton bonnet that completely covers every bit of hair, except for a strand on the forehead, although it takes a very young woman to carry it off gracefully; and he also draws a parasol, made of black velvet and *toile de jouy* linen, which is carried on the shoulder in an open position, with a defiant nonchalance, or in a closed position, like a rapier, to sustain a woman's graceful bearing as she strolls along the footpaths of ducal parks.

And that resonating debate on the pages of *Le Figaro*, between Mme. Marcèle Lender and Mlle. Claire Mistinguer, two giants of the fashion houses: the one, faithful to classic lines, to Hellenic pleats, to impeccable tunic dresses; the other, a devotee of whimsy and modern caprice: the rowdy debates of the Rue de la Paix fashion houses locked in that discussion of sublime frivolity... And Rubén, in the end, proves himself to be a judge of vanity, partial to what is *seyante*, to what favors the contours of the female body, to what reveals, with decency, its sinuosity and allows one to imagine the forbidden that lies beneath all the layers of fabric: cashmere cotton, fine linen...and he concludes by saying that in the midst of all that whimsical fancy, a woman of good taste can be recognized because she knows how to disdain the excesses, choosing genuine fashion instead, the bold and ingeniously unconventional touch that enhances the prestige of beauty.

And then there are the outdoor fashion shows, the latest in Parisian novelties: eliminated are the lavish salons and their courtly offices, the flurry of activity in the cutting rooms and the attendant clutter. And along the fine cinder paths, among the British gardens with their military-like rigidity, or in luscious corners with a French *sans façon*, among grassy arabesques and fragrant floral bas-reliefs, sometimes under the discreet shade of the trees or in the radiant luminescence of the autumn sun, the models wander about like strange heraldic apparitions. Over here, a group takes shape, looking like the motif for a painter's canvas; and over there, a white silhouette wanders off among the glossy branches, bending down to caress a fertile rose, to breathe in the perfume of the spikenards and to contemplate the aristocracy of a lily; in the distance, in the half-light of a gazebo, a figure vanishes like a poetic story...and in the meantime, hidden in the foliage, the orchestral blackbirds and the Bohemian sparrows sing an eternal hymn to eternal beauty.

"Our century, so eminently positivistic, has turned us into practical people...and not having more sky-blue in our aspirations, in our ideas and our lives, the woman puts it in her clothes because we can't live without a bit of heaven, no matter how small," he concludes, smiling at his female admirers, as he returns the prescription pad to the learned doctor.

All of them, enthusiastic and admiring, applaud him. But Eulalia sits in sullen silence, her hands resting on top of the tablecloth, the knot of her eyebrows darker than ever.

"Come now, fans, more fans!" Rubén demands, enchanted with himself. "Do you know that I've vouchsafed nights of love writing dedications on fans like these? And on mirrors?"

Necks stiffen, and the women start to murmur. He folds his arms and slowly tilts his head in homage to the delight of those memories.

"The unrivaled Monna Delza! My verses carried me, on immortal nights, to her coquettish chalet in the Bois-de-Boulogne, her pagan sanctuary! On the very evening of the premiere of Henri Bataille's *La vierge folle*, at the Odèon, where she reaped garlands and countless baskets of flowers, which filled not only her dressing room but the entire hallway, I too had my premiere. What a battle of suitors it was to win that precious jewel, the Golden Fleece! I came out the victor, and she left the theater on my arm. We drove off fast in her 40-horsepower automobile, she at the steering wheel, wrapped in white ermine, and at our feet a Bengali tigerskin for a rug... Imagine! The Muses of modern poetry, run over by the automobile! Thalia, Erato, and Euterpe, all fleeing along a bitter-smelling, undulating asphalt road, pursued by the threat of Michelin tires under the noisy splendor of the electric lights along Avenue Foch...! And in that little chalet in the Bois, her bedroom...silk intimacies, altar-cloths from the Louis XIII period, a coverlet for her lascivious bed, and sheets like *robes de fées*, those ethereal muslin gowns, and birds from across the ocean in Gothic cages, a profusion of hydrangea in Chinese vases, extravagant little dogs at play between our bare feet..."

In the distant kitchen, a tray full of plates and cups has crashed to the floor, but not a single head turns. And again Rubén is pursuing Eulalia's gaze.

"Perfume of myrrh in the braziers...Monna Delza's hair, cascading down, a nebulous and tormented mane, like those Paris nights. Monna Delza! *L'enfant gâté*! Coveted by Jewish tycoons, the luscious *gamine* whom I held in my Chorotega Indian arms...! The voluptuousness of such a discreet hour! A touch, a bite, a kiss, synthesis of eternity! Who would have said it, *mon frère* Louis! Upon my departure, beneath dawn's light, she lay naked in her bed. I, taking care not to waken her, left her a poem written on the mirror of her *boudoir*, in red lipstick. The title? *Mene, Tequel, Fares*...those mysterious words of Belshazzar's banquet."

From among the women in attendance, a discomfited Oh! escapes, which then turns into a soft roll of laughter. Eulalia, maintaining her distance, still refuses to look at Rubén, who now says:

"And do you know that en route to Nicaragua, I paid for the services of a harlot in New York with verses I wrote on her fan?"

The furtive laughter dissolves into a painful silence.

"Listen to this story," Rubén says, tapping the heavy silver knife against his empty glass. "It's one that will never appear in my autobiography. At nightfall I disembarked on the wharfs of that sleepless Babylon. I left my luggage at the Waldorf and went out for a stroll, letting fate take me where it might... At 123 Broadway I entered a certain place, discreetly illuminated by cheerful lights: it's called the One, Two, Three. A whorehouse, aseptic, like everything Yankee. It smelled of listerine. They were playing the Argentine tango "Quiero papita." Sensuous music. It's danced cheek-to-cheek, bodies apart. Afterwards...ah, afterwards!"

At the mention of the word whore, there's a great stir and many a blushing cheek, but now it's Eulalia who is laughing, disdainfully. Casimira tries to cover the eyes of her two daughters, wishing to shelter them from that vision of sin. Bishop Simeón coughs discreetly, his fingers pressed against his mouth.

One of the ladies, stunned, asks Casimira to read what Rubén has written on Salvadorita's fan, because the two little girls had handed him their fans as well. Casimira hurries to read the verses. They're already familiar with the poem.

"The *putas* looked after me as if I were King Belshazzar himself, and I ended up in the arms of one of them, a Dominican girl." Rubén ignores the interruption and the loud applause that appear to praise the poem. "Her name was Eleonora, like Poe's muse, a pale and haggard-looking girl. I had left my wallet back at the Waldorf, so I didn't have a cent on me to pay for her favors. Instead, I paid her by writing a décima on her fan, one that had been given to her as a gift by a Catalonian from Montjuic, a wine seller."

Rubén laughs, but no one else does. Suddenly Eulalia's voice rings out with a confused echo, like that of a broken church bell: "And your wife, oh, king of the harlots! What has become of her?"

The learned Debayle rises hurriedly to his feet and pulls the pages of his farewell speech from his pocket.

"Wait, Louis, sit down, no need to feel alarmed, I'll answer the lady." Rubén smiles, without a hint of annoyance in his demeanor. "My wife, dear lady, has been convinced that she should no longer pursue me, thanks to the advice of her brother, an innocuous clown named Andrés Murillo. A born social climber, he has been prudent for the first time in his life, and had her sign an agreement which obliges her to stop troubling me, all for the trifle of five thousand francs, which I have already deposited into the hands of that Lucifer of a brother-in-law. I had already turned over to him a similar sum when he'd taken it into his head to come and wait for me in Corinto, though it didn't sufficiently placate her at the time. It was almost all the money I had brought with me. How did I obtain the funds for the new transaction? By committing myself in advance to the widow Garnier in Paris, for a book that I haven't even written, concerning my trip to Nicaragua, and also by obligating myself to another book of selected verse and prose for the widow Mucci in Barcelona. I asked *La Nación* in Buenos Aires for a remittance and instructed my lover in Paris to sell my Pleyel piano and wire me the funds."

From his seat, the learned Debayle gestures in vain for him to be quiet.

"Because, *madame*, you see, I have a lover. She isn't some Parisian *grisette*, but a country girl from Navalsauz, a small village of goatherds in the Gredos Mountains. Illiterate. I've taught her to read. And as far as my wife is concerned, I hope never to see her again. Her brother forced me to marry her when I was an adolescent, employing the compelling argument of holding a pistol against my ribs, it's true. And she wasn't any virgin, that's also true. She had a liaison with a socially prominent old fellow, whom she visited until the very end, on his deathbed. And she invited me, her poor innocent sweetheart, to accompany her on her visits to spoon him his medicine in my presence. A theme fit for some dismal dime novel. Don't you think so, *milady*? I'll write it one day, don't worry..."

Eulalia has turned pale, but doesn't stir from her chair. Rubén sighs and looks over at the learned Debayle.

"Your farewell speech, Louis. You can begin now," he says.

Debayle straightens up and begins reading in a tense voice, which is practically inaudible at first. As he forges ahead with his flowery words, he gradually recovers his aplomb. He finishes. Everyone stands up to raise their glasses except Rubén, who remains seated, his glass of champagne before him, bubbling and abandoned. The string orchestra starts up again: another waltz, "Ruinas," by José de la Cruz Mena.

"That was an extraordinary toast," says Rubén, applauding him. "I'm not going to respond, though; I'm terrible when it comes to speeches. There are lies in what you said, white lies. It was a miracle that I ever entered the Jesuit school that you mentioned, an academy for sons of the rich, like you; and when my uncle Pedro Alvarado, a cloth merchant, a foolish millionaire who paid my tuition, found out I had fought with his son Pedrito over some childish nonsense, he cut off my funds. The priests notified me of this one lunchtime, do you remember? I was no longer even allowed to sit at the table. I was put out on the street to contemplate my humiliation. Afterwards, at the hour for soirées, I went to the door of my cruel uncle's house, where Pedrito was playing the piano, rewarded by forced applause. They may applaud him here, I prophesied, but the world will applaud me...! And on top of that, my Uncle Pedro Alvarado cheated me out of my mother's small inheritance, keeping it for himself... *Voilà toute la vérité, mon frère Louis.* Nothing at all like the happy childhood you spoke of. But here's my farewell homage to you, the person who so patiently puts up with the incorrigible neurotic that I am."

"A gift! What can it be?" Salvadorita claps enthusiastically as she watches Rubén take a tube wrapped in silk paper from his jacket.

"Open it," Rubén requests of the little girl.

The child undoes the knot and tears open the wrapping: the folios of the trial initiated against Debayle for having left General Selvano Quirino blind fall open for all to see.

Some of the guests who had stood up to get a look at the gift sheepishly return to their seats. Debayle thanks Rubén with a vexed nod of his head.

"You see, I got hold of the proceedings for you when Zelaya finally granted me an audience." Rubén tries to smile at the learned Debayle. "For myself, nothing. I've delayed my return trip in vain. They've named me ambassador, but there is no money in the public treasury to advance me anything, according to the secretary of the treasury, that noble ignoramus."

"They'll send you the money in Paris." Debayle has taken the papers from Salvadorita and tries unsuccessfully to keep the guests from seeing them. "It'll arrive with your credentials. I'm sure of it."

"In the meantime, I'll starve to death in Paris." Rubén's swollen eye now looks at Casimira with its sad ruby-colored reflections. "If only I had been born the son of a millionaire like my cousin Pedro! But for me to eat and survive, I've got to squeeze the bitter juice from my brains and turn it into ink. Casimira, your poet is a pauper. A pauper who must travel with a second-class ticket, in a cabin shared with strangers, hearing the distant clamor of the parties above in the first-class salon, a poet who owes his tailor for his silk suits, who is in debt for his trunks and his portable bathtub. Who buys his wine and medicines on credit. Who flees his landlords."

Casimira hugs her two little girls as if the embrace were meant for Rubén, who now turns towards the learned Debayle.

"And don't think that the handing over of those court proceedings came free, Louis. Zelaya saw it necessary to placate that strange lady, Galatea Quirino, and I had to write a poem for her bereavement. The poem, "Mater Dolorosa," was published in some horrible leaflet; you've probably seen it. She wanted to see you in jail. *Mais c'est impossible, un aristocrate en prison.* I had already told you as much."

The learned Debayle signals to Santiago Argüello to hurry up and recite once and for all the ode to Rubén, a tribute he has worked on for several days. Rubén notices the two men's discomfort, but ignores it.

"That I'm an incorrigible inebriate, that's what Zelaya's courtesans and lackeys tell him. They tarnish me! I'm not some tamale vendor like them! I'm Rubén Darío, damn it!" He bangs his fist on the table.

In a bowl next to each place setting, there's an orange with the flags of France and Nicaragua stuck in it, and beneath the orange, the menu printed on linen. Rubén removes the flag of Nicaragua. Santiago Argüello is already standing; he clears his throat in order to get everyone's attention.

"Sit down!" Rubén orders him, waving the little flag. "All of you, with your verses, you try my patience. Let Chiron the Centaur come!"

Chiron, who was washing glasses in the kitchen, hears the call from a distance and, as if he emerged from thin air, appears behind Rubén. Forcing a smile, Santiago Argüello takes his seat again.

"Recite something from your reading of Oviedo," Rubén asks him, sticking the flag of Nicaragua back in the orange.

Chiron thinks for a moment. He dries his soapy hands on the legs of his trousers and then begins reciting:
Fray Francisco de Bobadilla, commissioned in the year of our Lord 1527 by Don Pedro Arias de Avila, Governor of Nicaragua, to delve into the deeds and customs of the aboriginal Indians interrogated in the Plaza of Tesoatega, a Nagrandano chief who was called Miseboy, in the presence of officials and scribes who stood ready to record and attest to his words, and the colloquy took place in the following manner: Why do your people pierce their noses, ears, and the generative member? And the cacique Miseboy answered him: our noses and ears, for the wearing of adornments during our ceremonies; but with respect to the generative member, not all do it, but rather some rascals, for the giving of more pleasure to women.

Rubén laughs heartily, and the two little girls, Margarita and Salvadorita, also laugh innocently in their mother's lap.

Debayle, although furious with Rubén, flashes Chiron a reproachful look, wanting to dismiss him.

"Pay no attention to him, stay. Now recite 'The Meeting of the Centaurs,'" Rubén says to him.

"Another bit of ventriloquy?" Santiago Argüello asks.

"No ventriloquy at all," says Bishop Simeón, raising his hands as if to ask for a truce. "Chiron is a true prodigy."

"Then spare us that poem, Rubén. I find it very academic, dry, cerebral. None of the music of your 'Sonatina.'" Santiago Argüello has crassly raised his voice, seeking the approval of his table companions.

Rubén's face grows somber. With a display of disgust and boredom he takes a first sip of tepid champagne, and gently urges Chiron to return to the kitchen.

"*C'est lui qui ne comprend rien,*" Rubén says, as if talking to himself, and stands up. The bruise on his cheek now appears monstrous. There is already a wilted smell from the flowers woven into the wire canopy. The guests get up to leave, the discreet scraping of their chairs against the floor echoing the rustle of dried leaves blown by the wind.

Eulalia is the last to stand up. She removes the cloth rose from her bodice and, furtively approaching Rubén, she opens his hand to receive it, then closes it with warm pressure. At that she leaves, gathering her long skirt, dragging fallen petals in its wake.

Now Salvadorita runs to Rubén and hugs him around his legs. He bends down to kiss her, the cloth flower held tightly in his hand.

"Don't ever kill your nightingale," he whispers in her ear.

"The nightingale that shamelessly fills his gullet," says the goldsmith Segismundo.

"Let's not add a political chord to the lyre; it only has seven strings," Erwin says.

"Each time I see you, you grow more lukewarm in your opinions, my friend," says Segismundo.

"And as for you, all there is to life is bad-mouthing Somoza," Erwin says.

"Criticizing him. Is that all? Gentlemen, the nightingale of these lands deserves to have his neck wrung," thunders Segismundo.

"Lower your voice. Others have gone to jail for insinuating less," Captain Prío says, lowering his own voice.

"Do you suffer from fear, Captain?" Segismundo asks him.

"Neither fear, nor heroics," Captain Prío says. "But I don't like getting screwed like some asshole, all because of other people's imprudence."

"I get the sense that the owner of the establishment is inviting me to leave," says Segismundo, offended.

"Sit down, the session's barely gotten started," Rigoberto says, to calm him down.

"Let's be clear that I'm staying under protest," Segismundo says. "Captain, have them bring me another *nepenthe*."

"Perish the thought that we were conspiring, Captain," Norberto says. "This is merely a cheerful little table of your select clients. Somoza could come in here unarmed and no one would touch a hair on his head."

"Speak for yourself," Segismundo says. "Me, I don't know what I would do if I saw that man standing next to me."

"You don't sound like the Grand Master of the Máximo Jerez Lodge," Erwin says. "Masons can't spill the blood of another Mason because that would be like destroying the image which the Great Architect has created of himself."

"You're talking like the book of the Templars of Syracuse," Norberto says.

"There are dispensations," the goldsmith Segismundo says, looking fixedly at Norberto. "Although they were both Masons, Somoza had Sandino killed. The only thing that's prohibited by the Scottish rite is to look a Mason in the eye before he has to die."

"What a compassionate religion," Erwin says.

"Freemasonry isn't a religion, it's a universal fraternity," Norberto says.

"I see them as being real fraternal," Erwin says.

"I've just been initiated," Norberto says, and now he's the one looking at the goldsmith Segismundo. "I still don't have the right to wear the apron on the white uniform. Only my Grand Master can decide when I've reached the final step."

"Was Rubén a Mason?" Captain Río asks Rigoberto.

"Of course he was," Master Segismundo replies. "He joined the Lodge of Saint Denis, headed by Doctor Encause."

"Well, take a look at my notes," Rigoberto says. "Rubén calls the Masons 'terribly naive people.'"

"Impossible!" exclaims Segismundo, alarmed.

"He was the one who was naive, thinking he was a magician who could teach an illiterate child to read," Erwin says.

"You need to clarify for me whether Rubén allowed himself the luxury of traveling first-class aboard ship," Norberto says. "Because now you've got him in a second-class cabin like some nobody."

"New facts are continually emerging," Rigoberto answers.

"Facts that are continually emerging in your head," Erwin says.

"Just like Chiron's recital at the banquet," says Segismundo.

"And Eulalia's farewell with the cloth flower in her hand," Norberto says.

"Captain, please enlighten these skeptics," Rigoberto asks.

"Eulalia rode down this very street in her coach, returning home after the farewell luncheon," Captain Prío said. "Rubén left, carrying the cloth flower with him, and no one ever heard her recite poetry again."

"You yourself saw her pass by?" Erwin asked. "How old were you, Captain?"

"A year old."

"And you bade her farewell from this same doorway," Erwin said.

"I wasn't there when she died, but I know how it happened."

"And how did she die?" Norberto asked.

"It happened on a Wednesday afternoon, in August 1923," said Captain Prío. "She pretended that she wanted her portrait taken, and she called for Maestro Cisneros. He arrived with all his photographic chemicals, and when he wasn't looking, she stole the bottle of potassium cyanide, ran to lock herself in her room, and swallowed the whole bottle."

"And what about the inventor Godofredo?" Norberto asked.

"He had already died," Captain Prío said. "*The Rose Child,* an orphan at fifteen, went to live in her Aunt Casimira's attic."

"The mother-in-law of that swindling nightingale," said Segismundo.

"Always flogging a dead horse," Erwin said.

"Is the nightingale the one that sings when it's going to die?" Norberto asked.

"No, that's the swan of ducal parks," Captain Prío said.

"Not everything that's going to die needs to sing in its last moments," said Erwin.

"Probably to dance, though," Rigoberto said, placing his journal back in his imitation lizard portfolio.

It was already close to midnight.

The Barbarians, Cara Lutecia!

The taxi, a two-tone sky-blue-and-yellow 1952 Oldsmobile that still had whitewalls from its glory days with its previous owner, stopped with a screech in front of the La Merced Park at the end of its route through sunlit streets from the Pacific Railroad Station.

It was after four in the afternoon. At the front door, a maid wearing men's shoes and sweeping dust with listless swipes of her broom, stopped what she was doing when she saw *Bienvenido Granda*, the singing moustache, step out of the taxi. A year ago, during the intermission of the Matanzas Sound performance at the Teatro Teresita, the lights came on, and the singer, dressed in his puffy-sleeved rumba outfit, went down into the orchestra seats with a stack of photos of himself to sell to the audience. She had bought one from him. She even remembered the smell of toothpaste on his breath, as if he had just brushed his teeth.

Bienvenido Granda was paying the cab driver, while the preacher remained seated in the back. The woman returned to her sweeping, futile as it was because the wind blew the dust right back through the small door in the massive portal, but she never took her eye off *Bienvenido Granda*, who was already walking toward her. He examined the big house in detail while the preacher, Bible clutched to his chest, walked along the far sidewalk, glancing at the closed doors as if looking for a different address.

Already pulling away, the taxi driver hit the brakes and stuck his head out the window when he heard *Bienvenido Granda* suddenly shout and run toward him because he had forgotten his little cardboard valise. Bible under his arm, the preacher shook his head with a stern look of disapproval.

Seeing the little valise once more safely in *Bienvendo*'s possession, the preacher had every reason to keep shaking his head in disapproval. At that moment, *Bienvenido Granda* approached a fruit vendor who had set up her stand on the sidewalk outside the park, and with a yen for something sweet he bought a *piña de mamón*, after having taken his own good time in choosing the prettiest and best one of the bunch. Satisfied with his purchase, the valise in one hand and the tasty little fruit in the other, he at last approached the gateway.

"When did you get back?" the delighted woman asked while still sweeping away. She swept air while he put a *mamón* in his mouth, making its skin snap until the sun-red flesh of the fruit showed between his puckered lips.

The preacher couldn't hear *Bienvenido*'s reply, but it wasn't hard to imagine—the pit of the *mamón* pushed with delight from one side of his mouth to the other: *Keep your voice down, can't you see I'm in disguise? I ran off with a girl in San Salvador, from one of the finest aristocratic families there,* and so on... And before the woman knew it, *Bienvenido Granda* had slipped inside, disappearing into the half-light along with his little valise.

The preacher walked to the street corner, examining all the doorways along the way; then he crossed the street and came back down the opposite sidewalk, still surveying the doors, using the Bible as a visor against the glare of the sun. And now, to the surprise of the woman, who had been watching his dawdling approach, he stopped right in front of her. Alarmed, she glanced first at the Bible the preacher was holding up to shield his eyes and then at the lithograph of Pope Pius XII tacked on the front portal, faded from the rigors of the sun and rain; in profile, wearing the triple tiara, his finger in the air, the supreme pontiff didn't seem to be blessing but rather pointing to the gravity of the warning printed below his picture:

WE ARE CATHOLICS HERE
AND PROTESTANT PROPAGANDA
IS PROHIBITED

The preacher smiled at the Bible disdainfully, as if he had found it by accident on the train or next to the station's ticket window or in the taxi, and had no choice but to pick it up, but now no longer knew what to do with it. Would she accept it as a gift? The woman stepped back, frightened at the silent offer.

He too went in through the little door. The woman followed him anxiously; and, taking care to avoid even brushing up against him, she hurried ahead toward the hallway, separated from the front entrance by a wooden screen, to announce his presence. What did the pastor want? To pick up the religious pamphlets he was having printed! Hymns of the kind Protestants sing shut away in their churches. What good was the Pope's picture then, enduring the rain and the sun out at the front entrance?

Bienvenido Granda's purpose was very different. According to what he himself had told her (well, you already know the topic on which their exchange of words rested), he was there to order the handbills for the Sonora Sound's upcoming show. *Sonora*, once more in León! And now, while she went to announce him, the preacher stood waiting in the half-light of the hallway by the electric meter, watching the revolving numbers for lack of anything better to do. A delivery bicycle with a basket rested against the opposite wall.

Although there is no sign on the wall outside, a print shop operates in this spacious family mansion. The Cara Lutecia. The owner appeared a short while later from behind the wooden partition, cleaning his hands with a piece of flannel soaked in turpentine. A pinkish, smooth-skinned face with plump cheeks, reminiscent of the happy Mennen baby. On his head, the baby had a Basque beret that he had worn since he was a first-year law student.

The Heidelberg printing press was broken again, the happy baby informed the preacher, babbling the words like so many failed bursts of an outboard motor: he was behind schedule with printing the programs for the big concert of The Gypsy Boys of Spain at the Teatro González, and the concert was tomorrow.

Faced with such a detailed explanation, the preacher had forgotten to give the password agreed upon via correspondence and, finding it impossible not to feel himself a part of the beleaguered print shop, he was almost at the point of proposing to the cheerful Mennen baby that he himself go in search of a competent mechanic.

"*Mars is again approaching the Earth,*" the preacher finally said, determined to interrupt him, and he put the Bible back under his arm before extending his hand through the grating.

"And the tyrant shall be punished," the happy baby said, taking a moment to remember the agreed upon reply, releasing it as if the outboard motor had finally kicked in, and he opened the screen. Now, once the two men were face to face, he energetically patted the preacher on the shoulder, imprinting a trace of grease diluted by turpentine on his shirt.

In the hallway, the woman had abandoned her broom and was now polishing the floor while she hummed her favorite *Bienvenido Granda* song, "Room No. 22." Under her hostile gaze, which took in client and owner alike, the two men crossed the cloistered garden on their way to the print shop at the rear of the house.

Pieces of the Heidelberg press lay scattered on the floor in a pool of oil, like the remains of a dismembered animal; the pressman was busy cleaning the platen and rollers of the little pedal-operated printing machine, which looked more like a toy than anything else. It was only used to print raffle coupons and chits for cantinas, but now they were going to print the programs on it as a matter of emergency. In the meantime, in the next room, the typesetters, facing the wall and naked from the waist up, worked on their page frames, composing the type for a book they were getting ready to print.

To get to the office, separated from the workshop, you lifted a floral cretonne curtain hanging from a sash. Inside, what was always most immediately visible for any visitor was the massive mahogany desk, adorned with carved figures of Roman soldiers in plumed helmets, standing guard over a funereal urn that seemed to have beached itself there as if in the aftermath of some great flood; but for you, the most visible thing at this moment can't help but be what is lying on the desk: a little cardboard valise resting from its long and hazardous journey beside the cluster of *mamón* fruit, several of which were already missing.

Against the back wall, almost blocking passage, was a heavy mahogany armchair, the holes in its rush seat hidden under a folding mat of braided green plastic, the sort that taxi drivers use. On the other side of the desk, two rusty metal chairs. The big chair was occupied by a visitor who had been waiting for some time now; Rigoberto sat on one of the two metal chairs.

The armchair squeaked under the weight of the other visitor, perfumed with Eau de Vétiver cologne, the same kind used by Somoza. He was twenty-three years old at most, not much older than Erwin, the happy Mennen baby. You've already seen the two of them arguing at the cursed table. He looked like a prosperous cotton-grower, but he had gone broke three times and the National Bank was after him. Pests were always eating up the crops, that's true, but also a considerable portion of his bank loans had gone into hiring musicians for serenades and purchasing bracelets and necklaces and other little baubles that came from the goldsmith Segismundo, purchases he bought for himself and members of the opposite sex as rewards.

He was listening attentively to Rigoberto when the other two came in, and behind them the typesetter who followed

Erwin with proofs for the program for The Gypsy Boys of Spain's show, damp and sticky with ink, having just come off the press. Erwin hurriedly began correcting it, aided by Norberto who, from the big mahogany armchair, took charge of reading from the original typescript. Then finally they were left alone, confident that no one else would come in to interrupt them, except for the pressman on his way to Casa Prío for a round of beers, just a few blocks away.

While discussing what they called "the business," they seemed to forget about the contents of the little valise. But then they opened it again to stroke the "little beast" that slept, breathing peacefully, oblivious to their concerns. For months it had waited in the sunny window of the Sure Shot Gun Shop in San Salvador on Calle Segunda West, forlorn, as if it were never going to get out of there, the little snub-nose whimpering anxiously every time Cordelio peered through the shop window, impatiently wagging its mother-of-pearl backside, pretending to be asleep in its silk-lined case, yet always awake—but wait, don't despair, for he was a man of his word: he was going to set it free, he was going to take it home with him.

They finally released it from its chains thanks to the sacrifices of the goldsmith Segismundo, the hero of two seminal excursions, the last one of which nearly cost him his life, and to the sadly failing courage of the *Lion of Nemea*, as well as to the efforts of all the other voluntary exiles needed to stage *The Martyr of Golgotha*, under the direction of Lucio Ranucci (who at that very moment, lathered in soap, was shouting his Tuscan obscenities because the water in the shared bathroom at the Hotel America had suddenly gone off. Rigoberto will soon be telling his friends that they need to collect money to find Ranucci proper lodgings).

And so Rigoberto was able to begin his target practice under Cordelio's tutelage on a farm at the outskirts of Santa Tecla, not far from San Salvador, firing in the solitude of the coffee fields at a potbellied scarecrow, dressed in a jacket and tie and seated at a mock banquet table with glasses and bottles.

The cretonne curtain stirred, announcing the arrival of an intruder, so Rigoberto hurried to return the little beast (which had already been passed around from hand to hand four times) to its resting place in his undershorts. Torso glistening, *The Lion of Nemea* stood in the doorway, the curls of his shaggy hair dangling over his forehead. He smiled, revealing the dark gaps between his teeth.

Cordelio stepped forward, with the clear intention of pushing him out of the office, but *The Lion of Nemea*, like a victorious wrestler who has just left his opponent sprawled on the canvas, folded his arms and stood his ground, feet planted wide apart, a signal that nothing could budge him from that spot, not even, say, a flying leap from the fiercest of his silver-masked challengers, nor even a cataclysm provoked by the planet Mars in its fatal approach towards Earth.

"What are you doing here? How did you find us? Who sent you? How long have you been here?" Cordelio's questions were too fast and numerous for *The Lion of Nemea* to process them in an orderly way, so he began with the last:

"I arrived a short while ago, and I was helping feed the paper for the paper cutter. They're going to include Juan Legido's picture on the program," he informed them.

"And what did you hear us talking about?" Cordelio, alarmed, looked at the others, who in turn looked at each other, the bottles from a third round of beers dangling, useless, in their hands.

"You can't hear anything out there. If I had heard something, all the workers would have heard it too," he replied.

"Then, we'll see you later, okay," Cordelio said with a quick wave of his hands, as if shooing away a hen.

"No way, I'm a part of the business," he answered, without losing his composure.

"What business? There's no business going on here," Cordelio said.

"What business? The business I got my teeth knocked out for." And *The Lion of Nemea* spread his mouth open with his fingers to show them his missing teeth.

Cordelio looked at the others again, searching for support. Rigoberto couldn't help but laugh. Erwin and Norberto, looking concerned, didn't understand a thing. Where had this stranger come from to talk so self-confidently about "the business"? So the discussion between the two men, the preacher and the wrestler, progressed on its own; but every artifice, every explanation, every attempt to disguise the true situation on Cordelio's part was futile. And, in the end, after Cordelio's plea that he leave the office and whispered consultations among the four friends, *The Lion of Nemea* was brought into the scheme and assigned certain responsibilities, which you will learn about later.

However, before agreeing to include him in their little group, Cordelio made him kneel down and swear, with his fingers forming the sign of the cross, that he wouldn't repeat to anyone anything he heard from that moment on, or anything he was ordered to do. Would he swear to it? He would, and he kissed the cross formed by his fingers again and again.

"And now, show me the little beast asleep in the valise," he said.

Who was going to ask him now: What little beast? They showed it to him. And no sooner had the pressman been dispatched to Casa Prío for another round of beers than the little valise was quickly placed on the floor and on top of the desk Erwin unfolded a map drawn in India ink on a sheet of glossy paper, the same kind that was being used to print the programs for The Gypsy Boys of Spain.

Every block of the city's central grid had been sketched by Erwin in black ink. Towards the north, a red X marked the site of the Workers' Social Club, and a smaller X in green next to the Club on Primera Avenida marked the place where lookout A would be stationed; another even smaller X on the corner of Primera Avenida and Calle Real indicated where lookout B would be situated, and three more green Xs, running east to west, also along Calle Real, marked the positions for lookouts C, D, E, until it reached the last marker, lookout F, heading west in front of the Subtiava electric substation, marked in red.

Halfway down Calle Real, next to lookout C, stationed at the corner of Rubén Darío's ancestral home, the position of messenger O was marked in blue, and next to that mark there was a sketch of a bicycle, also in blue. On another section of the map, towards the south, marked in red, the liquor warehouse run by the León Municipal Revenue Department. It was here that the line marking the route of the bicycle ended.

Their heads joined over the map, which was held down at one end by a porcelain paperweight and at the other by a bunch of *mamón* fruit that had now suddenly found a new use. An alarm clock with two big bells that Erwin brought from his bedroom was also placed on the desk.

When Erwin indicates he's ready to start, Norberto sets both hands of the clock together, marking 12:00. Erwin, stuttering more than ever, explains the steps to be followed, his index finger, with its chewed fingernail, striking each point on the map. He keeps putting his ink-stained fingers to his mouth, which quickly becomes stained with the colors, too. Listen now to this account of the hectic exchange among the partners:

Erwin: When you hear the pow, pow, pow...
Rigoberto: Don't expect to hear loud blasts. It will be more like the sound of popcorn popping, like this (and he imitated the muffled noise of kernels popping in a pan).

122

Norberto: And what about the music? If the orchestra's playing, you won't hear anything with all that music.

Erwin: Do you think the musicians will still be playing? They'll be beating a path to the door!

Norberto: It's possible they won't catch on right away. Certainly the orchestra will be far enough from the guest of honor's table, and with all the noise of the dancers...

Rigoberto: Do we have a map of the Workers' Club yet? We still don't know where the table of honor will be, or where the musicians will be.

Erwin (Annoyed, he jabbered, and his ink-stained saliva dripped onto the map.): Then, when you hear the shots, Norberto, lookout A, you flash the headlights of your jeep three times. You should be parked next to the curb on the first street, here, facing Calle Real.

Norberto: They might not let anybody park anywhere near the Club.

Erwin (looks up at the ceiling and lets his arms drop to his sides): They'll assume the jeep broke down. It's been there since earlier in the day. You get there, it's already night, to try to start it, to drive off with it. That's why you'll test the headlights first, that's why you'll turn them on.

Norberto: It would be easier to have someone throw a rope with rocks tied at each end over the electric cable leading from the transformer on this corner (he pointed to the corner on the map, in the block where the Club is). That way you can cause a short circuit.

Cordelio: Too risky. The street will be crawling with soldiers and security agents. And it's possible that whoever it is, even if they don't shoot him on sight, won't have any luck short-circuiting the wires. He'll only have once chance.

Erwin (Growing impatient): Lookout B is stationed here, on the corner of the first street by Calle Real. When he sees Norberto, lookout A, flash the jeep's headlights three times, lookout B, turning back towards the Subtiava barrio, facing west, will then signal with his flashlight. Three times.

Rigoberto: We need a lookout B, he's key.

The Lion of Nemea (Pounding his chest): That's me.

Erwin (Observing him scornfully from head to foot): You won't do.

Rigoberto: It's all right. Let him. He gets a haircut that day and we buy him a shirt.

The Lion of Nemea: A shirt, okay. But get my hair cut, no way. This mane is my trademark.

Erwin (Addressing Rigoberto): He's your responsibility. (To *The Lion of Nemea*) With the flashlight, you too signal, three times. And here (tapping the map hard with his finger), at the corner of Rubén Darío's house, still on Calle Real, lookout C gets your signal, and he in turn signals three times with his flashlight.

Norberto (Bending over the map): Lookout C, and the other three, posted along Calle Real, D, E, F, all the way up to the electric substation in Subtiava, aren't covered yet.

The Lion of Nemea: I can get some guys from Subtiava.

Erwin (Quite alarmed): Absolutely not!

Cordelio: Forget about recruiting other people. That's all we need, to have you sitting in some bar in Subtiava and blabbing your head off about our *business*...

Erwin: It's my job to recruit those men: lookouts D, E, F.

The Lion of Nemea (Raising his arms in surrender): I take back what I said.

Erwin: Next to the electric power pole outside Rubén Darío's house, there'll be another man, messenger O, with a bicycle, here...

Norberto: There's no bicycle...

Erwin (Looking smugly serene): You've heard me say for days now that it's the print-shop delivery bicycle.

You saw it in the entry when you came in. But if you insist, then let's go, I'll show it to you, so you can touch it with your own hands.

The Lion of Nemea: That's right. The bicycle's there. I tried it out myself, and it works great.

Erwin: You tried it out? What are you talking about?

The Lion of Nemea: I saw it on my way in and felt like taking a spin. I took it outside and went for a ride around the block.

Norberto: Which means that somebody could steal it any time they want. And goodbye, bicycle.

Cordelio: Okay, we've got to get that bicycle out of there, and everything's set. And you, (addressing *The Lion of Nemea*) learn to respect other people's property.

Erwin (Sighing, disheartened): The man with the bicycle, messenger O, takes off (his finger tracing the route) until he reaches the liquor warehouse, which is south. Cordelio, you're there, waiting with your men...

Norberto: Can I ask a question?

Erwin (Looking up, hostile): Go ahead...

Norberto: Presumably the men Cordelio brings by train from El Sauce, if they do come, will be armed.

Cordelio: What do you mean, if they come? They're reliable. And they'll bring their pistols with them. The ones they use on their farms.

Norberto: Pistols. (Addressing Cordelio) You reckon that at the train station, under military surveillance the whole time, they'll let people get off without searching them?

Erwin: Forget that for now. In the meantime, the less said, the better. Cordelio sent me a letter, detailing every aspect of the attack on the liquor warehouse. I thought it was good.

Norberto: In a letter? With stamps? Van Wynckle's apprentices open all the mail.

Cordelio (To Norberto): A letter carried by a trustworthy courier. I wasn't born yesterday. I know they'll be searching everybody who gets off the train. That's why the weapons will be brought into León three days before. And, in any case, they'll all have their papers in order.

Erwin: So, the bicycle sets off...

Norberto: The bike can't go anywhere. Where's the rider?

Erwin (Ignoring him): The bicycle reaches Cordelio, waiting with his men, here. They attack the warehouse, and overcome the guards. Then they open all the taps on the liquor barrels, and it all comes rushing out. They set fire to it, and the flames can be seen all over León. And the glare will be all the more notable because the city will have gone completely dark. (A moment of silent absorption).

Rigoberto: Let's get back to the signals from the flashlights again, because it still won't be dark.

Erwin: The flashlight signal from lookout C (he brings his finger back to the corner where Rubén Darío's house is located) goes from here to lookout D. Lookout D repeats the signal, which lookout E receives, and sends it on to me, since I'm lookout F. I'm here with my people (he points to the corner of the electric substation), a group of five men, all armed. 22-caliber rifles and shotguns. (Looking up at Norberto) I already have the weapons and the men lined up. That's when we cross the street and overcome the guard, who's an old geezer and the only one on duty. He won't put up any resistance. I flip the switch, and all the lights in León go out. (looking up at Norberto again, this time in a commanding manner) Time?

Norberto (Picks up the clock and looks at the dial): Three minutes. Too long between the shots and the blackout.

Erwin: That's because you all keep interrupting! There can't be more than a minute and a half between the shots and the blackout.

Norberto (In Rigoberto's ear): I'd like to know what happened to my idea of short-circuiting the electric wires. It's less complicated. You shoot, and everything goes dark.

Erwin (Having overheard him): And I'd like to know what happens if you keep circling around *Zela the Moor's* house and don't show up at zero hour. I bet you'll say you couldn't get past the military check points.

Norberto (Smiling): You think that after this business is over, we'll be here discussing responsibilities?

Erwin (Pointing his finger again at the green X, a half-block from the Workers' Social Club, where Norberto, lookout A, is waiting behind the wheel of the jeep): The lights have gone out all over León. The fire, seen above the rooftops, lights up the sky, which has now turned orange and red. At the Workers' Club, no one knows what's going on. It's total chaos. The soldiers don't know what to do, whether to stay or run. Rigoberto then exits under cover of darkness. You've got the motor running. Rigoberto hops into the jeep and you take off for your farm, Palmira (his finger traces the jeep's route, from the point where it's parked, on the corner of Primera Avenida, and from there all along Calle Real, passing Subtiava all the way out to the highway to Poneloya). I go to my hideout and Cordelio to his. And wait for the next day.

Norberto (He cuts a *mamón* fruit from the bunch and puts it in his mouth): The only thing nobody has thought about is how Rigoberto is going to get into the party with the doors packed with guards.

Rigoberto: I'll get in on Rosaura's arm.

Erwin: No way! If she's not part of the plan, we can't put her
at risk.

Norberto: Right. It'd be the same as my getting into the jeep
to give the signals with *Zela the Moor* sitting next to
me. Our girls have nothing to do with anything that's
going on here.

Rigoberto: Let's just assume that everything's been set up so
nothing happens to me. Then, at the count of two,
we're covered in darkness, period.

Erwin: Without a doubt.

Cordelio: Nobody'll be checking at the doors. It's a public
fiesta. Besides, Rigoberto's a journalist. It's only
natural for him to be there. He'll be able to go in by
himself.

Norberto: And Van Wynckle? His new security system will
be launched there, at the convention.

Rigoberto: Look, we've got two weeks to figure out how to
get in.

It was already dark outside, and in the office the fluorescent
light on the ceiling was too high up to provide decent light
among the cobwebs. Erwin rolled up the map, and Rigoberto
picked up his little valise. They had decided to leave at ten-
minute intervals, and he was the first. In the next room, the
pedal-operated printing press had already begun operating
again.

"How much more practice do you think you'll need?"
Cordelio asked Rigoberto when he started for the door.

"A couple more times, only to get my hand limbered up.
Afterwards, I'll have to lock the little beast away and put
him to sleep with chloroform."

"You can practice at my farm at Palmira," Norberto said.

"Didn't we decide that the farm would be Rigoberto's
hideout? It can't be used for anything else," Erwin said.

"In that case, I have another place," Norberto said. "Cafarnaún, a farm where I once rented some land to grow cotton. I'll take you in my jeep."

"The two of you can't be seen together in the jeep," Erwin said.

"Cafarnaún's a good spot. I know how to get there by myself," Rigoberto said.

"And where will you keep the little beast?" Norberto asked.

"The best place in the world," Rigoberto said.

"We still need the poisoned silver bullet," Cordelio said. "The guy for that is the goldsmith Segismundo."

"Norberto will speak to him," Erwin said.

"Right. Norberto, this, and Norberto, that," Norberto said.

"Isn't he making you the engagement ring for *Zela the Moor*? You're the one, then," Erwin said.

"What engagement ring?" Norberto said. "I don't even have a pot to piss in."

"*Zela the Moor*!" Rigoberto exclaimed, turning around at the door. "I nearly forgot the most important thing!"

"Tomorrow night's the serenade with The Gypsy Boys of Spain," *The Lion of Nemea* said, throwing his arm round Norberto and grinning toothlessly from ear to ear.

TROPICAL INTERMEZZO

Curriculum Vitae
Somoza García, Anastasio

1896.

Born on the El Porvenir Farm, adjacent to the town of San Marcos. His parents are Anastasio Somoza Reyes, a coffee-grower, and Julia García, a homemaker. (According to the goldsmith Segismundo, unconfirmed rumors point to General José María Moncada, a native of the neighboring town of Masatepe, a real womanizer despite his caustic character, as his real father).

1914.

He gets an unidentified servant girl pregnant and is rushed off to the United States on the advice of his uncle, the physician Víctor Manuel Román y Reyes. He begins studying accounting at the Pierce Business School in Philadelphia. He learns English in his dealings with taxi drivers and cardsharps in the gambling dens on Market Street.

1915.

His bastard son, José (later called *The Ox-Cart Driver*) is born in Monte Redondo, a district in the municipality of Masatepe.

He meets Salvadora, a student at Beechwood College, run by the Benedictine nuns in Jenkinstown. (His other uncle, Dr. Desiderio Román y Reyes, to whose care he has been entrusted, practices medicine in Philadelphia. Look at this:

One Sunday his uncle asks him to accompany him on his rounds to see his patients at Saint Catherine Hospital, and among them is Salvadora, recently operated on for appendicitis. She had arrived barely a month before from a boarding school in Louvain, Belgium, because of the winds of war that were blowing in Europe, a prudent decision on the part of her father, the learned Debayle). Love at first sight. Courtship. Each Sunday she leaves the Beechwood campus, and he waits for her under the carillon clock of the Wanamaker Department Store.

1916.

The sweethearts return to Nicaragua on the steamship *Saratoga*. He asks for Salvadora's hand in marriage on the very day of Rubén Darío's funeral. Turned down by the learned Debayle, he decides to bide his time. (Salvadorita has brought back with her the custom of shaving under her arms, and her mother Casimira accuses him of having corrupted her, Captain Prío asserts).

He becomes friendly with the Marines, playing poker with them until dawn. He gets a job with the Metropolitan Power & Light Company reading residential electric meters, a job he loses through some intrigue on the part of the very same learned Debayle. The Rockefeller Foundation Sanitation Mission names him outhouse inspector, and he earns himself the nickname of Marshal of the Baton because of the baton-length flashlight he has to use in order to see down into the dark holes. He organizes boxing matches for the Marines.

1917.

He goes into making counterfeit money, in partnership with Justo Pastor Gonzaga and Filomela Aguirre, aka *The Alligator Woman*. The operation, set up in The Blessed Souls brothel, is discovered. Filomela is arrested, and because she keeps quiet, the others aren't caught. He proposes that the learned Debayle perform a sex change operation on *The Alligator Woman*, which opens the doors to the desired marriage.

1918.
Nuptials in the Cathedral Church of Managua.

1922.
Luis (called *The Good*) is born, the couple's first child.

1924.
A girl, Lilliam (called *La Coronada*), is born, the couple's second child.

1925.
The Marines leave Nicaragua, once peace has been secured, following a reconciliation of the two opposing political parties, the Liberals and the Conservatives, locked in bloody combat since 1854. His uncle by marriage, Dr. Juan Bautista Sacasa, is elected Vice-president.

He is named Party Chief of León. General Emiliano Chamorro, a Conservative, leads a coup d'état. The Marines return to re-establish peace when the Liberals, led by General Moncada, take up arms.

1926.
Anastasio (*The Bad*) is born, the couple's last child.

Leading a handful of peons from his father's farm, he tries to attack the headquarters of the Conservative Constabulary in Masatepe. He's wounded in the hand (the goldsmith Segismundo emphatically states it was only a scratch), and is arrested. He is placed under house arrest in the home of his father-in-law. The High Command of the occupying troops needs a personal translator for General Logand Feland, Supreme Commander of the occupying forces. Thanks to his father-in-law's efforts, he is hired. And freed from house arrest.

1927.

At Tipitapa, the Peace Accord of Espino Negro is signed (called Espino Negro—Black Thorn—-for the thorny branches of the tree under which the Armistice was sealed). General Moncada agrees to lay down his arms in exchange for the North American promise of backing his candidacy for president. One of the rebel generals, Augusto C. Sandino, refuses to surrender. The war of resistance begins in Las Segovias.

1928.

Private secretary to General Moncada, who wins the presidency (1928-1932) in free elections monitored by the Marines. (Here's where he begins to need you, boy, shining star of his fornications: Somoza arranges Moncada's nocturnal excursions to visit married women, choosing for him those domiciles where the husband is absent from the city: *dixit* Captain Prío.) A favorite of General Logand Feland, a favorite of the American minister, Mr. Matthew Hanna (an old son-of-a-bitch who played it sly, and the goldsmith Segismundo imitates an *affected way* of walking), a favorite of Mrs. Loretta Hanna, splendid in her maturity and much younger than her husband, but really not that young, my friend, a really strange old fogy: "Oh, you dirty scoundrel! Goddamned mother fucker taxi driver!" she used to exclaim in his arms; the favorite of General Moncada (an old leper, and the father of an even bigger leper, the goldsmith Segismundo heatedly declares; if he asked the general for something and didn't get it, he would see to it that his nocturnal excursions were ruined by sending a large Marine escort behind him, in two trucks, which obliged him to turn around and come back, grumbling; or he would employ a ruse to have the husband urgently called home.) Sandino's war of resistance continues.

1929.

Moncada dismisses him after discovering he has pilfered some money from a fund of American dollars destined for indemnifying the farm owners affected by the war against Sandino. Moncada's devastating words (spoken with a father's pain) were: *you're not a thief, my son, just a pickpocket.*

1930.

Moncada pardons him, following repeated requests from his aide-de-camp, Melisandro Maravilla, who unknown to Moncada had been an accomplice in the peccadillo.

1933.

His uncle by marriage, Juan Bautista Sacasa, assumes the presidency (1933-1937) after winning it in free elections (also monitored by the Marines). The occupying troops leave Nicaragua. He becomes director of the newly formed National Guard, with the rank of general because of the wound he received in the attack on the Masatepe barracks. He enlists Juan Pastor Gonzaga with the rank of colonel and names him Comptroller. He also installs Melisandro Maravilla with the same rank and names him Quartermaster. Sandino signs the peace accord with Sacasa.

1934.

Has Sandino executed. Juan Pastor Gonzaga carries out the arrest warrant, and Melisandro Maravilla commands the firing squad.

1936.

He incites the troops stationed in León to revolt. He overthrows his uncle, who boards a Mexican boat at the Port of Corinto to carry him into exile, still wearing the presidential sash across his chest.

1937.

Elected President of the Republic for a term which is to expire in 1941. A portrait of Benito Mussolini hangs in his office at the presidential Palace in Tiscapa. Mussolini sends him the gift of a small tank, which is admired with great interest at military parades. In an emotional speech, he declines the fervent demands by the Catholic Falange for him to be designated President-for-Life.

A Constitutional Assembly is installed which, as its first provision, extends his term of office as president until 1947, without any need for new elections.

1939.

Franklin D. Roosevelt receives him in Washington with state honors (which constituted, it was later learned, and don't go contradicting me because it's the truth, the goldsmith Segismundo advises Erwin, a rehearsal for the ones that would be held days later for King George VI of England. I'm not contradicting that. Go on, says Erwin). Questioned about this invitation, Roosevelt would respond with the now famous words: he is a son-of-a bitch, but he's our son-of-a-bitch.

Luis (*The Good*) and Anastasio (*The Bad*), accompany him on the trip, and stay on as boarders at the La Salle Academy on Long Island, New York.

1941.

He declares war on the Axis, a day before the United States.

Unknown to Salvadora, he has his bastard son José (*The Ox-Cart Driver*), who had been making his living in Masatepe driving an ox-cart, brought to him. He inducts him into the National Guard with the rank of sergeant, and assigns him a tutor to teach him to read.

1942.

He confiscates all the properties of German families in Nicaragua. (An armed assault by the gangster! He kept all their land holdings: coffee plantations, cattle ranches, sugarcane plantations. Just think, he sent Justo Pastor Gonzaga to finish the job, machine gun in hand. A Dillinger! Anybody would think Somoza had taken something from you, Erwin says to the goldsmith Segismundo. Are you of German ancestry? You certainly don't look it. I pay no mind to such sarcastic remarks, replies Segismundo).

Luis (*The Good*) enrolls in Louisiana State University to study agronomy. Anastasio (*The Bad*) is admitted to West Point.

1943.

The portrait of his daughter Lilliam (La Coronada) shows up on the one-córdoba bill, with an Apache Indian feather on her head. The archbishop of Managua, Monsignor José Antonio Lezcano y Ortega, crowns her queen of the Military Academy in a ceremony held in the Cathedral, attended by National Guardsmen dressed as Roman soldiers in Bakelite armor and helmets and bearing wooden lances.

1944.

He proposes an amendment to the Constitution that would make him eligible for re-election again, which is prohibited, in order to remain in office beyond 1947. A demonstration which he himself organizes on July 4 to back the Allies suddenly turns against him. The speech he wants to deliver from the balcony of the American Legation is received with intense jeering, and he has to remain silent. Serious disturbances follow for several days. The electorate, defiant, takes to the streets of Managua. He thinks seriously about resigning and leaving the country. He is saved by the last-minute providential intervention of General Moncada, who tricks the leaders of the movement, promising them negotiations that are never held. All the conspirators are hauled off to jail (Moncada, of course, Erwin says, who else, the man who fathered him, thus appeasing the goldsmith Segismundo's insistence that the general was Somoza's real father). Personal monopoly of the cement industry, matches, liquor.

1945.
Luis (*The Good*) returns from Louisiana without a degree. Anastasio (*The Bad*) returns as a West Point graduate. He names him Director of the Military Academy and introduces him to José (*The Ox-Cart Driver*), who becomes his assistant. ("Although he's older than you, you're of the same blood, and he'll be loyal to you like no one else," he says. And Segismundo adds: the history of Nicaragua is full of bastards, and although this one eats in the kitchen, he'll be happy so long as they let him dip his hand into the till).

1947.
He decides to sit it out and doesn't run for election. His candidate, Dr. Leonardo Argüello, whom he chooses because he's senile, is proclaimed the winner after a fraudulent recount of the votes that really favored the opposition candidate, Dr. Enoc Aguado. Oh, what a surprise! As his first official act as new president, Argüello orders his dismissal as Director of the National Guard. Stung by this treachery, he overthrows the new president, who had lasted but ten days. The National Congress names in his place Dr. Víctor Manuel Román y Reyes, his uncle, who is even more senile. (The same uncle who had facilitated his flight to the United States when he got the servant girl pregnant, don't forget, says the goldsmith Segismundo).

1949.
His uncle, the aged President Román y Reyes, dies of food poisoning from eating rotten fish. (Forget that business about

137

rotten fish. The gangster had strychnine put in his food with the help of a crafty cook, his staunchest supporter. Somoza was desperate to drape the presidential sash across his chest again, but the old man had refused to give up the ghost, and even took a lover to bed, a seamstress who worked in the presidential household).

1950.
He circulates the rumor that he's sick and near death. His personal physician, Colonel Heriberto Guardado (NG), makes certain to confirm the rumor in social circles. Eventually, he is elected president for another term (1950-1956), after negotiating a political deal with General Emiliano Chamorro, his traditional Conservative adversary:

A hot drawing room in Managua. Two wicker rocking chairs.
Somoza (*Fanning himself with a straw fan*): General, can I ask you a favor?
Chamorro (*Suspicious, his eyes hidden under the heavy folds of his eyelids*): Go ahead.
Somoza: *We're close to signing this pact...(he hesitates). I have a son, Luis...*
Chamorro (*Courteous*): *The engineer? I know him.*
Somoza (*Bashful*): *He calls himself an agricultural engineer, unjustly. But there are no laws here to punish a person for telling lies. (He laughs, slyly.) He doesn't have any work. I want you to allow me to make him a congressman, so he'll be kept busy. Why don't we lift that ban against the children of the president being ineligible? (He falls silent, and waits, his linen handkerchief, perfumed with Eau de Vétiver cologne, close to his mouth.)*
Chamorro (*He ponders, his eyes hidden beneath his eyelids*): *That...would open a lot of doors for your boy. In the event that the president is incapable of governing for any reason, his successor is chosen from among the congressmen...*

Somoza: *Luis? Luis, my successor? Don't make me laugh, General! (He laughs openly.) Someone who has no ambitions in life. That's why they call him Luis The Good. If I were asking you something for the other one, Anastasio...well, he's the one you'd have to look out for...*

Chamorro *(He thinks: I'll make a concession to a cadaver. Your cancer won't let you last much longer.): All right, then. But as a personal favor, not a political one.*

Somoza *(He rises up a few inches from the wicker chair and extends both hands to him): Many, many thanks, General. You don't know how grateful I am to you for this.*

(And what a favor it was! The goldsmith Segismundo pounds the table with the palm of his hand. With that pact, the dynasty was born! If Dillinger dies, his son will take his place. And Erwin says to him: who knows when that will be, because on the 21st, across the way from here in the Teatro González, old Tacho will be anointed for another six years, and that's how it'll be, per secula seculorum. Until someone comes along who'll risk his balls, the goldsmith Segismundo says. And Captain Prío says: that someone hasn't been born yet; and with that bulletproof vest, even less of a chance. Yes, Rigoberto says, looking against the light at the spoon he's just taken from his mouth: he hasn't been born.)

1951.
Owner of textile factories, ice and soft drink plants, footwear factories, cotton mills, coffee plantations, sugar refineries, salt production plants. He makes May 27, the First Lady's birthday, Armed Forces Day (in order to appease her because she has discovered the existence of José (*The Ox-Cart Driver*), Captain Prío says: she really lit into him, right there in the presidential office, in front of the Peruvian ambassador who had come to inform him of the gift of some horses from President Odría.)

1954.
An uprising of officers of the National Guard in April. All the ringleaders are tortured, castrated, and murdered. Luis (*The Good*) and Anastasio (*The Bad*) direct the interrogations with the diligent cooperation of José (*The Ox-Cart Driver.*) He builds a port, Port Somoza. He founds a merchant ship line, the Mamenic Line, to export cattle to Peru; an airline, Lanica. He controls the meatpacking business, including the hides and lard, through his own slaughterhouses. He also goes into raising pigs, fattening and slaughtering them. He establishes February 1, his own birthday, as Father's Day. José (The Ox-Cart Driver) begins to appear in family photos in *Novedades.*

1955.
He dedicates his own equestrian statue in front of Somoza Stadium.

1956.
He receives the overthrown leader Juan Domingo Perón and settles him in the Palace of Tiscapa. Perón becomes bored in Managua. (We've got to make him forget Evita, poor thing, to get him married here, so he'll invest his money in some big enterprises, the First Lady says to her husband when she sees Perón sad and dejected, spending the entire day up at the crater of the lagoon. God forbid! the alarmed husband replies. I don't need anybody involved in my business affairs. As soon as I can, I'll pack him off to Trujillo in the Dominican Republic. Trujillo? My God! That man's a dictator and a thief, she says to him).

In Panama, he attends the Continental Summit of Presidents, where he meets Dwight D. Eisenhower in person. Others in attendance: Fulgencio Batista (Cuba); Rojas Pinilla (Colombia); Pérez Jiménez (Venezuela); Castillo Armas (Guatemala); Manuel Odría (Peru); Bienvenido Trujillo (Dominican Republic). (Stop! You're making me sick! the goldsmith Segismundo says, with the face of a man about to vomit).

On September 21, on Mars's closest approach to Earth, he arrives in León aboard the presidential train, accompanied by the First Lady. His coach, furnished with wicker chairs, is the same one that General Zelaya once put at the disposal of Rubén Darío to carry him from the Port of Corinto:

> *Oh, Salvadora, Salvadorita...!*
> *Is he a king of gold or a king of love?*

Farewell Letter

León, September 21, 1956

Señora Soledad López
Confidential

Dearest Mama,

Even though you've never known it, I've always been active in resisting our country's ghastly regime. Since all attempts to make Nicaragua once again (or perhaps for the first time) a free and unblemished country have been in vain, I've decided, despite my friends urging me not to, to be the one who will try to usher in the beginning of the end of tyranny. If God wishes me to die in the attempt, I don't want anyone to be blamed, since this is entirely my own decision.

I trust you'll take all of this calmly and know that what I've done is a duty that any Nicaraguan who really loves his country should have done a long time ago. My efforts haven't been a sacrifice but rather a duty that I hope will be fulfilled. If you accept this the way I want you to, I can tell you that I'll feel happy. So then, let's not have any sadness, because to do one's patriotic duty is the greatest satisfaction that a good man, as I have tried to be, can aspire to. If you accept these things with serenity and with the clear idea that I've fulfilled my highest duty as a Nicaraguan, I'll be very grateful to you.

Your son who has always loved you dearly,

Rigoberto

PART TWO

Now You'll Have Life So You May
Poison Yourself

Captain Prío leaves his observation post to go downstairs and bring out the huge loudspeakers and place them by the door on the street corner, because it won't be long now before those attending the Great Convention will start filing out of the Teatro González. On the bar top, he shuffles through his collection of records, chooses an LP of John Phillip Souza's military marches, played by the Boston Pops Orchestra, cranks the volume on the record player up to full blast, and to the reverberations of "The Star Spangled Banner," marches back upstairs and resumes his position on the balcony.

In the plaza, *The Alligator Woman* is waving her arms as if she were conducting the orchestra. Walking backwards, she gets the demonstrators to follow her so they'll gather on the side of the plaza where she has wanted them to gather for some time now, in front of the Teatro González, up with their cardboard placards, up with the red cloth flags, up with their shouts. Get those people over here! What are those jerks doing up on the trucks? Orders repeated by her lieutenants, Catalina Baldelomar, with monumental buttocks, dressed in colorful taffeta, whom Captain Prío doesn't know but you do, and a local man, her brother, *Stone Face* Diómedes Baldelomar, perhaps forty years of age, also wearing dark glasses like *The Alligator Woman*, with a towel draped round his neck as if he had a cold.

Firecrackers boom, rockets go off, lit by the tips of cigarettes, and now Captain Prío leans over his balcony: his calculation has been correct. Somoza is just leaving the Teatro González to cross the plaza, surrounded by a throng of heads, hats, and military caps, going on foot to his mother-in-law's house. He makes a few brief statements into the microphone of the Gran Cadena Liberal Radio, and Erwin and Norberto, meeting for the last time that day, go into the print shop to listen; the pressmen, standing idle for the moment, have the radio tuned to Radio Darío, which is hooked into the national radio network:

Radio Announcer: General, what do you think of this display of affection? No one has moved, just waiting for you to come out.

Somoza: Ask the people of León, the people of León. I feel so moved I can't speak.

Radio Announcer: And the National Convention, how is it going?

Somoza: Like a train.

Radio Announcer: Is your candidacy a sure thing?

Somoza: I'm a soldier of the Mother Country, and a soldier of my party. If the National Convention decides that we should stick with the same man, then I'm that man.

Radio Announcer: May we inform our listeners where you are going now?

Somoza: Of course. To pay my respects to my mother-in-law. She's having a luncheon. Let's see if they've left anything for me.

Radio Announcer: You have heard the statements of his excellency the president... Listen, listen to the acclamations of the people of León gathered in Plaza Jerez, their enthusiasm and fervor reaching new heights...! Listen to the explosion of flares and rockets...! And at this moment, the president is making his way through the crowd and going to embrace one of its leading women! A warm embrace; she whispers something in his ear...and now, yes, General Somoza is leaving. Here's the woman he spoke to! What is your name, ma'am?

The Alligator Woman: (Out of breath.) Filomela Aguirre, at your service. Long live Somoza! Long live the Liberal Party!

Radio Announcer: What did you tell the president?

The Alligator Woman: Not to forget that we need a school in the Ermita de Dolores barrio, that countless children there are losing out for want of a teacher, and he promised to take care of it.

Radio Announcer: We'll continue with our live transmission as soon as we return. The affiliates can now leave the Gran Cadena Liberal, coming to you from Managua courtesy of Station X...many, many thanks. (A few seconds of static.)

Musical Theme: (First chords of the first movement of Beethoven's 5th Symphony.)

Voice of Jorge Negrete: Today is the 21st. What will happen on the 21st? (Musical bridge: Chopin's *Clair de lune.*) The 21st is here...the suspense is over...what we didn't tell you yesterday, today you can finally find out: *Tovarich*, the play of the year, a festival of laughs at the Teatro Darío, opens tonight at 8:00 p.m. sharp...bring your whole family, don't be left out and have others tell you tomorrow what happened on the 21st... (Men and women laughing. Applause.)

In the meantime, Captain, even though you aren't there to witness it, *The Rose Child* appears to be nervous because she can't get up from the table, which the waiters have already cleared. Moralitos has arrived, looking very military, his cap under his arm, to announce that *el señor presidente* is now on his way, that no one is to leave, please, the faces of the guests reflected in his Ray-Ban sunglasses. But lieutenant, she has to get back and go over the lines for her part one last time, her blond hair has to be done up with a bow, her costume needs some final touches, she has to see to *Zela the Moor*'s hair and outfit as well, a whole heap of things, and besides, to hear the rebroadcast of *The Right to be Born* over Radio Mundial at three in the afternoon, that is if the Gran Cadena Liberal hasn't taken over the airwaves for the rest of the day; there's so much she can learn from the vocal gymnastics of the female lead, Marta Cansino, despite the fact that Lucio Ranucci has advised her not to listen to such trash. Forget it. No one's leaving here.

And *The Alligator Woman*? Still under Captain Prío's gaze, *The Alligator Woman* can't leave the plaza. She'll have to stay there throughout the recess, making sure the supporters don't wander off through the streets at the very moment Somoza returns, and especially, when he leaves the Teatro González for the last time, once he's been declared his party's presidential candidate. And it won't be until then that she (he), surely it'll be dark by then, will be able to return to Baby Dolls to dress for the party at the Workers' Social Club.

Somoza has already entered his mother-in-law's house. Seeing the commotion outside die down, Captain Prío goes to close the shutters of his balcony window. *The Alligator Woman* takes advantage of the respite to slip off her shoes, because her feet are killing her from all the running back and forth she's been doing since early morning. She slips the shoes off without sitting down, possessing an uncanny sense of balance, like a heron disguised as a man.

Captain Prío adjusts the elastic of his bow tie and takes his place behind the bar next to the cash register. The conventioneers begin to fill up the tables, taking off their coats, which they drape over the backs of the chairs, and loosening their ties. And he himself is the one who keeps tabs on the orders in the midst of the din of voices.

Attentive to the bustling clientele, he forgets about *The Alligator Woman*, who has been too busy until now to get a bite to eat. She is standing, looking thoughtful, on the steps of the Teatro González, eating a big tamale with her fingers, the wrapping open in the palm of her hand. Obligingly, she offers the best bites to *Stone Face* Diómedes Baldelomar; between puffs on his Valencia cigarette, he chews gratefully. Thoughtful, I'd say, because of her silence, even though I can't ascertain anything in her expression, so well hidden behind those dark, triangular-shaped sunglasses, just like the ones that *Stone Face* Diómedes Baldelomar is wearing. Might she be thinking about that long-ago date of April 9, 1908? Then she was just a little girl, with sharp, pointy teeth. A girl of seven. Inside the now empty Teatro González, the blades of the ceiling fans continue to turn. Nobody who works there can get inside to turn them off because the security agents are guarding all the doors. So, again I'll let the pages of the calendar fly back under the blades of the fans, and you may join them in their flight. Listen:

Under the sun that toasts the cicadas a golden brown, she was walking hurriedly along the railroad track next to Lake Xolotlán, whose foamy, languid waves were lapping up against the track. Her knapsack swinging back and forth in her hand and her little pointy teeth visible, her mouth partly open from exhaustion, her bare feet flattening the dry sprouts of brush, as she hurried to catch up with her father who strode on ahead of her, annoyed at having to stop so many times, weak from hunger, but not daring to pick up the half-ripe mangoes rotting on the ground, even less to throw stones at the ones that could be seen through the thick foliage of the trees lining the path far into the distance. They were traveling alone, en route to León, making their way around the solitary Momotombo Volcano, whose black sand cascaded all the way down its distant barren slopes, but the invisible eyes of Galatea Quirino, *Our Lady of the Fields*, were watching them to make sure they didn't touch anything.

The fireworks-maker Apolonio Aguirre, alias *The Great Dragon,* and his seven-year-old daughter, Filomela Aguirre, later known to all as *The Alligator Woman* because of those sharp little teeth, had spent six months in the Santos Lugares jail, having been arrested on orders from General Silvano

Quirino, *The Little President,* when they were found cutting reeds and sticks on his property to use in making fireworks.

Now blind, after the ill-fated operation, he wanted to indulge himself one last time, even if it only meant hearing the sound of the hoofs of his big wild mule crunching the flat rocks on the road and smelling the fertile land in that October of heavy rains. Diminutive, as if he had stopped growing during puberty, his slanted Imbita-Indian eyes now dead and floating in a cloud of blue vapors, he undertook his farewell ride, one hand on the animal's rump as always, the other clutching the reins.

He came to a halt in the foothills of the Cosigüina Volcano, the border of the Santos Lugares properties by the Gulf of Fonseca, and, when he was changing bridles, accompanied by his overseers, he heard the sound of people walking through the reedbeds, out of sight, and sent his men to look for them. Brought before him, the father and daughter were sentenced on the spot as common thieves and hauled along as prisoners on the return journey, their hands tied in front of them to the saddletrees, stumbling along behind the horses, league after league, while *The Little President's* eyes burned with despair in their sockets.

The return trip took seven days and nights, silently passing the fields of indigo with their processing troughs, tinted crimson, the mounds of crushed sugar cane next to the grinding stone of the sugar mill, and the vultures sitting on the cowhides laid out in the sun to dry, encountering pack-mule trains carrying shipments of sugarcane sweets to Honduras and wagon trains filled with their cargoes of bananas, and in his nostrils the sharp fermented smell of drying tobacco and the bitter draft off the flats of salt extracted from the marsh. And then when he reached his hacienda next to Lake Xolotlán, they put him to bed on his old army cot, its hard leather as taut and sonorous as a campaign drum, and covered him with his tiger-striped blanket, and there he died on the morning of October 9, 1907.

He had not forgotten to have *The Great Dragon* and his daughter locked up along with the other reedbed thieves who had stolen firewood and fruits, tenant farmers who hadn't paid the taxes on their harvests on time, day laborers in rebellion against the laws of the Liberal revolution which ordered those rounded up on the roads to work without pay, and the Imabita Indians of his own race who struggled endlessly to cut down the wire fences so they could sow the lands bequeathed to them by royal decree, which they still considered theirs. At night, the prisoners were taken out in squads to make noise with rattles to frighten off the swarms of locusts that laid waste to the fields, and the ones who showed little zeal for creating a din awoke the next morning with their heads and hands clamped in stocks.

One December night, as the first light of day was filtering through the cracks in the roof of the jailhouse, which stank of urine and feces, *The Great Dragon* had heard the prisoners talk of a traveling prince who walked the streets of León on carpets of cracked wheat in colorful arabesque designs, just like those of Holy Week, who passed beneath triumphal arches covered with stuffed birds and fruits that stood out in bas-relief on woven wreaths of flowers. And *The Great Dragon*, embracing the little girl trembling with cold, was determined to meet that prince.

As luck would have it, he received a commission from *Our Lady of the Fields* to design an immense life-size image of *The Little President*, made out of fireworks, which was to be lit at dawn in front of the hacienda's chapel, following the midyear requiem mass. The portrait began to light up from its base, wrapped in a rosy-hued cloud, and the figure of the deceased, just as he was during the era of the Liberal revolution, gradually emerged in all his military trappings and stripes, his eyes, with the blue light *The Great Dragon* had placed in them, being the last to go out.

When the stick skeleton faded back into darkness, *Our Lady of the Fields*, who had watched the spectacle from the atrium of the chapel, ordered the fireworks-maker and his daughter to appear before her.

In one corner of the sitting room there was a clavichord which had stood forgotten and silent among animal harnesses and farm tools. Seated on a stool, she was busy kneading curds, her arms thrust into the bucket. The whey had soaked her long mourning dress which left only her feet exposed. Her long toenails were curled up like claws, because when she was very little they'd been scalded by water that had been boiling in preparation for skinning a pig. On her ruddy face, her nose rose up, haughty, above a mouth filled with gold teeth, and from the wrinkled nest of her eyelids the little ovals of her eyes surveyed father and daughter with curiosity.

The fireworks-maker approached, shielding himself behind the little girl.

"We're very poor, *Our Lady*," he dared to babble, transmitting the trembling in his gunpowder-stained hands to his daughter's little body.

"Our Lord was poor, and he died on the cross without complaint." *Our Lady of the Fields* seemed to be praying as she kneaded the curds. "You are free. Go in peace."

The Great Dragon took a brave step forward, pushing the little girl ahead of him.

"You, who can do anything, give me a letter to take to the prince," he asked her.

"What prince?" The hard shell of the little eggs of her eyes seemed to break.

"The one who came from far away, conqueror of death." *The Great Dragon* drew his hand across his forehead, mopping off the sweat. "The one who is paraded on a float under triumphal arches."

"Oh, that one." She leaned back on her stool, her indifference a form of disdain.

"My little girl can feed his swans." *The Great Dragon*, confusing her scorn for consent, took another step forward, causing his daughter to stumble.

"He's no prince, but a libertine, an accomplice of that outlaw who made my brother blind! The two of them together stole the files of the court case, and now he wants to flatter me with his pagan verses." She ground the words with rancor between her closely-bunched gold teeth.

Terrified, the fireworks-maker took a step back. But now she called the little girl forward, extending her arms to her, and he pushed her closer without hesitation.

"I'm going to send you to a place where there's a real prince, the prince of the righteous." And with a maternal embrace, she hugged the little girl who had been standing there the whole time, chewing on the hem of her dress cut from a coarse blanket.

"You mean, there's another prince?" *The Great Dragon* was astonished.

"Yes, a blessed prince, one who wants nothing to do with the things of this world and who will get to heaven with his works." Her cluster of gold teeth came loose in her mouth.

"A poor prince?" *The Great Dragon* dared to appear wary. "Without parks or swans?"

"Those swans are phantoms, fabrications of the mind of that Beelzebub." She was now rocking the little girl on her knees as if trying to lull her to sleep.

And *The Great Dragon* didn't understand why she held swans in such contempt because on the green-striped wallpaper on the wall between the two windows hung a heavy-framed painting where white-plumed swans sailed on the waters of a blue lake. There were naked nymphs bathing in the lake, and it was a swan, the leader of them all, that covered the most beautiful nymph with the beating of its wings, while she, swooning, surrendered herself to the kiss of his crimson beak.

"Passing fancies of my brother Selvano Quirino, may he rest in peace," she said, without looking at the painting. "That painting will be burned with the rest of his belongings on the first anniversary of his death. His godless books, and that instrument, they're all going straight into the flames." And she turned her head scornfully toward the clavichord.

They were now traveling on foot along the tracks under the April sun with a letter from *Our Lady of the Fields* for Saint Mardoqueo, in which she recommended his receiving the little girl at the Orphans' Hospice that she maintained in León. Under his shirt, thick with sweat and dirt, *The Great Dragon* carried the letter that smelled of whey, but his thoughts were constantly focused on the Prince of Swans who had come from afar, and he saw himself pushing his way through the crowds to get close to that float that rolled under the triumphal arches, and there he would offer himself as an artist of lights to entertain the courtesans at his Bohemian parties.

They were nearing the outskirts of León at last, and could see church towers beyond the vegetation of the market gardens and hear the church bells ringing, and they made their way along the tracks, between low brick walls, ravines, and trash dumps, barbed wire fences, open lots, roof tops bunched together next to the rails, until they reached the railroad station draped with blue-and-white banners and heard the train's long whistle rise above the music of the band. The prince was leaving. *The Great Dragon* caught a glimpse of him waving farewell to the crowd with his handkerchief from the window of his coach, which was already in motion. One moment he said goodbye and then almost immediately used the handkerchief to cover his eye, red as a ruby and swollen shut.

And, as the train was pulling away, he went about asking, eager to find someone who might know in what country the prince lived, and somebody finally responded that the learned Debayle, his intimate friend, was the only one who knew his address abroad. He went to knock at the door of the house next to the cathedral, already deep in shadow, and a little girl came to the door, wearing an Italian straw hat and playing with an open fan: her father wasn't home.

Did the little girl know the address of the prince who had gone away? Her mother, Casimira, knew it, said the little girl, and told them to wait. And they waited. The little girl returned with the address written on a card. The fireworks-maker didn't know how to read, so the little girl, joyful and talkative, gladly read it for him: Rue Corneille 17, Paris. Paris? Did the little girl know where Paris was? Far away, very far away; it would take many years by boat to reach Paris.

And the other little girl, the one with the pointy teeth, looked disdainfully at the know-it-all with the straw hat and showed not the least interest when the little girl began reading to the fireworks-maker what the prince had written for her on her fan, nor when her sister came to the door to claim that the prince had written much longer ones for her which she knew by heart: *Margarita, how beautiful the sea, and the wind carries with it a subtle essence of orange blossom...*

They left the two sisters fighting over their verses, and went looking for the hospice, the little girl trailing behind her father through the no-longer-euphoric streets of León and the framework of the triumphal arches, now devoid of birds or fruits, still standing bare on the street corners.

Saint Mardoqueo was busy serving dinner to the orphans, standing next to the wood-burning stove, feeling the heat of the flames against his emaciated, smooth-cheeked face. The orphans came over to him with their tin bowls and, after being served their soup, went to sit down in the corners of the refectory to eat in silence, their skinny bodies wrapped in the clouds of smoke from the fire that spread through the room like a warm mist.

He offered father and daughter a bowl of soup, which the fireworks-maker and the girl hungrily devoured without bothering to use a spoon, and then standing by the fire, he read the letter. When he recognized his patron's signature, he smiled beatifically and made the sign of the cross over the paper.

When he had more than twelve orphans following him through the streets, he had asked permission of Bishop Simeón to undertake a pilgrimage to Santos Lugares to ask the señora, a relative of his, for her support in establishing a hospice. And so he went, with his shepherd's crook pounding the dusty road, at the head of the troop of boys dressed like him with little coarse linen smocks, and he returned with her promise of help. The hospice was blessed by Bishop Simeón on October 17, 1905, two years before Rubén returned triumphant to Nicaragua; and this blessing put an end to the bitter dispute between the bishop and the saint.

Eight years earlier, at noon on the day before Palm Sunday, 1900, Bishop Simeón had gone to seek refuge in the garden to read the Argentine edition of *Profane Prose* which Rubén had sent him from Paris, together with a letter, replete with fond thoughts. As he was walking down the corridor with its Arabic tiles next to the alms room that was now used to store ecclesiastical garb, from behind the closed door he heard noises like someone in pain.

He knocked, cautiously at first, and then when no one responded, with greater force, until finally his vicar-general, Father Mardoqueo, appeared, clumsily buttoning the front of his soutane. The bishop pushed him aside angrily, then searched the darkened room for his accomplice. He found her behind the open door of a closet where white tunics and ecclesiastical robes hung, wrapped in the embroidered silks that had graced the top of a canopy.

Before him stood the Cathedral's clothes-presser, Estebana Catín, better known as *The Bengal Tigress*. She suddenly allowed the silks to fall. Her exuberant breasts trembled with her laughter, and as she lifted her head defiantly, her hair, soaked in oil, glowed like a dark halo, as unkempt as the mat of her pubic hair, while to the bishop's horror, a trickle of unholy liquid ran down her firm, plump legs. He turned away from this sight, lowering his head, and chased the woman out with such frantic gestures that the book flew out of his hands.

He went looking for the vicar and found him hiding in the choir at the end of the apse. Talking to him from a distance as if he were a leper, Bishop Simeón imposed upon him the immediate penitence of going through the streets as a beggar, dressed in sackcloth, a punishment that moved the city to tears because Father Mardoqueo, called to the priesthood as a child, had been destined for the bishop's throne.

The rivulets etched in his cheeks by his tears are what the fireworks-maker notices by the firelight as Father Mardoqueo finishes reading the letter.

"I can't," he said after stepping away from the flames. "We only take boys at the hospice."

"You can cut her hair," *The Great Dragon* pleaded.

"*Our Lady of the Fields* asks this of me," he brooded. "But what can I do?"

"Who's going to know it, your eminence?" *The Great Dragon* said, kneeling down on the ground.

"I'm not an eminence," Saint Mardoqueo gently corrected him. Then he looked at the little girl. "What's your name?"

"Filomela," *The Great Dragon* answered, and he went down on his other knee. "If it pleases you, you can call her Filomelo, with an *o*."

And without waiting for any further reply, he stood up and disappeared through the large dark opening of the refectory door, but soon afterwards he came back and, taking the little knapsack from his daughter's hands, undid the knot and placed everything he had in his pants' pocket inside it: a needle, a skewer, a piece of brown paper, a measure of potassium chlorate.

She came from powder. She had been born amidst a fountain of lights, when *The Great Dragon*'s fireworks operation, set up in their house in the Zaragoza barrio, caught fire one December night just as she was letting out her first bellow. The heavens flamed in rebellion with the explosion of the rockets, sparklers, and Catherine wheels that had been stored away for the Festivals of the Gritería, a great hoopla in honor of the Immaculate Conception, and *The Great Dragon* could only think of his ruin as he ran out of the house through the smoke with the infant girl in his arms, wrapped in tarpaper, just like a cherry bomb at festival time, the umbilical cord dangling from her like another wick about to be lit, while her mother was asphyxiated beneath the burning bedcovers of the shabby bed.

It was only when the beams of the roof were ablaze, with sparks flying and thunderous booming, before it fell into the flames that removed the paper wrapping from the infant, he saw the gash that marked her sex and, not finding anything else to cover her with, he shook the sparks from his felt hat and placed it over her arched little body.

Although at first she was so scared of the world that she clung to Father Mardoqueo's garments, her hair cropped so she'd look more like another little boy, she soon learned to run around on her own far from the gang of beggar-orphans that fanned out through the streets at the sound of the cowbell. She would deliberately get lost among the stalls in the markets, which were teeming with local merchants and outsiders, and would climb into the driver's seat of the wagons stopped next to the railroad station platform in order to get off the moving convoy at the outskirts of town, and she would return to the hospice late at night, alone, her little face flushed with her restless energy and her coarse woolen dress in tatters.

She would curse when the handouts were miserly and would return the half-centavo copper pieces, the over-ripe bananas and rotted fruit, showing her little pointy teeth and shouting that they were orphans, not parrots. She sneaked into houses while brashly banging her tin cup, shamelessly raiding people's pantries, and even porcelain flower vases started showing up on the altar in the hospice chapel, requisitioned by her hands from sitting-room tables. And she would even stroll into cockfight pits, disdainful of the gamblers, grabbing the bills from the fistfuls in their hands, or into crap-shooting dens where she would spirit away her cut from the gamblers' winnings, indifferent to their threats and reprimands.

By the age of twelve, she was in charge of going from door to door, every Friday, with the apostolic letterbox, a pine box with a padlock and a slot for the faithful to insert the letters they had written to Saint Mardoqueo. They paid one *real* for a stamp for each letter deposited in the letterbox, and he answered all of them.

One Friday afternoon early in December, when she was off in the wilds of the barrio Ermita de Dolores on Calle Paso de Carretas, where the houses began to spread out among the wire-fenced orchards, making her rounds with the apostolic letterbox, she came to a house she had never seen before. She entered the courtyard and found a group of little girls in white tunic dresses playing with little clay cups and plates, watched over by a girl with menstrual pallor.

Without knowing it, she had happened upon Talía, *Terrestial Light*, sister of Saint Mardoqueo, who watched over *The Blessed Souls*. Happy that the apostolic letterbox had found her in her confinement, she wanted to write to him, so that while *The Alligator Woman* remained amidst this delightful and novel company and soon became the leader of their games, she leaned against the open window onto the courtyard, trying to think of what to write, the pencil pressed against her lips.

She had been expelled from convent school after the nuns discovered her romantic involvement with Sister Brígida, the plump and genial singing instructor who absentmindedly strolled about the cloister, her sheets of music safely tucked under the front of her starched habit, and *Terrestial Light*'s father, *Goliath*, barred her from his house. Left to fend for herself, she went off to found her own kind of hospice for orphan girls.

Saint Mardoqueo woke up sitting at his desk the next morning, trying in vain to think of a reply to the letter written in clumsy handwriting and filled with misspellings that had so horrified him. Rather than begging his forgiveness, his sister confessed to him certain sins that she refused to renounce; the nun, using a whole page to explain herself because, wise in ways of foolishness, they still pleased her memory; and the brothel of underage girls, preferred by furtive clients who could return home without any hint of odor that could announce their whereabouts, except for a faint aroma of sour milk, which was her livelihood. And he had the dreadful feeling that, even though she had not said as much, she was asking for his connivance.

And he was still thinking about his sister that afternoon, unable to find the proper reply to her letter, when, on his return from an audience with Bishop Simeón, he entered the refectory of his orphanage and found that the boys had raped the little girl. Crying with rage, the stain of blood still wet on her shift, she was threatening them with ferocious curses, and brandishing her father's skewer, which she had run to get from her knapsack as soon as she had managed to escape their clutches. She had already wounded one of them in the stomach when Saint Mardoqueo finally succeeded in disarming her, cornering her while he tried to clamp her down, and defending himself against her sharp little teeth. He fell on his knees and prayed disconsolately, the obscene insults the girl continued to shout at the boys bubbling like a sulfuric soup in his ears, and then without even daring to look at her, told her that she could no longer remain under that roof.

She snatched the skewer from him and tied up her knapsack, setting off through the streets, following the smell of gunpowder that would lead her to *The Great Dragon*. After a great deal of walking, she finally found him in a courtyard in the Subtiava barrio, kneeling on the ground by the light of an oil lamp. He felt the girl's presence at his side, barely turning his head before continuing with his work, pressed to finish the fireworks portrait of Colonel Moses Pendleton (USMC) which was to burn at midnight in the Plaza Jerez.

When *The Great Dragon* stood up to search his pocket for a coin, the wicks that he had to place across the framework of the portrait became entangled like parasites across his body, and he hardly noticed the blood still gleaming on the little girl's shift like the crimson explosion of a firecracker. Seeing her make no gesture to take the coin from him, her hands still gripping her knapsack, he put it back in his pocket and kneeled down again to continue his work, soon forgetting that she was still there. He was also unaware of it when she rushed back out into the street, trying to settle in her little head with hair shaved over the ears, like the cavity of a reed, the decision to change herself one day into a real man, to sometime be able to pee in a long stream standing up.

But that would come later, with time. For the moment she was in pain from the scratches on her now tarnished little box, where hair had begun to sprout like tender grass. Blood was still coming down her skinny legs in little streams, and as she walked along the cobblestone streets she was disturbed by a feeling of scorched numbness.

Back in the patio playground, and ignoring the questions put to her by *Terrestial Light,* who had come outside to empty the chamber pots on the flowers growing on the graves, she went inside to a room where the playful music of a polka was being scratched out on a violin. She wiped away the tears that stung like shards of glass on her angry little face. It was her birthday.

"What graves were those?" Norberto asked, intrigued.

"The graves in the cemetery of your great-aunt, *Terrestial Light*," Segismundo said, throwing his arm out in front of him. "That's where they buried the fetuses when they got the young girls pregnant."

"They buried them in the same boxes those big spools of thread came in," Captain Prío said with great solemnity.

"Like pet cats you don't like to throw on a rubbish dump when they die," said Erwin, laughing quietly.

"Among her clients were doctors who performed those abortions," Rigoberto said, and he looked at each of them. "I'm glad to see no one's calling me a liar now."

"Am I mistaken, or do your notes show that Chiron and *The Alligator Woman* were born on the same day?" Captain Prío asked Rigoberto.

"December 6, 1900, a few minutes apart," Rigoberto said. "Chiron in the Laborío barrio, *The Alligator Woman* in the Zaragoza barrio."

"But does he know he's Saint Mardoqueo's son?" Norberto said.

"Bishop Simeón never told him the truth," Rigoberto said. "He only knows that he was born in an outhouse. He has all that written down in his memoirs."

"That's quite a story, indeed," the goldsmith Segismundo said. "Why in an outhouse?"

"Faced with the hostility of her other celibate Sisters, *The Bengal Tigress* locked herself in there until the moment she gave birth," Rigoberto said. "And she had to cut the umbilical cord herself with a paring knife."

"Why such hostility if they already knew she was a libertine?" the goldsmith Segismundo said.

"She wasn't any libertine," Rigoberto said. "Just like her other two sisters, she was a Daughter of Mary."

"As chaste as the Daughters of Mary of Father Olimpo Lozano, your violin teacher," Erwin said.

"I don't get it," Norberto said. "And when Bishop Simeón finds her naked in the closet? It seems like he's going to jump on her, too, to screw her."

"Nevertheless, Saint Mardoqueo was the only man she ever had," Rigoberto said. "And her celibate Sisters never suspected that her belly came from a priest."

"Can you imagine a more tragic fate? The most erudite of the centaurs born in shit," the goldsmith Segismundo said.

"That portrait of Colonel Pendleton that was mentioned burned right out front here at the end of the gala *soirée* the Social Club gave him," Captain Prío said. "The learned Debayle gave the speech in his honor."

"There goes the Captain again, swearing he saw all this from his tender cradle," Erwin said.

"Even though I was asleep in my cradle upstairs, my father was looking out from the balcony and saw the portrait light up," Captain Prío said.

"And this business about being born at the same hour and the sky aflame with fireworks is an opera," said Erwin.

"That's how destinies intertwine, to the sound of wailing and great commotion," Norberto said.

"The destiny of a mute lunatic and a procuress," Erwin said.

"Didn't Chiron take Rubén's brain to *The Alligator Woman* after he stole it?" Norberto said. "That's a new crossing of their destinies."

"Before that, destiny brought them together in the cemetery, you'll hear that part later," Rigoberto said.

"It remains to be seen if destiny will bring them together again in the future," said Norberto.

"Even now Chiron still takes the same route every afternoon to go and have dinner at her brothel, the same route he took that day with Rubén's brain," Captain Prío said. "Only at a more leisurely pace."

"I ran into him there not long ago," Rigoberto says.

"And what were you doing there, my dear poet, in a place like that?" asks Segismundo.

"Dropping off a love letter someone was sending to a girl there," says Rigoberto.

"One of the courtesans?" the goldsmith Segismundo says.

"No," Rigoberto says. "For the girl who looks after the rooms and tends bar downstairs."

"It doesn't fit how *The Alligator Woman* ended up at The Blessed Souls if she didn't want anything to do with men after she was raped," Norberto says.

"And where was she going to go?" Captain Prío says. "Besides, look at the model she had. *Terrestial Light* didn't want anything to do with men either, and she became the owner of a whorehouse."

"Such a tormented soul, and she ended up as one of Somoza's henchmen," the goldsmith Segismundo says.

"You're going to make me cry out of pity," Erwin says.

"Aside from the theft of Rubén's brain, there are many bridges to cross before we get to Somoza," Rigoberto says. "I hope I can finish reading you all of this before the 21st."

"My dear poet, are you going to marry Señorita Rosaura before the twenty-first, and leave us to go off on a honeymoon?" the goldsmith Segismundo asks. "There are just a few days left now if those are your intentions."

"No," Rigoberto says. "Why turn one person's troubles into the pain of two?"

"So?" Segismundo asks.

"I have a long trip ahead of me, and I don't know if I'll be coming back," says Rigoberto.

Pearls of Basra

In the San Felipe barrio, *The Chronicle* occupies an adobe house painted a lively, brothel blue. It has three doors facing the street, two of them with wood louvers. Not as tall as the other houses on the same block, squeezed between The Heraldic Funeral Parlor and The Mercantile School of Commerce, it looks as if it is sinking under the weight of its red-clay roof tiles.

The newspaper had passed through many hands since the days of its founder, the politician, Escolástico Cisne, father of Gaspar, Melchior, and Balthazar, the three kings of moneylending. It was next acquired by Dr. Absalón Barreto, during the period of the crimes of Oliverio Castañeda, the poisoner, when Rosalío Usulutlán worked there. Now, having fallen on hard times, it's the property of Rafael (Rafa) Parrales. He bought the old machinery and the filing cabinets with a loan he got from doña Casimira, his godmother, and never repaid.

After getting out of bed this Friday, the 21st of September, like any other day, even though today he's got less time to spare, Rafa Parrales is sitting in the doorway of the middle entrance, which doesn't have any louvers and is the only one that provides access to the editorial offices, the typesetting areas, and his own rooms at the far end of the house. Soon he'll have to go to Plaza Jerez in order to be there when Somoza and the First Lady make their entrance into the cathedral.

All he's wearing are striped pajama-pants and an iridescent silk kimono that hangs open, revealing his muscular chest, a product, as we already know, of his endless body-building exercises. A hairnet keeps his hair in place. His prominent nose is even whiter from the talcum powder, and his aging face shows the effects of the frequent massages

he gets during the home visits of the barber, one Ovidio
Parajón, with whom, behind closed doors, he enjoys singing
duets from Bellini's *La Sonnambula*, with Rafa Parrales in
the role of Elvino:

Sposi or noi siamo...

And while he works with the scissors on the head of his
partenaire (and as he had done, to his eternal honor, with
Rubén's lifeless head—) sending locks of hair showering to
the floor, Ovidio Parajon responds, in the role of Amina,
straining his voice until it achieves a soprano's texture:

Sposi! Oh! Tenera parola!

In the evenings, Rafa Parrales usually sits in the same
doorway in the same bedroom attire, not to kill time as he is
doing now, but rather because he's eager to do some fishing,
the fishing line in his hand, and for bait a thousand córdoba
bill with Somoza's profile set inside the oval. At the sight of
some unsuspecting passerby, he furtively abandons the bill
on the sidewalk and runs to hide behind the door he's left
ajar, turning off the light, and between his fingers the silk
reel which he continues reeling in until the fish, in pursuit
of the mysterious bill that is dragging itself along the
pavement, suddenly bumps into the fisherman, and falls into
his arms.

When he does this, most of the time he provokes insults
and threats of physical aggression, but on a sufficient
number of occasions his stratagem works, and he succeeds
in getting the passerby to accept, in exchange for the
thousand córdoba bill, an invitation to withdraw with him to
his living quarters in the rear of the house where a record
player urges upon the listener the delights of dancing in a
discreet half-light.

But the passerby who is approaching this morning is Rigoberto, and from a distance Rafa Parrales recognizes the bolero he is whistling: "Two Crosses." His heart beats anxiously beneath his firm pectoral muscles, and he stands up, opening his mouth with two rows of perfect teeth, dentures par excellence, in a big Kolynos toothpaste smile. Rigoberto is surely bringing news from Norberto, the most unexpected of his conquests after the unforgettable serenade two Saturdays ago from tomorrow, performed in front of that very same door by The Gypsy Boys of Spain.

That night, after their gala performance at the Teatro González, The Gypsy Boys of Spain had climbed into the Queen Mab waiting outside for them, a pickup that ran the Poneloya beach route and had seats facing each other like its sister, The Pegasus Traveler. At Rigoberto's invitation, Norberto hopped in the back with them and found himself pinned between musicians and instruments, and you already know how uncomfortable this kind of transportation is for the boys in the band. Rigoberto, sitting up front next to Juan Legido, then gave the driver instructions to the San Felipe neighborhood rather than the San Juan neighborhood where *Zela the Moor* lived, a request that Norberto never could have suspected, not from his position of confinement with his arms wrapped around the double bass entrusted to him out of necessity.

The Queen Mab pulled up in front of the Heraldic Funeral Parlor, which was next door to *The Chronicle*. In the hope of getting a request for its services, the funeral home didn't close until after midnight, and at that very moment a client happened to be inside, picking out a casket. She was the first to see the musicians, dressed in their bolero jackets, climb out of the truck with their instruments. Norberto was the last one to get out because they took their time to relieve him of the double bass in his embrace, and by then The Gypsy Boys of Spain were already harmonizing under a street lamp, around Juan Legido, who continued crossing himself to exorcise the sight of the burlap-covered caskets in the mortuary.

Norberto rushed to him to explain the mistake, but it was too late because the instruments sounded out as if they were blaring through Captain Prío's enormous loudspeakers. And it wasn't only the owner of the funeral home and his client who hurried outside; every door on the street, and beyond, was suddenly illuminated; their door handles clicked open, and the sidewalks filled up with people in nightgowns and pajamas.

In the midst of the musicians, Norberto tried to flee but found it impossible. Mario Rey gracefully stepped forward in front of the closed door, and his voice rose above the chorus of violins to sing "Two Crosses," the first song the suitor himself had chosen of three, before hopping on the truck. And when Mario Rey repeated the verse, *for two loves that died without understanding each other...*, the door opened without a sound, as if it had simply vanished into thin air. Rafa Parrales, drenched in Chanel No. 5, flashed the orchestra his denture-perfect, resplendent smile, emotion making him draw in his nostrils, his talcum-powdered face whiter than ever. And when he saw Norberto, he opened his mouth in a gasp of surprise and greeted him, with concealed delight, bowing his head.

The musicians were now tuning up in order to follow up with "True Affection," and by now there was a real commotion in the street.

"That's not the girl's father," Juan Legido told Norberto, carefully studying Rafa Parrales.

"It's her uncle, a real nut, and extremely dangerous, and he's armed," Norberto whispered to him.

"What?" Juan Legido said with alarm. "What happened to your friend? He guaranteed me there'd be no danger."

"Forget about my friend." Norberto took Juan Legido by the arm. "Let's get out of here, before that brute pulls his gun."

But the musicians were already playing and Juan Legido took his place in front to sing, though feeling uncertain, *who was to blame, I don't want to know, I don't know if it was me or destiny's desire...*

"All right, now, let's get out of here," Norberto begged him as soon as the other finished.

"Hey, he can't be too displeased; in fact, he's smiling," said Juan Legido.

"He's pretending to smile," Norberto said.

"Well, the truth is, he looks pretty happy to me," Juan Legido said. "The only thing that surprises me is that the girl hasn't come out."

"How is she going to come out with that nut standing at the door?" Norberto said.

Mario Rey finished singing "Lisboa Antigua," and Rafa Parrales applauded in a slow and deliberate way, and with another nod of his head, his gaze still resting upon Norberto, he then closed the door just as quietly as he had opened it. The musicians climbed back into the Queen Mab, and amidst the provocative laughter in the street, which mystified Juan Legido, the crowd of bystanders returned to their houses.

"The secret of this unfortunate incident is safe with me, brother." Over his shoulder, Norberto heard the voice of *The Lion of Nemea* just as the truck started up, with all the musicians safely inside. There he was, naked from the waist up, as always. Even from a distance you could tell he was drunk.

"What secret!" Norberto said. "Even my two spinster aunts, who live on that corner, came out to hear the serenade."

"In that case, there's nothing I can do!" *The Lion of Nemea* said. "If the word's already out, it's already out. You can always count on me. But it's your ass. I won't tell."

"What?" Norberto said. He didn't know whether to laugh or cry. And when all was said and done, he laughed.

"Death to Somoza!" *The Lion of Nemea* suddenly shouted.

"Are you nuts? Do you want to get us arrested?" Norberto said.

"Brother, there's no way for the plan to fail! It's all in black and white on paper, it's perfect. Me here, you there, the other guy over there. And pow pow pow. We'll be rid of that piece of shit!"

His boozy voice was probably being heard all over León. And telling him off or getting angry wouldn't do one bit of good—that much was obvious.

"Let's go have a drink, it's on me," *The Lion of Nemea* roared.

"I'm inviting both of you, if you like." It was the voice of Rafa Parrales. Once more the door had quietly swung open. And before Norberto could think, *The Lion of Nemea* leapt up on the doorstep.

"You two can pretend I'm invisible," he said. And as if they were going to have their picture taken together, *The Lion of Nemea* had grabbed Rafa Parrales around the waist, the latter looking at him with some amusement, wrinkling his nose.

Before going inside, Norberto cautiously looked up and down the street, but there was not a single door left open. They entered the pinkish half-light of the living quarters. Rafa Parrales maintained a delicate composure even though *The Lion of Nemea* ended up quickly falling asleep on the chaise longue where he had settled. Heaven's gifts couldn't be trifled with. And he talked more than anything else about baseball, a pleasant topic for Norberto, who, having forgotten about the business of the serenade, was more concerned about knowing whether this hermaphrodite might have heard some of the reckless words spoken by the wrestler who by now was snoring with his mouth open.

But nothing in his mood or words seemed to justify that suspicion; he was too busy cultivating a future rendezvous.

And with that Norberto said goodbye, leaving *The Lion of Nemea* wrestling in his dreams on the chaise longue, snorting loudly but still fast asleep. He awoke there in the morning, in plain sight of the printing press workers as he found his way to the street, the strangest of conquests for the owner of the house.

"Forget it," Rigoberto says. "The problem with Norberto is that he's very shy."

"And if he comes with you?" Rafa Parrales follows Rigoberto over to the old desk where the newspaper's only two typewriters are sitting.

"And what am I going to do at the party?" Rigoberto inserts a sheet of paper into the carriage of the typewriter. "Play the role of the sleeping *Lion of Nemea*?"

"We'll have a little drink, you listen to a record, then you retire, saying you're sleepy." Rafa Parrales takes a nail file from the pocket of the kimono and starts filing his nails.

"I need an advance on my salary." Rigoberto begins typing at a furious pace. His typing skill allows him to look at Rafa Parrales at the same time.

"Blackmail." Rafa Parrales blows on his fingernails.

"One good turn deserves another." Rigoberto fumbles for the little lever that changes the direction of the ribbon spool.

"How much?" Rafael Parrales bites off a cuticle from his thumb.

"My entire salary for October, I've got a lot of debts." Rigoberto resumes his typing and stares at him.

"You're taking advantage." Rafa Parrales puts on a martyr's face. "All right. Your entire salary for the month of October. But it's got to happen today."

"Today's the big bash for Somoza." Rigoberto stops typing and rests his arms on the typewriter. "Aren't you going? And besides, I'm in *Tovarich*."

"Of course I'm going." Rafa Parrales raises his eyebrows. "We'll meet after the party, I meant to say. And after your play. I'll wait for the two of you here, at midnight."

"Can I bring the cast from *Tovarich*?" Rigoberto types one last line and pulls the sheet of paper from the typewriter.

"Phew, that's a lot of people!" Rafa Parrales scrunches up his face. "And besides, that includes Norberto's girlfriend and her mother, too!"

"All right then, just him." Rigoberto inserts a new sheet of paper and starts hammering away. "And my loot?"

Rafa Parrales walks happily over to the metal box and returns with the bills in his hand, spread out like a fan.

"A deal's a deal." He waves the bills in Rigoberto's face.

"Norberto only likes Black & White, the one with the two little dogs on the bottle, like Somoza." Rigoberto takes the money, and without counting it, stuffs it into his imitation-lizard portfolio. "And don't be so cheap. You couldn't even offer The Gypsy Boys of Spain a toast."

"Don't blame me for what happened with The Gypsy Boys!" Rafa Parrales lays his hands against his chest. "Out of the blue. How was I supposed to think clearly at that time of night?"

"Final period to my front page article on Somoza's candidacy, nothing but praise." Rigoberto pulls the second sheet of paper from the typewriter, picks up the other one, and hands them to Rafa Parrales.

"This will be in Monday's edition." Rafa Parrales takes the two pages and fans himself. "Everything on today's front page carries my byline."

"That's fine, they can read my article afterwards." Rigoberto inserts another sheet in the typewriter. "And put Somoza's picture in there for me, one that's not so old. The last ones you published are from the time he was running counterfeit money with *The Alligator Woman*."

"A loose tongue like that will get you in trouble." Rafa Parrales looks more closely at the pages. He has his eyeglasses in his kimono, but he never puts them on in the presence of other men. "What do you get out of going around as the opposition?"

"Opposition?" Rigoberto looks offended. "You need to read what I wrote there."

Rafa Parrales places the pages under a paperweight, circles the desk, and comes up behind Rigoberto.

"Do you know Lt. Moralitos, head of that new security bureau?" he asks.

"Only by sight." Rigoberto has to twist his neck to see Rafa Parrales. "His mother is a neighbor of my girlfriend, and I've seen him at the door sometimes when he goes to visit her."

"And what's supposed to happen today, the 21st?" Rafa Parrales lays his hands gently on Rigoberto's shoulders. "All day long, Radio Darío has been saying: 'Wait for the 21st.' What's happening on the 21st?"

"That's my publicity for *Tovarich*, which opens tonight, the 21st." Rigoberto slowly taps the keyboard, underlining the title of the article that he's about to begin: "Triple Crown for Orestes."

"Moralitos says it's subversive propaganda." Rafa Parrales moves away from Rigoberto now, hands in the pockets of his kimono. "And he's investigating you. He's checking up on your movements in San Salvador with Cordelio Selva."

"Let him investigate me." Rigoberto tries to type, but cannot concentrate.

"Cordelio Selva bought a revolver in a gun shop in San Salvador two months ago. And they think he's entered the country on the sly, with the weapon." Rafa Parrales looks at his watch, and then puts it up to his ear. "Did this piece of shit stop running?"

"And how do you know all that? Did Colonel Maravilla tell you?" Rigoberto looks at his watch. "It's 9:20."

"What an inquisitive fellow. The only thing I can tell you is they have photos of this Cordelio Selva at all the military checkpoints into León." Rafa Parrales has approached the door that leads to the printing press and shouts inside, asking for the time. They tell him it's 9:20.

"You don't even believe me when I give you the time." Rigoberto pulls the sheet of paper from the typewriter, slowly turning the platen, crumples it up, and tosses it on the floor. "If they're like the photos of Somoza that you put in the paper the last time, I don't think they'll recognize him."

"Truthfully, you don't know Cordelio Selva?" Rafa Parrales loosens the sash of his kimono.

"That Moralitos is an asshole." Rigoberto takes a clean sheet of paper and crumples it up without even using it. "He was checking up on me at the Casa Prío. If he had something on me, he would have arrested me and taken me to Managua."

"If you wanted, you could be in Managua working at *Novedades*, and no one would suspect you of anything." Rafa Parrales begins removing his kimono. "But you never wanted that."

"I've been thinking about it." Rigoberto looks at the keyboard as if in search of some lost letter. "I like the idea of going to Managua with a good salary. And then I could get married."

"*The Man* is crazy about getting bright people. I'll talk to him today." Rafa Parrales looks over his shoulder as he moves away, his torso naked except for the kimono now draped over his shoulders like a cape.

Rigoberto gets ready to type the article he's titled "Triple Crown for Orestes," using the pseudonym of *Mister Hit* as his byline, but first he rummages around in his portfolio for the journal where he keeps the averages for Orestes *'Chimpanzee'* Hernández: *80 RBIs, .403 batting average, 23 home runs, the sensational Cuban slugger, batting clean-up for the León Samsons baseball team, well on his way to capturing the triple crown, his closest rival being Pedro Naranjo, another Cuban, with the Boer Indians club, who doesn't represent any threat to him for the moment after having fallen into a deep slump in the last few games.*

He looks around for the file-photo plate, the one with Orestes Hernández leaning on his bat, one knee on the grass, and dusts it off before laying it on top of the typed pages next to the typewriter. And inserting a new sheet of paper, he turns the platen cylinder with resolve, ready to begin copying the baseball averages from his journal. It's the same one that also contains his notes on Rubén Darío, as well as the letter to his mother, which he'll leave within sight on the upper shelf of the clothes closet where she keeps the money from her grocery store earnings in an English crackers tin so she'll be sure to find it the next day.

Then Rafa Parrales, now dressed, goes by, and before leaving he squeezes the rubber bulb hidden at his waist so that Rigoberto sees the Hawaiian woman hula on his tie. And he's barely out the door when the print shop workers begin horsing around in the shop, feigning punches with Kid Dynamite, the boxer who is doing time at the Veintiuno Prison after having knifed his wife in a jealous rage. Because he's a trustworthy convict, Colonel Maravilla loans him to Rafa Parrales on workdays to turn the heavy wheel of the printing press.

It's 10:00 a.m. already, and sirens can be heard in the distance. Somoza is arriving at Plaza Jerez. Rigoberto goes to hand in his article on Orestes Hernández to the chief typesetter, an old man with long hair, wearing a shirt that's missing all its buttons, and who's fit to be tied. He shows him the mess: with a left jab, Kid Dynamite had knocked his glasses off, which were tied to his ear with a shoe lace because one of the stems was missing, and, during all the melee, the other stem and one of the lenses got crushed under the feet of the printshop workers. Rigoberto opens his portfolio, pulls out a ten-córdoba bill, and hands it to him, and the workers send him off with a round of applause, Kid Dynamite himself enthusiastically joining in.

As for me, if you'll excuse me, I have to leave Rigoberto. We'll catch up with him later at the Hotel América. There are so many details to take care of today. Now I have to accompany Norberto to the branch of the National Bank—which he finds closed—where he had an appointment to arrange pending matters related to overdue debts from his previous season's cotton crop. The Palmira, his farm on the Poneloya road, the last of his assets, is at risk of foreclosure, but it's clear that nothing can be done today, not with the bank employees all in the plaza. He gets into his topless jeep and drives over to the Pearls of Basra jewelry shop to pick up the silver bullet.

In *Novedades*, in the section called Tales of Mystery Taken from Real Life, Erwin had read of a crime carried out by a jeweler from Alabama who used a perforated bullet injected with the tiniest dose of potassium cyanide, diluted in juniper oil, then soldered shut with tin.

On Saturday morning, September 8, when Norberto showed up in the jewelry store to carry out the assignment entrusted him by his associates, the following dialogue took place between him and the goldsmith Segismundo in the privacy of the jeweler's workroom at the back of the store:

Norberto (Cautious): Maestro, the great false prophet is coming to León.

Goldsmith (Looks at him, without removing the jeweler's loupe held in his right eye, underneath his bushy eyebrows): It's a disgrace, brother. A disgrace for us and for the harmony of the universe that the beast will set his hoof on these streets.

Norberto (Looking up at the ceiling): Let's not forget that the planet Mars is approaching Earth.

Goldsmith (Bringing the acetylene torch closer): And as our brother, the great Rubén, used to say: *a great flock of crows stains the celestial blue.* Brother, the antichrist has been born. And to our shame, in Nicaragua.

Norberto (Leaning his elbows on the railing that separates him from the goldsmith's workbench): But Mars is favorable to us, and the supreme will of the Great Architect of the Universe could manifest itself.

Goldsmith (Working the acetylene torch, a white flame flares up, and the room is filled with the strong smell of burnt kerosene): The will of the Great Architect does not work alone. A hand that will execute his will must take the lead. And that hand does not exist, brother. This is a country of eunuchs. Men grow fat more easily when they have no balls.

Norberto (Leaning his body over the railing and lowering his voice): That hand exists.

Goldsmith (The acetylene torch, lit, dances in his hand, and he seems to forget that he can get burned): Hands to steal, to falsify. Concealed hands that only know how to give the finger. I know of no other kind of hand.

Norberto (Steps back before the bright flame of the torch): And what if I tell you that those balls exist, too?

Goldsmith (Shuts the flame down): Those words sing a different tune. Lucky the man who has them. As far as I know, the only one who could have witnessed the spectacle of some monstrous testicles was the learned Debayle.

Norberto (He laughs, intrigued in spite of himself): What do you mean, Maestro?

Goldsmith (He removes the loupe and his eye appears red): When Sandino, our brother, anointed in the Yucatán Lodge, passed through León in 1926 on his way to the San Albino mines, he was suffering from swamp fever, contracted in the Huasteca camps in Tampico. He went to see the learned Debayle at the Maison de Santé. Debayle asked him to undress completely, and he was absolutely stupefied when he saw the size of his patient's balls, enormous and rose-colored like a phoenix's eggs.

Norberto (Reflecting): That explains why, when they killed him, they had to bury him in two clandestine holes. One for his body, the other for his balls.

Goldsmith: No. That was the case of the bar owner Basilisk and his hernia. (He places the loupe back in his eye.) When he saw that marvel, the learned Debayle asked Sandino for authorization to publish a monograph giving anatomical details of the wonder. He wanted to measure them, weigh them. But the hero refused. Chiron witnessed it.

Norberto (Resolutely): Would you be willing to help raise the phoenix's balls from the ashes?

Goldsmith: It's the phoenix that rises from the ashes, not the balls.

Norberto: What's the difference? Are you willing?

Goldsmith (He stands up, places his hands on his hips, aching from sitting for so long on his bench): Slow down, and watch your step. In these matters, a misstep brings unpleasant consequences.

Norberto: The hand has the weapon in its grasp. The bullets are ready. But one of them must be made of silver to fulfill the Salomonic Cabala of the hierarchy of noble metals. And so that nothing will fail, the bullet must be equipped with a mortal venom.

Goldsmith (He picks up his tweezers and deposits them in a container of alcohol, his jeweler's lens still in his eye): Be very careful, lest they fuck you good for listening to such wild ideas.

Norberto: I'm telling you this under oath, maestro, looking to the west, like the Hyperboreans of old. (He turns to face west and bows his head three times.)

Goldsmith (He takes a step towards Norberto, grabs him by the arm): Swear by the compass and the Great

Architect's square that you're not playing with me. And give me the sign of the double embrace of the Knights of the Temple.

Norberto: I swear by the compass and the square. (He raises his hand in oath.) I give you the double embrace of the Knights of the Temple. (He embraces him twice.)

Goldsmith (He deposits his lens on the table, like a throw of the dice): Now, tell me your revelation.

Norberto: On September 21, exactly, when Mars completes its final revolution around the earth, the impure blood of the beast will be spilled before midnight. After that, Mars will begin to move away and our protection with it. And the poisoned silver bullet must be of your making, maestro.

Goldsmith: And the cartridge?

Norberto (He searches in his pants' pocket): Here it is. It's a question of extracting the lead bullet, molding one of silver, perforating it, and filling it with potassium cyanide.

Goldsmith (He takes the bullet, brings it to eye level): That's a simple job. The rest isn't so simple. Getting it into the beast.

Norberto: Trust me, everything is ready.

Goldsmith (He takes the bullet over to the table, sits down on his bench, and examines it through the loupe held in his eye): The beast is a Mason, 33rd Degree, consecrated by the Lodge of Managua.

Norberto: The Cabala of Rhadames says that the Degrees of the tyrants are spurious.

Goldsmith (He sets the bullet in the vise, tightens the handle to hold it in place, takes a pair of pincers): Can I ask you one final question, brother?

Norberto: Proceed, maestro.

Goldsmith (He manipulates the pincers to extract the lead bullet from the casing): That hand of vengeance, is it yours?

Norberto: No. But it is the hand of a just man.

Goldsmith (He takes the pincers over to a small plate and drops the lead bullet onto it): Is that just man a member of the brotherhood?

Norberto (Categorically): No.

Goldsmith (He removes the shell casing from the vice, blows on it): Then, that makes things easier. Even though the Degree of the beast is spurious, remember what the Scottish rite dictates: a brother cannot look upon the face of another when he murders him. Melisandro Maravilla, at the last moment, had to turn his face away from Sandino.

Norberto: Neither you nor I will be there to look the beast in the eye.

Goldsmith (Straightening up again): All right, but you've got to swear that this business remains a secret between the two of us. I don't want any buzzards feasting on me in some empty lot because of someone's treason.

Norberto: I swear. (Raises his hand.)

This time, Norberto finds the goldsmith Segismundo showing a client a collection of costume earrings mounted in a box lined with red felt. When the client leaves without buying anything, the goldsmith Segismundo goes back into his workshop and returns with a ring box. He opens it in front of Norberto, and the silver bullet appears between the folds of silk. The operation, apart from being laborious, required the following steps:

a) Getting a hard wax mold by utilizing the discarded lead bullet as a casing.

b) Pouring an alloy of silver into the mold, 75% silver, 25% lead.

c) Polishing the piece once it has cooled, first with a burin, then with a No. 5 steel file.

d) Setting the piece in the vise. Perforating it with a fine bit, previously adjusted to the drill.

e) With a subcutaneous hypodermic needle using a solution measured to fit the glass plunger, injecting potassium cyanide diluted in a solution of juniper oil into the perforation.

f) Sealing the hole with tin, continuously polishing the outer facing of the seal, again with the No. 5 steel file and finally with a No. 8 fine sandpaper.

Both are engrossed in silent contemplation of the jewel in its box when Rosaura comes in, holding one of her little brothers by the hand. Smiling happily, she shuffles towards them in her rubber-soled sandals, a handkerchief tied around her head and pink plastic curlers in her hair. The goldsmith Segismundo raises his voice in a strained falsetto:

"This kind of ring isn't made everyday, my friend."

"And a person doesn't get married everyday." Norberto, turning in Rosaura's direction, smiles at her, the ring box already tucked inside his shirt pocket.

"I see that you're getting ready for a party," Segismundo tells Rosaura, his robust hands resting on top of the display case gleaming in the sun.

"I'm going to the nomination banquet with Rigoberto," Rosaura says, radiant, leaving the goldsmith Segismundo speechless.

"Rigoberto, a patriot, in that den of bootlickers," he finally says, indignantly.

"That can't be, Rigoberto taking you to the celebration," says a surprised Norberto.

"What do you mean it can't be?" Rosaura asks. "I already got two invitations."

"You need invitations?" Norberto says.

"Of course, they're required," Rosaura says. "Not just anybody can get in. You have to show them at the door. They're numbered."

"Why so much security for a party of sheep?" Segismundo says between clenched teeth.

"But Rigoberto has a part in the premiere of *Tovarich*," Norberto says.

"It's nothing. Anybody can make an entrance and say: Good evening," Rosaura says.

"Good evening, *little master*," a somber Norberto corrects her.

"And how can I help you?" the goldsmith Segismundo asks Rosaura, unnerved by this latest bit of news.

"I want to see some wedding rings," she says, and blushes.

Segismundo, with a dry, professional air, takes several ring boxes out of the display case one by one and sets them on top of it.

"When's this wedding?" Norberto asks, puzzled.

"As soon as he gets a job at *Novedades*, we'll get married and move to Managua," Rosaura says, and she picks up one of the ring boxes.

"At *Novedades*? How could he commit such treachery?" the goldsmith Segismundo says, and the ring boxes he is still holding fall on top of the showcase.

"I really have to be on my way," Norberto says in a rush, and he's gone.

"And I'll look for my ring someplace where they're nicer to their customers," says Rosaura, and she returns the unopened boxes to the goldsmith Segismundo.

The misunderstandings in this dialogue call for some explanation: unbeknownst to me, that morning, Rigoberto had stopped by Rosaura's house in the San Juan neighborhood, which is why I haven't been able to give you an account of it until now. As I've already said, this wasn't an easy day.

She had sent her little brother out to search for him all over León, and he found him on the way to the Hotel América. As if she'd won a raffle, when she saw him from the doorway coming down the street holding her little brother's hand, she showed him the invitations that had been a gift from her neighbor, Lt. Moralitos's mother, who doesn't go to parties, and she kept on insisting until Rigoberto finally agreed. Really, you mean it? It was going to be such a grand party, and it's all free. Would he come by for her at 9:30? Yes, she should be ready at the door; he would pick her up.

And then, not knowing at what moment or why, with so much on his mind, he had started to tell her about his chat with Rafa Parrales concerning the job at *Novedades* while she stood on the top step at the door and he was seated on the step below. The next thing he knew, he heard her enthusiasm take flight, and he didn't dare cut short her wedding plans as she dealt them out like cards from a deck, and that's how she arrived at the cost of wedding rings and the money she'd saved from sewing baseball caps at home. He even walked a block with her on her way to the jeweler's, and holding his portfolio up to shield his eyes from the sun, he watched her hurry off, hand in hand with her little brother.

This means that Lucio Ranucci will be missing an actor from the cast of *Tovarich*, but Rigoberto isn't about to tell him this because, as of now, he sees that he's a bundle of nerves, pacing the corridor of the Hotel América with the face of a tragic character in need of sleep. But it really is such a small part that the director could easily play it himself when he realizes that Rigoberto hasn't shown up in the dressing room to put on Anatole's striped vest, the butler at the mansion of Princess Ninoshka Andreyevna (*The Rose Child*) who is exiled in Paris. You already know that all he has to say at the end of the first act is: "Good evening, sir," after opening the door for the exiled prince, Fedor Sergeievich (*Jorge Negrete*), the princess's disconsolate suitor; and after hanging the visitor's overcoat in the closet, to disappear forever from the stage.

That prince, Fedor Sergeievich, buffeted by age and ailments, and forced to earn his living in Paris working for a pharmacist on Rue Vaugirard, is going to take his customary seat in the Voltaire armchair next to the samovar, where no one will pay attention to what he says, again and again made a fool of by the fickleness of Princess Ninoshka Andreyevna, who is secretly in love with her young cousin, the captain of the hussars, Vasili Ivanovich (Tirso the Albino), despite the fact that she's already in the autumn of her years. But the one Vasili really wants is the younger princess, Natasha Petrovna (*Zela the Moor*), and if he doesn't win her hand, he would much prefer to turn himself into a *satori* and live out his days as a hermit.

Nervous and out of breath, Lucio Ranucci, the sleeves of his customary white silk shirt now nearly transparent and rolled up to his elbows, rushes up to Rigoberto, brushing the blond locks from his forehead with his familiar gesture. Curtain time is fast approaching, and the strict military vigilance in effect throughout the city has made everything more difficult; the electricians and carpenters have had their tools confiscated, the lead actress and her daughter, who are also in charge of wardrobe, are nowhere to be found. *Jorge Negrete* arrived a moment ago to inform him that the loudspeaker truck cannot take to the street without a special permit, and Ranucci reprimands him for showing up in his stage costume with his top hat under his arm, Negrete arguing that such publicity was more eye-catching, as if it were a circus performance. The Italian's blue eyes, already watery, are filled with copious tears.

Rigoberto takes two Valium from his portfolio and hands them to Lucio Ranucci, who contemplates them for a moment in the palm of his hand before swallowing them without any water.

"When the cast comes out to take its bow, don't forget to mention that the publicity campaign was mine," Rigoberto says.

Of course. He'll have him step forward, and then he'll ask for an ovation just for him, even though his part in the play was so small. To merely open the door and say, "Good evening, sir."

The Sorrow And Dread of this Terrible World

The lunch hour has passed, and in the sleepy heat the National Military Band, led by Captain Ramiro Vega Miranda, takes its place on the steps of the Teatro González and launches into the waltz, "The Loves of Abraham," with a drowsy beat. With the addition of a few more musicians, and a change of some instruments, the band will transform itself into a tropical orchestra to play that evening at the party to be held at the Workers' Social Club.

The conventioneers, dazed from rum and beer, have come trickling out of the Casa Prío, taking their time returning to the Great Convention, which will delay reconvening until the arrival of the president and presidential candidate. Captain Prío picks up his lunch, one plate covered by another plate, sweating between his hands, and returns to his lookout post. As he mounts the stairs, they creak with the same hollow echo that Eulalia made when she came downstairs from Rubén's room, impregnated with the seed of glory.

That seed of glory, who now waits at her Aunt Casimira's home for her turn to be greeted by Somoza, had seen her father on his deathbed, and afterwards upon the catafalque lying in state in the Auditorium of the University of León, a distant effigy—brain already removed—among acetylene gas lamps and floral arrangements. Unaware that this was her father, her little blond ringlet-covered head peeped from among the satin petals of a rose fashioned from the ribs of a parasol, to discover the wax-colored form draped in a Greek tunic crowned with myrtle, while her mother recited "The Rose Child": *crystal, gold and roseate, dawn in Palestine, the three kings come to adore the king...*

The Rose Child will be briefly greeted by Somoza, who has finally arrived at his mother-in-law's house, and despite that lady's insistence, as she barks a stream of orders from her wheelchair for them to serve her son-in-law lunch in the dining room, closed off by stained-glass windows and never, or hardly ever, used, he has declined to join them because there's no time. He walks over and embraces her—a thousand thanks, but I don't have time. Before heading back to the Teatro González, he'll have a turkey sandwich with tomato and lettuce in his rooms at the Municipal Palace, and one with tuna and a glass of malted milk, all brought from Managua in thermoses by his aide-de-camp, Colonel Lira. And now he is greeting all those present, each one by name, for he's a champion in the art of remembering names, nicknames, and faces, a master in the art of allowing those who so wish to show their intimacy with him, like Dr. Balthazar Cisne, who bends over to catch his ear, and he assents, calls to one of his aides: jot this down for me, it's important. Everything is important.

And now he's in front of *The Rose Child*, kisses her on her forehead, and she catches a scent of his Eau de Vétiver cologne, although faint, the same as Norberto's, when he comes every night and pulls out his handkerchief: so now you're an actress? I knew it, he accuses her with his finger. Is it true that the work is called...? *Tovarich*, she helps him, and Somoza turns toward Van Wynckle, then to Moralitos. First they told me that it was a Communist work—so many Russian names. And Moralitos, expressionless: yes, sir, he assents, and the whole time Van Wynckle's playing with his pen, not taking any notes, paying no attention to the topic. But we looked into it, and instead it's about Russians fleeing Communism, Somoza laughs, and he kisses her again, now on the cheek, and gives her a hug; what's more, they've given me publicity for my candidacy. And he raises his voice so they all can hear him, still hugging *The Rose Child*: What will happen on the 21st? The announcement of my candidacy, of course! Somoza forever! Long live Somoza! And they all respond to the Viva, applauding and laughing. Then he makes

187

a motion to leave, but Rafa Parrales follows him, and also whispers in his ear and Somoza stops for a few seconds, seconds that seem like an eternity for anyone not privy to their conversation.

And if you want to hear what he says to him, come closer; and you too, Captain, listen, up there in your lookout, and you weaving sisters, awake now, for it's time to take heed and make ready the threads of your labor: General, I've got an excellent candidate for you to take to Managua to work at *Novedades*, a serious boy, intelligent, alert. You won't regret it. And Somoza calls his secretary over, jot down that name for me so I don't forget it. Then he leaves, goes out into the street amidst the swirl of bodyguards, and Rafa Parrales remains with the secretary, I'll write it down myself, he says, solicitous, and in his own hand he writes in the notebook the secretary holds up for him, rushing because he can see he's being left behind by the presidential retinue: *Rigoberto López Pérez, as a journalist for the newspaper* Novedades. *He may be reached through Rafael Parrales, director of The Chronicle, tel. 234, León.* (Exhibit Number 6). Oh, sad seamstresses! What twisted threads you are readying to stitch your cloth!

But now, I must not let Captain Prío eat lunch all alone on his balcony, the plate in his hand, chewing while he looks out over the plaza, his eyes alert while he swallows his food, watching Somoza and his entourage return to their temporary quarters and disappear around the corner of Calle La Rambla. *The Alligator Woman* is lying on a bench, her felt hat covering her face, apparently indifferent to the music the band is playing, her head resting on the legs of *Stone Face* Diómedes Baldelomar, who is lazily smoking a cigarette.

There's something else, Captain. Chiron has just taken his customary perch high up in the bell tower of the cathedral, beneath the Atlas supports, and he leans outward to peer down on the plaza, a book in one hand. Had he spotted *The Alligator Woman* earlier, moving about the plaza? I wonder if he knows that the distant bundle draped in red, stretched out on the bench, is she (or he)? You've already heard that he eats supper everyday at her brothel.

As children, without knowing each other, their paths might have crossed at some cockfight or dice game, where he was called upon to recite and she was begging. But when they did meet properly, she was on top of the pedestal of a fallen angel and he used a stack of books to help her get down. They had both turned twelve that day.

Who better to help me with that story than Dr. Balthazar Cisne. He's returning home on foot, hurried along by *The Rose Child* who doesn't want to miss the rebroadcast of *The Right To Be Born*, while Lucio Ranucci is drowning in his anguish. Dr. Balthazar Cisne is still disturbed by the fact that Rafa Parrales, that degenerate, had more time at Somoza's ear than he, even though both of their requests were duly noted; his: four fluorescent lamps to illuminate Rubén's statue, which is going to be erected in the little park in front of the Church of San Francisco; the other request, written in that fool's own hand, was as far as he could make out intended to benefit Rigoberto. (I'm not going to be the one to tell him what lines Rafa Parrales jotted down in the secretary's notebook, written in ink the color of blood, redder than the fiery glow of Mars as it approaches Earth; the seamstresses have guided his hand, forcing it, the way grade-school teachers do with children who resist penmanship.)

Allow Dr. Balthazar Cisne to continue on his way without distractions because I will need him later. And let the blades of the fans, as black as ravens' wings, in their incessant fluttering, help him turn back the pages of the calendar. They won't lie idle for a single moment in what remains of this day, nor will the seamstresses in their weaving. Come, there's still much to see. To begin with, it's the evening of December 6, 1912.

Chiron has sat down beneath the canopy of his favorite mausoleum. He has placed his bundle of books on the step next to him and lit the wick of the Coleman lamp that he always brings along. Around him the wings of the marble angels seem to flutter with a muted noise.

Bored with his role as a child prodigy, he had begun to withdraw to the solitude of the Cemetery of Guadalupe to read without any distractions. At first, he had been called upon to recite in the solemn sessions of the Athenaeum of León, afterwards at wedding banquets and First Communion breakfasts; in time he was relegated to a customary role in the city's Sunday concerts in the parks, and he no longer dared walk past cockfight pits, gambling dens, and saloons, because they would grab him off the street and make him recite "The Head of Rawí" amidst the soft wailings of drunkards and gamblers.

He had started to write himself, but the members of the Athenaeum never wanted to hear his own poetry. And now, thankfully, they had forgotten him and rarely troubled him. The first among them was the learned Debayle, who had never paid him much attention anyway other than to look on him as a curiosity of nature. He still swept the rooms at the Maison de Santé and disinfected the scalpels and forceps after the operations, storing them in the glass cabinets, and when night fell he would withdraw to the cemetery with his stack of books and his lamp.

That night, while reading Ibsen's *John Gabriel Borkman* again, in a little blue-bound volume that Rubén had left him, he heard the sound of boots on the path, hedges being trampled, voices speaking coarse English, and childish drunken laughter that interrupted his reading.

A bottle landed on the mausoleum canopy and smashed, and as a precaution, he lowered the wick of the lamp until it was nearly extinguished. Then, in the moonlight, he saw them. They came tripping over the graves with young girls in white tunics drunk and kicking in their arms or astride their shoulders. They pulled the ones who were afraid along by their arms, and when some managed to break free, they were pursued amidst festive shouts, while the others forced open the wrought-iron doors, shoving the naked girls inside the crypts and feigning voices from beyond the grave.

Right next to Chiron, one man had drunkenly succeeded in tearing off one of the young girls' tunics, ripping it from her shoulder after a bitter struggle that had cost him a bite on his face: the ferocious bite of some sharpened little teeth. The blood ran down his milk-white chest, but he didn't seem to realize it. Another soldier had climbed onto a pedestal and tried to push over the statue of an angel with folded wings, and amidst much jubilant shouting it finally landed face down on the ground, breaking apart at the neck. The soldier who had undressed the young girl finally noticed the blood, and to get back at her, laughing the whole time, he handed her over to the others, who then lifted her onto the empty pedestal. Terrified, the young girl tried to get her balance, holding her arms out wide, without daring to jump from that height as they demanded.

When they left, followed by the other young girls running after them, leaving her on top of the pedestal, her crying had grown so muffled that Chiron, standing at the foot of the column, couldn't hear it. He climbed up on his stack of books to reach her, persuaded her to sit on the edge of the pedestal, then had her slide down into his arms. When she grabbed him around his neck, with the two of them about to fall, he felt the cold shiver of her naked little body against his chest; and before he set her down, he asked her to hold still, because she was laughing now, and he was laughing too, and very close to his face that strange alcohol breath.

Chiron went to pick up her tunic, and torn as it was, she hurriedly slipped it on over her head. The two of them left the cemetery together, and he walked back with her all the way to The Blessed Souls, the halo of the lamp spreading before the footsteps of two people who had come into the world together, you remember, one a centaur and the other a soul from purgatory, one born amidst an explosion of fireworks and the other in the clandestine darkness of an outhouse.

On that evening of her birthday, *The Alligator Woman* had no sooner received the white tunic of a blessed soul from the hands of *Terrestial Light,* than the Marines from Camp Pendleton, returning from the *soirée* to honor the commander at the Social Club, reached the brothel, already closed, and worked up all the dogs in the neighborhood with the honking of their car horns.

Without knowing what time it was, squeezed in between knees and military boots and belts in the back seat of the first car she had ever gotten into in her life, and with a hulk of a Negro at the wheel, darting around the potholes in the streets like some enormous insect, she clung to the neck of one of the Marines who was pouring bourbon into her from his canteen and whose sweat smelled like goat's milk.

But wait. An hour before that *Our Lady of the Fields* had been crushed under the wheels of a cart carrying a load of molasses when the team of oxen, frightened by a coral snake, had backed up. Tearful and frightened in the face of death, she then appeared in a vision to Saint Mardoqueo, who was still on his knees praying for the little girl who had been despoiled. And shimmering in the bloody atmosphere around her, with her staved-in head a mess of blood and molasses, *Our Lady of the Fields* warned him that her family would shoot it out over the Santos Lugares estates in a Holy War that was about to begin.

Despite that first night of wild shooting, while some escaped from houses under siege and others knocked on the doors of the armories demanding munitions, the gala *soirée* to honor Colonel Pendleton was held in the rooms of the Social Club, even though decimated by wakes. Many of those present packed pistols under the coattails of their tuxedos, on their guard, and *The Great Dragon*'s masterpiece, a portrait of Colonel Pendleton, burned majestically at midnight in Plaza Jerez after a speech by the learned Debayle, the sound of the firecrackers strung along the wooden framework mingling with the sound of gunfire in the distance.

Worried over the outbreak of the Holy War, Bishop Simeón was returning to his Episcopal Palace after saying early morning mass when he ran into Chiron, who was waiting for him at the door to hand him a document. He read it at the breakfast table. It was a detailed report of the facts concerning the events at the cemetery, every line quivering with a telegraphic sense of outrage. From the outset, he had recognized the same elegant and concise style that Rubén used in writing for Buenos Aires's *La Nación*.

At noon he went to the cemetery, where he held a ceremony to sanctify the grounds anew. The caskets of the first victims of the Holy War were lined up along the paths next to armed kinsmen waiting for the gravediggers, who couldn't keep up. But despite the mourning, the city was already boiling with protests against the desecration that had taken place, and Colonel Pendleton was quick to order the reading of a military edict on every street corner, denying that those under his command were in any way responsible.

"I'm going to write an editorial denouncing those vandals, even though they may well burn my newspaper down," Dr. Escolástico Cisne told Bishop Simeón, angrily fanning his face with his hat as they left the cemetery.

"We need proof...up until now, the conduct of the American soldiers has been beyond reproach." Incredulous, the learned Debayle sought to distance himself from such reckless talk.

"I have the proof. An eyewitness account." Bishop Simeón stroked the cross on his chest.

The learned Debayle looked at him in alarm.

"Even with proof, it would be an isolated incident," he finally responded. "Without the American forces, this country would fall into anarchy. Chaos, Monsignor."

"Chaos is what those sons-of-hell are sowing," Dr. Escolástico Cisne said, again furiously fanning himself. "Red-faced gorillas, that's what Rubén himself called them! Monsignor, will you let me have that document? I'm going to print it."

Without saying a thing, Bishop Simeón, to the visible dismay of the learned Debayle, took the report, which he had under his cloak, and handed it to him. And that afternoon, *The Chronicle* printed it in its entirety on the first page, bordered in black, in six-point type, the only ones they had enough of in the type cases.

Very early the next morning the Marines ransacked the Maison de Santé, smashing down doors and breaking the glass cabinets and furniture amidst the clamor in the wards of the sick, whom they knocked out of bed with rifle butts. And when they entered the ward in the back courtyard, the shots they fired into the air sent the mental patients running outside, helter-skelter, into the streets.

They went looking for Chiron, who wasn't there but at the Episcopal Palace where Bishop Simeón had taken him to sleep as a precaution. But they got wind of this, and did not hesitate to barge into the Episcopal quarters. Chiron escaped from them by jumping out the window of the council room, and they pursued him until they caught up with him in the atrium of the cathedral. There they gave him the first blows with their rifle butts. He broke free and went running out the main door, but they finally managed to subdue him in the baptistry, hitting him at will, on the head and in the ribs, leaving him prostrate in a pool of blood.

In the meantime, another patrol had entered the offices of *The Chronicle*, tossed the boxes of movable typeface that scattered all over the sidewalk, taking a hammer to the plate-beds and the pedals of the presses and smashing them to bits, and then they led Dr. Escolástico Cisne away, in handcuffs, to the Marine barracks in front of Plaza Jerez.

Bishop Simeón, aided by his servants, carried Chiron to the Maison de Santé. The learned Debayle, upon receiving word of the assault, hurried over from his house in his *robe de chambre* to suture the boy's wounds and bandage his head. Three days later, Chiron woke to find himself in the little hole-in-the wall where he lived, next to the ward for the consumptives and the lunatics. He came to, but he'd lost the ability to speak. And he returned to his normal duties alongside Debayle, who personally directed the repairs to the doors, the room dividers, the glass cabinets, and took the opportunity to hang on the wall, next to the portrait of Stendhal, the photograph that had been taken of him next to Rubén, the two of them sitting in the garden.

But now we have to leave the Maison de Santé and make our way over to the railroad station. Listen to the sad whistle of the train that's pulling into León at midnight on January 7, 1916, three years later. It's Rubén who's returning. The yellow squares of the train windows pass in front of the closed doors all along the tracks.

How completely different is this return from the 1907 apotheosis that *The Great Dragon* had heard them tell about during his time at the Santos Lugares prison. You've seen the photographs taken by Maestro Cisneros. However, this time only a small group approached the step of the coach as the locomotive came to a stop at the platform illuminated every few steps by the Standard lanterns the Marines from Camp Pendleton were holding in their hands, patrolling back and forth with their rifles slung over their shoulders. Bishop Simeón, Debayle, two orderlies with a stretcher. Chiron. And in the shadows, standing back from the platform, near the station gate, Eulalia, the first wrinkles at the corners of her lips, and a little girl with golden ringlets clutching her hand.

Wrapped in a tartan rug, Rubén appeared at the door of the train, his eyelids heavy and drooping, his beard gray. He staggered before stepping down, helped by Rosario Murillo, and his swollen belly was exposed when his blanket fell open. Behind him, his brother-in-law Andrés Murillo got off the train.

The greetings were brief, reserved; and Rubén remained silent. But when he saw Chiron, who was helping the orderlies to prepare his stretcher, his eyes lit up.

"Chiron the Centaur, my son," he called out to him with open arms. "I heard about your misfortune."

Chiron let Rubén embrace him and, using spirited hand gestures, tried to tell him something. Struggling to understand, Rubén forced a laugh. He rejected the stretcher, rejected Debayle's arm and his wife's solicitous attention, and trusted Chiron to help him walk, his head bent down under the brim of his fedora. When he reached the entrance, he stopped as if he heard someone calling to him; he turned around and saw Eulalia in the dark shadows, the little girl still holding her hand. Fearful of an unpleasant incident, Debayle urged him to go on, and Rubén continued on his way to the carriage that was waiting for him at the foot of the steps in the small square.

"The Maison de Santé," Debayle instructed the driver.

"There's no need to abhor the forgotten empress, the deposed queen," Rubén told Chiron, who could feel the poet's head, resting in his lap, burning up with fever.

"You're going to get well," Debayle told him, his hands resting on the handle of his walking stick to steady himself against the lurching of the coach.

"Thank you, Louis," Rubén said, and he placed his burning hand on top of Debayle's.

I regret the discomfort of this trip, but there's no time to lose; it's now February 2, 1916, and we must be at Rubén's side in his sickbed in the corridors of the Maison de Santé while still mindful of what's going on outside. You may enter once more.

In the empty room, with whitewashed walls smelling of carbolic acid, Rubén rested on a cot made of black iron under a lilac mosquito net that seemed to envelop him in a light mist. Small white specks floated in the halo of light streaming in through the skylight high on the wall. Debayle was rocking in a wicker chair next to the cot, softly stroking his goatee and explaining to him the nature of the operation that he would have to perform in order to extract the pus from his liver, using the Maydl-Reclús trocar. His back to him, Rubén said nothing.

While this scene was taking place, which for the moment showed no signs of outward conflict, outside there was a storm brewing. Eulalia had shown up early at the Maison de Santé in defiance of the efforts of Debayle, who could not keep her away any longer. She went immediately to look for Rosario Murillo. She caught her in a state of *déshabillé* on her way to the bathroom, a bottle of mouthwash in her hand. They were soon talking in the garden beneath a grapevine, where each had dragged her own chair.

Rosario Murillo, without raising her voice, as if in a friendly chat between two old friends, had already called Eulalia a whore, just as she had done years ago. And while Andrés Murillo watched them from the corridor, their conversation went like this:

Rosario: I know all about you two. My wife's heart tells me everything...(with her hand on her heart).
Eulalia: Your wife's heart! That brother of yours planned this whole charade...(casting a calculating glance at Andrés Murillo). At the point of a pistol, he made him promise to marry you. And you were no virgin.
Rosario: You're lying, you're lying...(straining to control herself).
Eulalia (Smiling, with feigned sadness): An infamous plot to ruin the life of a naive boy and save yourself from dishonor.

Rosario (Raising her chin): Enough! The infamy is yours. Faced with the impotence of your husband, you seduced Rubén just so you could have a child...you wanted to have the child of someone famous...what am I saying!... A daughter!

Eulalia: You were a decrepit old man's lover, but he was able to give you money, and your brother, too. (Lifting her gaze to the sky, trying to appear indifferent.) Don't bother to deny it! Rubén told the whole story at a banquet! You yourself fed your lover his medicine!

Rosario: I don't know why I stay here listening to you. You've got the reputation of a lunatic...a neurosthenic... (standing up, as if the meeting were over). You offend the memory of a dead man. And regarding Rubén's account of things, remember his weakness...his artificial paradise, as he calls it...

Eulalia (Without releasing her prey): He was perfectly sober when he made that public confession. The way you took him in! His dark heron, he called you in his verses! The poor man!

Rosario: You harpy! A thousand times over, a harpy! I'm his wife, and you're his lover. (Challenging her, hands on her waist).

Eulalia: Yes, his wife. The wife he never could stand, the wife he always wanted to divorce. You went to France, sent by your brother. Rubén slept with you one night, befuddled with drink, and that was enough to stop the divorce proceedings...

Rosario: Well, this you can count on, that daughter of yours won't get a cent. Everything that Rubén leaves belongs to me as his legitimate wife... (Emphatically pointing to her chest with her index finger) And the glory, too!

Eulalia (Also standing up): Take all you want! But Rubén never loved you!

Rosario: Nor you, either!

Eulalia: How wrong you are! (She runs her hands over her body and finally let's them rest on her belly.)

Rosario: Whore! A thousand times over, a whore! (She steps forward and raises her hand, ready to slap her.)

Eulalia (She steps back, amused): Calm yourself, señora. If you lay a hand on me, be prepared to get the worst of it. I have a gun in my purse. It would be the final straw if you still had that little flask of vitriol in your gown from so long ago. Good day.

Eulalia went to sit down on a sofa in the corridor, leaving Rosario with her hand still in the air, and when her brother came over to her, she began sobbing and leaned against his shoulder while looking furiously at the other woman who was placidly smoothing her skirt, preparing herself for a long wait.

Rubén, in the meantime, had called Chiron in to ask him if he still had the copy of Ibsen's *John Gabriel Borkman*, and when he brought the slim volume, Rubén, with difficulty, settled himself among the pillows on the bed, had him bring him his gold-rimmed glasses and pull back the mosquito net, and sitting Chiron down on the bed next to him, read to him in a low voice that Debayle could barely hear from the rocking chair: *You've sacrificed my life for love! Do you understand? The Holy Scriptures speak of a mysterious sin for which there is no redemption. I didn't understand what sin that was, but now I do. The crime that no repentance can erase, the sin that grace does not reach, is the sin of sacrificing a life for love!*

"The two of them are arguing outside, aren't they?" he asked, handing the book back to him. Chiron nodded.

"You ought to read this terrible passage to Rosario so she'll shut up," he told him. "Too bad you can't do me that favor."

Taking advantage of the distraction, Debayle pulled out his monogrammed handkerchief, a prearranged signal to his assistants already standing by in the doorway, next to the folding screen. The odor of cologne from the handkerchief gagged Rubén.

"You smell like a *cocotte*," he said, wrinkling his noise, and again he turned his back to him.

Debayle laughed, understanding. The handkerchief still in his hand, he hurried his assistants, who were setting out vials and instruments on the little table with rubber wheels.

"I'm not going to anaesthetize you," he told him. "I'm just going to put a cocaine poultice on the hepatic region."

"Eat a load of shit," Rubén replied, covering his head with the sheet.

One of the assistants began helping Debayle into a white surgeon's gown stained with old traces of blood. The others wheeled the little table over to him. On the enamel trays, the scissors, the trocar, and the scalpels tinkled against the dark vials.

Rubén suddenly turned over. He leaned down, making the springs in the bed squeak, and feeling around on the floor tiles with his hand until he found the porcelain chamber pot, he threw it without much force at Debayle. The chamber pot landed at his feet, wetting his shoes with urine and splattering his gown.

Alarmed, the assistants pounced on Rubén, pinioning him with their arms and legs.

"You're behaving like a nursery-school kid," said Debayle, shaking the spatter from his shoes.

"Chiron, don't let this man touch me!" Rubén could barely be heard to say.

Chiron looked at Debayle for a second and made a move to approach the bed.

"Stay back or it will go very badly for you," the learned Debayle warned him very calmly.

"Doctor! Can you hear me? Is something wrong?" The voice of Rosario Murillo was heard behind the door.

"Nothing, señora, please be calm," replied Debayle.

They removed Rubén's pajama top and covered his eyes with a piece of black linen. An assistant disinfected the skin on the lower half of his stomach with a solution of phenol and marked two points with a blue pencil. Chiron was sobbing in a corner of the room, where the learned Debayle had confined him.

There was a courteous knock on the door, and Debayle, angered by another interruption, ordered Chiron to go and open it. It was his brother-in-law, Dr. Juan Bautista Sacasa. Smiling, he handed Chiron his hat.

The learned Debayle was now putting on his rubber gloves while he waited for the application of the cocaine compress in the area to be punctured

"Doctor, save me from this barbarian," Rubén said when he heard the voice of the other surgeon."

"This is a useless procedure," Dr. Sacasa said, leaning against the back of the bed and smiling obsequiously, as if Rubén could see him.

"Then why don't you act like a man and put a stop to it, damn it?" Rubén's voice was growing weaker by the moment.

"I'm very sorry, my dear poet, but you know how hard-headed Louis is," Dr. Sacasa said, winking at Debayle.

"You're nothing but a grinning nonentity," Rubén told him, his head drooping to one side.

Debayle vigorously drove the trocar into one of the two points that had been marked by the pencil. A cry of pain filled the room, and Chiron covered his face with the hat he had forgotten to hang up. One of the assistants approached with a receptacle. A stream of thick blood, black as ink, flowed out through the mouth of the trocar when the learned Debayle pushed down on the plunger.

"I told you," Dr. Sacasa said, with a triumphant smile. "There's no pus."

"Let's proceed to the next marked point," Debayle ordered his assistants, ignoring his brother-in-law.

"No, no!" Rubén begged. "They're going to kill me!"

They held Rubén down again. Chiron was crying, his face hidden behind the hat. Once more Debayle drove the trocar in, and this time the scream reached the street. In the corridor, Rosario Murillo and Eulalia stared at each other, trembling.

The assistant again brought the receptacle over. The learned Debayle pushed down on the plunger. Once more, the blood, dark and thick, slowly flowed out.

"So then, the poet's liver was healthy?" said Segismundo, unbuttoning his shirt. It was hotter than ever that night.

"No. It was completely destroyed," Rigoberto said, fanning himself with his journal. "Advanced hepatic cirrhosis. The punctures hastened his death."

"A sponge saturated with anise," Captain Prío said, going to empty the cigarette butts filling the ash tray.

"That learned Debayle!" Segismundo said, suddenly indignant, hitting the table with his fist.

"The only reason you're indignant is that Debayle gave a gala party for Colonel Pendleton," Erwin said, stretching in his chair and yawning.

"The learned Debayle was a Yankee lover, everybody knows that," the goldsmith Segismundo said. "I'm indignant about his famous operations. Just listen to poor Rubén screaming, helpless in his hands."

"The prince returned to León to die in an iron bed, among butchers," Captain Prío said.

"His grand parties in the aristocratic salons of Europe were left far behind," Norberto said.

"What aristocratic salons and what grand parties are you talking about?" Erwin said. "In a rundown boarding house in Barcelona, Francisca, his wife, with their little son, going hungry. That's what he left behind."

"In that boarding house in Tibidabo, Francisca was washing the dishes when she heard the shouting outside about the death of a prince," Rigoberto said. "She ran to buy the newspaper, and that's where she read about it."

"And it was the prince of Castilian letters who had died," Captain Prío said.

"And isn't it true that she was illiterate?" Erwin said.

"Rubén taught her to read, the same as he did with Chiron," Rigoberto said.

"He would have been better off if he'd devoted himself to teaching in elementary school, as Debayle pointed out to him one afternoon," Erwin said.

"And in his will he left Francisca all the rights to his books," the goldsmith Segismundo said. "So much for Rosario Murillo's clamoring!"

"You heard Eulalia? Now there's no doubt that I'll be related to Rubén Darío," Norberto said.

"Of course, but those pages are written in collaboration with your father-in-law," Erwin said.

"The only information Dr. Balthazar Cisne contributed had to do with the orgy in the cemetery, and the retaliation taken by the Marines," said Rigoberto.

"Then that dialogue between Rosario Murillo and Eulalia, Norberto's grandmother, is your doing," Erwin said.

"No," Norberto said. "I lent Rigoberto a journal in which that blowup between the two of them was recorded by Eulalia."

"So you, too, are dedicated to historical research instead of finding a way to pay off your bank loans," Erwin said.

"I didn't have to research anything," Norberto said. "*Zela the Moor* took the journal out of her mother's closet."

"The one who's really doing some research is Moralitos," Captain Río says. "But it's about those sitting around this cursed table."

"What's that?" Erwin asks him, stuttering, and no longer laughing.

"He came here this morning with several security agents, saying they were here to check out the place for the arrival of *The Man*," Captain Río says.

"Is it possible Somoza's coming to Casa Río?" Norberto asks with the look of someone who has swallowed medicine.

"Don't interrupt," Erwin says, cutting him off with a wave of his arm.

"For them this house is on the perimeter of their surveillance," Captain Río says. "They even searched the toilets."

"And he asked about us," Erwin says.

"He had each name typed on some pink sheets he pulled out of a folder," Captain Río says. "He called you 'the regulars' and me 'the proprietor.'"

"He didn't say 'the cursed table'?" Erwin asked.

"No, the name the security people have for you is just that, 'the regulars,'" Captain Río says. "They know your addresses and occupations."

"And did that gentleman happen to inquire about me?" the goldsmith Segismundo asks.

"They have you down as a fanatic of the worst sort," says Captain Prio.

"What a great favor they do me, those assassins," Segismundo says.

"And what's the point of having us on that list?" asks Erwin.

"Because all of you 'regulars' are all checked off as enemies of *The Man*," Captain Río says.

"But I'm not mixed up in any politics," Norberto says.

"It's called prevention," Rigoberto says. "They want to have us on edge, scare us."

"The one he asked about most was you," Captain Prío tells Rigoberto. "He's been checking into what you were up to in El Salvador."

"In El Salvador?" says Segismundo.

"From what I could gather, they've been tracking Cordelio Selva," Captain Prío says. "And they believe that Rigoberto's involved with him in some way."

"Who's this Cordelio Selva?" Erwin asks.

"A very brave patriot," Segismundo says.

"In El Sauce, Cordelio Selva was taken in by Father Olimpo Lozano, who later took in *Jorge Negrete*," Captain Prío says. "From there he went off to enroll in the Caribbean Foreign Legion, making off with the priest's woman and money from the poorbox to be used for the cause."

"Save those stories for another time, this is serious business here, Captain," Erwin says, unable to stop his stuttering.

"And why doesn't Moralitos just ask me, instead?" Rigoberto says.

"They have their methods," Captain Prío says. "If I were you, I'd get out of León until this whole damned thing blows over. There are only three days left before the convention."

"I can't run out on *Tovarich*," Rigoberto says. "The whole scheme for promoting it will fall apart."

"Moralitos kept coming back to that," Captain Prío says. "He thinks your publicity has a double meaning."

"When the 21st arrives, he'll realize there was no hidden meaning," says Rigoberto.

The Sad Princess

Before leaving that morning, Rigoberto had asked his mother to make him his favorite dish for lunch: rooster soup with meatballs. The rooster in today's soup, a gift from *Jorge Negrete*, is none other than Lucifer, defeated the previous Sunday by a single mortal thrust in the first flurry of feathers by The Archangel Gabriel, the cock owned by Father Olimpo Lozano. And after that fatal thrust, to the sad regret of his owner as well as of his blood brother Beelzebub, Lucifer had gone to sleep the sleep of the just in the grocery store freezer, cradled among the purple and rose-colored popsicles tinged with his blood.

Rigoberto serves himself two helpings of steaming soup, and then withdraws to his room, which smells of dirty socks, to take a nap, but first he closes the shutters on the window facing the patio because he prefers the dark, though that way the suffocating air makes the room even hotter and clammier.

He wakes up bathed in sweat, not knowing what time it is. He jumps up to open the window, fearful that night has fallen, but before he even sees the clock the intensity of the light outside tells him he has plenty of time. It's 2:20 in the afternoon. He gets dressed and goes out to the hallway to wash his face and splash some water on his hair in a small sink that drains out through a pipe at the foot of a lime tree in the patio; the tree is always in bloom and full of fruit.

Father Olimpo Lozano, his violin teacher, has also taken a nap in the hammock in the hallway in his underwear after he'd returned from the luncheon for the First Lady. He woke up when he felt the nervous weight of The Archangel Gabriel on his gassy, bloated stomach after the bird leapt up on him, lonely on its own in the ecclesiastical residence where he wandered around fancy-free.

The gamecock is staring at him beady-eyed, and the priest, still submerged in his stupor, smiles back at him, but then suddenly he has the feeling that someone else is standing in the hallway looking at him. He sits up, places the bird carefully down on the floor as if it were made of porcelain, then gropes around for his white cotton soutane which is lying on a stool next to his military cap, hurrying because he knows that someone's caught him in this state of undress.

"Don't trouble yourself," he hears a voice say. "The worst would have been to have found you in the arms of some woman in that hammock!"

Giving up trying to get dressed, Father Olimpo Lozano rummages in his soutane for his glasses.

"Here they are, they fell on the floor," comes the voice again.

Now that he has his glasses on, he can get a good look at him. The louse hasn't changed after all these years. He's shaved off his sideburns, a little heavier perhaps, more tanned; but he's the same.

"You ran off on me with all the money from the poor-box," he says.

"That was centuries ago," Cordelio says. "I thought you wouldn't even remember it."

"And that wasn't the half of it," says Father Olimpo Lozano.

"Diana Coronado came with me of her own free will," Cordelio says. "I didn't force her."

"The poor child," he says. "So helpless, and to have lost her virtue with the likes of you."

"Stop pretending she was so innocent," Cordelio says. "She knew the most indecent positions, and you taught her every one of them."

"And what became of her?" the priest asks, dressing in earnest, slipping into his saffron- and avocado-stained soutane, with the captain's epaulettes.

"How should I know?" Cordelio replies. "She was happy as a clam with me in Cuba, the Dominican Republic, Costa Rica. But when we got to Guatemala, she ran off with a high-ranking officer when the Arbenz revolution came along. I never saw her again."

"Bumping people off, stirring up revolts, that's what you were up to in those other countries. That was what you used the *reales* from the alms box of Our Lord of Esquipulas for," he says. His soutane is buttoned crooked, so that the top button is out of place.

"I didn't even take a thousand córdobas," says Cordelio. "And you should have seen how heavy that sack of coins was."

"Not even a thousand córdobas? You big liar, it was the whole collection box full of donations! If you'd just waited till the penance was over before running off!" Now he's managed to put his rubber sandals on over his socks.

"Some day I'm going to pay it all back," Cordelio says.

"I'm not holding you to it," Father Olimpo Lozano says. "Why did you come to Nicaragua?"

"Why should I lie?" Cordelio says. "I came to organize an uprising against Somoza. But I'm going back disappointed. That man is stronger than ever."

Father Olimpo Lozano pokes around in his soutane, finds a toothpick that he puts into his mouth.

"Somoza is in León," he says.

"I found out too late that I'd stumbled into the lion's den," Cordelio says.

"So, then, you're not going to hang Colonel Melisandro Maravilla by the balls?" Father Olimpo Lozano asks him.

"Me?" Cordelio says.

"You swore a long time ago that you were going to make him pay for your father's death." Now he's picking at a tooth, eyes closed.

"Maybe because I was a boy then and thought vengeance was the answer," Cordelio says. "And now, you're my father."

"Why don't you tell me what you want from me," Father Olimpo Lozano says. "Simply by coming to this house, you've put me in danger."

"I want you to give me a place to sleep for tonight," Cordelio says.

"Not for a minute!" Father Olimpo Lozano says, shaking his head vehemently. "They'll make things miserable for me the rest of my life. You're all they talk about up there. They already know you're back in Nicaragua."

"No one will know," Cordelio says. "Just for tonight, and I'll be gone by morning. I promise."

"Promises!" he replies. "Just like you promised the time I caught you in a *tête-à-tête* with Diana Coronado. That's how far your lack of respect went. And then you ran off with her, and the reales."

"I left you the Victrola," Cordelio says.

"I sold it; I didn't even get a hundred pesos for it," Father Olimpo Lozano says.

"Records and all?" Cordelio asks him.

"Not even if they had been made of gold," he says. "And if I hadn't threatened those thieves from my pulpit with hellfire and damnation, I'd never have gotten the Victrola and the records back at all."

"I haven't anywhere to sleep tonight," Cordelio says. "I'm not even going to approach *Jorge Negrete*. He's a coward."

"You think anyone who doesn't do what you want is a coward," Father Olimpo Lozano says. "Besides, he's very busy with a play. He's about to become an actor."

"You see, all the more reason," Cordelio says.

"My *Archangel Gabriel* ate his Lucifer alive," he says, looking at the cock who has stayed quiet the whole time, standing between the two of them. "The poor boy, I felt sorry for him. But a fight is a fight."

"We arrived in Nicaragua together, on the same boat," Cordelio says. "That's where I got to know Lucifer and Beelzebub."

"See what a loyal brother you have. He didn't even mention a word about it," Father Olimpo Lozano says. "And when you ran away, he did a good job covering your back for you. It wasn't until the next morning that he came to tell me, figuring that you were long gone by then."

"You were sleeping it off," Cordelio says. "You spent the night drinking like a fish with those musicians from Masatepe. Don't you remember? The two of us carried you to bed."

"I started off going at it with Maestro Lisandro Ramírez to see who could play the best variations of 'The Carnival of Venice' on the violin," Father Olimpo Lozano explains. "We played and we drank. And that's why we were getting smashed."

"So now you're blaming it on the violin," Cordelio says.

"Didn't the two of you split the loot from the poorbox?" Father Olimpo Lozano says.

"What a fine way to thank my brother for staying with you and looking after you when I took off," Cordelio says.

"Looking after me? He began absconding with my best fighting cocks. He said they'd died of dropsy," Father Olimpo Lozano says. "And then one day he disappeared, too. A few years later he turned up here in León, already the owner of a bar."

"He's gotten rich," Cordelio says. "And look at me."

Father Olimpo Lozano picks up the Archangel Gabriel and strokes his crest.

"What a nice way to repay me, the two of you, for taking you in when you were destitute," he says. "All right, you can stay. One night, and no more."

"Great. I'll be back later," Cordelio says.

"How can you even think of walking around with the whole National Guard out on the streets?" Father Olimpo

Lozano says. "If you don't stay here now, in hiding, you can't come back."

"I have to pick up a passport so I can get out of the country," Cordelio says. "That's why I came to León."

"A fake passport, no doubt," Father Olimpo Lozano says.

"I'm not going to ask Moralitos for a real one," Cordelio says.

"I always wind up doing what you want," Father Olimpo Lozano says.

That conversation is still going on as Rigoberto enters his mother's neighborhood store. His mother, who has just finished with a customer, wants to ask him something, but he says they'll talk later, that he's running late. The customer, a widowed harness-maker named Lisímaco Arturo Bejarano Ortiz, a resident of El Calvario neighborhood, bought two Mejorales for his headache, paid for them with a one-córdoba bill, was getting his change, and declared that he did not speak with the person in question, but that he seemed in a hurry and very nervous.

A truck with loudspeakers mounted on the cab is making its way along the street in front of the store, blaring out garbled Vivas! with bullfight music in the background. From the truck's side rails, shorn-headed recruits in oversized uniforms are tossing match books with Somoza's portrait out into the street, and the children fight and scrabble noisily to pick them up.

It's now 3:00 p.m. As Rigoberto walks along the street, he can hear the afternoon radio broadcast of *The Right to Be Born* because all the radios in the neighborhood are tuned to the World Radio Network, YNW, 740 on the AM dial. The actors' voices flow out into the street over the transoms, issue forth from bedrooms and kitchens, pursuing him along the sidewalk only to await him at the next street corner, where other passersby are also listening, heads together, and an electrician repairing a meter has stopped halfway up the ladder with his ear glued to the laments, the supplications, the sighs of the radio soap.

The Rose Child has finally had a chance to sit down in her living room next to the sky-blue bakelite Telefunken radio on top of the locked glass cabinet where the pawned articles are kept, each with its cardboard tag. Her hands grip the arms of the rocking chair to stop the involuntary rocking back and forth, her attention fixed on the dial's magic eye that flutters with each musical flourish, and in her lap, the Countess Ninoshka Andreyevna's deep-crimson velvet dress that she hems during the commercials for FAB, the detergent that gets out the drab.

From the hallway, her daughter, *Zela the Moor*, is also listening, the script on the table next to her, because she's got to go over her part. But she forgets about her lines, the ones Lucio Ranucci himself had marked in red pencil, and on the back of a sheet she makes a sketch of Albertico Limonta's features, which are exactly like Norberto's, only a little thinner, and if she had a green crayon handy she'd color his eyes green, which is the way the narrator describes them on the radio.

Dr. Balthazar Cisne is pacing back and forth between the hallway and the living room, fuming because his wife wastes her time on such foolishness instead of hurrying over to help Lucio Ranucci. He, too, still keeps one ear tuned to the program. Deep down he's afraid of what might happen: if don Víctor del Junco doesn't get his voice back, Albertico Limonta will never find out who his mother is; an attack of apoplexy is very serious, as confirmed by his never-erring friend, Dr. Atanasio Salmerón, a member of the Board of Directors of the Rubén Darío Honor Society.

And it is he, despite his apparent disgust, who gestures to Rigoberto to remain silent when he sees him approaching with his imitation-lizard portfolio under his arm, indicating to him in pantomime to sit down. A short time later, the magic eye contracts into a writhing spasm to the opening bars of Tchaikovsky's piano concerto No. 1, and when the musical jingle praises FAB soap for the last time, he furtively goes over to the radio to turn it off with a vindictive twirl of the knob while the commercial can still be heard coming from the other houses in the neighborhood. *The Rose Child*, already familiar with how the program signs off, lifts her glasses to dry again the tears from her eyes and goes to her room, her costume cradled in her arms.

Without wasting a minute, Dr. Balthazar Cisne drags a rocker over to sit down next to Rigoberto, a volume of the complete works of Rubén Darío in his hand, ready to continue the discussion on which verses are to be engraved on the base of the statue. This, supposedly, is the purpose of Rigoberto's visit.

As a matter of personal pride, Dr. Balthazar Cisne doesn't tell him that his attempt to approach the First Lady to invite her to inaugurate the statue has failed. Instead he lets him know that General Somoza thought the request for proper lighting was very important, and that it was duly noted by his secretary. And suddenly closing the book, he draws his chair closer and glances at the door before speaking.

"The people in charge of Somoza's security are really on the lookout for Cordelio," he says. "Every time I hear his name mentioned, my heart skips a beat."

"And what do you have to be worried about?" Rigoberto asks.

"You assured me you were no longer mixed up in politics, which isn't true," Dr. Balthazar Cisne says. As far as Lt. Moralitos is concerned, Cordelio's the devil himself."

"They've blown it out of all proportion," Rigoberto says.

"Not at all," Dr. Balthazar Cisne says. "And you and I in the same boat with him!"

"That Moralitos is simply trying to make himself look important," Rigoberto says. "He wants to prove he's got more pull than Colonel Maravilla."

"You've got that right," Dr. Balthazar Cisne says. "Ever since the colonel sent him to Managua under arrest when he was his warrant officer here, he hasn't forgiven him."

"General Somoza is fully aware of your clever way of promoting the premiere of *Tovarich*," he hears *The Rose Child* say. She's just come out of her room, dressed as Princess Ninoshka Andreyevna because she needs to measure her gown.

"And why would a president concern himself with trivialities?" Rigoberto says.

"He doesn't concern himself with those things; he's got Lt. Moralitos for that," says Dr. Balthazar Cisne.

"Isn't it an American who's heading up the security bureau?" remarks Rigoberto.

"His name is Van Wynckle," says Princess Ninoshka Andreyevna. "A very serious gentleman. He speaks perfect Spanish, with an Argentine accent. You'd think you were listening to Luis Sandrini."

"And what does Somoza think of my publicity?" asks Rigoberto.

"That you're doing him a great favor because everybody probably believes it's all for his candidacy," says Dr. Balthazar Cisne.

"And did he mention my name as the author of the ads?" Rigoberto asks.

"Why lie? No, he never mentioned your name," says Princess Ninoshka Andreyevna, feeling bad about disappointing Rigoberto. "And we didn't exactly have time to explain it to him, either."

"It's better this way, don't worry about it," Rigoberto says. "He shouldn't know about me. What for?"

"Well, I think he already knows about you," says Dr. Balthazar Cisne.

"And why in the world should he know about me?" Rigoberto asks.

"I didn't hear it myself, but I've been told that some guy named Rafa Parrales asked them to give you an important position, I don't know exactly which one," says Dr. Balthazar Cisne.

"Why didn't you say so before?" Rigoberto says. "I hope it was a good job. I wouldn't mind being Head of Liquor Warehouses."

"Those are high-ranking positions," Dr. Balthazar Cisne says.

"Well, I wouldn't take just any dumb job," Rigoberto says.

"Let's get started," Dr. Balthazar Cisne says, and he opens the book, pointing to the page where he's done some underlining. "What do you think of this for one of the sides? *And for me today León is like Rome or Paris.*"

You already know that the inscription on the *frontis* has been decided upon: *oh, Salvadora, Salvadorita...!* Princess Ninoshka Andreyevna is at that moment about to offer her opinion, and while the words are still in her mouth, she hears the clatter of Norberto's Jeep engine in the distance. *Zela the Moor* hears it too and runs to the living room dressed as young Princess Natasha Petrovna, wearing a gold lamé gown, slowing her pace at the last minute as she goes toward the door. Norberto hasn't appeared yet. Dr. Balthazar Cisne, peering above the rim of his glasses, and Princess Ninoshka Andreyevna, peering above the rim of her glasses, stop the girl in her tracks with their icy stares: Norberto had better not be coming to take her for another spin in his Jeep, and much less, with her dressed as young Princess Natasha Petrovna, because such daring has already led *Zela the Moor* to be grounded.

Norberto's convertible Willys Jeep is nothing but a chassis, wheels, steering wheel, and two front seats. A jeep like a creole colt, without harness or reins but very suitable for a slow jaunt around the track, which is how he likes to drive, easing up in front of the houses where the girls bring their rockers out to the street in the sun, or next to the high-curbed sidewalks where they play *desmoche*, and Norberto can toss his cards without getting out of his Jeep, a Jeep for driving up to open-air bars on tree-lined patios, the gear shift in neutral, the motor turned off, then sitting down at a table, being served, making toasts, drinking; a Jeep for driving *Zela the Moor* around in full view of all, even if they both swear that these are clandestine jaunts.

He's turned off the motor and comes to the door enveloped in Eau de Vétiver cologne, all flattery, all smiles, all gentleness. He greets Princess Ninoshka Andreyevna, who lets herself be kissed on the cheek, and he holds out his arms to Dr. Balthazar Cisne, who only offers him his hand, then he goes over to young Princess Natasha Petrovna and shakes her hand. He is about to greet Rigoberto but stops and instead pulls out a little ring box from his pants' pocket. That's the prearranged plan.

"The ring," he says, allowing the ring box to be seen.

Silence, a painful silence. The ring? Young Princess Natasha Petrovna's anxiety spreads like a rippling veil in a storm over the head of Princess Ninoshka Andreyevna, and Dr. Balthazar Cisne feels its undulations brush against his face. Rigoberto could easily claim the box and put an end to the misapprehension. The script says it's his engagement ring. But he only smiles, playfully, in Norberto's mournful face.

Another visitor will thwart the denouement of this scene. Taking off his little Tyrolean hat, the goldsmith Segismundo comes in. Don't think this is an unexpected visit. He always stops by Dr. Balthazar Cisne's house on the way to his jewelry shop after he's had lunch at a neighborhood eatery, where he likes to converse over dessert with the students. As soon as he entered, he saw the ring box in Norberto's hand and recognizing it, is able to conceal his puzzlement. He sits down in a rocker and asks young Princess Natasha Petrovna for a glass of water, which she brings with trembling hand from the kitchen in a large coffee cup.

"It's stifling outside," says Segismundo, sipping the water.

"It's as hot as the devil," Dr. Balthazar Cisne agrees, his eyes still fixed on the ring box.

"No," Segismundo says. "There's only one devil, and he's here in León. And if I'm burning up, it's from rage."

"You shouldn't get sulfurous about politics," Dr. Balthazar Cisne says, finally resigned to closing the book.

"It's not a question of politics," Segismundo says after finishing his glass of water. "It's a question of public health. The air smells of sulfur, of the devil's shit."

"Are you referring to General Somoza?" Rigoberto asks him.

"Who else?" the goldsmith Segismundo ripostes harshly.

"You've got to judge leaders with a cool head," Rigoberto says.

"A cool head? What are those words doing in your mouth, my dear poet?" Segismundo asks. "The one acting with a cool head is that gangster. He doesn't blink an eye when he orders his butchery."

"Let's leave that to history," Rigoberto says. "Only history can judge a country's leaders."

"I can't believe what I'm hearing! Then, it's true," the goldsmith Segismundo says.

"What's true?" Rigoberto asks.

"That you're going to that party of boot-lickers, as your fiancée told me," Segismundo says.

"I'm only going because I have to accompany her," Rigoberto says.

"What about your part in *Tovarich*?" asks Princess Ninoshka Andreyevna, who has been standing there, her eyes also glued to the ring box.

"No matter, I'll get to the party late," Rigoberto says.

"According to what I heard at lunch, the invitations for that party are numbered," says Dr. Balthazar Cisne. "Moralitos himself will be watching the door."

"I'm sorry, I had forgotten that the three of you just came from lunch with that gangster," the goldsmith Segismundo says, looking derisively at Dr. Balthazar Cisne, who prefers to play dumb about the whole thing.

"Lt. Moralitos is too important a person for the job of doorman," Rigoberto says.

"Well, my dear poet, seeing that they've already sent you your invitations, you've got nothing to worry about," Segismundo notes with the same sarcasm.

"Moralitos has to be there," says Princess Ninoshka Andreyevna, turning to her husband. "They said especially because of that man, that Cordelio Selva. They've been looking for him like a needle in a haystack, even showing his picture around."

"A person I've not had the pleasure of meeting," Dr. Balthazar Cisne hastens to add, without anyone having asked him.

"I have!" the goldsmith Segismundo says, and he looks defiantly at Dr. Balthazar Cisne, and then at Rigoberto. "I've had that honor."

"Be careful no one hears you," Dr. Balthazar Cisne says. "The streets are crawling with spies."

"Of course! We've got to be careful!" says Segismundo, getting up.

"It's not such a big deal, sit down," Princess Ninoshka Andreyevna says, in truth wishing he would leave because he's delaying the denouement.

"No, I'm going," the goldsmith Segismundo says, standing in front of Norberto: "From what I hear, it's true about the job at *Novedades* too."

"So that's the job they were going to give you!" Dr. Balthazar Cisne says to Rigoberto. "Congratulations."

Segismundo, who has already put on his little Tyrolean hat at the door, suddenly turns toward Norberto. He still can't pin down what he's doing there displaying that ring box that holds such a grave secret.

"And that ring box?" he says to Norberto in a disapproving way.

Rigoberto, lips sealed, doesn't go to his aid either.

"It's a wedding ring," Norberto says, and he doesn't even know why he's smiling.

Young Princess Natasha Petrovna, again caught between panic and joy, backs up to the door leading to the hallway. Princess Ninoshka Andreyevna can't avoid moving her lips in prayer. Dr. Balthazar Cisne, with the volume of the poet's complete works in his hand, puts on a stern face, as he thinks he should, given the weightiness of the moment.

"The ring is for him," Norberto finally says, and he goes over to Rigoberto, holding out the ring box. "I was looking for him all day so I could deliver it to him as he asked."

Rigoberto takes the box, but he doesn't put it in his portfolio. He plays with it, rolling it around on his fingers, not looking at it, and he barely raises his eyes to see young Princess Natasha Petrovna, who has hidden her face in her hands. Princess Ninoshka Andreyevna, expressionless, goes to sit down in her rocker.

"We'll look at the verses tomorrow, doctor," Rigoberto says. He puts the ring box inside his portfolio and walks toward the door.

"We'll see each other at tonight's performance," Princess Ninoshka Andreyevna says in a faint voice from her chair.

The goldsmith Segismundo, ashen-faced, is waiting for Rigoberto at the door.

"So then you have a role in tonight's play," he says in an unexpectedly loud voice, even for him.

"A small contribution, nothing, really," Rigoberto says.

Anatole, hunchbacked and nearly blind, has been the family servant for three generations. He left his own daughter, the widow of a railroad man, in Moscow, to follow the princess to Paris. Too old now for other duties, he has nothing to do but open the door when the little bell rings.

"He's also been in charge of the publicity for the play," says Princess Natasha Andreyevna in the same languid voice as before.

"Yes, I know that already, all that about what will happen on the 21st," the goldsmith Segismundo says, not taking his eyes off Rigoberto.

Rigoberto waves goodbye with his portfolio in his hand, and leaves, but Norberto runs after him and the two stop on the sidewalk. And then, when he finally pulls himself away and is about to disappear around the street corner, the goldsmith Segismundo takes off his little Tyrolean hat and holds it against his chest.

The Music Box That Holds My Treasure

Come with me quickly now and stand next to Captain Prío on his balcony, just in time to see Somoza leaving the Teatro González amidst renewed shouts, Vivas, and firecrackers. By unanimous vote, he's just been nominated as the presidential candidate for another term (1957-1963), and the sirens of the Benemérito Fire Engine Company join the static-laden uproar from the Grundig radio, again turned up to full blast downstairs at Casa Prío.

See *The Alligator Woman* as Captain Prío sees her, at the rear of the crowd streaming across the plaza, wildly gesturing to reignite the hurrahs of the demonstrators following Somoza, more unruly now but less numerous than in the morning. And that other one, up there, that's Chiron, high above the plaza once more, in the cathedral bell tower, standing under the protection of the Atlas supports. Hands on his knees, he peers down into the abyss to follow the procession, occupying an even better vantage point than that of Captain Prío on his balcony. To Chiron's eyes, the swirl of people around Somoza is slowing down as it moves farther away from the center of the plaza, and for all the efforts of *The Alligator Woman* and her lieutenants, the demonstrators are gradually dispersing and lagging behind, so that the ice cream vendors now have little trouble pushing through the thinning ranks with their carts.

The streetlamps are already lit now that it's getting dark. Somoza has entered his quarters and the demonstrators begin disbanding in earnest. When he does come out on the balcony for the last time, accompanied by the First Lady, there won't be much of a crowd left to hear him because most of them are scrambling for places on the dump trucks and the cotton freight transports. Meanwhile shadows fill the plaza and extend into the side streets like a silent tide, engulfing all the objects in their path: cement benches, groomed laurel trees, trucks, crates, demonstrators alike. Above the rooftops, a cloudless sky glows with the colors of a bedside lamp.

Should it occur to *The Alligator Woman* to raise her head for a moment, she would see Chiron before he's swallowed by that darkness. And she does raise her head. She removes her felt hat, waves it joyfully, and he mimics her greeting in return, and then gestures again to let her know he'll be joining her shortly at Baby Dolls because it's nearly time for dinner. Two close threads in the warp of the tapestry the seamstresses have begun to close-stitch without haste, unconcerned that night is falling because they don't need their eyes to work their stitches well.

And suppose one of you were to leave your spot on the balcony and go over to the Teatro González, which is also now falling under the darkness of night, would you find the fans still on? I doubt it; all the security agents are gone by now and the employees, tired of having to stand around doing nothing, must have turned them off, at last, as an act of regaining control.

Better to stay where you are. *The Alligator Woman* and Chiron, who are now exchanging goodbyes with hand signals that make them laugh out loud, can easily take us where we need to go, back to February 16, 1916. It's growing dark then too, and you mustn't miss what's happening there. The whole city is on tenterhooks. Rubén is dying. He has just received the final rites from Bishop Simeón.

The crowd was praying on its knees with a sustained murmur at the doors of the Maison de Santé, lit by the acetylene gaslamps, and the tolling of a small bell emanating from the hospital was suddenly drowned out by the knells of the cathedral's main bell echoing across a mauve-colored sky. At the head of the procession the seminarians from the San Ramón Academy sang *Laudate Dominum*. Enveloped in a haze from the censers, Bishop Simeón held the monstrance aloft as he walked under a blue canopy carried by four canons of the church behind a troop of secular clergy, and so they proceeded until they entered the cathedral.

With a ceremonial candle still in her hand, Rosario Murillo was praying at the prie-dieu before the improvised altar while Chiron was sweeping up the withered flowers. Behind the lilac-colored gauze of the mosquito net, Rubén was lying curled up on his side, wrapped in a thick, gray blanket, snoring lightly, his mouth slightly open. Between his fingers he clutched the silver crucifix that Amado Nervo had given him in Paris when they shared the same rat-trap in Faubourg Montmartre, and that he always carried with him in his travel *nécessaire.*

Eulalia was still in the corridor, but having lost the battle, she was forced to witness the viaticum ceremony from a distance. Her decision to get her daughter Leda inside the Maison de Santé to watch with fright the comings and goings that whirled around Rubén's final moments, instead of reinforcing her position, had completed her defeat, as Debayle used the excuse of that provocative act to forbid mother and daughter any access whatsoever to the room.

The learned Debayle had already gotten from Andrés Murillo the promise to cede to him sole ownership of Rubén's brain. Standing aside from the bed, the two conversed in hushed tones while consulting a sheet of paper. If you move closer, you will see the people who were authorized to enter the room from that moment on, out of the many waiting impatiently in the corridor. After being called together, they tiptoed quietly in: the poet Santiago Argüello, representing the Athenaeum of León; the poet Manuel Maldonado, for the Athenaeum of Masaya; the artist Alejandro Torrealba, so that he could make a charcoal sketch of the dying man; the painter Alejandro Alonso Richi, permitted to enter with his easel, palette, and box of paints; Maestro Cisneros, with his tripod, box camera and nail-studded case; José López, the maker of religious figures, to set the plaster mold for the death mask; and the barber, Ovidio Parajón, to perform the cadaver's *toilette*.

At the far end of the corridor, now empty because the visitors not on the list had left, Eulalia's indignant sobs could be heard from time to time. Each time, Rosario Murillo, who had taken her place next to the bed, would lift her reddened eyes to defy that stubborn crying, which Chiron, off to himself by the door, was silently copying.

Debayle kept watch over the rattling sound of Rubén's breathing, and from time to time placed his ear close to his chest, disdaining the stethoscope hanging from his neck. At the foot of the bed, Andrés Murillo held an Ingersol pocket-watch in his hand, never taking his eyes off the dying man. At one point, Rosario Murillo left her place at the bedside, approached her brother, whispered something to him, and exited the room. She was going to the bathroom.

Shortly thereafter, the learned Debayle again leaned close to Rubén's chest, rapidly signaled Andrés Murillo, who with a quick pull stopped the watch, then held it up for all to see that the hands had come to rest at 10:15 p.m. Rosario Murillo, who had returned at that moment, put her hands up to her mouth and let out a little scream.

Santiago Argüello and Manuel Maldonado bumped into her in their rush to get through the door to announce the news, and there was a momentary white flash because Maestro Cisneros held up the magnesium palette to fix the moment in time. But before the two men reached the street, a rumbling swept through the night, like the announcement of an approaching storm. The crowd outside burst out in a fearful clamor.

Chiron, who still didn't dare approach Rubén's bed, stared into space, and there was a new rumbling, this time deeper and more powerful, like the booming of the artillery on Cardón Island some time ago; it rattled the coffered ceiling and scattered a fine film of dust. It was the

Momotombo Volcano: the screaming in the streets confirmed it. A spattering of sparks lit up the sky in the east.

And now a herd of bare feet and big clumsy shoes swept into the Maison de Santé, as if the doors had opened by themselves before the shadows that filled the corridor and halted at the threshold to lay their bouquets at his door, lit up by a clarity that seemed to rise up from the body itself, rocking in the barque of the poet's bed, the lilac sheer sails of the mosquito net billowing out in the warm air that beat against the skylights, bringing with it the ever more distant echo of the volcano's rumblings.

The Alligator Woman was in that procession of coachmen, whores, winos, butchers, drovers, washerwomen, card-sharks, merchants, wagoners, and delivery boys, and as she entered the room she saw Chiron leaning over the keel of the barque, yes, in the act of closing the eyes that still stared into the mist where the swans that had watched over the sleep of *The Great Dragon* drifted. And among the dark faces gathered around the bed, she also saw the face of a child with golden curls who contemplated the prostrate prince with amazement. A rose bud, *The Rose Child,* who the day after tomorrow, on the second of the vigil nights, will fall asleep from boredom among the satin petals of an artificial rose.

At midnight, and with the doors of the Maison de Santé locked, the body was transferred to the basement morgue behind the building, beyond the ward for the consumptive and the mentally ill. Accompanied by Andrés Murillo, the learned Debayle went down to the morgue with his entourage of assistants, all wearing hospital aprons. He was prepared to remove the brain.

Leaning on his walking stick, Andrés Murillo watched. They handed the scalpel to Debayle, and as he traced the line of incision on Rubén's forehead, the scalpel shone like a star in his hand. He carefully lifted the scalp and folded it back. They handed him the saw, and its fine teeth began to bite tenaciously into the bone of the cranium. Finally, with a creaking sound, the skull opened and the brain mass was exposed. He feverishly cut the ligaments, took the brain in his hands, and with it now free of its fetters, he lifted it up in front of his eyes, searching for the best angle in the artificial light.

"Here it is!" he said. "The private vessel of the muses! Here it is!"

"Put it on the scale, I want to know how much it weighs," Andrés Murillo told him, pointing to the brain with the tip of his walking stick.

Debayle carried the brain over to the scale and deposited it onto one of the pans, which he first covered with a piece of gauze. In the other pan he went about placing weights of various sizes.

"One thousand eight hundred fifty grams!" he exclaimed, after adding up the sum of the weights. "Astounding! The brain of the average Caucasian adult male weighs no more than one thousand three hundred seventy-five grams."

"What other brain has weighed more than this one?" Andrés Murillo asked, and he went over to add up the numbers engraved on each weight himself.

"None, that I know of," the learned Debayle answered. "Victor Hugo's brain weighed one thousand five hundred twenty grams. Schiller's, one thousand five hundred ten. Those of Cuvier, Abercombie, and Dupuytren, even less. There's no comparison!"

"Put it in the jar of formaldehyde," Andrés Murillo instructed him.

"Wait a moment." And the learned Debayle called to one of his assistants. "Write this down, write this down!"

"Hurry up. It can get damaged," Andrés Murillo urged him.

"Abundant formation of the frontal lobes and of the parietal lobes of the left hemisphere," the learned Debayle quickly dictated while pointing to the brain with the scalpel.

"You've got to leave all this for later," an impatient Andrés Murillo said, pounding the floor with his walking stick.

"The Brocca convolution stands out," the learned Debayle continued dictating. "And the Reil insula remarkable, quite remarkable. A deep Sylvan fissure, and no less so the Rolando."

"Get it into the formaldehyde right now, I'm telling you," Andrés Murillo said, hanging his cane on his arm, making ready to grab the brain himself.

Alarmed, Debayle stopped him. He carefully lifted the brain and deposited it at last into the frosted jar filled with formaldehyde. He then proceeded to fill the empty cavity with sawdust, and after replacing the piece of skull, set to work sewing up the skin of the forehead with horsehair, using delicate stitches.

"Later I'll delve carefully into the morphology of the meninges," he was saying while sewing up the forehead. "The size of the Brocca convolution troubles me. I want to surpass the study that Antomarchi made of Napoleon's brain."

Andrés Murillo, now pacing restlessly in the confined space of the morgue, let him go on talking. And while Debayle worked with the needle, he silently went over to stand next to the jar holding the brain.

Glancing up to ask for more thread, Debayle saw him take possession of the jar.

"What are you up to?" he exclaimed.

"Taking what belongs to me," Andrés Murillo answered.

"What!" The learned doctor abandoned his work and went to confront him. "You promised me, doña Rosario promised me..."

"If we hadn't, you wouldn't have removed the brain," Andrés Murillo said. And holding the jar with some difficulty under the arm where his cane also hung, he opened the morgue door.

"You're taking something that's rightly mine!" Debayle

shouted, and without removing his apron, he ran to stop him, grabbing him by the coat sleeve as he started up the stairs.

"Right, what right?" Andrés Murillo said, barely turning around.

"A scientific right!" Debayle was beside himself. "What you want to do is to sell it. Don't be so shameless!"

"There's no greater right than that of the grieving family," Andrés Murillo responded, tearing himself from Debayle's grip and disappearing up the stairs.

The learned Debayle, perplexed, hesitated a moment. Then he too raced up the stairs, gathering his gown about him. Panting, he reached the back courtyard, and ran in the direction of the hospice, passing through the mental ward, but he barely managed to see Andrés Murillo's coattails as he disappeared through the door of the reception room at the end of the corridor. Running as fast as he could, he finally caught up with him just as he was about to get into a waiting horse-drawn carriage, and to the surprise of the Marine Corps sentries who were making their normal rounds, the two men confronted each other in the middle of the street.

"You're not taking it with you!" shouted Debayle, hoarse with anger.

"Yes, I am taking it!" Andrés Murillo shouted, even louder.

They started to struggle furiously. The jar fell to the ground and shattered. The liquid poured out, and among the shards of opaque glass, the brain lay exposed on the cobblestones. The Marines raised their rifles and surrounded them.

Hearing all the shouting, Rosario Murillo, who was resting in one of the rooms at the hospital, rushed out into the street.

"My God! What's all this?" she exclaimed, putting her hands to her head.

"This person wants to rob you of your husband's brain," said Andrés Murillo, pointing with his cane first to Debayle and then to the cobblestones, where the brain now seemed to have shrunk in size.

"Not theft, señora! You authorized me to preserve it for my phrenological studies." Debayle, who was still wearing his rubber gloves, bent down to pick up the brain.

"Hide that thing, doctor, hide it!" At the sight of the brain, Rosario Murillo covered her eyes.

Just then, a black automobile appeared around the corner, its headlights illuminating the scene. Major Cyril Appleton, León's Chief of Police, got out, followed by his driver.

"What the hell is going on?" he asked the sentries.

"No idea, sir," said one of them, snapping to attention.

Carrying the brain, the doctor stepped forward and spoke in French to Major Appleton, who didn't understand a word.

"Take that damned thing to headquarters!" he ordered, covering his nose.

Obeying orders, one of the Marines demanded Debayle hand over the brain.

"Let me put it in another jar. It can't be left out like this, exposed to the air," the learned Debayle pleaded, and he gestured with his lower lip toward the broken glass scattered across the stones.

Major Appleton understood the request. A contrite Debayle, escorted by two Marines, went inside, carrying the brain. Rosario Murillo returned to her room, while her brother stood in the street, trying to argue his case with Major Appleton, who by now was smoking with a vacant look in his eyes and not paying the least bit of attention. The soldiers returned with the jar, got into the car where Major Appleton was already waiting, and sped away.

Later, sitting on the edge of his desk at headquarters with the urn next to him, he tried to decipher a note the widow had sent him via her brother, who was waiting on a bench in the vestibule for a reply:

Dear Major:

It is a scandal and an outrage that my husband's brain should remain at police headquarters. I beg you return it to me immediately, as I am the legitimate heir of all his properties.

Sincerely yours,

Rosario Murillo, Widow of Darío

The major raised his eyes from the note and was taken aback to see Chiron, who was watching him, more out of curiosity than concern. He could swear that he was smiling at him. And then, completely forgetting about him, he looked away, absorbed in his contemplation of the urn.

A few moments later, Major Appleton looked at the open door, knowing he'd closed it when he came in, and then at his automatic pistol in the gunbelt hanging on the wall behind his chair. And in what he considered a surprise move, he jumped up to grab his pistol. But when he pulled it out to take aim at the intruder, he found himself alone in the office again. The brain had disappeared from the desk. In the silence, the open door shone with the reflection of yellow paint under the electric light.

Pistol raised, he ran across the vestibule, passing a swirl of soldiers rushing to the arsenal to get their rifles, and behind them, Andrés Murillo, completely at a loss as to what was going on. Chiron ran wildly through the streets, a chorus of whistles at his back, the sound of a warning gunshot, and then another, but he was running at a gallop, eating up block after block, his clumsy shoes pounding the pavement, his back soaked with sweat, until his pursuers lost sight of him.

At the sound of someone running, *The Alligator Woman* got up and saw him come through the courtyard's main gate, panting, with the urn in his hands where the brain, submerged in an amber liquid, sloshed back and forth like a great jellyfish. He handed it to her and his first gestures, after releasing his benumbed arms, were to warn her to be careful or it would break. Both of them were fifteen at the time. She laughed. And hadn't he run all those blocks at the risk of dropping what he had brought there? What had he brought anyway? They put their heads together, and Chiron's fingers sketched arabesques on the glass, pointing to the Medusa's hair.

And when the *blessed souls* woke up, they were delighted to find the party room cleared of the furniture *Terrestial Light* had delivered to *The Alligator Woman* according to a precise inventory on the day that she went off to take possession of Cafarnaún, one of the nine properties in dispute, because her relatives, who were fighting the holy war and were clients of the brothel as well, had agreed not to stand in her way.

At one end of the bare room, the urn rested in a washbasin sitting on the brothel's most prized piece of furniture, a settee with funereal carvings that resembled a gondola. The tapers projected onto the glass of the urn the violet reflections from the rust-tinged washbasin, as if beyond the maze of branches of the madrone tree, the corozo palm, and the mignonette that decorated the altar, the jellyfish were stirring in the depths of a subterranean cave.

"So, that dream about his head being pulled off was a prophecy," said Segismundo.

"My father spoke of the episode involving Rubén's dream in some statements he made to the Chilean magazine, *Ercilla*," Captain Prío said, addressing Erwin. "I have it upstairs if you want to see it."

"Such a colossal head!" Segismundo said. "I wonder what his hat size was?"

"Seven and a quarter inches," Rigoberto said. "He needed a special mold."

"And is it true that they dressed and undressed him like a mannequin each night for the vigil?" Erwin asked. "One night in a Greek tunic, another in his ambassador's uniform for the court in Madrid. The last night in tails."

"It's not recorded whether they put his size seven-and-a-quarter hat on him," Norberto said.

"All because he was adored like a saint. Everybody in Nicaragua knew his poetry by heart from having read it so much," Captain Prío said.

"In fact, his poetry had hardly been read at all in Nicaragua, Captain," Rigoberto said, checking his journal. "According to the Customs' records, the total number of books imported in 1906 was one thousand three hundred twenty. How many of those were Rubén's? No one knows. Perhaps not even fifty of them. And not one of his was printed here."

"He was adored by all the rest of the drunks," Erwin said. "A country of illiterates doesn't care about poetry."

"And the funeral? No one has ever seen a funeral like it," Rigoberto said.

"However much an alcoholic as he may have been, he was a great man and they buried him in grand style," Captain Prío stated approvingly.

"Even though he was carried through the streets without his brain. The music box," said Segismundo.

"What came out in the newspapers about the theft of the brain?" Norberto asked.

"Nothing," Rigoberto said.

"At least you admit to your own lie," Erwin said.

"No one was interested in divulging the theft," Rigoberto said. "Major Appleton, because he didn't want to look ridiculous. Andrés Murillo, because he believed that it was a Yankee scheme to keep the brain, and he didn't want any problems. And Debayle, because he thought they had secretly returned it to Rubén's widow."

"Everything neatly sewn up," Erwin said.

"I've seen the brain's burial place," Rigoberto said. "Chiron showed it to me."

"Where is it?" asked the goldsmith Segismundo, standing up as if ready to go look for it.

"In the courtyard of the brothel, where they buried the fetuses," Rigoberto said. "If anyone wants to go see it some day, there's a rosebush on top of it."

"A spy for the Somozas, gravedigger for the most portentous brain of all time!" Segismundo said, sitting down again.

"And there in the brothel, I saw the funeral gondola, too," Rigoberto said.

"What funeral gondola?" Norberto asked him.

"The settee shaped like a gondola where they put the brain for viewing," Rigoberto said. "*The Alligator Woman* has it in a room where she keeps old knick-knacks. I offered to buy it from her, and she said yes."

"And what do you want that settee for?" Captain Prío asked.

"I don't know," Rigoberto said. "It's a relic. When I've got the hundred pesos she wants for it, I'll buy it from her. I'd also like to buy the Ingersol watch that marked the hour of truth, but that is really hard to get."

"*The Alligator Woman* doesn't have it," Norberto says.

"No," Rigoberto says. "Moralitos has it. Rubén bought the watch in New York, the 21st of January, 1915. It's marked in his ledger book."

"A drunk who kept a ledger book?" Erwin says.

"Here are the expenses I copied from that day," Rigoberto says: "*Newspapers and crackers: 50 cents. Trolley: 10 cents. Lunch: 70 cents. Two dozen Gillette blades: 80 cents. An Ingersol watch: one dollar.*"

"A really cheap watch," Norberto says.

"And a bottle of whiskey, who knows how much," Erwin says.

"That day there was no bottle," Rigoberto says, closing his journal. "Whenever the bottle appears on the list, it says: *M H D.*"

"And what does that mean?" Norberto asks.

"*M H D* means *Mi Hermana Doliente*," Rigoberto says. *My Suffering Sister.*

"Don't tell me that a hired killer like Moralitos is a devotee of Rubén's!" the goldsmith Segismundo says.

"That watch is the cause of his longlasting quarrel with Colonel Maravilla," Rigoberto says. "Moralitos won it from him playing poker. The next day Maravilla regretted having bet it, ordered him as his subordinate to return it to him, and when Moralitos refused, he sent him to Managua in handcuffs, for sedition."

"That was when Somoza, his baptismal godfather, sent him to the Canal Zone for special training, to distance him from the quarrel," Captain Prío says.

"What I can't figure out, my dear poet, is why you so often frequent *The Alligator Woman*'s place," Segismundo says to Rigoberto, looking at him inquisitively.

"I only went there once because I had to pawn something," Rigoberto says. "My mother took sick, and I needed money."

"You told us you went to the brothel to drop off a letter," Erwin says.

"I forgot about that," Rigoberto says. "Twice, then."

"And what was it you pawned there?" Norberto asks him.

"Yes," Erwin says. "What was it?"

"Whatever it might be, *The Alligator Woman* is an honorable person," Rigoberto says. "Whatever you pawn there is quite safe."

"*The Alligator Woman,* honorable!" says Segismundo, and laughs a disdainful laugh.

"The day after tomorrow, the 21st, my time is up," Rigoberto says. "That day, before nightfall, I'll go to get back what I pawned."

"I wouldn't put any crazy thing past you," Erwin says, looking somber.

"Nothing crazy," Rigoberto says. "Just a matter of necessity."

A Prodigious and Fatal Destiny

In the almost noiseless and desolate afternoon, Rigoberto approaches the Pacific Railroad Station, his portfolio under his arm like any old bill collector for caskets bought on the installment plan. A hot breeze sweeps small whirlwinds of garbage from the Mercadito into the station entrance; there are no customers or vendors in the market at this hour of the day, the stools of the fried-food eateries are stacked on the tabletops, the Avenida Debayle is empty of traffic, and San Juan Park behind him is completely quiet.

Ovidio Parajón, comb behind his ear, is leaning against the door of his barbershop, The Flowers of Cytherea, perusing the pages of an old edition of *Screen*. Rigoberto is happy to see him because he lacks the details of the *toilette* for Rubén's dead body, and is about to engage him in conversation when he becomes aware of a tenor voice in the distance, which swells like a wave in the afternoon sun, the crest unfurling in a plume of flashing sound, ready to crash at any moment and flood the soporific air. Recognizing the severity of the threat, the barber abandons the doorway and runs inside to protect the mirror, but it's too late. Shattered by the powerful wave that has swept through his shop, it smashes to the floor along with all the hair clippings, while the wave crashes on through all the houses in the neighborhood, pounding the cupboards, destroying plates and glasses that explode into an endless spray, knocking down pots and pans that hit the floor with a dull clatter.

Jorge Negrete, dressed as Prince Fedor Sergeievich, comes out of a toilet at the far end of the courtyard across the street, still singing, and he goes to wash his hands at the sink while the air continues to resound to his song. From there he greets Rigoberto with a wink. The old Oldsmobile,

235

loudspeakers on top to blare out commercials, is visible under a zinc-roofed lean-to among the gamecock cages.

Ovidio Parajón is sobbing again over his mirror and sweeps up the pieces along with the hair clippings, and even though he forgives the offender each time because he himself suffers from the same passion for singing, such entertainment ends up costing him a bundle. And now Rigoberto, not wasting any time, jots down everything Ovidio remembers and dictates to him while he is sweeping: *he waited for the body to be brought back from the morgue, now dispossessed of its brain. They left him completely alone to do his work. He trimmed hair and beard with Spanish Fígaro-brand scissors, making sure to hide the sutures on the forehead, and as he combed he dabbed on some perfumed hair lotion, softened in camphorated alcohol; he dyed the white strands of hair with a charcoal color pomade, applied with a new toothbrush, then used a makeup brush to powder lips and cheeks with Belle Femme rouge, a French import; he put mother-of-pearl polish on his fingernails. With a barber's whisk he put lavender talcum powder on hands and neck. The roosters were crowing by the time he finished. People came in to see his work and were amazed. They all asked for locks of hair as a remembrance, which he gave them. Debayle, more than a little upset over the theft of the brain, looked crestfallen.*

Rigoberto puts his journal back in his portfolio and now he does go across the street in search of *Jorge Negrete* who, carrying a roll of toilet paper under his arm, has just climbed the steps to the porch door to enter his office at Radio Darío, part of his own home. He's waiting there for Rigoberto to give him the bill for the advertising expenses, typed out on the typewriter that has broken down so often it works with its guts exposed. His top hat and baton props are resting on the desk.

Cordelio is supposed to arrive from El Sauce on the five o'clock train. The Alka-Seltzer electric clock on the office wall shows it's already 5:10, and no one has yet heard the train whistle blow as it nears the station.

"Tomorrow, when we count the money, you'll be the first to get paid," Rigoberto says, returning the papers to him. "The box office will bring in more than enough to put up two statues."

"Another Judas play, only instead of Nazarene robes, the actors will be in swallowtails." Behind Rigoberto's shoulder, Cordelio's voice sounds as he comes in carrying a canvas bag. The bag looks very light.

Jorge Negrete leaps to his feet and is seized by a fit of coughing which turns into a nervous laugh.

"Brave I'm not, brother, just look how I'm trembling," he says, and holds out his hands for Cordelio to see how they're shaking.

"I hope you're not going to chase me from your house out of fear," Cordelio says, setting the bag down on the floor.

"This is a public place, people come in that I don't even know," *Jorge Negrete* says, who, unable to quiet his hands, finally puts them in his pants pockets.

"You told me on the boat that if I needed you, to look you up," Cordelio says. "You offered me your house as a hideout. Was that the liquor talking?"

"In this house? And what about María Félix? María Félix gets nervous at the drop of a hat," *Jorge Negrete* says, and he laughs again, uneasily.

"She's going to be in *Tovarich*, too," Rigoberto informs him.

"If she's brave enough to go on stage, she's not going to get scared just seeing me," Cordelio says. "Besides, there's no need to tell her who I am."

"Are you asking me for a place to sleep? Seriously?" *Jorge Negrete* asks him. "Because, if you're in León, it can't be for anything that's legit."

"I came to have a talk with Somoza, to see if he'll give me a pardon," Cordelio says. "I can't stand it anymore, going around with a fake name and hiding out."

"In that case, nobody better than your father the priest," *Jorge Negrete* says. "What could be better than waiting for Somoza's answer in a priest's house?"

"Are you crazy? After I ran off with Diana Coronado?" Cordelio says.

"No, brother, don't be afraid to go see him," *Jorge Negrete* says. "Yesterday, Thursday of Holy Week, after mass, he spoke to me about you, with tears in his eyes."

"Tears of rage," Cordelio says.

"Of forgiveness, because he's around National Guardsmen, and he knows they can come for you to kill you," *Jorge Negrete* says.

"He's got to offer you the same forgiveness because half the money in the alms box was yours," Cordelio says.

"Even when you're in mortal danger, you still can't stop slandering people," *Jorge Negrete* says, rubbing his still sweaty palms on the lapels of his tuxedo.

"Do you always help him say mass on Thursdays of Holy Week?" Cordelio asks him.

"It's a habit that stuck with me," *Jorge Negrete* says.

"Do you remember when you showed up barefoot at the rectory in El Sauce, with your feet full of chiggers?" Cordelio reminds him.

"You, a ward of the church, didn't want to let me through the door," *Jorge Negrete* says.

"From then on my father the priest sinned more with cockfighting than with women. The only thing I had to seduce him with was my Victrola," Cordelio says.

"You were stupid to be afraid of me. You can see how well we both made out," *Jorge Negrete* says, aimlessly opening and closing the drawer of his desk.

"But seeing you with your gamecock cages and your knives hanging round your neck, I thought to myself: Here's the one who's come to take your place, Cordelio."

"Let's stop all this gibberish," *Jorge Negrete* says, looking at the door. "María Félix could be here at any moment with my coffee."

"And you, poet," Cordelio says to Rigoberto. "Can't you find me a place to hide for tonight?"

"Well, that's not so easy," Rigoberto says. "But I'll see what I can do."

"Don't even think about putting him up with Rafa Parrales, that would be like sending him straight into the hands of Colonel Melisandro Maravilla."

"You run me out of your house, and yet you care where I go," Cordelio says.

"Aren't we brothers?" *Jorge Negrete* replies.

"I'll leave this bag with you, while I look for a hideout," Cordelio says."

"No, brother, take your bag with you," *Jorge Negrete* says.

"Don't bust my balls, it's the least you can do for me," Cordelio says, and he puts the bag under the desk.

Outside in the courtyard, the light seems too intense to them, almost blinding, even though it is nearly dusk. It's already past 5:00.

"Did you come by train? I didn't hear any whistle," Rigoberto says.

"They stopped the trains today," Cordelio says. "The only one that's running left early with the demonstrators. I had to come in a cattle truck."

"Moralitos is on your tail," Rigoberto says.

"I know," Cordelio says. "All the heads of the cattlemen's associations are going around from ranch to ranch with my picture, asking about me. I was asked to leave two of the places where I was hiding. Out of fear."

"And the men?" Rigoberto asks him.

"I haven't heard anything," Cordelio says. "But I got the pistols. They're there in the bag."

"What kind of pistols?" Rigoberto asks.

"Old ones, ranch guns," Cordelio says. "It's what I was able to find. But they'll do."

"If the men don't show up, we won't have anyone to give them to, anyway," Rigoberto says.

"We'll have to look for other men," Cordelio says. "There's still time."

"No, there's no time. Better call off the business with the liquor warehouse," Rigoberto says.

"Besides that, I got sick," Cordelio says. "Been suffering from malaria. Even now, I'm burning up with fever."

"You look it," Rigoberto says, touching his cheek with his hand.

"I know what you're thinking," Cordelio says.

"What am I thinking?" Rigoberto asks.

"That I'm not even worth shit," Cordelio says.

"It's not your fault," Rigoberto says.

"I was desperate to get here, even thought about getting on the train with the demonstrators," Cordelio says. "I would have come into León, shouting Viva Somoza."

"No need to push your luck that far," Rigoberto says.

"I already did," Cordelio says. "I showed up at the rectory to ask my father for a place to stay. He's putting me up for tonight."

"It's a risk. But if he doesn't turn you in, it's a safe place," Rigoberto says.

"I've got no other," Cordelio says.

"Erwin still needs a lookout C for Calle Real," Rigoberto says. "You'll have to be that person now. Go find him."

"Erwin's really going to be pissed with all my screw-ups," Cordelio says.

"Nothing to be gained by getting pissed," Rigoberto says. "I've got to be going now. All I have left to do is reclaim the little animal."

"Reclaim it?" Cordelio asks.

"I pawned the revolver at a brothel," Rigoberto says.

"At a brothel!" Cordelio exclaims. "You could have asked Erwin for a loan."

"The cheerful Mennen Powder baby had his Heidelberg printing press confiscated," Rigoberto says. "The magistrate showed up the day before yesterday with a bunch of lawyers and secretaries, and it was taken away in a truck. The press operators are playing baseball in the street."

"And in which whorehouse did you pawn it?" Cordelio asks him.

"At Baby Dolls, *The Alligator Woman*'s place," Rigoberto says. "And it wasn't for the money, but to keep it in a safe hiding place."

"At *The Alligator Woman*'s?" Cordelio says. "That's a safe place for sure!"

"Like your father's rectory," Rigoberto says.

A reporter from the news program *Evening Flash*, as thin as a stick on a skyrocket and barely eighteen years old, enters the courtyard on his bike and greets Rigoberto from a distance. He leaves the bike and comes over, laughing.

"Take a look at this hot news, poet," he says, pulling out his notebook from his pants' pocket:

An individual named Manfredo Casaya, known as The Lion of Nemea, *showed up very drunk this afternoon at the offices of the daily newspaper* The Chronicle, *demanding to speak to the editor, Dr. Rafael Parrales, from whom he intended to extract a sum of money; it was explained to him that he had not returned as yet from the lunch in honor of the First Lady, which was being held at the home of the aforementioned's widowed mother, doña Casimira Debayle. He didn't believe the information they gave him and tried to get in all the way to the bedroom to look for him, shouting obscenities against Dr. Parrales the whole time, accusing him of an unmentionable relationship with Norberto N., well known in the city as the manager of León's professional baseball team. Faced with such an attitude, the printing pressman, Kid Dynamite, confronted him. The shirtless madman struck the boxer in the mouth, and when he saw him bathed in blood, fled on foot.*

"And you're going to report that on the news?" Rigoberto asks him.

"Without mentioning the matter of the obscenities," the reporter answers, still laughing, and he races up the stairs, two steps at a time.

"The great wrestler finally put an opponent on the mat," says Cordelio.

"You'd better get over to Erwin's," Rigoberto says. "Now it's two lookouts we need."

"Let's go together," Cordelio says. "And we've got to find Norberto. If we cancel this business, it's got to be amongst all of us."

"Cancel the business? That's crazy," Rigoberto says.

"And what if you leave the revolver where it is, and we use one of the ones I brought?" Cordelio says.

"One of those clunkers? And what about the jewel?" Rigoberto asks, patting his portfolio.

"I'm just saying not to keep taking risks," Cordelio says.

"Risks!" Rigoberto says, and he laughs. "I still need to get the invitation. They'll be demanding it at the door."

Now they've fallen silent, with Cordelio restless, as if in a cage.

"There's something I have to do," he says.

"There's nothing to do but leave me to do my part," Rigoberto says. "We'll say goodbye here."

Rigoberto walks to the small square at the railroad station, wakes up the taxi driver who's asleep in the back seat of the only cab in sight, and gets in. The taxi sounds as if it's dropping old cans behind it as it goes rumbling along the streets of San Felipe in the Ermita de Dolores barrio on the outskirts of León where the streets turn into ravines. It's already dark when the taxi stops in front of the gateway to the playground at Baby Dolls. Rigoberto asks the driver to wait for him, and he turns off his headlights.

The mud wall of the house has lost some of its daub. Under the eaves, almost rubbed out, a drawing of a woman in high heels, her overly small head thrown back, sipping from a champagne glass held by no one, more as if she were drowning in bubbles that look like soap suds. The string of light bulbs along the eaves illuminate nothing with their rotten-fruit glow except the stench of garbage and the urine that comes seeping out from under the closed doors.

"Well, if it isn't *Bienvenido Granda*," he hears as he crosses the playground.

Sergeant Domitilo Paniagua, dressed in civilian clothes, wearing a *Five Stars* baseball cap, has just come from taking a pee, and steps in front of him.

"A sight for sore eyes, sergeant," Rigoberto says, putting his hand up to his temple as though it were a salute.

"When I saw you from a distance, I thought: what a small world, here's *Bienvenido Granda*, the man who wrote that letter for me," Sergeant Domitilo Paniagua says.

Rigoberto wants to continue making his way to the house, but the sergeant grabs him by the arm.

"You put some outrageous things in that letter that you didn't read to me," he says.

"What outrageous things?" Rigoberto asks him.

"All that nonsense about the Martians that you and I had talked about," Sergeant Domitilo Paniagua says, and he squeezes him arm harder. "You said that Minerva Sarraceno should find out if I was like the Martians, without any little pecker or anything."

"When she read the letter in my presence and came to that part, she died laughing," Rigoberto says.

"And you were laughing too, at my expense," says Sergeant Domitilo Paniagua.

"I had to gain Minerva Sarraceno's trust," Rigoberto says, not attempting to break his grip.

"Did you want to steal her from me with your jokes?" Sergeant Domitilo Paniagua asks.

"What makes you think that!" Rigoberto exclaims. "The thing is, I like coming here."

"And what does that have to do with anything?" Sergeant Domitilo Paniagua says.

"What could be better than a friendship like hers when you're in a bind?" Rigoberto says. "When I came back the next time, since I didn't have anything to pay with, she was sweet enough to suggest to *The Alligator Woman* that she allow me to pawn something instead."

"You should never have written those things with my signature on it," Sergeant Domitilo Paniagua says, letting go of him.

"Tell me one thing," Rigoberto says. "Did Minerva Sarraceno give you a second look or not?"

"She's just become my girlfriend," Sergeant Domitilo Paniagua says without changing his gruff tone of voice.

"So?" Rigoberto asks, and the sergeant no longer detains him. But he catches up to him at the door.

"That letter," says Sergeant Domitilo Paniagua. "Minerva Sarraceno gave it back to me, and I've burned it. If I find out that you're going around talking about it, I'll fuck you up good."

And he takes Rigoberto by the arm again, to lead him inside. The metal-top tables are empty except for Sergeant Domitilo Paniagua's, where there's a solitary bottle of beer and a glass with some residual foam. On the folding chairs up against the wall, three or four women in rubber sandals, with a trace of makeup, are sitting quietly. Rigoberto takes his journal out of the portfolio and makes a few notes: *it's a long time since any of them has worn a doll dress and a straw hat. They look more like maids who have finished their day's work. How long did that style last after Somoza changed the name of the brothel and did away with the white tunics? Ask* The Alligator Woman.

"Are you by any chance going to write another letter for me, like that last one?" Sergeant Domitilo Paniagua says.

"I'm taking notes for an investigation," Rigoberto says.

"Investigation? Investigations are my department," Sergeant Domitilo Paniagua says.

It looks as if there's no one behind the bar, except for some movement under the counter. And when Minerva Sarraceno straightens up, she laughs heartily simply at seeing Rigoberto.

The Alligator Woman wasn't in the habit of pawning things. But Minerva Sarraceno had accompanied him when he made his request, biting her handkerchief as she listened to him tell his sad love story one more time, backing up his promise that as soon as he paid off his debts and retrieved the pistol, he'd return to El Salvador to take his revenge. And afterwards, he had them laughing with the story of the invincible wrestler and the labors of a master jeweler who was a stud and nearly lost his life in combat; they knew the wrestler, *The Alligator Woman's* pal from the Subtiava barrio, a bum all his life. And they also knew Maestro Segismundo; he visited Baby Dolls, but early in the afternoon so he wouldn't be seen by any of the other customers.

Without moving from behind the counter, Minerva Sarraceno looks from one to the other of them and laughs harder. And still laughing, she gets two beers from the bottom of the cooler and takes them over to them.

"And your Judas play with the Italian, what became of that?" Sergeant Domitilo Paniagua asks Rigoberto.

"It wasn't a Judas play, but *Tovarich* that Ranucci finally staged," Rigoberto explains.

"So, the Italian was happy in the end," Sergeant Domitilo Paniagua says.

"That's how it worked out," Rigoberto says. "And I became an actor."

"You're a loafer," Sergeant Domitilo Paniagua says.

"You haven't told me what brings you to León, sergeant," Rigoberto says then.

"They recruited me for the security detail, for *The Man*'s visit," Sergeant Domitilo Paniagua says.

"And where do they have you posted?" Rigoberto asks.

"I was at the door of the Teatro González for the morning watch," Sergeant Domitilo Paniagua says. "Later tonight they've got me posted at the door of The Workers' Club for the party. I'm under Lt. Moralitos's command."

Rigoberto is about to pour the beer into his glass and stops in midair.

"I thought the security forces from Managua were going to be at the doors," he says, and then he fills his glass.

"The guards at the doors are the responsibility of Fifth Company," Sergeant Domitilo Paniagua says. "That was Lt. Moralitos's decision. Since we're from here, we know everybody."

"But sergeant, you're not stationed in León. Do you know people so well that no one can get by you?" Rigoberto asks.

"I can't speak for the others. But the thing with me is I have a knack for faces," Sergeant Domitilo Paniagua says. "You, for example. I'd recognize you in the pitch-dark."

"You mean to say that you wouldn't let me in at all if I wanted to attend that party," Rigoberto says.

"Not even if you changed into a monkey," Sergeant Domitilo Paniagua says.

Rigoberto sips his beer, and suddenly puts the glass on the table.

"I've got to take my fiancée to that party, Sergeant," he says. "But I don't have an invitation."

"If you don't have an invitation, you're screwed," Sergeant Domitilo Paniagua says. "Each person has to turn in his invitation at the door. The invitation has a number, and whoever comes in has to be registered on a list, with his number next to it."

"Who came up with that lamebrain scheme?" Rigoberto asks.

"Lt. Moralitos," Sergeant Domitilo Paniagua replies.

"How odd that a nothing lieutenant can give orders to you, commanded by a colonel," Rigoberto says.

"Moralitos isn't just any lieutenant," says Sergeant Domitilo Paniagua. "He answers to some Yankee. And the Yankee hands down orders to him and no one else."

"What's more, he's happy he can go over Colonel Maravilla's head because of the way he held him back," Rigoberto says.

"Oh, yeah," says Sergeant Domitilo Paniagua. "The argument over a famous watch."

"All right, so let's see," Rigoberto says. "I show up with my fiancée. There's a commotion at the door, everybody wanting to get in. And then, you give me the high sign, and let us pass."

"How come you won't have an invitation if you're from a newspaper supporting *The Man?*" Sergeant Domitilo Paniagua asks.

"It's shameful, but the editor, who's a real fag, gave them all out to his lovers," Rigoberto says.

"What a degenerate!" Sergeant Domitilo Paniagua says.

"And so I was left without an invitation. And my fiancée pestering me because we can't go to the party," Rigoberto says.

"The problem is that Lt. Moralitos will be supervising things at the door," Sergeant Domitilo Paniagua says.

"There are three doors," Rigoberto says. "As soon as he leaves the door where you're posted, you give me the high sign."

"It looks like you've studied the whole thing," Sergeant Domitilo Paniagua says.

"Necessity is the mother of invention," Rigoberto says.

Sergeant Domitilo Paniagua stands up.

"You're not to tell anyone that I did you this favor." he says, admonishing him.

"Have another beer," Rigoberto says.

"I'd like to, but I can't; they're waiting for me at headquarters. They're going to give me a coat and tie," Sergeant Domitilo Paniagua says.

"Well, I'm going to have another one, so here's to my fiancée until *The Alligator Woman* returns and I pay back my loan," Rigoberto says.

"What was it you pawned here?" Sergeant Domitilo Paniagua asks him, suddenly very interested.

Rigoberto slowly wipes the suds from his moustache with his fingers.

"A revolver," Rigoberto says.

"A revolver?" says Sergeant Domitilo Paniagua, frowning under his baseball cap.

"It belongs to somebody else, and I should have returned it to him a long time ago; it belongs to that fag editor at the newspaper," Rigoberto says.

"And what did you need with a gun?" Sergeant Domitilo Paniagua asks him.

"That Protestant preacher who was with me on the boat sent me a letter threatening to kill me because of a woman I stole from him in El Salvador," Rigoberto says. "He didn't know anything about us, but they wrote to him from his congregation there, telling him that she was going to have my child. That's why I asked to borrow the gun."

"And did you finally get things straightened out with him?" Sergeant Domitilo Paniagua asks, sitting down again.

"No. Somebody bumped him off at a cockfight in Somoto, far from here, last Sunday," Rigoberto says.

"Well then, your troubles are over, and so are my doubts," Sergeant Domitilo Paniagua says.

"What doubts are you talking about," says Rigoberto.

"Whether the man in this photo is the same as that preacher of yours," Sergeant Domitilo Paniagua says, and he pulls a photo out of his shirt pocket.

It's a very faded photo of Cordelio, taken years ago at a table in a bar somewhere because you can see the glasses and bottles in the foreground, part of a naked shoulder, and a glimpse of a woman's head.

"He looks like the preacher, but it's not him," Rigoberto says, handing back the photo.

"The man in this picture is Cordelio Selva," Sergeant Domitilo Paniagua says.

"I've heard a lot of talk about him," Rigoberto says.

"They sent me this photo the day after you got off the boat. What a coincidence," Sergeant Domitilo Paniagua says. "Did I tell you at that time that we were already looking for Cordelio Selva? That I didn't have his photo?"

"I don't remember any of that," Rigoberto says.

"Well, once I had his photo it was like a thorn in my side," Sergeant Domitilo Paniagua says. "Wondering about the likeness."

"That surprises me, Sergeant, because you can recognize a face even in the dark," Rigoberto says.

"You can imagine how important he was if they were circulating his mimeographed file along with his picture," Sergeant Domitilo Paniagua says.

"What did the file say about him?" Rigoberto asks.

It said that Cordelio Selva drifted here and there engaged in Communist activities in the Caribbean, and that he could enter Nicaragua secretly at any time, and that he went around with a Victrola and records in a sack, visiting the camps in the cotton regions and the shacks on the banana plantations where the workers slept, charging each couple a peso to play them one song to dance to; all this was after he had fled the deadly bullets that rained down on the people of Mina La India in 1937, after his father, Euclides Selva, a storekeeper, had incited the miners to rise up; then one night in 1940 during a religious procession in El Sauce, Father Olimpo Lozano took Cordelio in out of pity after he had been badly beaten up in some doorway while being robbed of his Victrola and a bunch of records; and just so you can see how evil his heart is, he ran away again during another procession with all the alms of the penitents of the Church of Santo Cristo de Esquípulas.

"Everyone knows that he ran off with a woman that the priest had been keeping," Rigoberto says.

"If that's true, they didn't put it in the report," says Sergeant Domitilo Paniagua.

"But surely they must have put it in the report that Colonel Maravilla was the one who put down the uprising at Mina La India."

"Of course," says Sergeant Domitilo Paniagua. "And I'll tell you a secret."

"Tell me," Rigoberto says, edging closer.

"Colonel Maravilla is scared to death of this man because he believes that he's going to kill him one day," Sergeant Domitilo Paniagua says. "All because of what they did to his father, who was the one behind the strike: they strung him up by his feet and hung him upside down in a well, pretending they were going to drown him, and the rope broke. That's what happened."

"And Colonel Maravilla was there?" Rigoberto asks him.

"Was he there? He's the one who tied the rope around his feet and hung him upside down in the well," says Sergeant Domitilo Paniagua. "He wasn't a colonel yet, a captain at most. *The Man* himself had sent him from Managua to put down that strike."

"All right, if I happen to come across anything about this Cordelio Selva, I'll let you know, sergeant," Rigoberto says.

"There's a reward," Sergeant Domitilo Paniagua informs him.

"In that case, we'll go halves," Rigoberto says.

"I hope that pervert doesn't end up shooting one of his lovers when you return his pistol to him," Sergeant Domitilo Paniagua says. "Those quarrels between fags can be bitter."

"It's a pistol that probably won't even fire," Rigoberto then says.

"If it didn't work, they wouldn't have given you anything for it here," Sergeant Domitilo Paniagua says. "*The Alligator Woman*'s too sharp for that."

"It's worth something because it's a historic relic. It belonged to the learned Debayle," Rigoberto says.

"The learned who?" Sergeant Domitilo Paniagua asks.

"General Somoza's father-in-law, the very doctor who operated on *The Alligator Woman*; a sex-change operation, to make her into a man," Rigoberto says. "The pistol was a gift from doña Casimira to that fag Parrales. He's her godson."

"That's nonsense. Sure as shooting, *The Alligator Woman* was born that way, with that little dick of hers and all the rest," Sergeant Domitilo Paniagua says. "And make sure you don't get any ideas about bringing that gun with you to the party, even if it doesn't work."

"I'm going straight from here to return it to its owner," Rigoberto says.

No sooner has Sergeant Domitilo Paniagua disappeared into the shadows of the courtyard than someone, having entered without Rigoberto hearing him, makes his way over to him among the tables. It's Chiron; he's come for dinner, as he does every evening, with a book under his arm as always.

Minerva Sarraceno says she won't be long, she'll bring him his dinner, and he gestures to Rigoberto, asking him what he's doing there at that hour. And what about the play? Today is the 21st. There's plenty of time for everything, Rigoberto says, and Chiron sits down beside him. What are you reading? Chiron is reading none other than *Tovarich*, an edition published in Buenos Aires by Emecé Publishers; it's a so-so play, well, less than so-so, he indicates, gesturing with his hand.

And Rigoberto pulls out his journal from the portfolio. This operation which the learned Debayle performed on *The Alligator Woman*, did it turn out all right or didn't it? he asks Chiron. Not in the least. The artificial penis got infected and ended up pulling away from the sutures. Chiron makes a gesture as if removing something useless from between his legs: from that moment on, the pee poured out of her as if it were coming through a broken pipe. Debayle had hired Maestro Cisneros to take a photograph of her before the operation, naked, and he was going to take another one following the operation when the scars had healed. But there wasn't to be a second photograph. He found the one taken before the operation between the pages of a surgical textbook after Debayle's death, before they cleared everything out of the Maison de Santé, and he kept it. She has her head covered with a black hood like the executioner in a novel. He can't show it to him. No one has ever seen that picture, and *The Alligator Woman* doesn't know he has it. Don't write anything down about that. Chiron places his hand on the open pages of the journal.

Outside in the street comes the sound of a noisy motor from a truck that's approaching and then stops, and there are voices, the voice of Catalina Baldelomar breaking into guffaws, and then the truck starts up again and pulls away. And the combative voice of *The Lion of Nemea*, drunk as a skunk.

The Alligator Woman enters with her entourage, and the girls, all smiles, get up from their seats to greet her in silent jubilation; Minerva Sarraceno also approaches, but it's Chiron she's focused on as he celebrates her arrival with an elaborate display of mime. Catalina Baldelomar recognizes Rigoberto, pushes the chairs aside with her big buttocks, and goes over to give him a festive embrace while her brother *Stone Face* Diómedes Baldelomar takes up a guard position next to the courtyard door, smoking a Valencia cigarette. And *The Lion of Nemea*, frightened when he spots Rigoberto, but pretending not to know him, heads straight for the bar and asks for a drink, pounding the top of the counter with his fist. Minerva Sarraceno isn't impressed and walks right past him on her way to the kitchen to get Chiron's dinner, giving the loudmouth a hard look.

Rigoberto, in turn, pretends not to know *The Lion of Nemea*. He doesn't have the inclination or the time to do battle with him. It's after 7:30. He sees *The Alligator Woman* go down the hallway; he follows her and catches up with her as she is unlocking the padlock to her room.

"I've come to pick up my article," he says, counting out all the bills at once.

"What's the hurry?" she asks, trying another key.

She knows quite well what his hurry is. To settle a score. His Salvadoran fiancée's uncle, the one he's going to kill, had tricked her into going for a ride one Sunday in his car to Santa Tecla, invited her to have a drink at a bar, then drove her, already tipsy, to an isolated factory of his that made imitation English sauce under the pretext of showing her how the fake Perrins Sauce was made, with soy sauce, pepper from Chiapas, and tamarind honey, and there, among the kettles and jars, he took her by force.

"I want to make sure I'm on board *La Salvadorita* tomorrow," Rigoberto says in reply to *The Alligator Woman's* question.

"Those kinds of debts are collected on the spot, or they're best forgotten," she says. "You already had your chance."

"They're forgotten until they're repaid," he says.

"So hot to kill a man," she then says. "And there's no guarantee you won't get killed too in this escapade."

She locks the padlock again on the bolt of the now-open door. She turns around and removes her dark glasses. Rigoberto had never seen those eyes, so little accustomed to light, which even in the half-light of the hallway can't stop blinking. Little rat eyes that shine in a milky halo like copper coins.

"Tell Minerva to give you the pistol," she says, handing him the bunch of keys. "You can pay her."

Then she goes into her room and, without turning on the light, calls to him when he's already on his way down the hall.

"You've got to be careful you don't get mixed up with any lushes like my neighbor's stepson," she says. "From the moment he climbed onto the truck with the rest of us, coming back from Plaza Jerez, he was blabbering about I don't know what plan for today, the twenty-first. He says that he's part of it and that you are, too."

"The only plan that I'm a part of is promoting *Tovarich*, a stage play, which Chiron's carrying under his arm," Rigoberto says. "We're putting it on today, the twenty-first. And tomorrow I'll be out of here."

"Go have them get your pistol, then," she says from out of the darkness.

"What's that story I've heard, that the year after Rubén Darío's death, the girls here began dressing up like dolls?" Rigoberto asks. "Wearing flared dresses and straw hats."

"Don't go believing those stories," she says and turns on the light.

Stone Face Diómedes Baldelomar is the only one left in the room, still standing by the door that leads out to the courtyard. Chiron left after he ate, and Catalina Baldelomar has also left to get dressed for the party, with her gaggle of followers too. All the better, he tells himself when he sees *The Lion of Nemea* has also left. And now that he has the gun back, he walks past *Stone Face* Diómedes Baldelomar, who doesn't return his greeting, makes his way to the toilet stall at the back of the courtyard and, sitting on the seat under the light of the yellow bulb screwed into a socket in the ceiling, he inserts the silver bullet into the cylinder. Then tosses the lead bullet and the ring box down into the hole.

Standing in the dark courtyard, he sees *The Alligator Woman* in the distance, counting receipts at the bar with Minerva Sarraceno. She's already put on the outfit she's wearing to the party: a checkered shirt, a tie painted with a quetzal whose tail is made of real feathers, a Borsalino felt hat with a red hat band and, pinned to the lapel of her sport coat, a campaign button with Somoza's picture on it.

And then he sees her stealthily circle the bar and reach out to stroke the back of Minerva Sarraceno's head. She shivers from the touch, then turns to embrace her, ardently rubbing herself against *The Alligator Woman*'s body. While they're caressing, neither seems to notice that *Stone Face* Diómedes Baldelomar is still standing at the door, expressionless, Valencia cigarette in his mouth.

And it's not because her soulmate is watching her that *The Alligator Woman* covers her face with her Borsalino hat, and Minerva Sarraceno's, too, now that she's kissing her without removing her dark glasses, and she kisses her and puts her hand between her breasts. Rigoberto goes out to get back in his taxi.

May Pubescent *Canéforas* Drink To You

Captain Prío peers out into the plaza one last time. In an unenthusiastic encore, the one-time Marshal of Latrines has again appeared on the balcony in response to the scattered round of Vivas rising from the shadows, the First Lady by his side. Both greet the sparse gathering with a mechanical wave of hands, as if they were really standing before a packed arena, and then they disappear, arms around each other, behind the illuminated windows.

It's almost 7:30. And while the First Lady puts herself in the hands of the hairdresser in her retinue, who dresses in white like a nurse, Somoza has time to lie down for a while, fully dressed. Without a sound, his aide-de-camp Colonel Lira carefully lays out on the back of the velvet sofa, part of Colonel Melisandro Maravilla's formal set, his dark blue cashmere suit, made to order by Fine Suits by Gómez; his starched white shirt, impeccably ironed; a tie with a pattern of green geometric diamonds and his sanforized *Fruit of the Loom* underpants; and at the foot of the sofa, his shiny black patent-leather shoes, the shoes of a magician or a dancer, and inside each one, a dark-blue nylon sock.

It's after 8:00 when he gets up, having managed only a short nap. Sitting on the bed, he looks through the pleated folder with the reports that arrived that day from Managua via motor express, and with a blue-and-red double-tipped pencil, he marks the margins of things that get his attention. Then, wearing a striped terrycloth bathrobe, he gets up and goes into the bathroom to shower.

The bathroom is far down the hall from the makeshift room where he's been resting, and I ought to remind you that the rooms, private quarters, reception area, and all the other rooms being used by the president are really public offices that have been cleared of their desks and filing cabinets.

Certain difficulties arise (previously experienced, if you recall, by Lucio Ranucci) because once he's soaped up, he turns the shower on only to discover there's no water; and naked, covered in soap suds, he has to go to the door to yell to Colonel Maravilla about his predicament. Security agents race downstairs to get the Fire Department to come to the rescue: a couple of buckets of water taken from a water tanker is the only way he can finish his shower.

In the reception room, where there are open suitcases in every corner, thermos bottles, Thompson submachine guns, rifles, ammunition belts and small boxes of ammunition, the high-ranking officers in their white dress uniforms laze about in wicker rocking chairs, already set for the party to begin. Colonel Maravilla is one of them, although he's sitting off to one side away from their conversation, the dark skin of his bald spot shining like a piece of polished leather. Colonel Justo Pastor Gonzaga (NG), the chief of staff, as chubby and pink as a plastic doll, and blind as a bat besides, and Colonel Heriberto Guardado (NG), Somoza's personal physician, graying and curly-haired, and wearing thick tortoise-shell glasses, are conversing alone out on the balcony, fanning themselves with their military caps; the two of them look more like impersonations of military officers than anything else. Van Wynckle, still on his feet, not looking for a place to sit down, wearing a suit that's even more wrinkled than it was in the morning, with his crewcut and thick beads of sweat dotting the forest of bristles on his scalp, looks incongruous in this setting.

Somoza comes out from his quarters, arranging the cummerbund high above his big potbelly, his shirt pockets, as a result, practically coming down below the waist of his pants, and the fragrance of Eau de Vétiver permeates the reception room. All stand at attention until he, with the slightest of signals, orders them at ease.

That's when Colonel Lira approaches with the bulletproof vest, ready to help him into it, as if it were a royal mantle. But he waves it off, visibly annoyed.

"Mister President, I do beg you. Please, put the vest on," Van Wynckle asks him in his suave but imperious Argentine accent, staying right where he is.

"Mind your own business," Somoza says in a severe tone of voice, then he laughs, pleased with himself. The officers smile, looking at each other.

"This is my business, Mister President," Van Wynckle replies, his head tilted, his eyes half-closed.

"You're much too serious. Too serious," Somoza says, looking at the others, still amused, and he lights a cigarette.

Colonel Lira disappears with the vest. Van Wynckle pulls out his notepad, and looking at Somoza all the while, jots something down, as if he were a reporter.

"Mister President," he now says, still looking down at his pad, "*that woman* you approached outside the theater, who is she?"

Somoza looks at him surprised, as if he doesn't remember.

"He means *The Alligator Woman*, Chief," Colonel Gonzaga says from the balcony.

"Oh, that one," Somoza says, laughing. "If you want to call her a woman. It's a long story. Is there some problem with her?"

"No," Van Wynckle replies. "Simply curious. A strange woman."

"Indeed," Somoza says. "But loyal. Very loyal."

"I don't doubt it," Van Wynckle says.

"General," Colonel Gonzaga says, approaching him, leading the doctor by the arm. "Heriberto here wants to ask your permission to go to Chinandega for his daughter's fifteenth birthday party, but he doesn't dare."

"What an ass you are," Somoza says. "You already missed the first dance with her. Go on, and take her this little present from me." And he pulls out his wallet, and then a thousand-córdoba bill, bearing his own likeness.

And now the First Lady comes in, dressed in a blue taffeta gown with a sheer surplice, a sequin-embroidered hat, high-heeled shoes, also embroidered with sequins to match her purse, an emerald-studded necklace, thick gold and silver bracelets, and an ermine stole on her arm.

An old doll, the goldsmith Segismundo would say. The reason she's so weighted down by a luxury bordering on insolence is that, in the opinion of her beloved Tacho, who's an expert in dressing dolls: "Wealth is to be flaunted." The slogan is obeyed by wives and mistresses of the high-ranking officers of the National Guard every waking moment and under every circumstance, and the First Lady, despite her lineage, sets the tone for what is known as "the fashion of a Guardsman's woman": each one of them wishes to wear, on every occasion, whatever is most expensive, incongruous and gauche, including, for example, that ermine stole she'll show off at the party despite the stifling heat in León.

"And what about your bulletproof vest?" she asks, sounding authoritarian, which brings a smile of hope to Colonel Lira's face.

"I've been baking in that shit all day, and I'm not putting it back on," he says.

"We're not here for everyone to do as he pleases," she says, raising her voice.

And with a gesture of annoyance, he opens his arms for Colonel Lira to come and put the vest on him under Van Wynckle's impassive gaze.

But just then there's a commotion at the door. Moralitos strides into the room, all tensed up, fists clenched, followed by three civilian agents who appear quite calm, carrying their submachine guns with complete nonchalance.

"What's going on?" the First Lady asks while she adjusts the clasp of one of her earrings.

"I've taken Cordelio Selva prisoner," Moralitos says, clicking his heels.

"Thank God!" exclaims the First Lady, still fumbling with her earring.

Colonel Maravilla leaps from his rocker and rushes up to Moralitos. Van Wynckle, annoyed by the fuss, crosses his arms as he does every time that he's about to receive a report, but this time he takes a few steps back, ready to see how his student handles himself.

"How did it happen, son?" Somoza asks, calmly approaching him, and he leaves Colonel Lira standing behind him, with his hands extended, still holding the vest.

"He was walking by the Church of the Good Shepherd, toting a canvas bag with him, not an hour ago," Moralitos informs him. "In front of the atrium, an officer from one of the roving patrols I'd sent out earlier ordered him to halt, and all he said was: 'You got me, I'm Cordelio Selva.' And there were four pistols in the bag."

"Where do you have him?" Somoza asks.

"Down at La Veintuno jail, sir. Incommunicado," Moralitos replies.

"Leave him there, I'll take over from here," Colonel Maravilla says, and Moralitos barely glances at him.

"Don't anyone think about touching him," Somoza warns. "Take him to Managua by jeep under armed guard and hold him there for me. I'll deal with him when I return."

"How do you know he's Cordelio Selva?" Colonel Maravilla asks Moralitos.

"Because first I went to get Father Olimpo Lozano, and I didn't move the prisoner until the priest had identified him for me," Moralitos replies, but directing his response to Somoza.

"He's my chaplain," Colonel Maravilla informs Somoza.

"As well as Cordelio Selva's adoptive father," says Moralitos, and now he does turn to look at Colonel Maravilla.

"But a real Somoza loyalist," says the First Lady, who has finished fixing her earring. "He's not to blame for the misdeeds of somebody he took in out of charity."

"With all due respect, señora, I must inform you that when he had the prisoner before him, he burst into tears," Moralitos says, again clicking his heels.

"I'll answer for him," Colonel Maravilla says, containing his anger.

"I have reasons to suspect that Cordelio Selva was hiding in the rectory of the Calvario Church," Moralitos says, chewing his moustache.

"Leave the priest alone," Somoza says, and embraces Moralitos. "Congratulations, son. You've taken a weight off my shoulders."

"Just the same, put the vest on," the First Lady says.

"No, forget it," Somoza says. "You kill the dog, you kill the fleas."

"Mister President, may I however..." says Van Wynckle.

"No *howevers*," says Somoza. "And cancel all that nonsense about checking the doors at the party. Let everybody in."

"Yes, sir," Moralitos replies, coming to attention.

Cordelio Selva, a prisoner? That indeed is an unforeseen turn of events, Captain. The three weavers, because they're in a rush, got the threads mixed up, that is if they're capable of making a mistake, being blind and all. But we don't want to investigate any further at this point, lest your attention be drawn away from the issue at hand; let's leave the presidential couple heatedly arguing over the bulletproof vest and security details, family matters as far as they're concerned, and let's turn our attention to Rigoberto, who can use his master key to open the doors we have to pass through. Rigoberto, who at this hour knows nothing of Cordelio's arrest. He's also gotten dressed for the party. He has already placed the letter for his mother on the top shelf of the closet, next to the portfolio where he keeps his journal. Look for that journal, read it quickly, for tomorrow it will be gone. Just for openers: Rubén will be buried today, February 13, 1916, at the foot of the statue of Saint Paul in the cathedral, and what's more, there will be a marriage proposal during the funeral.

Night had already fallen and at each street corner the funeral procession stopped to allow the orators, standing on chairs or on tables pulled out on the sidewalks by helpful hands, to be heard high up on the balconies, draped with the national flag trimmed in mourning, while the hoarse clamor of the National Military Band's tuba could be heard several blocks away, too far back in the garish crowd to interrupt the eulogies.

The learned Debayle was waiting to make his speech on the balcony of the Maison de Santé, the last station for the funeral cortège before it turned toward the cathedral. Basket-bearing maidens in sheer tunics and golden sandals, their mouths painted vermillion, led the procession in two columns, sprinkling roses from the wicker baskets they carried on their shoulders. Rubén's body, dressed in white peblum, crowned with myrtle, was being carried on an open bier, by request of the Athenaeum of León, under the blue silk episcopal canopy with its gold tassels, raised on silver poles, which the students of Law, Medicine, and Pharmacy took turns holding up. On her brother's arm, Rosario Murillo was walking behind the bier, without anyone in the city seeming to notice her.

Behind them came the highest-ranking authorities in their formal black attire like a dense flock of buzzards—the prelates of the Church Council dragging their flowing capes of red taffeta; members of the city council bearing the city's coat of arms with the crowned lion rampant, his left paw resting on an azure globe; the societies of the learned professions in squadrons beneath their insignias; and the artisan guilds with the banners of their trades. Then, the allegorical floats teeming with little girls—Poetry: a white swan, silk reins in its beak, held by the muse Calliope;

Victory: a headless angel, the three Graces embracing one another at her feet; Fame: a Parthenon among whose columns appeared a troop of Bacchantes raising their trumpets to the sky; The Thankful Motherland: the Momotombo Volcano, fashioned out of papier-maché, with its smoking crater, and leaning against the volcano, Pallas Athena clasping a shield. And last, the common people bearing palms.

The procession finally stopped at Debayle's feet, and the din of voices slowly died away. The gaslights hanging from the eaves to illuminate the balcony reached the blue silk episcopal canopy with their glow. With the papers for his eulogy trembling in his hands and tears veiling his eyes, he began by exalting Rubén's prodigious brain, and he was about to offer the facts concerning its supernatural weight when from deep inside the Maison de Santé the distant murmur of Chiron's loud wailing reached the street.

Listen to it. Struggling to break the bonds of its restraint, his voice ceased being a murmur and flew unbounded toward the crowd, passing through courtyards and doors like a gale-force wind, moving in whirlwind fashion out to the lonely precincts of the city gathered in mourning. Debayle tried to go on reading, tried to ignore Chiron, but the gusts that seemed to be blowing from those incomprehensible wails tore the papers from his hands. No one was listening to him now, all ears tuned to that impassioned voice until it finally subsided, its fury now but a whisper. Admitting defeat, Debayle put his papers away, and the procession once more resumed its march to the cathedral.

From the top of the atrium stairs, Bishop Simeón released seven white doves, symbol of the seven theological virtues, which disappeared into the dark night. The body was now being ushered in through the main door, covered with scattered petals that were being snatched away by the crowd, on its way to the open crypt at the foot of the statue of Saint Paul, while the clamor of the crowd swelled beneath the vaulted ceiling, mixed with the thunderous sound of the cathedral choir singing *Miserere Domine* and the chords of the National Military Band playing the "Farewell" march composed by its director, Maestro Saturnino Ramos.

Not a few Canephor maidens, muses, and bacchantes had already fallen asleep in their mothers' laps, their baskets empty and the hems of their tunics soiled with dust and pigeon droppings, when someone indiscreetly approached Debayle who, quite downcast, was closely watching the work of the bricklayers. It was Anastasio. He was wearing a brown corduroy suit, not at all appropriate for a funeral.

The words exchanged between the two men as they stood next to the crypt amid the clanging of buckets of mortar, the tapping of hammers, and the scraping of trowels—quite challenging as you can see—were these:

Somoza: Doctor, will you allow me to introduce myself? I am Anastasio Somoza (smiling, he extends him his hand, there in the close quarters next to the crypt). What I did was nothing. (Accompanied by two Marines, and now it's clear that from the start he was going to charm them with his skills, he had entered the Maison de Santé in search of Chiron to silence him. One can assume that Debayle knew absolutely nothing of that frustrated attempt).

Debayle (Dryly): I don't know what you're talking about. *Pardon.* (He turns his back to him).

Somoza: I need to consult with you.

Debayle (Turning around. He looks him over): I hold my consultations in the Maison de Santé.

Somoza: Only you can cure what ails me, doctor. Salvadorita and I are in love. We love each other.

Debayle: What? (He struggles to regain his composure.) This is a funeral, *monsieur*. I beg you to get out of my sight. (The lime that the bricklayers are pouring into the mixture makes him sneeze several times.)

Somoza: I know that this is not the moment. (Solicitous, he

offers Debayle his handkerchief, which the doctor
rejects, of course, already having his own in his
hand). But as long as you say no, a death knell will
sound in my heart, just like those bells. (Sure enough,
the bells of the cathedral ring out twice as loud just
then, majestically, a signal that the crypt is about to
be sealed).

Debayle: And just who do you think you are? (And he thinks:
What duck laid this egg?).

Somoza (Wounded, he maintains his composure): I'm an
honorable young man. My father owns a coffee
plantation in San Marcos. I've studied accounting. I
can speak English. *Of course, I do.*

Debayle: Look here, if I catch you anywhere near my house,
I'll call the American military police.

Fortune, queen of capriciousness. Anastasio stayed in
León, all because he wasn't going to give up his endeavor,
and thanks to the influence of the Marines, he got the job
reading electirc meters. He made an enemy of his father who,
faced with his unexpected return, was not disposed to give
him a single dime. Every month he eagerly awaited making
his round to his sweetheart's house, placing the ladder which
he carried on his shoulder against the wall to read the meter:
climbing to the next-to-last rung, he took longer than normal
to write down the figures in his meter book, while
Salvadorita stood at the bars of her window. In this difficult
situation, they exchanged languorous looks and deep sighs;
their colloquy over, he would take his ladder and station
himself at the house next door. When Debayle found out
about these maneuvers, he arranged for his dismissal from
the Metropolitan Light & Power Company.

Anastasio went back to the Marines, his poker buddies,
and they got him the job as inspector of privies. So all at
once he could be seen carrying a bucket of creosote from
house to house and an unusually long flashlight that allowed

him to see down into the depths of the latrines. Debayle had chain-flush toilets, so in his case he didn't run the risk of the latrine marshal showing up at his residence, and he left Anastasio to himself, to carry on with that job.

Meanwhile the Holy War raged on, the calm of León's sweltering midday interrupted by sudden gunshots on street corners; and beneath the roar of all that shooting, he conceived the idea of intervening in the lawsuits that were being waged over the ownership of the Santos Lugares properties in the courts, whose louvers and desks were stained with the blood of the ferocious litigants. How? you ask. Listen to this:

Justo Pastor Gonzaga, a shyster lawyer whom he had met at the Marines' poker tables, profited by getting secret favors from the judges. And with the promise of a part of the spoils, Anastasio devoted himself to looking into those cases where one could buy a ruling without too much fuss once the weakest of the litigants had agreed to a purchase price. With what resources was he going to purchase anything? With his miserable latrine marshal's salary? No. By making counterfeit silver dollars with the minting press he had brought with him from Philadelphia in his trunk, along with the rest of his meager belongings.

And because he wanted to become rich at any cost, Justo Pastor Gonzaga took him to see *The Alligator Woman*, who wanted to be a man at any cost. And the die, along with the casting forge, the ingots of tin and copper, and the little sacks of silver filings to mint the fake coins, were transferred to a shed in the playground of The Blessed Souls brothel, once all parties had reached an agreement.

A bit of bad luck. The bloodhounds from Camp Pendleton raided the clandestine factory when the shiny new coins, astutely minted in operations that lasted through the night, began to circulate through León's bars, gambling houses and cockfight pits; and *The Alligator Woman*, along with the forge, the minting stamps and what not, was driven off to Marine barracks, again squeezed in between boots, knees and military belts in a convertible, that rooted its way along the streets like a pig pushing its way through a crowd.

When *The Alligator Woman* was brought in, along with the noisily unloaded counterfeiting apparatus, Anastasio, in shirt sleeves and suspenders, his brown corduroy suit-coat hanging on the back of the chair, was playing poker with the Marines in the barracks' vestibule, the thick smoke of Camel cigarettes floating above the table. He didn't put down the cards he held in his hand. Justo Pastor Gonzaga, who had gotten up to go to pee, tiptoed back to the scene, not knowing whether to flee or to stay.

The Marines burst out laughing at the familiar figure of *The Alligator Woman* in her white tunic as leader of the blessed souls, now in handcuffs. High-stakes gambler that he was, Anastasio decided to laugh too, not knowing what card to play next if, out of revenge, she pointed him out as the owner of the dies, the ingots, and the rest of the confiscated materials and apparatus. But not then nor ever did she denounce him. And thanks to Justo Pastor Gonzaga's intervention and circuitous dealings with the authorities, he succeeded in getting her released.

That was when he convinced her to change the name of the brothel to Baby Dolls, like the one he had known on Market Street in Philadelphia. He made arrangements at the Metropolitan Power & Light Company, where he had friends, for them to run a line out to Paso de Carretas Street, and one night when she was returning from Cafarnaún, after paying *Terrestrial Light* her salary, she found her house lit up as if on fire. He advised her to curl the girls' hair into dyed gold ringlets, put them in straw hats and petticoats, and he himself taught them how to flutter their big false eyelashes like real dolls.

His longing for Salvadorita's hand still seemed a far-off dream. But *The Alligator Woman* insisted on being a man. If it had not been for her insistence, the marshal of latrines might have remained trapped in the grip of his rotten luck forever, pounding the streets of León in his rubber-soled shoes looking for privies that needed to be inspected. But he wrote a letter to the learned Debayle, proposing the operation.

It could not have come at a more opportune moment. The doctor's enemies at the Medical Society of León were gaining the upper hand, insistent that no one should forget his past mistakes. His clientele at the hospice was being decimated. And in the wards at the end of the courtyard there only remained a few consumptives, sitting in Viennese rocking chairs and crocheting, and a few uncontrollable mental patients from good families chained in their cells.

The learned Debayle answered him with a carefully typed note, which Chiron delivered to his room near Saint Mardoqueo's hospice. He asked him to come see him at the Maison de Santé at 5:00 that afternoon. He was there on the dot, naturally; and here is the dialogue of that meeting, so different from the previous one:

Debayle (Very courteous and affable): Take a seat, please.
Anastasio (Depositing his marshal's flashlight on the desk
    with a dry thud): Thank you very much.
Debayle (Feigning a serious expression): For scientific
    reasons, I'm interested in the case.
Anastasio (Twirling his Panama hat between his fingers):
    Let's get down to brass tacks, doctor. Half and half. I
    open the doors to glory for you, and you open the
    doors to happiness for me.
Debayle (To himself: "At least, he's good-looking, that can't
    be denied. And he's got guts."): Is the young lady
    you speak of in your letter prepared to go under my
    scalpel?
Anastasio (He shifts forward in his chair): Ready, and eager.
Debayle (Pressing his fingertips together): Still, I would need
    a medical consultation with her, to evaluate her

anatomical condition.

Anastasio (Even farther on the edge of his chair): I'll bring her tomorrow, provided that...

Debayle (He sighs): Are your intentions honorable?

Anastasio (He stands up, very erect): I officially ask you for Salvadorita's hand.

Debayle (He too stands up and extends him his hand): For the time being, you can visit my house. (With a gesture of his mouth, he indicates the flashlight.) And give up that baton, Marshal. That trade doesn't belong in my family.

Please note that on that very night, with the interview concluded, Anastasio arrived at Baby Dolls brimming with joy, his broad-brimmed Panama hat leaping in his hand, no longer carrying his inspector's flashlight, which he had broken to bits against the curb as soon as he left the Maison de Santé. He was just stopping by because Salvadorita was waiting for him in his first official visit as her fiancé. For her part, *The Alligator Woman* felt a tremendous urge to pee and went into the darkness of the old playground to try to practice standing up and creating the long stream she so wished to be able to produce. Lifting her crinoline doll's dress, she dropped her bloomers and took aim at the trunk of an orange tree. She couldn't, of course; her time hadn't come yet. And the unruly and messy stream completely soaked the flared leggings of her bloomers.

But now open the door to the operating room in the Maison de Santé. Because this is a clandestine operation, the learned Debayle has only one assistant to aid him, Chiron, who witnessed everything with a mixture of happiness and misgiving. Was *The Alligator Woman* going to finally have what she had desired so badly all her life? Ready to give it his all, using the wood-fired oven, he had sterilized the instruments with greater care than ever: the scissors, the hemostatic pincers, clamps, catgut, and scalpels which the hand of the learned Debayle, the back of which was as red as a ripe *guineo* banana, arranged as his first action on the strip of gauze covering the little metallic instrument table which was beginning to rust. And after helping him on with his rubber gloves, having first sprinkled them with talcum powder, he tied his mask around the back of his head with a firm knot.

The Alligator Woman tried to smile at Chiron from the operating table, but she was gripped by fear; and at that moment Debayle placed a cotton compress over her nose and poured a little stream of chloroform onto it. Within a few minutes she was fast asleep, her lips just far enough apart to reveal the two rows of her pointy teeth.

Scalpel in hand, the learned Debayle saw in a lightning flash the moment President Sadi Carnot handed him his diploma, *summa cum laude,* during the Sorbonne's formal graduation ceremony, while a blizzard of snow was falling outside; he saw Championnère smiling at him from the dais—after all he'd been his most favored student; he saw Clemenceau, his companion on those nights on the town, applauding him from the balcony, flashing him the bottle of champagne hidden under his overcoat for their celebration afterwards. And in another flash he saw the treatise in which he would describe in French the surgical solution for the case, with before and after photographs. His name would once more appear in the *Revue de Hautes Etudes de Médecine,* leaving that pack of dogs at the Medical Society of León speechless.

So he began. With an artist's pleasure, not feeling the least bit tired, he operated on his subject, opening, tying, suturing, while at his side Chiron kept the books open to the illustrations he pointed to: a modification of the genital-urinary apparatus thanks to precise incisions according to the studies made by Felix Guyon; the formation of an artificial penis according to Beaumont's method; Dartigues's testicular graft. And finally, with night already upon him, he placed bandages like stars over the wounds where there once had been small breasts, removed by his knife in accordance with the Poll-Kelly surgical manual. At that, with a supreme gesture of triumph, he pulled off his mask.

"I still need to verify the success of that operation," said Rigoberto. "I've got to talk to Chiron."

"Ask her yourself," Norberto said. "Haven't you two become good friends?"

"The goldsmith is the one who's friendly with her," Rigoberto said, lowering his voice. "He goes to her brothel early so no one will see him."

"What are you saying about me, little man?" asked Segismundo, coming in the door.

"Is it true that you're a client of Baby Dolls?" Norberto asked from across the room.

"I don't answer police interrogations," Segismundo said, alarmed.

"Then, it's true!" Norberto said.

"It's crucial to know if the operation left her the way she wanted, or not," Rigoberto insisted, looking quite pensive.

"Crucial, for what?" Erwin asked.

"To know if she harbors any hard feelings toward Somoza," Rigoberto said.

"Hard feelings?" asked the goldsmith Segismundo, sitting down. "She's capable of sacrificing her life for that gangster!"

"Has she herself confessed as much to you when you visit Baby Dolls?" Norberto asked him.

"I don't get intimate with transvestites, the way you do with pederasts," the goldsmith Segismundo said, hot under the collar.

"She wields a lot of power that comes straight from Somoza," Captain Prío said.

"Power in a whorehouse?" Norberto said.

"Do you think the power to report someone is a small thing?" Erwin asked him. "She can choose her victims, in secret. It's like finding yourself on a road at night at the mercy of a wild beast."

"She's simply a person who's devoted to running her business," Rigoberto said.

"That woman, or whatever she is, is a dangerous spy," Erwin said. "Anybody who has dealings with her knows where she stands."

"But according to the notes of our good poet here, she'll get to heaven before Saint Mardoqueo," the goldsmith Segismundo says.

"All brothel owners inform the National Guard about what they hear their customers saying," Rigoberto said. "If they don't, their businesses will be shut down."

"*The Alligator Woman* is more than just a spy," Captain Prío says. "She runs León's Popular Fronts for Somoza. She's the one who's going to fill the plaza tomorrow for Somoza."

"She's got Catalina Baldelomar here in the markets for that, and *Stone Face* Diómedes Baldelomar out in the sticks," Erwin says.

"All I know about Catalina Baldelomar is that she got it on with Tirso the Albino," Rigoberto says. "But he didn't get her pregnant, because otherwise you'd have seen the fetus light up in her big belly like a bulb."

"Her brother is the dangerous one," Erwin says. "He had the job of castrating bulls in the Lechecuagos district. He took a liking to knives and turned into a killer."

"All this talk about castrating gives me the chills," the goldsmith Segismundo says, squeezing his legs together.

"Debayle would have needed several days to castrate you," Norberto says.

"Thank you very much," the goldsmith Segismundo says. "With such flattery, you've made amends for that earlier matter, my dear pupil."

"As proof that he's carried out the order to kill someone, he cuts off the victims' hands and brings them to Colonel Maravilla in a sack," Erwin says.

"Or else he cuts off their ears," Norberto says. "I had a tractor driver that *Stone Face* pulled out of his house one night. And when they found the body, it had no ears."

"Now you're the ones who are exaggerating," Rigoberto says.

"No, my dear poet," Captain Prío says. "Whenever it's my turn to be on duty at the bar, there's *Stone Face*, just sitting there, waiting for orders to take care of some dirty business. And the day that Moralitos showed up here, he was with him. He stood watch at the door."

"Tomorrow *Stone Face* is going to be very busy at Moralitos's side then," Erwin says.

"He won't be with Moralitos," Captain Prío says. "I already told you that putting people in the plaza is the job of *The Alligator Woman* and her cronies."

"And since Captain Prío is going to be very busy tomorrow, too, we should be leaving," the goldsmith Segismundo says, already on his feet. "This place will be filling up with vultures, and you've got to get ready to serve them."

"As long as vultures pay, I'll serve them," Captain Prío says.

"Since we can't hold our session here tomorrow, take this table away so it doesn't get contaminated, Captain," Norberto says as he gets up to leave.

"That won't be necessary, we'll bless it again later with the proper libations," says Segismundo.

"Let's invite Moralitos to come make peace with us tomorrow. That way our session will be properly protected," Erwin says, getting up with a big yawn and putting on his Basque beret.

"Don't forget to come by at noon to pick up your ring," the goldsmith Segismundo tells Norberto.

"Another ring!" Erwin exclaims. "In your previous life you must have been a Babylonian whore. And one of the high-priced ones."

"The ring isn't for me," Norberto says.

"That thing about a previous life is called metempsychosis," says Segismundo.

"Why do you want to know if *The Alligator Woman* harbors ill will towards Somoza?" Erwin asks Rigoberto on their way out.

"Because then I'll know for sure what she's capable of," Rigoberto says.

Would You Go Hunting for the
Bloody Tigers of Evil?

Somoza will attend the fiesta without his bulletproof vest, that's how it has been plotted by one of the sisters who likes to spring surprises. Emaciated, with bags under her eyes, she cuts the thread of the fabric with her sharp teeth lest the noise of her rusty old scissors get the attention of her other two sisters who are humming along as they work in the darkness, weaving the tapestry. But those other two had agreed some time ago to play a trick on the jokester, because this is how the daughters of the night like to amuse themselves: on his way to the big party, Rigoberto stops at Casa Prío, unconcerned about any bulletproof vest because he intends to fire from a crouching position, aiming below the belt the way he did practicing on the scarecrow.

It's past 9:00. The visiting members of the Great Convention are still coming into Casa Prío, filling up the large room, engaged in noisy conversations that sound like speeches, greeting one another with big hugs and making their way over to the bar, holding their money aloft to get a drink, as if placing bets. But it's not long before they begin filing out in groups on their way to the fiesta or to their rooming houses to the sound of military marches playing at full blast for the last few minutes on a record made by the Boston Pops Orchestra. One of them, a skinny fellow with a pock-marked face, who had called Rigoberto *Bienvenido Granda* when he saw him come in, approaches the corner where the cursed little table is located to say goodbye, loudly patting him on the back, as if they had known each other all their lives.

Rigoberto's already having his second helping of tutti-frutti sherbet. He scrapes the iridescent surface of the scoops resting in an aluminum cup, and without letting go of his spoon, runs his tongue over his fleshy lips to savor the clear sweetness of the shavings. Does he look at his watch? No. Captain Prío does not remember him appearing to be in any hurry, proof of that being the delicate way he savors the sherbet. Nerves? Under the table, his feet, in the brown moccasins he had sent over to the San Juan Park for a shoeshine while he was getting dressed, are constantly shifting, but that doesn't prove anything; it's just an old quirk of his.

His curly hair glistens with Glostora hair cream. His preppy, sky-blue suit is a light gabardine, and his pearl gray tie has a sketch of a pale butterfly drinking from the calyx of a marble-colored iris. Is it possible he feels like ordering a third serving of tutti-frutti? He does. In San Salvador, Manlio Argueta's ice cream parlor didn't make it the same way.

Captain Prío finally comes over to sit down with him, carrying a *Mantovani and His Orchestra* LP that he has retrieved from behind the counter where he keeps all his records. With things having quieted down, he wants to put on some instrumental string music as soon as the marches end.

Didn't it surprise Captain Prío that Rigoberto wasn't on stage for his part in *Tovarich*, which was probably beginning about then at the Teatro Darío? Didn't it surprise him that he was going instead to the fiesta in Somoza's honor? It did surprise him, and in each case, he asked him about it. And his questions were answered as follows:

"I've already finished what I had to do, Captain. Rubén will have his pedestal."

"What can I do? Rafa Parrales has me on assignment at the fiesta. He wants a front-page feature for tomorrow's paper."

And Rigoberto had scarcely finished his explanations when they both looked up, as if to the sound of someone calling them. Standing motionless in the doorway was the goldsmith Segismundo, his shirt soaked with sweat, squeezing his Tyrolean hat in his hands.

"I saw the whole thing," he says, walking over to them.

"Have a seat," Captain Prío offers, but he just looks at Rigoberto and doesn't respond.

"I was coming out of the Church of the Good Shepherd about 7:00, and don't anyone ask me what I was doing in a church," he says, short of breath. "And I saw them stop him. He was alone. He didn't put up any resistance. They searched the canvas bag he was carrying, and three National Guardsmen on patrol raised their Garand rifles simultaneously. Even from where I was, I heard that dry, menacing sound. I thought they were going to kill him then and there. But what they did was handcuff him and put him into the jeep. You could hear them communicating by radio. They didn't move, just stayed there, maybe fifteen minutes, then Moralitos showed up in another jeep with more soldiers. Father Olimpo Lozano was with him. Moralitos had them take the prisoner out of the jeep. He got him down on his knees, yanked his head up by his hair, and shined the flashlight in his face for the priest to get a good look at him.

"It was Cordelio," Rigoberto says, looking thoughtful, almost distracted.

"I recognized him right away," Segismundo says, and he collapses in the chair.

The record with the marches has come to its end with "Semper Fidelis," so Captain Prío gets up to take it off, but he doesn't put the other one on.

"I had already given up hope of finding you, my dear poet," Segismundo tells Rigoberto. "I looked for you at your fiancée's place, then I came running here. This was my last hope."

"Is she still waiting for me?" Rigoberto asks him.

"At the door," the goldsmith Segismundo says. "You're not taking her to the party, right?"

"No. I'm going alone," Rigoberto says.

"Don't worry about her then," says Segismundo. "I'll take her to a safe place."

"You're the one who needs a safe place," Rigoberto says.

"She's the first one Moralitos will look for," says Segismundo.

"And what safe place do you have in mind?" Rigoberto asks.

"I have someone who can take her to Puerto Morazán so she can board the boat leaving tomorrow," Segismundo replies.

"What I don't get is how she's going to agree to leave," Rigoberto says.

"Thanks to a little piece of paper you're going to give me," the goldsmith Segismundo says.

Captain Prío is still arguing with one of the waiters because he's just learned that some customers, members of the Great Convention, left without paying their bill. He is interested to see that Rigoberto is hurriedly writing something.

"Tell her there are serious complications that you'll explain later; that you're going on ahead, that you'll wait for her at the port, that the only way you can get married is by going to El Salvador together. That there is no other way. That she should trust me, that you're sending the engagement ring with me. I'll supply the ring," Segismundo says.

Rigoberto raises his eyes.

"And how do you think this whole trip can be arranged between now and morning?" he asks him.

Segismundo looks at him without blinking.

"Because it was my own escape I was planning," he says. "I'm utterly ashamed to tell you this. But I got scared."

Rigoberto busies himself folding the little piece of paper before handing it to him.

"Then in any case you go with her," he says. "You've done your part."

"Fear is a really fucked-up thing, like a sickness," the goldsmith Segismundo says, and he puts the piece of paper in the lining of his Tyrolean hat. "But I'm over it now."

"I hope I get over it, too," Rigoberto says, giving him a faint smile.

Captain Prío, who hasn't finished arguing with the waiter and is threatening to fire him, sees Segismundo stepping off the sidewalk to head very singlemindedly toward the plaza. Rigoberto, who is already at the door that opens onto Calle Real, turns quickly to say goodbye.

It's already after 10:00 p.m. Motorcycle sirens announce that the presidential cavalcade is on its way to the fiesta. Rigoberto stops under the light of a streetlamp on the corner of Calle Real, which Erwin had marked in blue ink as lookout B on the map. There's no one there. He never smokes, but tonight he craves a cigarette, and pats his shirt pocket as if he always carried a pack with him. He turns down the first street and sees the patrol at the next corner guarding the access to the block where the club is located. He crosses over to the soldiers' side and raises his hand in greeting. They just look at him, sullen-faced under the shadow of their helmets.

Next to the curb, in the exact place marked in red ink on the map lookout A, Norberto's jeep is parked, and when he passes by, he brushes his fingers against the metal of the vehicle. Up ahead, Somoza's bulletproof limo, motorcycles, and military escort vehicles, the drivers leaning against the open doors. Inside, the military band is just finishing the national anthem.

Colonel Lira had run towards the platform where the National Military Band was sitting, waving his handkerchief, and as if caught by surprise by the music, Somoza froze in his tracks, hand on his chest, fingers pointed towards his heart, right next to the First Lady who's trying not to blink. The radio announcer from the Gran Cadena Liberal climbed onto a chair and held out his microphone to catch the distant, garbled sounds of the music just as it was ending, so he hurriedly gets down from the chair and tries to approach Somoza to request a few words from him, dragging along the cable and getting it tangled in the feet of those in attendance. The couple moves forward amid the applause, smiling to left and right as Moralitos opens a path for them, until they finally emerge from all the pushing and shoving that leaves the announcer far behind them, into the western end of the old adobe house where those invited to the table of honor are waiting at their places, ministers and local government officials with their wives.

Rigoberto has gone into Conny's neighborhood store next to the club, where he hears a radio, with a crocheted doily on it, playing at a low volume and the radio announcer complaining about the noise and asking for a little more order. He buys a little box of twelve Adams chiclets for one córdoba, and from his wallet hands the owner, Conny Aguilera de Cáceres (forty years of age, married, her living quarters above her store) a five córdoba bill and receives four one-córdoba bills in change. The wallet (Exhibit Number 5), kept in his right pants pocket, has three clear plastic picture-pockets, all empty.

As it is 10:30, the first dance is going to begin. Rafa Parrales, who is circling around the table for the guest of honor, heads toward the orchestra platform, and with a mischievous air, he whispers something to Colonel Vega Miranda. The musicians, in khaki uniforms and black ties, each one seated in front of a music stand with NGO, the orchestra's monogram, on it, leaf through their music, and when they're ready, Rafa Parrales takes the microphone to ask Somoza to come forward and dance with the First Lady to the sound of a Peruvian waltz titled "My Little Southern Star," the couple's favorite song, which he will have the pleasure of singing in their honor. There's applause. Moralitos, his back pressed up against the wall, behind the table of honor, gives a quick signal to the security agents, and he himself moves forward to clear a path to the dance floor. The people squeeze together around the tiled floor, curious to see the couple dance.

The waltz ends, there's more applause, Rafa Parrales thanks the couple, and Rigoberto is now at the door. Sergeant Domitilo Paniagua, with a necktie that's so tight it looks more like a hangman's noose, the tips of his shirt collar bent up, hears from the door that they're now going to play Dámaso Pérez Prado's "Mambo No. 5," and he feels so thrilled, so eager to dance he's embarrassed. Tapping his foot to the rhythm, he happily signals Rigoberto to go on inside, along with all the others who are entering in droves, and amid all the shoving he winds up in the swirl of people around the dance floor where more applause and enthusiastic Vivas break out because Somoza is going to dance again, this time with the club's carnival queen, Señorita Azucena Poveda Siles, eighteen years old, a resident of the Zaragoza neighborhood, a typewriting and stenography student at the Mercantile Academy.

His arms held high and fists closed, mambo, how delicious the mambo, Somoza, challenging the young girl who raises her elbows, austerely marking the rhythm, barely smiling, her upper lip with little droplets of sweat, and he rhythmically lowers himself in front of her until he's crouching, mambo, how fantastic it is, practically touching the heels of his shoes with his buttocks, then coming back up to a standing position, impulsively, enthusiastically, again to the sound of more applause and Vivas, and laughter, and whistling, and the mambo still playing, he hugs her tight and kisses her near her mouth while the photographers' flashbulbs go off.

Openly rejoicing, the announcer describes the scene down to the last detail. Rigoberto, on the perimeter of the circle, applauds too, smiling, and follows Somoza with his eyes as he returns to the table of honor, watches him sit down and sees Colonel Lira hand him a handkerchief perfumed with Eau de Vétiver cologne which he uses to wipe away his perspiration and, discreetly, the rice powder left on his mouth after having kissed the club's carnival queen. The colonel goes to his valise to bring back a bottle of Black & White, and serves him a double shot.

The orchestra begins a new set with Bobby Capó's rhythmic bolero, "Cinnamon Skin." Rigoberto looks at his watch. It's 10:45. He buttons his jacket, and doing a *paso doble* around the wooden trays filled with glasses the waiters are carrying aloft, he heads for the hallway where the girls, seated in tight rows on folding chairs, are docilely waiting to be asked to dance, paper plates with sandwiches and pastries in their laps.

Señorita Ermida Toledo Granera, an assistant who works at the counter at the Munguía Bakery, twenty-two years of age, five feet-two-inches tall, brunette, straight hair, a scar on her chin from smallpox, with no criminal record, gets up without hesitation when asked to dance, even though she doesn't know the person, not even by sight. Rigoberto leads her out onto the dance floor, offers her a chiclet, and puts another one in his mouth. And from the moment he's taken her around the waist, dark eyes cinnamon skin that drive me crazy, he makes his way through the couples who struggle to push him back, *me importas tú, y tú,* and *you* until he's opposite the table of honor, *y nadie más que tú.*

Somoza is halfheartedly listening to Rafa Parrales, who is leaning over to show him that afternoon's edition of *The Chronicle*, while the guests at the table of honor, not many of whom have gotten up to dance, have begun talking louder now that the bolero is over. The smoke from Somoza's Lucky Strike cigarette, dangling from his silver cigarette holder, unfurls in lazy circles in front of his freckled face, climbing in ever fainter and more dispersed spirals toward the giant portrait behind him, where Moralitos stands guard, the portrait of a younger Somoza staring out into the distance in starched uniform and a Marine Infantry expeditionary hat, two small metallic rifles crossed above the hatband, his hands gripping the broad belt holding his pistol.

He nods, still listening, puts the cigarette holder down on the ashtray, and now his fingers toy with the matchbook which also bears his likeness, the same as the ones the military truck had distributed by the fistful in the streets earlier that day. On the tablecloth, within reach of his hand, his pack of cigarettes (from which a very self-assured Rafa Parrales takes one), the ashtray that Colonel Lira empties every so often, and the glass of Black & White. The First Lady, who has barely sipped her ginger ale, listens to Rafa Parrales, nodding yes with her head without looking at him, so that no one on the dance floor will miss her smile, which is not directed at anyone in particular.

The musicians quickly flip through their folders for the sheet music for "La Múcura," a mambo rhythm, and they begin playing. It is 10:50. More couples go out onto the dance floor, some are already dancing. Standing by their music stands, the musicians take their mouths from the mouthpieces of their trumpets and saxophones and sing in chorus *mama I just can't deal with it, I just can't deal with it.* Somoza breaks away for a moment from his chat with Rafa Parrales and turns toward the First Lady, rhythmically moving his shoulders, as if trying to get her to dance. She gives a fleeting smile, and playfully shoos him away with a wave of her hand.

Rigoberto is careful not to lose his spot on the dance floor, without breaking the cadence of his hands, feet, and waist, and smiling all the while at the girl who is dancing focusing on the movement of her own feet and chewing on her chiclet *girl, who broke your little clay jug*, then he takes her by the waist, inviting her to bend her torso just as he's doing, and turns in a circle until he's facing the table of honor. He raises his hands as though he's playing the maracas *Saint Peter who helped me how come you made me call him,* then suddenly lowers them to his chest, and crouches down spreading his legs *the jug's on the floor mama, I just can't deal with it.* Worried, Moralitos takes a step forward: he's seen him put his hand into his jacket *I just can't deal with it,* and all of a sudden there's the small revolver taking aim, the little black beast about *your little clay jug,* to spit fiery vomit, dazzling swipes of its claw, muffled reports, like Chinese firecrackers. As if he's suddenly overcome by sleep, Somoza doubles over in the First Lady's lap, and she holds out her arms to catch him, spilling her glass of ginger-ale *I just can't deal with it,* then the louder report of Moralitos's automatic pistol blasts out *I can't deal with it,* all the musical instruments fall silent one by one, the cowbell clanging without response until finally only the rattle of the drums is left, and all the dancing couples rush for the exit, stumbling over each other, knocking down the music stands, a stream of high-heeled shoes across the floor; amid the screaming and pushing someone has crashed into the bass drum and the cymbals clash, the waiters flee dropping their trays on the floor, while at the table of honor there's no one but Somoza and the First Lady who's cradling him, and opposite them the solitary dancer, abandoned by his partner, hunched over in his final dance step, bathed in blood, his legs slightly apart, the empty revolver still pointing upwards from below the table. From his hiding place behind a column, Rafa Parrales pokes his head out and, unable to control his voice, shouts:

"My dear poet! What are you doing down there?"

As if that were a signal of sorts, the mouths of the Thompson submachine guns open fire on the crouching dancer, who now begins a fresh, violent, uncoordinated upward movement and then sinks down again, knees bent but still refusing to touch the floor, shaking as if the cymbals, the maracas, and the *quijada de burro* were still playing and then the body, jerking frantically as if in response to the blare of trumpets, finally slumps forward and the head knocks against the talcum-powder-dusted dance floor, while the little black beast scurries a few feet away from his open hand.

And there's a final shot at point-blank range, because Colonel Justo Pastor Gonzaga, holding his nickel-plated pistol high in the air, has approached the cadaver lying in a pool of blood slowly spreading across the tiled floor, and groping myopically towards the target, bends down and blows his head off. This gratuitous shot, ringing out in the silence following all the machine-gun bursts is too much for the First Lady: desperately, she clutches her husband's head as if to shield him from the noise, and screams:

"Justo Pastor! Where's Heriberto?"

As if he had shrunk inside his uniform, Colonel Gonzaga can do nothing but look at her from behind the thick lenses that magnify his eyes.

"The general gave him permission to go to another party in Chinandega, señora," a frightened and solicitous Colonel Lira informs her, again rummaging in his valise for some medicine he knows he doesn't have there. Finally, he pulls out a barbershop-size bottle of Eau de Vétiver cologne and uncorks it so that he can splash some of it on Somoza's temples, slapping it on as if he were trying to revive someone who had fainted. Rafa Parrales comes over and starts to fan him with a copy of *The Chronicle,* as though he had passed out from the heat.

"You mean there's no doctor? Nothing but shitheads around Tacho!" the First Lady screams, enraged. "Then call an ambulance!"

"There's no phone here, señora," says Colonel Lira, who by now is in tears.

"Have the motorcycles go for an ambulance," she orders.

Another person is heard shouting, but his tone is more controlled:

"Don't let anyone leave!"

Despite the fact that he's been there all along, Van Wynckle seems to have just arrived. As soon as he hears him, Moralitos grabs a submachine gun from the hands of the first soldier he sees and takes off shouting orders for them to follow him to the doors, where there's a huge struggle to get to the street, a raging mob Sergeant Domitilo Paniagua is trying in vain to control with his few, ill-prepared men. Shoes, women's purses, eyeglasses, hats lie crushed in the stampede.

We'll let Moralitos worry about the doors. There's more to be gained by sticking close to Van Wynckle on the dance floor, where a strange quiet now reigns, Rigoberto riddled with countless bullets, and Somoza opposite him, lying unconscious in the First Lady's arms at the center of the now deserted table of honor.

Van Wynckle strides toward the First Lady. There's no time to wait for an ambulance, they've got to take the limo to get the president to the hospital right away, so he calls over three agents to help Colonel Lira carry him to the door in his chair. And just as they're lifting him, Van Wynckle turns and sees two people who have silently approached Rigoberto's body. The she-man, his face heavy with make-up, still holding the newspaper he was showing the president. And the he-woman, dressed in an outlandish jacket and tie, dark glasses and felt hat. It's her. Earlier he had asked the president who she was, out of curiosity.

Separately, the two of them examine the disfigured body that's been cordoned off by the guards. They know him. Van Wynckle can sense their fear, almost like an odor. Somoza is carried out on his chair as someone shouts that the prisoners seated on the floor are to be moved out of the way. Van Wynckle steps out onto the dance floor, eyes narrowed and head pulled back, like someone who's choosing melons at the market on a Saturday, and he tells the man next to him, another queer egg, without taking much notice of who he's giving orders to, to take them both prisoners. Handcuff them.

It's obviously a moment of great confusion. The security agents, eager for Van Wynckle to give them orders, stare at each other, bewildered. The order, which seems as bizarre as the person receiving it, is directed at *Stone Face* Diómedes Baldelomar who, even on this festive occasion, is wearing a towel draped around his neck. They're ordering him to take his own mother (and someone who's much more than that to him) prisoner, but he's not taken aback, and rushes to carry out the instructions, his hand already on the handle of the long-barreled Colt which he always carries stuffed down his trousers.

Armed by Moralitos with a rifle and told to shoot to kill if anyone tries to escape, Sergeant Domitilo Paniagua watched as *Stone Face* Diómedes Baldelomar prodded *The Alligator Woman* at gunpoint, along with some strange-looking fellow he didn't know. He looked puzzled as they, in handcuffs, were forced to sit down on the floor with the other prisoners, very close to the door because there was no longer enough room inside. But Moralitos looks even more puzzled as he returns from the street where there was a more-than-suspicious-looking jeep, which is now being checked out by his men with their flashlights.

He heads straight for *The Alligator Woman* to ask her what's going on, and repeats the same question, with even greater bewilderment, to *Stone Face* Diómedes Baldelomar, while ordering Rafa Parrales, who's babbling uncontrollably, to shut up. And even though the two, mother and son, have little to say, he doesn't need to force an answer out of them because Van Wynckle is already standing next to him.

"She knows the assassin," he says.

"That's her job, sir, to know the president's enemies. She's my agent," Moralitos says. "I also know him. His name is Rigoberto López Pérez."

"López Pérez," Van Wynckle says, and he pulls out his note pad. "You were having this man followed?"

"Very closely, sir," Moralitos says. "Cordelio Selva had trained someone in marksmanship in El Salvador. It could be him. They bought the gun there."

"The gun was hidden at Baby Dolls and the dead man went there earlier this evening to get it," *Stone Face* Diómedes Baldelomar suddenly informs them.

Taken by surprise, Moralitos turns to look at him.

"Be sure of what you're saying," he warns him.

Van Wynckle calmly takes the gun from his coat pocket (Exhibit Number 1), and unfolds the handkerchief it's wrapped in.

"Is this the gun?" he asks him.

"That's the one," *Stone Face* Diómedes Baldelomar says.

"Who was holding it for him?" he asks him.

Stone Face Diómedes Baldelomar slowly turns his head towards *The Alligator Woman*. They look at each other, but no one knows what's going on behind either of their dark glasses.

"You had the gun in your possession," he says, with a hint of compassion in his voice. "On orders from you, Minerva Sarraceno returned the gun to the dead man. And that naked wrestler was on the truck with you, talking about an assassination attempt, and I warned you: you've got to report this. But you told me not to pay attention to drunkards."

"I want that other woman, Minerva, here, immediately. And I want that wrestler," Van Wynckle orders Moralitos.

Filled with rage and a sense of betrayal, Moralitos shakes his head and stares at *The Alligator Woman* who remains expressionless behind her dark glasses. Then he grabs Van Wynckle by the arm to take him aside a few steps.

"I've got the wrestler," he says.

"Is he an important piece of the puzzle?" Van Wynckle asks.

"No," Moralitos says. "He's one of my agents, a good-for-nothing, he complicates things. I recruited him to place him in San Salvador. And when López Pérez returned to Nicaragua, I kept him on his tail. I was never able to find out if he followed him all the way here or not."

"That doesn't sound good," Van Wynckle says. "How could that agent of yours have been talking about some kind of attempt today and you not know anything about it?"

"He came looking for me yesterday, to ask for some money," Moralitos says. "I reprimanded him and told him to follow López Pérez because of the suspicions I already had. But he took the money I gave him and drank it up and caused a big fuss. Better to lock him up, I decided. When my men finally found him, he was leaving Baby Dolls."

"But he spoke of a possible attack," says Van Wynckle.

"Because that was what he was given instructions to find out about," Moralitos says. "But he's nothing more than an irresponsible drunk and a loudmouth."

"Maybe he got drunk on purpose," Van Wynckle says. "And maybe he never reported back to you because he was mixed up with them. That happens in this business."

"It's possible," Moralitos says.

"And in this business, when you're talking about betrayal, you've got to follow your nose," Van Wynckle says. "Do you understand me?"

"Yes, sir," Moralitos replies. "I understand you very well."

"Take the case of that woman, or whatever she is," Van Wynckle says. "Even tonight the president thought she was absolutely loyal. And yet she had already handed the assassin his gun."

"There's nothing more we can get out of the wrestler," Moralitos says, turning his head towards *The Alligator Woman*. "But she's got a lot she can tell us."

"When they find out, the president's two boys won't want us to do anything with anybody here," Van Wynckle says. "She and all the others will have to be interrogated in Managua. Cordelio Selva, first; he's probably already in custody there."

"Cordelio Selva was smart," Moralitos says. "He got what he wanted. I already said that nabbing him had been too easy."

"Oh, no, not exactly," Van Wynckle says. "*The president, poor soul,* he himself opened the doors for the assassin."

From his post at the door, Sergeant Domitilo Paniagua had heard Moralitos state the name of the dead assassin, had heard *Stone Face* Diómedes Baldelomar say that he recognized the weapon, and had also heard the order to bring Minerva Sarraceno in. And when Van Wynckle and Moralitos withdrew to have their conversation, he first became uneasy, then downright scared. Just as he had wanted to dance the mambo before, now he wanted to run. But we'll leave him there at the door, because he won't budge until Moralitos gives him another order. The fear that makes him want to run also keeps him from moving.

Instead, come with with me to the San Vicente Hospital. While they are waiting for the surgeon (agents had been sent to his house to look for him), Somoza lies unconscious on a stretcher in the corridor outside the deserted operating room. Only the First Lady and Colonel Lira are with him. Because she knows none of them and distrusts them all, she's ordered that the doctors on duty be locked in the kitchen along with the orderlies and nurses, so the patients in the wards lie unattended, a soldier at each door and the lights on.

To the delight of his wife and aide-de-camp, Somoza shows signs of coming around: he opens his eyes partway, and it's then that the following dialogue takes place. Listen closely:

Somoza (Slurring his speech): Where am I?
She (Taking him by the hand): In the hospital, the doctor's on his way.
Somoza (His eyes closed again): Who shot me?
She (Grimacing, her lips trembling): Some little piece of shit Communist worker.

Somoza (Half opening his eyes again): What happened to
him?
Colonel Lira (He affectionately bends over the stretcher): He
already got what he deserved, General.
Somoza (Fidgeting, restless): They killed him?
Colonel Lira: Yes, General.
Somoza (His eyes shut again): The dummies...should have
taken him alive...to tie up the loose ends...of the
plot...now at least...get them to cut off...his balls...
(An uncomfortable silence). So they can...give the
Guard...egg drop soup...with my compliments... (He
smiles).

He falls back into unconsciousness, that smile still on
his lips. Egg drop soup. A cheerful spirit even under the worst
of circumstances, capable of jokes that people like Colonel
Lira are accustomed to taking seriously. The First Lady, with
a lifelong habit of taking them for what they are, takes the
handkerchief perfumed with Eau de Vétiver that Colonel
Lira hands her, the last clean one left in the valise, and dries
the cold sweat from her husband's brow.

Then footsteps are heard in the corridor, the sound of
military boots, the clanging of canteens, the thud of rifle
butts against the tiled floor. The doors swing open and Dr.
Apolidoro Arana appears, barefoot and in striped pajamas,
black bag in hand. A swarm of soldiers in battle gear
accompany him. They had gone to pull the surgeon from his
house, and brought him to the hospital on the back of an
army truck: the First Lady had remembered his name on the
way to the hospital. He's a distant nephew of hers.

"Get out of here! What is this?" she shouts at the
soldiers, and they take off, frightened.

Impassive, the surgeon had barely murmured good
evening. With a trembling hand that he gradually succeeds
in controlling, he takes a manometer out of his bag and takes
the wounded man's blood pressure; he searches around for

his light, then raises Somoza's eyelids and examines the pupils; he takes out a thermometer, and loosening the president's tie, opens the blood-stained shirt and takes his temperature under the armpit, and finally he listens to his chest. And as if he had someone there taking notes, he dictates: blood pressure 90 over 70. Pulse, irregular. Pupils, dilated. Body temperature, 100. Heartbeat, irregular.

He takes the stethoscope out of his ears, and looks around as if it's only now he realizes that the vestibule outside the operating room is empty.

"We've got to get the president undressed to examine the wounds," he says. "I need help."

"No one else is allowed in here," the First Lady replies. "I don't trust anyone. Let Colonel Lira assist you."

"All right, come over here, help me," the surgeon says, after reflecting for a moment.

"No one's allowed to undress the chief," Colonel Lira says, stepping between the surgeon and the stretcher. Confused, the doctor directs a questioning look at the First Lady.

"You, do as he says," she orders Colonel Lira. "Lend him a hand."

"No one's allowed to see the chief naked," he insists, his eyes filling with tears.

"You stupid shit!" she yells, shaking him by the lapels of his uniform. "Do as I say or get out!"

Colonel Lira wipes the tears away with the back of his hand.

"I can do it by myself," he says at last, and proceeds to undress the president.

He's strong, and really doesn't need any assistance. He lifts Somoza up with one hand to remove his shirt and next his bullet-riddled pants, which he pulls down over his feet. He unties his shoelaces, holding one shoe at a time, not letting them drop to the floor but carefully setting each one down in turn. And once he has the body undressed, he carefully folds the shirt and pants.

The surgeon then approaches the stretcher, surgical scissors in hand, and he looks again at the First Lady in a mute appeal for the authority to go ahead and cut away the sanforized undershorts, soaked with blood. With a nod of her head, she indicates he should proceed.

With one cotton swab after another, he rapidly wipes away the blood glistening in the mat of hair that covers the prominent belly, throwing the soaked swabs on the floor. Four wounds. One in the left abdominal region near the groin; another in the pelvis, which has perforated his prostate; one in the right thigh, and another minor one, below the knee.

And the old wound that Colonel Lira wanted no one to see, the modest buttonhole through which he voids into a rubber sac, affixed to his skin with adhesive tape, the remains of gala banquets and big country-style meals. Oh, what shitty luck! the goldsmith Segismundo would say. Was it for this you became a counterfeiter and a latrine marshal? And what would you do about diarrhea?

The Party's Over

Captain Prío hears them from his bed, sounds that seem far off in the distance, first a shuffling of footsteps and then muffled cries. And as the drowsiness of sleep dissipates, much closer, vehicles braking to a halt, screams, insults, and threatening voices. He gets up, without turning on the light, and from behind the window, which he cautiously approaches, he can make out the crowd of people filing into the plaza, the men holding up their pants and shuffling their shoes along on the ground because their belts and shoelaces have been confiscated, the women barefoot or hobbling on just one heel, their party dresses torn to shreds, a new demonstration minus the fireworks, minus the music, minus the placards, and minus the shouts of Viva Somoza.

Now more prisoners come pouring out in waves from all sides of the plaza, being brought either on foot or in orange-colored trucks and military jeeps that squeal to a stop at street corners, taken into custody in bars, pool halls, brothels, and gambling houses, opponents of the regime sought out in their bedrooms because they're on the list, members of the Great Convention pulled from boarding houses, likewise suspicious, as also is anyone who has his door open, or who looks out of it, or who goes out to get some medicine, or comes home late at night.

And Captain Prío is on his balcony, hidden among the shadows, asking himself what could have happened when he hears them pounding on the doors of Casa Prío downstairs. They've come to take you into custody, too, Captain. One of the security agents who was on patrol around the plaza that night informed Moralitos that you spent the evening playing spirited marches at full blast to celebrate the assassination attempt that was to take place, proof that you were part of the conspiracy. Moralitos believes anything is possible. And even if it weren't so, he has more than enough reasons to want to interrogate you about one, or maybe several, of your regulars; and all the more so when he learns who had come by for a dish of sherbet, already dressed for the party.

The rounded-up prisoners are being ushered into the vestibule of Police Headquarters, and that's where they take the captain, a short distance from Casa Prío, just one block away, in his underwear and wrapped in the sheet he had on when he answered the door, and they're shoving him unnecessarily because at no point did he offer any resistance.

The windows of the two floors of the police headquarters blazed brilliantly on this night of great commotion, casting scattered reflections on the rose-colored walls. Higher up, behind the columns of the railing around the perimeter of the roof, a battery of .50-caliber machine guns is aimed at the prisoners in the plaza, the shadows of the soldiers manning the weapons moving about, restless in the dark.

And on the steps of the plaza, Captain Prío finds himself next to the goldsmith Segismundo, who is being brought in, hands tied behind his back with his own belt and a nasty weal on his head that's bathing his face in blood. For now, there is no concrete charge against him. But the security agents who, on orders from Moralitos, have stayed behind to go through every last corner of his jewelry shop (where they will brazenly steal everything there is in the glass display cases) are going to find the lead bullet minus its casing in the shop's trash can (Exhibit No. 3), and then his real agony will begin.

Obviously there are no greetings exchanged in that encounter, much less any chance for the goldsmith Segismundo to ask Captain Prío, although he might think it: is the bastard dead, or only wounded? Someone finally kicked the shit out of him through that hole in his fat belly. Can't you smell the stink drifting this way, Captain? Yes, all of you should know that some very strange events are going to take place in the vestibule, and you're fortunate to have those two firsthand witnesses there.

On one side, under the stairwell, lies Rigoberto's naked body, his head pointing towards the door of the guardroom, where Van Wynckle and Moralitos are now seated in close proximity, facing each other on either side of the desk. Traces of sticky blood, already dry in spots, cover the red and yellow diamond tiles on the floor. Captain Prío had seen the body almost as soon as it was brought in, but he doesn't know who it is. Pressed against him, Segismundo gives him the details bit by bit, glancing at the body with a mixture of compassion and pride. When he hears this, Captain Prío feels a churning in his guts that releases his sphincter muscle; he wraps the sheet tightly around himself, and pretends he hasn't heard.

It was impossible for Captain Prío to have recognized him, with his head smashed in and the body riddled with bullets as if he had the smallpox. And neither he nor Segismundo could have known they had cut off his testicles because you couldn't see the mutilation for all the blood. That strange, bloody mass lies inside a jar of alcohol, which can be seen on the desk in the guardroom every time one of the security agents opens the door to get orders.

The Alligator Woman, expressionless behind her dark glasses, and Rafa Parrales, who can't stop trembling amidst his fits of tears, know what it is. Despite the blood that's still pouring from his head wound and clouding his vision, Segismundo is so astounded at seeing them on the other side of the vestibule that he dares to nudge Captain Prío, who is no less stupefied at seeing *Stone Face* Diómedes Baldelomar playing the role of *The Alligator Woman*'s stern sentry; she, his loving mother, who only today had fed him by hand and rested her head on his legs.

When Moralitos arrived from the hospital, they had been put on the back of the truck where Rigoberto's body lay, the last of the prisoners to be taken out of the Workers Club. And they heard him very clearly shouting the order from the seat of his jeep, a submachine gun across his knee, to unload the body again in order to cut off his balls, at the request of the president; and the guards, spies, and security agents standing around the jeep were glad, for if the general had breath enough to ask for delicacies like that, then his wounds were not fatal.

And who other than *Stone Face* Diómedes Baldelomar to carry out that order. Get a move on, you're just the man, Moralitos had told him, calling him over to the jeep. Quick to obey, he ran over to Moralitos and said he preferred to do the job up there; but as he didn't want to leave his two prisoners, he got them up on the truck and then from the side-rail asked someone to shine a flashlight for him while he worked. Moralitos ordered Sergeant Domitilo Paniagua, who was just getting out of the jeep because he had taken him along to the hospital as his spur-of-the-moment driver, to go over and help with the flashlight.

Stone Face Diómedes Baldelomar completely stripped the cadaver laid out on the truckbed, and squatting, the lit Valencia cigarette in his mouth, began the operation with a knife he had taken from his bag, steady and meticulous about his work, his arm moving back and forth in strong, deep thrusts, each time asking Sergeant Domitilo Paniagua for more light and berating him because the flashlight was shaking too much. When he had finished, he folded his knife and put it away after cleaning it on Rigoberto's torn clothes, then went to the side of the truck to hold up the bloody mess for Moralitos and the others, and there were laughs and shouts of joy. But, also, all of a sudden, a voice of alarm because someone had jumped down from the truck and was now running along the street, someone who wasn't carrying a weapon but a flashlight, and the patrol watching the cross street on the north corner ordered him to halt, and Moralitos took off running, too, shouting for them not to shoot, but by then the sound of the fusillade was already over, its echoes reverberating down the street, and Sergeant Domitilo Paniagua fell headlong onto the road, the flashlight still shining.

"That son-of-a-bitch ran because he was in on the whole thing," shouted Moralitos, enraged. "Now him, too. We're not going to be able to find out shit about this mess!"

Rafa Parrales had edged up against *The Alligator Woman* so he wouldn't fall because his knees had buckled under him as soon as *Stone Face* Diómedes Baldelomar took his knife to the corpse, but she had pushed him away with a violent shove of her elbow; and when he heard the burst of shots afterwards he didn't think he could stay on his feet, and even less so when they dumped Sergeant Domitilo Paniagua's body on the back of the truck, practically on top of Rigoberto's naked cadaver. And when he was going up the steps to the entrance of the police headquarters, and they were just taking Rigoberto's body down from the truck, he had to grit his teeth and swallow the mouthful of bile that rose from his stomach, scared they'd beat him if he vomited.

Captain Prío can hear the wrenching sobs from the plaza, the pleading voices followed by emphatic and vile threats screamed back at them, ordering them to shut up, and meanwhile the military jeeps are unloading more and more prisoners in front of the headquarters, people arriving still in their pajamas or underwear, or like him, wrapped in a sheet they had to pull off their beds, and one of them who is sick is carrying his IV bottle with him.

Lined up against the wall, they're prohibited from moving or sitting down, and from his position in the middle of the vestibule, an officer covers them with a Lewis machine gun, moving it in a slow circle, as if it were the arrow on a roulette wheel just about to stop. And now the arrow is pointed at Minerva Sarraceno who is quietly sobbing and biting her fists; Segismundo recognizes her from his furtive visits as the girl who laughed so much behind the counter at

Baby Dolls, and he feels the vague desire to pay her his respects, as is his custom.

And there are two who are still wearing their white, full-dress uniforms, although their epaulets have been torn off: Colonel Melisandro Maravilla, who is trying in vain to hold onto the slippery surface of the wall as if he were standing at the edge of an abyss, and Colonel Justo Pastor Gonzaga, who is examining everything all around him through thick lenses with his shortsighted eyes. These old cronies of Somoza have also been arrested on orders from one of the two boys, Luis (*The Good*), via a radio message from Managua. Van Wynckle's mind works like neat stitches, like those of the sisters who tonight have much to weave and many loose threads to cut off; but these boys are one step ahead of him, to the total satisfaction of Moralitos, who offered to arrest his old enemy, Colonel Maravilla himself; if everything happened right under the nose of the military officer in charge of the plaza, and he didn't do anything to stop it, he has to be involved, Luis (*The Good*) reasoned through the receiver; and so does the one who shot the assassin in the head in order to silence him.

Van Wynckle didn't have the guts to explain to Luis (*The Good*) that the wasted shot fired at a dead man had been nothing more than a supreme act of servility. But his own reasoning is along similar lines: on the desk he has the copy of *The Chronicle* that Rafa Parrales was showing Somoza when the attack occurred, and he's written in the margin: Exhibit No. 2 with one of the many pens he carries in his shirt pocket; and in his notepad he's recorded that he heard Parrales address the assassin as *poet*, immediately after the attack—an obvious proof of friendship, which will have to be dealt with in the interrogation.

You already know the five-shot snub-nosed .38 caliber hammerless Smith & Wesson revolver with black finish and mother-of-pearl handle as Exhibit Number 1. The lead bullet that they find in the goldsmith Segismundo's shop, amidst the bits of sandpaper, you already know, too, as Exhibit Number 3. And Exhibit Number 4 will be the silver bullet, the only one that missed its target: just look at the sisters laughing, baring their decayed teeth.

Thanks to their recent training by Van Wynckle, the ONS technicians are now combing the scene of the assault for bullets and shell casings—until the emergency operation at the hospital being performed by Dr. Apolidoro Arana is finally completed, no one knows how many are in Somoza's body, and they find the silver bullet embedded in the wall under the giant portrait. A grave matter for Segismundo when Van Wynckle makes the inevitable connection with the humble lead bullet they're going to find in the shop's trash can, and more serious still when the technicians discover the perforation and the remains of potassium cyanide in the silver bullet.

And now the actors from the cast of *Tovarich* make their entrance, taken into custody when they were on their way to La Fuente Castalia to celebrate the opening night's rousing success. They've been brought from the plaza because Van Wynckle, convinced by Moralitos's arguments that the play was part of the plot, has included them in his notebook— before him, Prince Fedor Sergeievich, his mouth swollen from a blow that knocked out one of his teeth, and leaning on him, the chambermaid, all in black, wearing a starched cap, and her beautiful face, despite its double chin, streaming with tears; Lucio Ranucci, his Roman emperor's nose seeming more pointed than ever, his golden hair all tousled and his face as white as Carrara marble, whiter than Tirso the Albino's who can see nothing, his vision blinded by the black aniline dye used to paint eyebrows on him; young Princess Natasha Petrovna, next to her mother Princess Ninoshka Andreyevna, in long gowns and hairdos with costume tiaras, and behind them, smiling as if he were accompanying them to a party, Dr. Balthazar Cisne.

From his modest vantage point, Captain Prío, who swears

he'll never smoke again in his life if he gets out of this mess, even though he's already wishing they'd offer him a cigarette, stares at Rigoberto's corpse again now that the procession of actors has ended, and he suddenly thinks about Erwin, that there's no way he's not involved in the conspiracy. For his part, when he sees the young Princess Natasha Petrovna, Segismundo thinks about Norberto. Either they're holding him in the plaza or they're out looking for him, or they may not know that he was in on the whole thing. Without any opportunity to get a look at Van Wynckle's notepad, there's no way for him to know that Norberto's jeep has been towed to police headquarters and that they're already out searching for the owner. And for Erwin too, Captain, because he's a close friend of the jeep's owner.

But now, the high spot of the evening has arrived. There's a squealing of brakes, a slamming of doors, a jumble of footsteps. Escorted by a ring of machine guns, the First Lady appears in the vestibule, the diaphanous blue tulle covering her shoulders spotted with blood. She hasn't been detained, that would top everything. She's merely come to speak to her two sons in Managua via the radio. Tall, worn out, but still attractive, that's how Captain Prío sees her come in, while Segismundo doesn't want to see her, for fear that the rush of delight he'll feel will give him away.

"Attention!"

Moralitos's command explodes in the vestibule, and officers, soldiers, and armed agents heed the order with a display of emotion and respect, the officers saluting, their hands trembling at the edge of their caps; but it's also out of fear, Captain, a naked fear that they could be facing the same bad luck as those other two officers in their dress uniforms, who are also standing at attention; and among the other prisoners, no one dares move a finger, except for Rafa Parrales who steps forward, handcuffed, showing his perfect teeth with a face that says, look at me here, señora, what madness, but the powerful blow of a rifle butt to the pit of his stomach sends him reeling back against the wall like a broken doll.

The heels of her party shoes click against the floor in military fashion as she heads for the guardroom, but when she reaches the corpse, she stops, and all the prisoners clearly see her spit on it several times: the sound of saliva spurting from between her clenched teeth reaches Segismundo.

Van Wynckle hands her the microphone for the RCA radio apparatus and Moralitos brings her a metal chair, but she speaks standing up. Captain Prío and Segismundo can see her the whole time, because they can't close the door properly with all the people inside. Here, then, is the dialogue that all the prisoners and you can hear quite clearly:

Luis (*The Good*) (His voice, blurred, whines between pockets of static): How's my papa? How's my papa? Over.

She: He's doing fine, doing fine. He's just come out of the operation, operation. They won't have the pleasure of seeing him dead, of seeing him dead, those sons-of-bitches, those sons-of-bitches. (And she emphasizes these words directed, no doubt, at the prisoners outside in the vestibule.) And how's your brother? Your brother? Over.

Luis (*The Good*): He's like a madman, mama, like a madman. He wants to bomb León with planes, with planes. Over. (The voice fades in and out of Captain Prío's hearing.)

She (She clasps the microphone, brings it close to her mouth. And she shouts into it, hoping to control the waves of static in which Luis's voice becomes lost): Tell him I want him to calm down, to calm down. Convene the National Congress, the National Congress. You have to assume the presidency, the presidency. Over.

Luis (*The Good*): Everything's under control, in that regard everything's under control, Mama. The deputies of the regional departments, of the regional departments, they're already on their way to Managua. It's urgent that those who are in León for the convention, for the convention, come immediately. Over.

She: I read you, I read you. They'll be dispatched by express train, express. Put your brother on, put your brother on. Over.

Luis (*The Good*): Here he is, Mama, here he is. Over.

Tacho (*The Bad*) (Prolonged static): Did they get everyone involved in the plot? In the plot? Over. (It's some time before his nasal voice can be heard, and it fills Captain Prío with great fear, especially when he hears the sobbing. Segismundo thinks he sounds like a spoiled little kid who needs consoling. Another day, years later, he's going to get his wish to bomb León; Captain Prío can't even suspect that night that his own establishment will go up in flames when that happens.)

She (Van Wynckle holds up his notepad for her to read): They're looking for a certain Erwin, an Erwin...in a search of his premises, his printing press, they found a plan for the attack. And a Norberto, too, a Norberto. His jeep was parked in front of the place, a getaway car for the assassin, for the assassin. They'll get them, don't worry. (Moralitos nods.) And Cordelio Selva. Selva, who's already been taken to Managua, to Managua. Over.

Tacho (*The Bad*): They've already brought him to me. Tell Van Wynckle that I'm personally conducting the interrogation, with the best methods. (Van Wynckle can't hide a little smile.) It's tough, Mama. It's tough. Over.

She: I know, I know. But listen, don't do anything crazy, anything crazy, no planes, no planes. Call up the barracks, the barracks. Declare a state of emergency, a state of emergency.

Tacho (*The Bad*) (Again there's a delay in hearing his voice, again just bursts of static in the radio, like the echoes of hurricane winds): It's all right, mama. It's all right. I read you, Mama, I read you. Over and out.

When she hears Norberto's name mentioned, young Princess Natasha Petrovna lets out a deep sob which, thanks to her mother's promptly stifling it with her hand, will not be noted by Van Wynckle. Stunned by the unforeseen revelations, Segismundo lowers his head as if under the weight of a load of bricks, and Captain Prío mentally crosses himself again and again.

The First Lady leaves the guardroom, with Van Wynckle and Moralitos behind her. Her eyes fall upon *The Alligator Woman*'s dark glasses, two blind patches that make the First Lady stop in her tracks. Moralitos feels obligated to snap them off her face, and now those beady eyes of a wine-cellar rat are indeed looking at her, the rough bristles of her moustache, cultivated by the use of milk of figs, trembling at attention. She doesn't know how much she owes this (fe)male prisoner, her handcuffed hands gripping the pants she had always longed to wear. The First Lady owes her her wedding veil, Captain. But what does that matter now? Van Wynckle cranes his neck, and presses his mouth to her ear:

"Did you keep the murder weapon for the assassin?" he asks *The Alligator Woman*, and the surprise of the question makes her shake her head agitatedly.

And there's Van Wynckle at her ear again.

"A brothel!" she exclaims, horrified.

But as well as being horrified, she's disconcerted. She wrinkles her nose. And Captain Prío also senses the arrival of a little whiff of excrement because *The Alligator Woman* has shit in her pants, something he fears could happen to him, too. *Stone Face* Diómedes Baldelomar dares to laugh, but Moralitos shuts him up with a grunt.

"Is this a man or a woman?" the First Lady asks again, turning to Van Wynckle who, taken by surprise, shrugs his shoulders.

And later, before sending her to Managua with the rest of those in custody, he'll have her put in a cell and stripped of her clothes in his presence; and since she's soiled herself, he has them wash her down with buckets of water and put her into a pair of army pants. Once in Managua, he'll type up a report with the results of his investigation. And now, many years later, when Captain Prío can read that report, which never got to be part of the proceedings of the Council of War, he smiles. After giving the matter lengthy consideration, Van Wynckle concluded that she was a woman.

And what does the First Lady say to Colonel Maravilla, now that she's standing in front of him on her way to the door? It can't be anything very pleasant because she's furiously waving her jewel-laden hands in front of his sallow face and he, feeling defenseless, finds himself forcing a smile, his bald head shaking back and forth in denials. She hasn't deigned to look at Colonel Gonzaga, who has tried to intervene with a few words of his own. And they take them to the second floor, handcuffed, after Van Wynckle protests to Moralitos in English about why they're holding them there with the rest. They're still army officers.

"And what about this one?" the First Lady asks now, looking at a crestfallen Prince Fedor Sergeievich. And again Van Wynckle is at her ear, after he's consulted his notepad.

"I'll show you what's going to happen on the twenty-first!" she screams.

And in a fit of rage, her cyclamen-red nails raked deep furrows across those powdered cheeks, and the maid in her white cap who tries to protect him only makes her even angrier, and the furious fingernails dig into his throat without anyone intervening; no one but she can decide when her fit will end.

Now Captain Prío sees her stop, reconsider. He sees her turn her gaze upon the corpse, thrown under the spiral staircase. He sees her look at Van Wynckle.

"Who else in this group knew the murderer?" she asks, breathing hard.

Despite the anguish of the moment, Captain Prío cannot help noticing Van Wynckle's big clownish shoes as he again approaches the First Lady's ear.

"What are you waiting for, find out!" she says. And retracing her own footsteps, she goes over to stand next to the corpse.

"Just take a look at him, all of you, take a good hard look at him, and then go back to your places. No one say a word," she orders them.

Van Wynckle furrows his brow, unhappy with how this is being handled but not daring to put in his two cents, and he pulls out his notepad.

Dr. Balthazar Cisne, Princess Ninoshka Andreyevna, and little Princess Natasha Petrovna want to go together, but she doesn't let them. She seems not to recognize them, there are no family ties here.

"It looks like you put on a black tie because you knew what was going to happen," she says.

He's about to protest, but *Stone Face* Diómedes Baldelomar gives him a shove. Van Wynckle makes a notation in his log: black tie.

Captain Prío, careful to keep his sheet wrapped tightly around him so he won't end up naked as he walks, steps in front of the corpse. The bullet holes that looked like a black smallpox to him before now look to him like wild animal bites. The shot to the head had disfigured him, but that was *Bienvenido Granda*'s bushy moustache, and those were his fleshy lips. And his curly hair. Despite the blood, the Glostora hair cream still gleamed.

"Now, all those who recognize this man, raise your hands," she orders once they've all had a look at him.

Captain Prío barely has enough nerve, and Segismundo hesitates at first, but then he raises his hands, bound together with his own belt. To Van Wynckle's astonishment, a forest of hands goes up. One who doesn't raise his hand is Rafa Parrales.

"Come on, you," the First Lady then says. "Are you going to tell me that you don't know him?"

"He's the poet," he replies, and trying to wipe his nose with his shackled hands.

"Everybody's a poet here," the First Lady says. "It's his name I want."

"Rigoberto López Pérez," he says, barely audible.

"A friend of yours, right? You had good reason to keep Tacho distracted with the newspaper," she says then. "You, you piece of shit, without even a pot to piss in. It was my family that gave you that pot!"

And finally she leaves, the hard clicking of her heels fading on the sidewalk, hidden behind her entourage of bodyguards and uniformed military officers, leaving behind the disconsolate wail of Rafa Parrales and the bitter sobs of young Princess Natasha Petrovna, now freely accompanied by her mother, Princess Ninoshka Andreyevna.

And now prepare yourselves to witness the last of the events of this night of static, squealing brakes, military commands, insults, interrogations, moaning, people soiling themselves out of terror. And running.

But before we proceed, there's the unavoidable question: did the First Lady see, while holding the radio microphone up to her irate mouth, the bloody mess of Rigoberto's testicles floating in the jar of alcohol? It was in front of her, on the desk. From no to highly unlikely, Captain Prío maintains. If she saw the jar, she could well have thought it was a fetus, evidence of some clandestine abortion; it was, after all, police headquarters; and besides, it has already been remarked that she was not in the habit of taking her husband's jokes seriously, unlike the gentle and loyal Colonel Lira. But who transmitted such an order, Captain? Colonel Lira? Would Moralitos have paid any attention to him?

Then listen to this: when the blade of *Stone Face* Diómedes Baldelomar's razor cut through the tendons and ligaments, the odor of semen that spurted from the blood had traveled far enough to reach someone with a certain keen sense of smell, and the owner of that nose went through the heavily patrolled streets of the city searching for that scent. He pursued it until he finally found the truck parked in front of police headquarters, and hoisted himself up to look over the side, where he saw only one body, a body with a thick stain of blood on his stomach, and his tie twisted around his neck as if he had been hanged.

He waited. He's old now, but he knows he has one more race to run. He takes a deep breath. He looks up at the illuminated windows, and higher still, toward a sky of murky brilliance and scattered clouds. Mars, wrapped in bloody splendor, is again bidding farewell, moving off among the constellations on its return trip to the depths of the firmament. And while the prisoners are being handcuffed in pairs to be taken to Managua, Captain Prío unhappily manacled to Rafa Parrales, the goldsmith Segismundo to Lucio Ranucci, Prince Fedor Sergeievich to Dr. Balthazar Cisne, and so on, no one sees him cross the vestibule toward the guardroom where Van Wynckle is still making notes for his report, half-listening to Moralitos, and there's a distant hum of voices on the radio. No one sees him get to the door of the office, but then they do see him take off running, the jar in his hands. Raising the alarm, Van Wynckle chases after him, and there's a crack of shots corner after corner as he flees at full gallop down the long blocks of closed doors until at last he's out of sight, the jellyfish of testicles held tight against his chest, another Medusa, like that other one many years ago, a Medusa stirring, awake, moving to the rhythm of his running, his rough shoes beating against the pavement, his back bathed in sweat, heading for the deserted brothel, towards the fountain of darkness and oblivion, towards nothingness.

Managua, 1985, 1993, 1997
Pollensa, Mallorca, October, 1997

Postscript

On the morning of September 22, Somoza was transferred by Sikorski helicopter to the Military Hospital of Managua. The following day, President Dwight D. Eisenhower sent a team of surgeons from the Walter Reed Army Hospital, headed by Major General Leonard D. Heaton, aboard a U.S. Air Force Constellation. His first decision was to take the patient, aboard the same plane, to the Panama Canal Zone, where he was admitted to Gorgas Hospital. Operated on for a second time, his system suffered a shock from which he did not recover. Somoza died on September 28th at five o'clock in the morning. He was given a twenty-one-gun salute at Albrook Air Force Base. His body was returned to Managua on a C-54 military transport plane.

Eisenhower, after attending a breakfast with his wife Mamie to honor disabled veterans of the Korean War, appeared in the East Garden at the White House to declare that the United States had lost a loyal friend, a victim of the bullets of a Communist zealot, *a loyal friend of the United States of America victim of the dastardly attack made upon him by a Communist fanatic*, according to a teletype message transmitted by United Press (UPI).

The state funeral, which lasted a week, was held under a strict state of emergency. Somoza received honors as a Prince of the Church accorded him by the Archbishop of Managua, Monsignor Alejandro González y Robleto, and General Leónidas Trujillo sent a full-scale military band decked out in black-and-gold uniforms to play at his funeral.

The country's jails were packed. It is calculated that there were nearly five thousand prisoners, the most dangerous held in the installations of the Presidential Palace on top of Tiscapa hill.

Norberto turned himself in on October 11th. That same day the body of Manfredo Casaya (aka *The Lion of Nemea*) turned up on the road leading to Fortín de Acosasco. Erwin was captured on October 14th on Juan Venado Island, near León, on the Pacific coast. Along with Cordelio Selva, the authorities put them in cages next to the animals in the presidential house's zoological garden (tigers, lions, and panthers), where they rotated other prisoners who were prime suspects, or when they wanted to get incriminating confessions out of them.

The interrogations were carried out in person by Luis (*The Good*) and Anastasio (*The Bad*), with José (*The Ox-Cart Driver*) always a diligent helper. In addition to the use of cages next to the wild animals, the methods included immersion in pools of water, electric shocks, exposure to intense lights, and prolonged beatings. Sartorius Van Wynckle and his nascent security team aided the two brothers throughout. Moralitos brought *Stone Face* Diómedes Baldelomar in from León, a most useful person for that kind of work.

Luis (*The Good*) was elected president in February 1957 for a six-year term (1957-1963), although there was no time to change the campaign materials (matchbooks, key rings, ashtrays, plastic cups) that had his father's picture on them.

Anastasio (*The Bad*) already held the position of Director of the National Guard. Following the death of his brother Luis (*The Good*) in 1967, he took complete power, sharing it only with his own son, Anastasio Somoza Portocarrero (*The Baby*) and with his half-brother José (*The Ox-Cart Driver*), whom he made a general. Elected president twice, the first time for the term of 1967-1972 and the second time for the term 1974-1979.

Erwin, Norberto, and Cordelio were sentenced to thirty years imprisonment by the Council of War, which was still operating under the code and regulations of the United States Marine Corps.

Rafael (Rafa) Parrales died in March 1957 as a result of the grievous torture that damaged his nervous system and caused him to lose an eye. The goldsmith Segismundo Mestayer was sentenced to twenty years and was pardoned in 1963.

Filomela Aguirre (aka *The Alligator Woman*) was exonerated by the Council of War. She remained in Managua, became an informant for the ONS, and set up a fireworks factory, which Minerva Sarraceno, who had also been exonerated, inherited upon her death in 1971.

All the members of the cast of *Tovarich* were exonerated. In 1956, Lucio Ranucci was taken on foot and deported somewhere along the Costa Rican border. Captain Prío was also exonerated.

Colonel Melisandro Maravilla was sentenced to five years' imprisonment and a dishonorable discharge. Colonel Justo Pastor Gonzaga was exonerated and went into retirement.

Lt. Anastasio Morales (*Moralitos*) continued his career in the Office of National Security (ONS). In 1970 he murdered the Sandinista prisoner, David Tejada, in his jail cell, and confessed to having thrown his body into the crater of the Masaya Volcano. In 1971, free despite the sentence imposed on him by the Council of War, he murdered the army doctor who had reported Tejada's death as the result of torture. In prison again, he fled to Guatemala after the 1972 earthquake that destroyed Managua, and opened an Argentine steak house.

On May 12, 1960, Erwin, Norberto, and Cordelio Selva were murdered in their cells in the Air Force prison under the pretext that they were attempting to escape. The forensic examination of the dead bodies showed that all three of them had been castrated alive.

Stone Face Diómedes Baldelomar was tried and sentenced as one of the principal authors of the assassination of journalist Pedro Joaquín Chamorro on January 10, 1978.

He was pardoned in 1996 for health reasons and returned to his home district of Lechecuagos.

Anastasio (*The Bad*) was overthrown by the Sandinista revolution and fled to Miami on July 17, 1979. That same night he had the caskets of his father and his brother Luis (*The Good*) removed from the family crypt in the Managua cemetery to be taken with him to Miami.

On September 17, 1980, he died in Asunción, Paraguay when the Mercedes Benz in which he was traveling along Avenida España was attacked by bazookas and rifle-fire from the windows of a residence that the Argentine conspirators had rented in the name of the singer Julio Iglesias.

LIST OF CHARACTERS

Abelardo Lira, Colonel (NG): Somoza's aide-de-camp.

Alligator Woman, The (Filomela Aguirre): At the age of seven and disguised as a boy, Filomela entered the boys' orphanage in León run by Saint Mardoqueo, with the blessing of Bishop Simeón and with funds from his sister *Terrestrial Light's* Blessed Souls brothel, which was later inherited by *The Alligator Woman*. Somoza, who frequented the brothel before his marriage to Salvadorita Debayle, entered into a counterfeiting operation with *The Alligator Woman*, for which she didn't name Somoza when she was arrested. Out of gratitude for her silence, Somoza sought to provide *The Alligator Woman* with the means for the sex change operation she had longed for, which was performed unsuccessfully by Doctor Debayle. As a Somoza loyalist, she became a willing agent for Lt. Morales's secret police operations.

Anastasio Morales, Lt. (NG) (Moralitos): a government official in the Office of National Security headed by the American agent Sartorious Van Wyncklc.

Anastasio Somoza, General: President of Nicaragua (1947-1956). Called "the man" by the people of Nicaragua. Given the nickname of *Tacho* by his wife Salvadorita.

Andrés Murillo: brother of Rosario Murillo, *La Maligna*.

Apolidoro Arana: The surgeon who operated on Somoza the night he was assassinated; a distant nephew of the Somozas.

Apolonio Aguirre (*The Great Dragon*): an illiterate pyrotechnic and father of Filomela Aguirre. Apolonio and his daughter spent six months in the Santos Lugares jail, cruelly imprisoned by General Selvano Quirino when he discovered them cutting reeds and sticks on his property to be used for making their fireworks. As fate would have it, Apolonio is later commissioned by *Our Lady of the Fields* to build a giant fire works figure of her deceased brother, General Quirino, after which she provided him with a letter of introduction for his daughter to enter Saint Mardoqueo's Orphans Hospice in León.

Aunt Bernarda: Darío's half-blind, impoverished aunt, living in the house on Calle Real in León where Darío spent his boyhood.

Balthazar Cisne: A money-lending lawyer and usurer, President of the Rubén Darío Honor Society, rescuer of the Rubén Darío statute commissioned in Italy and incorrectly put ashore at the port of La Unión in El Salvador where it became lost for a period of time. He is the husband of *The Rose Child* (Leda Sacasa) who bore him a daughter, *Zela the Moor*.

Basilisk: Grandfather of María Félix and owner of the Fuente Castalia Canteen.

Bienvenido Granda: Nickname for Rigoberto López Perez because of his likeness to the Cuban singing star of that era who sang with La Sonora Matancera Orchestra (The Matanzas Sound); journalist, and assassin of Somoza.

Captain Prío: Owner of Casa Prío and observer of the scene on the day of Somoza's entrance into León in 1956 for the great convention at the Teatro Gónzalez.

Casimira Sacasa Debayle: Somoza's mother-in-law; wife of the learned Doctor Debayle, mother of Margarita and Salvadorita; sister of Dr. Juan Bautista Sacasa and Godofredo Sacasa; godmother to Rafael (Rafa) Parrales, owner of *The Chronicler* newspaper.

Catalina Baldelomar: Merchant woman aboard the *La Salvadorita*, which is en route from El Salvador to Nicaragua. She has great regard for *The Alligator Woman* whom she looks upon as a kind of surrogate mother.

Chiron: Though mute, the learned doctor Debayle's assistant; tutored by Rubén Darío who supposedly infused him with the *numen*, "the spirit of the muses," by taking his head between his hands the day Rubén made his triumphal return to Nicaragua in 1907; Chiron is the boy who carried the flag of Nicaragua when Darío came ashore at the Port of Corinto; a sacristan of the cathedral; he is the illicit son of the priest Saint Mardoqueo and the rectory's young clothes presser, *The Bengali Tigress*, Estebana Catín; though illiterate, he became a voracious reader under Darío's tutelage; devoted to the great poet.

Colonel Heriberto Guardado (NG): Somoza's personal physician, not in attendance at the banquet celebration the night Somoza is shot because he had gone to Chinandega, with permission from Somoza to celebrate his daughter's fifteenth birthday party.

Colonel Justo Pastor Gonzaga (NG): Somoza's chief-of-staff and crony, a shyster lawyer who introduced Somoza to *The Alligator*

Woman in 1916 and helped him to buy up properties of the Santos Lugares holdings by intervening in lawsuits and offering the litigants a buy-out price (with counterfeit silver dollars made in partnership with *The Alligator Woman*).

Colonel Melisandro Maravilla (NG): Commander of Company 5 under Somoza; commanded the firing squad that executed Sandino in 1933; former aide-de-camp to General Moncada (Somoza's real father, according to the goldsmith Segismundo); an accomplice of young Somoza in 1929 in pilfering funds that had been set aside for indemnifying the farmers; in 1937, as a captain, he was sent by Somoza from Managua to put down a miners strike in Mina la India, and was responsible for the death of Cordelio Selva's father, who was behind the uprising,

Cordelio Selva: One of the conspirators in the plot to kill Somoza, disguised as a Protestant preacher aboard *La Salvadorita*; the purchaser of the assassination pistol in San Salvador; according to the goldsmith Segismundo, "a brave patriot." Cordelio Selva was a drifter, involved in Communist activities in the Caribbean. He had fled the deadly bullets that had rained down on the people of Mina La India when the miners rose up in 1937, incited by his father, Euclides Selva, a storekeeper, who died at the hands of Colonel Melisandro Maravilla, then a captain. Cordelio had sworn to take revenge on the colonel for his father's death.

Desiderio Lacayo (*Goliath*): A businessman, father of three children: Eulalia, the priest Saint Mardoqueo, and *Terrestrial Light*.

Diana Coronado: A girl who was being kept by Father Olimpo Lozano; Cordelio runs off with her to Guatemala. She does not appear in the story.

Domitilo Paniagua: The sergeant in charge of the Nicaraguan port of entry, Puerto Morazán. Later assigned to security during the banquet to celebrate Somoza's nomination to run for a third term, he dies that night in a hail of bullets fired by National Guard soldiers in a case of mass confusion following the attack on Somoza.

Escolástico Cisne: Politician and founder of *The Chronicler* newspaper, father of Gaspar, Melchior, and Balthazar, the three money-lending *magi*.

Estebana Catín *(The Bengali Tigress)*: She does the ironing for the rectory; impregnated by Saint Mardoqueo, she gives birth to Chiron.

Euclides Selva: Cordelio Selva's father, a storekeeper in Mina La India, accused of inciting a rebellion of the miners and put to death by Colonel Melisandro Maravilla.

Eulalia: Daughter of *Goliath* (Desiderio Lacayo); Rubén Darío's lover who gives public recitations of his verses; she takes her own life in 1923 with an overdose of potassium cyanide.

Father Olimpo Lozano: The violin-playing, cockfighting priest, fond of drink and women, who took in Cordelio Selva and *Jorge Negrete* when they were homeless and wandering the streets of El Sauce; he was Rigoberto's violin teacher and Casimira's confessor; it is said that he has fathered many children.

Filomela Aguirre (*The Alligator Woman*)

Francisca: Darío's mistress in Spain; he abandoned her and their small son in Barcelona; she was washing dishes when she heard news of his death; he had taken her as his mistress before his return to Nicaragua in 1907; though she was illiterate, he taught her to read as he did Chiron; Darío left her all the rights to his books, a source of contention with Rosario Murillo.

General José María Moncada: President of Nicaragua (1928-1932). It was said that he was Anastasio Somoza's real father, according to the goldsmith Segismundo.

General José Santos Zelaya: President of Nicaragua in 1907.

General Selvano Quirino: "The Little President," a favorite of President Zelaya; Quirino was an Imabita Indian and brother of *Our Lady of the Fields*; he went blind during an operation performed by the learned Doctor Debayle in his desire to have his eyes made blue.

Godofredo Sacasa: An inventor, the invalid husband of Eulalia, injured when thrown from a horse and then victimized by the learned Doctor Debayle's botched operation to repair the damage.

Goliath (Desiderio Lacayo)

Jorge Negrete: Nickname of don Olinto Poveda because of his resemblance to the Mexican star of the silver screen of that era.

José (*The Ox Cart Driver*): General Somoza's bastard son by an unnamed servant girl, before he married Salvadorita.

José Cisneros, Maestro: The photographer who took Darío's picture in the garden of the Hotel Lupone at the Port of Corinto upon his triumphant return to Nicaragua in 1907.

José Prío: Father of Capt. Prío; owner of the Casa Prío at the time Darío conducted his liaison with Eulalia upstairs in the bedroom now used by his son, Capt. Prío.

José Santos Zelaya, General: President of Nicaragua at the time of Darío's return to Nicaragua.

Josías Arburola Reina: The name that Cordelio Selva gave to Sergeant Domitilo Paniagua at Puerto Morazán when he enters the country incognito as a Protestant preacher, claiming to be a Honduran citizen.

Juan Bautista Sacasa, Dr.: Henri Debayle's brother-in-law who warns against the operation the learned doctor is about to undertake on Rubén Darío; Casimira's brother, and Somoza's uncle through marriage to Salvadorita; President of Nicaragua (1933-1937), he ordered the capture and execution of the rebel general Augusto Sandino.

Julio Selano: Darío's personal secretary.

La Maligna: Rosario Murillo, Darío's ex-wife.

Leda Sacasa: *The Rose Child*, Eulalia's daughter, supposedly fathered by Rubén Darío.

Louis Henri Debayle (the learned doctor): Somoza's father-in-law; intimate friend of Rubén Darío; father of Margarita and Salvadorita for whom Darío wrote verses on their fans at the breakfast reception to honor him in 1907; husband of Casimira; quack surgeon who leaves tragedy in his wake; performs a horrific operation on Darío in 1916 after which Darío's brain is preserved.

Lucio Ranucci: Italian stage director, jailed by Sgt. Domitilo Paniagua for supposedly uttering a curse against Nicaragua.

Manfredo Casaya (*The Lion of Nemea*): A wrestler and secret agent for Lt. Moralitos who sent him to El Salvador to trail Rigoberto.

María Félix: Wife of don Olinto Poveda (*Jorge Negrete*), so nicknamed because of her likeness to the beautiful Mexican silver screen actress who starred opposite the singing matinee idol Jorge Negrete in several films.

Minerva Sarraceno: She is in charge of Baby Dolls in León, sought after by Sgt. Domitilo Paniagua with a love letter written for him by Rigoberto.

Monsignor Simeón Pereira y Castellón: Bishop of León; he happens upon his vicar-general, Saint Mardoqueo, in consort with *The Tigress of Bengali*; although he knows that Saint Mardoqueo fathered Chiron, he never reveals the man's identity to the boy.

Olinto Poveda, don (*Jorge Negrete*): The cockfighter aboard *La Salvadorita*, accompanied by, his nephew, Tirso the Albino, sailing from El Salvador to the Port of Morazán in Nicaragua.

Onofre Bellorino: Rubén's tailor and valet, given to strong drink and suffers from delirium tremens.

Our Lady of the Fields (Galatea Quirino): Sister of General Selvano Quirino; she became a powerful landowner upon the death of her brother who owned vast amounts of property known as Santos Lugares or Cafarnaún; she brings a lawsuit against Dr. Debayle for the operation performed on her brother which left him blind; a relative and patron of Saint Mardoqueo who provides funds that maintain Saint Mardoqueo's Orphans Hospice.

Ovidio Parajón: Darío's private barber, the one who prepares the great poet's hair and makeup for burial at the time of his death in 1916 and who, forty years later, is Rafa Parrales's private barber, joining him in a bit of operatic singing when he attends to his toilette.

Pedro Alvarado: Darío's wealthy uncle who cheated him out of his mother's small inheritance; he threw Rubén out of his house when the latter became embroiled in an argument with his son Pedrito.

Prince of Swans: The epithet given to Rubén Darío, grand poet and national treasure of Nicaragua.

Rafael (Rafa) Parrales: A homosexual and a sycophant in his dealings with the First Lady; current owner and managing editor of *The Chronicler* where Rigoberto is employed as a journalist; Rafael bought the old machinery of *The Chronicler*, fallen into disrepair over the years, with a loan from his godmother Casimira, which he never repaid.

Rigoberto López Pérez: Called *Bienvenido Granda* because of his strong likeness to the popular Cuban singer of that period, with the Matanzas Sound, La Sonora Matancera Orchestra; he was carrying the little valise with the pistol Cordelio Selva purchased in El Salvador which he would use to assassinate Somoza.

Rosarillo Murillo (*La Maligna*): Rubén Darío's wife.

Rosaura: Rigoberto's fiancée; she appears briefly in a scene in The Pearls of Basra jewelry store when she comes in with one of her little brothers to look at some engagement rings. She has hopes of moving to Managua if Rigoberto gets a job there as a reporter with *Novedades*.

Rubén Darío: Nicaragua's national poet and hero, ambassador to France, known for his drinking and womanizing; he wrote one of his most famous verses, *Margarita, How Beautiful the Sea,* on the fan of Casimira's daughter Margarita in 1907, sister of Salvadorita, at the Port of Corinto upon his triumphant return to his native land.

Saint Mardoqueo: Vicar-General of Bishop Simeón, brother of *Terrestrial Light*; a priest who is called a saint before his time and who runs the Orphans Hospice that took in Filomela Aguirre (*The Alligator Woman*) in 1907 when she was a child.

Sartorius Van Wynckle: The FBI agent sent by J. Edgar Hoover to oversee Somoza's security and the training of his security force.

Saturnino Ramos, Maestro: The conductor of The National Military Band, composer of the military march titled "Welcome" to greet Darío on his return to Nicaragua.

Segismundo Mestayer, the goldsmith: The owner of the Pearls of Basra jewelry shop in León, known for his sexual prowess and outlandish sexual endowment, and designer of the poison silver bullet that Rigoberto would fire to kill Somoza.

Stone Face (Diómedes Baldelomar): Catalina Baldelomar's brother, a sadistic cutthroat henchman for Somoza; like his sister Catalina, he regards *The Alligator Woman* as a kind of surrogate mother.

Tacho: Salvadorita's nickname for her husband.

Terrestrial Light: (née Talia) sister of Saint Mardoqueo and Eulalia, inherited the lands of Cafarnaún from *Our Lady of the Fields* when the latter was run over and killed by an ox cart; *Terrestrial Light* was expelled from the Catholic girls boarding school when her romantic involvement with Sister Brigida, the music teacher, was discovered; subsequently barred from her house by her father *Goliath*, she goes off to fend for herself and founds The Blessed Souls Hospice; that orphanage is really a brothel in disguise.

The Rose Child (doña Leda Sacasa): Daughter of Eulalia, supposed love child of Rubén Darío and Eulalia, wife of Dr. Balthazar Cisne and mother of *Zela the Moor*; orphaned at age 15 after her mother, Eulalia, takes her own life in 1923, she went to live with her aunt, Doña Casimira.

Tigress of Bengali (Estebana Catín): The young, voluptuous domestic who did the ironing for the cathedral; impregnated by Saint Mardoqueo, she gave birth to Chiron.

Tirso the Albino: Nephew of Olinto Poveda (*Jorge Negrete*), child of Eufrasia Poveda, Olinto's sister; Tirso is supposedly the result of a curse placed by Saint Mardoqueo against all Nicaraguan girls who had children with the Marines stationed at Camp Pendleton, stating that the child of such a union would be born without any color.

Zela the Moor: The daughter of *The Rose Child* and Dr. Balthazar Cisne, enamored of Norberto.

HABITUÉS OF "THE INFAMOUS LITTLE TABLE" AT THE CASA PRÍO
CONSPIRATORS IN THE PLOT AGAINST SOMOZA

Erwin: The baby-faced owner of the *Cara Lutecia* print shop; he has the look of the Mennen Powder Baby; he is slightly younger than Norberto and wears a Basque beret he has worn since his first year of law school.

Norberto: Twenty-three years old, he likes to wear the Eau de Vétvier cologne that is a favorite of Somoza's; one of the conspirators in the plot to kill the dictator; *Zela the Moor*'s suitor; he went broke in the cotton business and is in arrears in repaying the bank.

Rigoberto: *Bienvenido Granda*'s look-alike; a journalist for *The Chronicler*, the keeper of a journal with all the meticulous notes on the lives of Rubén Darío and Somoza, and their family histories; trained under Cordelio Selva in El Salvador to assassinate Somoza.

Segismundo Mestayer: The owner of The Pearls of Basra jewelry shop; an ardent anti-Somoza opponent.

GLOSSARY

aeda: Greek poet

aigrettes (Fr.): tufts or plumes of feathers

aguardiente: a grain alcohol; strong spirits

Bienvenido Granda: popular Cuban singer with *La Sonora Matancera* Band; because of Rigoberto's strong resemblance to the singer, the people around him nickname him Bienvenido.

camisas judías: a type of blouse popular at the time; square-necked, puffy-sleeved Spanish chemise

campesinos: farmers; rural folk

casa de putas: house of prostitution

Casa Poloni e figlio: Poloni & Sons, Ltd.

'est lui qui ni comprend rien (Fr.): It's he who understands nothing

charro: Mexican horseman

ocotte (Fr.): slut, prostitute

copain (Fr.): friend, companion

culo: asshole, jerk

Dr. Balthazar Cisne: In Latin America, members of the legal profession bear the title of doctor.

déshabillé (Fr.): undressed; state of undress

di piccolo non avea altro che la statura (It.): the only thing small about him is his stature

dulce de panela: a soft, conical-shaped sweet, made of processed sugar cane wrapped in its own leaf which is then peeled back to break off pieces

El gitano señorón: "The Gypsy Gentleman"; a popular ballad sung by Juan Legido with Los Churumbeles de España Orchestra, The Gypsy Boys of Spain.

gamine (Fr.): scamp

grisette (Fr.): a floozy; a girl from the working class

Gran Cadena Liberal: the Great Liberal Radio Network

guaro: a cheap rum

guaro lija: a very strong rum

guanacaste: a huge, green leafy tree, with wide branches

hijo del alma: someone who is much loved

jícaro (also, *guira*): calabash-tree

Judea: a popular religious drama; the *Passion of Christ*

La Défense: a well-known prison in Paris at the time

La Maligna: the Evil One, the She-Devil, the Malevolent One (almost in the sense of a malignancy); the Malignant One

La Salvadorita: the ship owned by the First Lady, Salvadorita Somoza Debayle, the one on which the conspirators Cordelio Selva and Rigoberto arrive from El Salvador.

La Vierge Folle: "The Foolish Maiden" by Henri Bataille (1872-1922)

leche de higuera: a milky-like oily extraction squeezed from the seed of the fig-tree, sometimes used as a purgative for intestinal parasites; according to popular folklore, used to grow a mustache.

l'enfant gâté (Fr.): spoiled child

Lisboa Antigua: "Old Lisbon"

Louis Quatorze: Louis XIV

luminarias: festival lights, a tradition in Latin countries

Mais c'est impossible, un aristocrate en prison (Fr.): But that's impossible, an aristocrat in prison

Manuel Bernal: well-known in the 50s for his recitals of poetry on the radio

Mercado Municipal: City Market, Municipal Market

merde (Fr.): shit, hell, damn (expression of astonishment)

mon frère (Fr.): my brother

mon pauvre ami (Fr.): my dear friend (literally, poor friend)

nécessaire (Fr.): dressing-case; travel kit; toilette; grooming kit

nepenthe: a strong alcoholic drink

NG: National Guard

Novedades: *The News*, the Somoza party-line newspaper published in Managua

numen (Grk.): poetic muse, inspiration

ONS: Office of National Security

panida (Grk.): poet

partenaire (Fr.): partner

passementerie (Fr.): lace; beaded embroidery and florets borrowed from Iranian decoration

piña de mamón: a tropical fruit with a hard green shell, with a pinkish, acidic pulp, and seeds

puerto: port

puta: vulgar term for prostitute; bitch

"Quiero papita": "I Love Daddy," a tango love-song of the period

réclame (Fr.): an advertisement, sometimes with a jingle

red (baseball) caps: symbol of the Liberal Party in Nicaragua; Somoza loyalists

Revue de Hautes Etudes de Médicine (Fr.): Journal of Higher Studies in Medicine

robe de chambre (Fr.): dressing gown

secrétaire (Fr.): a style of desk of the Louis XIV period

serre-tête (Fr.): fashionable woman's hat of the period, something like a flapper's hat of the 1920s, based on Rubén Darío's sketch of it in the learned Debayle's prescription pad.

seyante: that which is becoming

silver-toothed buffaloes: a line from a Darío poem, likening the rich Yankees to silver-toothed buffaloes, perhaps with the image of Teddy Roosevelt in mind.

The Gypsy Boys of Spain: *Los Churumbeles de España* as they were known in the 50s, identified by their flamenco style of song and lyrics; lead singers were Juan Legido and Mario Rey; their cassettes and CDs are still available.

The Matanzas Sound: *La Sonora Mantancera* as they were known in the 50s for their tropical music, with Bienvenido Granda as the lead singer; their cassettes and CDs are still available, with an image of Bienvenido on the front.

Tovarich: a 1933 play by French dramatist Jacques Deval (1890-1972); the play combines bubbly comedy with harsh political undertones; the plot presents Russian aristocrats in Paris, exiles from the 1917 Revolution, forced to become servants and common workers in order to survive, yet maintaining their dignity and giving their money back to benefit the people of Russia; the word *tovarich* in Russian means comrade.

True Affection: the ballad is "Cariño verdad" sung by Juan Legido

Two Crosses: the ballad is "Dos Cruces" sung by Mario Rey

Virgen del Hato: Virgin of the Fold

Voilà, toute la vérité (Fr.): There you have it, the whole truth

Yankee: a common pejorative term expressed as yanki (sometimes *yanqui*), in the Latin countries; it is directed at North Americans who are viewed as imperialists.

Curbstone Press, Inc.
is a non-profit publishing house dedicated to multicultural literature
that reflects a commitment to social awareness and change, with an
emphasis on contemporary writing from Latino, Latin American,
and Vietnamese cultures.

Curbstone's mission focuses on publishing creative writers whose work
promotes human rights and intercultural understanding, and on
bringing these writers and the issues they illuminate into the
community. Curbstone builds bridges between its writers and the
public—from inner-city to rural areas, colleges to cultural centers,
children to adults, with a particular interest in underfunded public
schools. This involves enriching school curricula, reaching out to
underserved audiences by donating books and conducting readings
and educational programs, and promoting discussion in the media.
It is only through these combined efforts that literature can truly
make a difference.

Curbstone Press, like all non-profit presses, relies heavily on the
support of individuals, foundations, and government agencies to bring
you, the reader, works of literary merit and social significance that
would likely not find a place in profit-driven publishing channels, and
to bring these authors and their books into communities across
the country.

If you wish to become a supporter of a specific book—one that is
already published or one that is about to be published—your
contribution will support not only the book's publication but also its
continuation through reprints.

We invite you to support Curbstone's efforts to present the diverse
voices and views that make our culture richer, and to bring these
writers into schools and public places across the country.
Tax-deductible donations can be made to:
Curbstone Press, 321 Jackson Street, Willimantic, CT 06226
phone: (860) 423-5110   fax: (860) 423-9242
www.curbstone.org